THE
LESSONS
WE
LEARN

THE
LESSONS
WE
LEARN

A Homefront Mystery

Liz Milliron

First published by Level Best Books/Historia 2022

This novel is entirely a work of fiction. The names, characters and incidents portrayed in it are the work of the author's imagination. Any resemblance to actual persons, living or dead, events or localities is entirely coincidental.

Author Photo Credit: ErinMcClainStudio.com

First edition

ISBN: 978-1-68512-048-1

Cover art by Level Best Designs

This book was professionally typeset on Reedsy.
Find out more at reedsy.com

For my family, who kept me (mostly) sane through a very difficult year. I love you all.

Praise for The Homefront Mysteries

"As WWII is being fought overseas, an entirely different battle is being waged on the home front, in Buffalo, New York. Milliron offers an authentic glimpse into the life of a woman on the cusp of coming into a new world of her own making as she fully embarks on becoming a private investigator. Intriguing, charming, and a delight to unravel the mysterious murder of her dear friend's father, readers will truly enjoy Betty, the memorable, plucky PI."—L.A. Chandlar, award-winning author of The Art Deco Mystery Series

Chapter One

March, 1943

When I was little and I did something wrong, Pop would punish me. Later, he'd ask if I learned my lesson and 'course I said yes. I knew that if I didn't, he'd punish me again. Back then, I thought those were the hardest lessons I'd ever learn, way worse than anything school could come up with. What I didn't know was that the lessons you learn as an adult are much tougher than anything you face as a kid. Maybe 'cause they're a lot more life-changing.

I sat on the front steps of my house, the cold of the concrete seeping through my slacks. Cat, my gray and cream stray, was curled on my lap. Spring was doin' its best, but winter didn't want to let go, even if the snowfall so far had been light.

My oldest friend, Liam Tillotson, who preferred to be called Lee, stood a pace away, smoking a cigarette and staring off toward the lake. The chill damp couldn't make his bum leg, the one he'd broken in a childhood tire-swing dare, feel any better.

"Is your dad back yet?" I ran my hand over Cat's back.

Lee flicked his nearly-spent butt into the gutter. "Nope and I'm just as happy he isn't."

"You aren't worried about him?"

Lee shrugged. "Betty, I already told you. He's gone off before, when he's too drunk to find his way home. Or too ashamed, which always leads to

1

another bender. Either way, it means peace for Mom, the girls, and me."

I knew Mr. Tillotson had been hitting the bottle pretty hard ever since last summer when he hurt his back. I also knew he was a mean drunk. No wonder his family was glad he was staying away. But this time, Lee had told me it had been almost two weeks since he'd disappeared. I'd have thought Lee or his mom would at least have reported him missing. "What about your mom?"

"I talked to her this morning. If he doesn't show up by my birthday, she'll call the cops. I honestly think it's a waste of time. He'll stagger in at some point and won't even know what day of the week it is."

"Has he been to work?"

He stared at Cat. "Nope. They called last week looking for him. This was maybe the second day he was gone. The boss said if Dad didn't show up the next day he'd be fired. We got another call the following morning. No Dad."

"Then all you've got is your job."

"And anything Mom can pick up." Lee didn't seem too worried about it. Then again, I didn't know how much dough Mr. Tillotson had been bringing home. Or how much of it he'd been spending on booze.

"If you need any help, let me know." We weren't swimming in money at my house, but I knew my folks wouldn't let the Tillotsons, who had two girls about the same age as my brothers Michael and Jimmy, go without.

"No sweat. Mom's good with the budget and I'm making more than fair money at GM. I've been able to pick up a little overtime. Not having Dad around helps, to be honest."

"I could ask around, see if I can scare up any dope about him."

"Nah, that's okay."

"I wouldn't even charge you."

His voice turned sharp. "I told you, leave it alone. We're fine."

"Okay, okay. Keep your shirt on." I scratched Cat under his chin. "Changing subjects, your birthday is in two days. What do you want?"

His expression smoothed out and the tension disappeared from his shoulders. "An end to the war so Tom can come home, marry you, and we can all hang out together again?"

Lee and Tom, my fiancé, had been friends nearly as long as Lee and I had. I knew Tom had made Lee promise to keep an eye on me while he was off fighting with the 1st Armored Division. But even though 1943 was young, I didn't see an end to the conflict in sight. "Things are bad in Poland," I said. "I wouldn't be surprised if there were a lot of Jewish refugees soon. The Nazis are really beating them up." Just yesterday the papers had been full of stories on how the Germans were fighting the Soviets in Kharkov. I wouldn't be seeing my sweetheart for a while.

Lee's face sobered. "I read that." He stuffed his hands in his pockets. "Honestly, I don't need much for my birthday this year. Well, nothing you can give me."

* * *

Two hours later, I sat at my kitchen table, my other friend, Dot Kilbride, at my side. I'd just finished telling her about my chat with Lee earlier.

"He's really not concerned?" Dot asked. Dot's first name was Dorothy, but nobody called her that 'cept her folks.

"Nope." I turned to my sister, Mary Kate, who was reading a recipe, her bottom lip caught between her teeth. "You got everything?"

"Yeah," she said, turning a page. "It won't be a big cake, but you and Dot scraped up enough to make it and I can do a bit of real frosting."

"Swell." We'd saved and traded coupons for a couple of months so Lee would have a cake on his birthday. Since I was competent, but not great, in the kitchen, I'd bribed Mary Kate into helping us. I couldn't solve Lee's problem with his father, but I could give him a treat. "Anyway," I said, returning my attention to Dot, "I offered to poke around and Lee got testy. I get the feeling he'd be glad if his dad never showed up again."

Mom came into the kitchen. "Who'd be glad if his dad never showed up?"

"We're talking about Lee and Mr. Tillotson," I said. "He's been missing for a while, close to a couple of weeks. I was with Lee earlier and he wasn't particularly keen on solving that mystery. He thinks Mr. Tillotson is off on another bender and, well, good riddance to bad rubbish."

3

Mom pursed her lips. "Liam is a good boy. I won't say he's right, but..." She paused, mashing her lips closer until they were nothing but a thin line. "I should run over later and see if Nora needs anything. I have some old clothes from Mary Kate that might fit the Tillotson girls."

At that moment, Pop entered. "What about the Tillotson girls?"

"Gee-whiz!" Mary Kate grabbed the recipe book. "Mr. Tillotson is missing, he's a drunk, Lee's happy, and Mom is going to check with Mrs. Tillotson to see if she needs anything. Now would everybody please go away? I can't work when the kitchen is jam packed like this."

I smothered a grin and led Dot from the kitchen, Mom and Pop following. We went to the living room and sat. "I guess Mary Kate takes her work seriously."

Pop packed and lit his pipe, puffing until a cloud of sweet-scented smoke hung in the air. "What's this about John Tillotson?"

I told the story for a third time, adding Mom's concerns about Lee's little sisters. "I still think I should call Detective MacKinnon down at police headquarters. This all feels fishy to me."

Pop wagged his pipe stem at me. "You'll do no such thing. Not if Lee asked you to stay out of it. He's a grown man. Until and unless he asks for help, you mind your own business, young lady."

I knew my folks didn't approve of Mr. Tillotson, his drinking and the way he treated, or mistreated, his family. He'd come home rip-roaring drunk last September, cussing a blue streak, barely able to walk a straight line. Pop and some other men in the neighborhood guided him home. That night Mrs. Tillotson had shown up at our house boasting a shiner under her left eye and telling a flimsy story about walking into the door. I'd seen my parents' dark looks and silent condemnation. Despite all this, they held to their "don't speak until spoken to" position.

I wasn't so keen on staying mum.

Dot shot me a look. "What are you gonna get Lee for his birthday?"

Our talk turned to potential birthday presents and how pleased Lee would be to get a real cake.

I participated with half my mind on the gabbing, but the other half firmly intent on finding Mr. Tillotson. I had Sam MacKinnon's home telephone number, saved from my last case when I'd had reason to contact him late at night. As soon as Dot left, and I was sure my family wouldn't hear me, I'd call him, whether it was a Sunday or not.

* * *

It was nearly four o'clock before I had a chance to telephone Detective MacKinnon. Dot went home, Mom and Mary Kate had settled in to do some sewing, and Pop was napping in his armchair. My brothers were nowhere to be seen and prob'ly wouldn't be home until supper at six. It was the perfect opportunity.

"Hey, Detective," I said when he answered. "It's Betty. Sorry to bother you on a Sunday."

"No you aren't. At least you aren't sorry enough not to call me." His words said he was angry, but his voice was cheerful. "It's okay. I'm used to weekend work. What do you want?"

"It's my friend's dad." I ran down the story of Lee's missing father. "Have you heard anything?"

"If Mrs. Tillotson didn't file a missing person report, I'm not sure I would," Sam said.

"What about John Does? You got any of them downtown? Or drunks who are passed out and can't identify themselves?" I gave him the details of Mr. Tillotson's description. "That sound familiar?"

"Not offhand. I would have to check with the office." He paused and I assumed he was writing notes. "I'll see what I can do. Should I call you back?"

"Why don't we meet later at Teddy's over on South Park, not far from my house?"

He paused. "Are you going to be able to get there without sneaking out?"

The last time I'd met Sam it had been late at night and turned out to be, well, a disaster when I got home. But I thought maybe I had a good chance now. "I'm gonna try. Be there at seven. Wait until seven-thirty. If I don't show by then, I'm not coming and I'll call you."

He agreed and I hung up. I went back to the living room. "I'm going out after dinner. I prob'ly won't be too long."

Mom looked up from her mending. "Where are you going? Somewhere with Dot?"

I took a deep breath. "No. I'm meeting Detective MacKinnon."

Pop opened one eye. "Is this about Mr. Tillotson?"

Oh boy. I decided to go with the truth since lying hadn't done me any favors in the past. "Yes." I held up a hand. "I know what you're gonna say, Pop. That it's none of my business. But this is my friend's father. Lee's like a brother to me. What if his dad is lying down in the morgue, with no one to put a name to him? If I can get some answers, doesn't Lee deserve that?"

Pop opened the other eye and said nothing, just fixed me with a stare. Then he closed his peepers again. "Don't be out past nine."

Chapter Two

I got to Teddy's a little before seven. Sam hadn't arrived yet, so I paid for two mugs of java and selected a booth in the back, where he could have his back to the wall and see the room. I'd noticed he liked to sit that way.

He arrived about five minutes later and slid into his seat. "You either didn't have trouble sneaking out or you're getting a longer lead." He added a splash of milk to his coffee. "How much do I owe you?"

I waved. "This one's on me. I told my folks the truth, that I had to talk to you about Mr. Tillotson. I don't think they like this whole private detective gig, but it seems they've accepted it at least. Now if only it paid enough for me to quit my day job. Doing investigations only at night or on the weekends is tough."

"I can imagine." He took a sip. Then he pulled out his notepad. "John Patrick Tillotson. Age forty-five. White male, black hair, brown eyes, no distinguishing marks or features. Last seen mid-afternoon on Tuesday, March second, around three-thirty in the afternoon. Currently employed by General Motors. Known to be a drinker. That's what you told me, correct?"

"That's Lee's dad."

Sam made a hmm noise and consulted his notes. "That description doesn't match any of our current John Does in the morgue nor anyone who is passed out in the drunk tank."

"Darn it." I played with the thick, white ceramic mug. My work as a private dick meant I was able to treat myself to a real coffee now and again, and I always relished the taste.

He pocketed the notebook. "Where was he last seen?"

"At home. He headed out mid-afternoon on the second, maybe a little later. He was s'posed to work second shift at GM, so that's where his wife thought he was goin'. He shoulda been home between midnight and one in the morning."

"She didn't hear him come in. Was that unusual?"

"Mrs. T was in bed, obviously. But Mr. Tillotson, well, he wasn't a quiet guy, even when he wasn't bending the elbow, if you catch my meaning."

"When he was drinking."

"Yep." I took a sip. "But him not coming home wasn't out of the ordinary. If he went to the bar after work, sometimes he didn't get back until the early morning. She sent the girls off to school at the normal time. It got to be nine o'clock and she still hadn't seen him. Even by the time the girls got home that afternoon, there'd still been no sign of her husband."

"Does he have any friends? Co-workers who can say whether he made it to work?"

I thought. "I'll have to ask Lee. I assumed he would have mentioned it if his dad never showed up at the plant that day, but it's possible he didn't know, 'specially if they worked different shifts. As far as Lee is concerned, the less he sees his dad the better."

"First rule of investigating. Never assume." Sam lifted his coffee mug.

"Didn't you mention a different rule one last time we talked?"

He grinned. "First rule of investigating. There are many first rules."

* * *

I stopped by the Tillotson place on my way home. Lee was in the living room helping his sister, Emma, with her math homework.

He tapped her paper. "You forgot to carry the one." He stood. "Keep goin' kiddo. I have to talk to Betty." He beckoned me into the kitchen, where he leaned against the counter. "What's shakin'?"

I thought about shucking off my coat and sitting, but I decided against it.

I wouldn't be there all that long. "I talked to Sam MacKinnon about your dad."

"Aw, Betty. For the love of—"

"Hear me out." Why was he so dead set against doin' anything? "He says there isn't anyone in the morgue among the John Does who matches your dad's description. No one in the drunk tank sleepin' it off matches, either."

"Okay. Can we leave it now?" He pushed away from the counter and took a step toward the door.

"Lee, what's up with you?" I hadn't intended on askin' the question, but the words burst from my lips. "This is your father. I know you don't like him, but aren't you in the least bit worried, or curious, about where he is? He's never been gone this long before. Somethin' could be wrong."

He cupped a hand to his ear. "Betty, do you hear that?"

"I don't hear anything."

He lowered his hand. "Exactly. It's quiet, peaceful even. Mom is out with some friends down at the church. Emma is doin' her homework. Anna is in her room, folding laundry. A normal, quiet evening."

"What's your point?"

"If my old man were here, he'd be passed out drunk in an armchair and Emma would be holed up in her room. Anna would be, too. Mom would be so embarrassed she wouldn't go out. Or, he'd be bellowin' and rantin', throwing stuff, pitching a fit over some imagined thing, and nobody would get anything done. I'd be afraid to go to work. What would happen to Mom and the girls if I wasn't here to stop him?" He crossed his arms over his chest.

As he spoke, the light dawned. The Tillotson house wasn't like my home. Our place was noisy, sure, but it was a happy sound. We all loved each other and looked out for one another. Lee's family might indeed be better off without the "man of the house." Lee, who wouldn't turn nineteen for another two days, might be better suited to protect and care for the women. Still, they needed to know. Didn't they?

Lee cocked his head. "What are you thinkin'? I can tell it's somethin', so spill."

I bit my lip. "I hear what you're sayin'. But Lee, if you value all this peace, and you care so much about your mom and sisters, you should find out what happened to him. 'Cause if he's not comin' back, you have some decisions to make."

"Like what?" he scoffed. "I already take care of everything. I fix things around the house and it's my paycheck that pays the bills." He turned, took a step, then faced me again. "Fact is, Betty, I don't give a damn what happened to the old drunk. I don't care if he's dead. It just doesn't matter."

Chapter Three

Two days later, after Dot and I got home from our jobs at Bell Airplane, where we built P-39s, we took the birthday cake to the Tillotson house to set things up for when Lee got home. "Did you bring the present?" I asked, as I laid out forks and plates for the cake.

"Yep. I found some fancy paper in my basement, so I was even able to wrap it real nice. It was a good idea of your dad's, buyin' Lee a new wallet. Thanks for goin' halves with me."

"No sweat. Pop said a man should have a nice billfold for his cash and stuff. We were lucky to find a leather one at a good price." I uncovered the cake. Mary Kate had written "Happy Birthday Lee" on the top with the leftover icing, which she'd figured out how to color blue.

"Wow, that's swell." Dot admired the confection from all angles. "I think your sister has a future as a baker. I'm so happy she helped us out. This is much nicer than anything I could have made."

I lifted my eyebrows. Dot hated baking. The fact she'd even considered making a cake was a mark of how special she wanted the party to be 'cause I don't think she would have done it for anyone else, even me. "She'll be some sort of cook, that's for sure."

"Just think. Next year, Lee will be twenty. He's not a kid anymore." She glanced at me. "Still no sign of Mr. Tillotson? I don't want him ruinin' the night. I want everything to be perfect."

"Nope, not a peep." I put out some napkins. I'd never let her know it, but her concern amused me. Back in November, Dot had been all about dancing with as many boys as possible and having fun. That had sure changed. "I

11

still think it's strange, but it doesn't seem to bother the rest of the family."

Mrs. T came into the kitchen. Since her husband had disappeared, she looked better, younger. The purplish smudges under her eyes had faded and there was a spring in her step. "What's strange?"

"We were just talkin' about—" Dot sucked in her breath as I stepped on her foot.

"About how we were able to get our hands on the stuff for the cake," I said, covering Dot's mutterings. "It's not easy gettin' eggs and all, even when you have the coupons."

If Mrs. T noticed any awkwardness in the conversation, she didn't let on. "Oh, my, yes. Every week I have to barter with the shopkeepers, even when I have the means to buy certain things." She clucked her tongue. "Betty, you must tell Mary Kate how lovely this cake is. She's such an angel to make it. I couldn't have done half as good a job."

Anna and Emma bounded into the kitchen. "He's coming, he's coming! We saw him out the front window, standing on the curb finishing a cigarette."

"Places everyone," Mrs. T said. She waved the girls into a corner and shut off the lights. Dot and I took up our spots on the far side of the table.

A minute or so later, we heard the front door and Lee's voice. "Mom? Where are you? Are the girls done with their homework? Why's it all dark? Did we blow a fuse?"

"We're in the kitchen," Mrs. T called.

The minute Lee entered, she flipped on the lights. "Surprise!" we all yelled. "Happy birthday!"

His jaw dropped and for a moment he was speechless. "What the...where'd you get a cake?"

"Betty's sister made it," Anna said. "Hurry up and cut it."

"Happy birthday." Dot went over and kissed his cheek.

I didn't say anything about that. "Sorry we don't have any candles for you to blow out." I'd always known Lee was sweet on Dot, even if it had taken her some time to feel the same.

He'd blushed a little when Dot kissed him, but he covered any embarrassment by ruffling Anna's hair. "No matter. Wow, a real cake. Thanks."

"And presents," Emma said. "C'mon Lee, Mom said we couldn't have no cake until you got here."

"You couldn't have *any* cake," her mother said in a reproving tone. "First we have to sing Happy Birthday."

There was a rousing, if slightly off-key, rendition of the song, then Lee cut. "I'm surprised you didn't bring your sister," he said, as he handed me my piece.

"She wanted all of us to have enough." I licked a bit off my finger.

As we ate, Lee opened his presents. "This is swell," he said, looking at the new wallet. "Thanks. My old one is falling apart."

"It was Mr. Ahern's idea," Dot said, her face flushed with excitement.

There was a knock on the door. "Are we expecting anyone else?" Lee asked.

"Not that I know of," said Mrs. T. She looked out the kitchen window. "It's a man in a trench coat."

"I'll get it." Lee pushed away from the table.

I followed him to the front door. When he opened it and saw Sam MacKinnon standing there, he said nothing, but the smile slid off his face.

"Liam Tillotson?" Sam asked. He showed his badge. "Detective Sam MacKinnon, Buffalo PD. May I come in?"

* * *

Lee pulled me aside while Mrs. T led the detective to the living room. "Can you join us?"

Dot came out of the kitchen. "What's going on?"

"Detective MacKinnon is here," I said. I turned to Lee. "Are you sure?"

"Is it about Lee's dad?" Dot asked.

"Can't see why else the police would be here." I refocused on Lee. "You haven't answered my question."

"Yes," he said. "You know this guy better than I do. Dot?" He turned to her.

"What?"

"Would you watch the girls and keep them busy? I don't wanna have them busting in on us only to hear their dad is dead."

She gave a mock salute. "Absolutely. I'll keep them out of the way." She returned to the kitchen.

I heard her cheery voice as she talked to Lee's sisters. Then I faced him. "Detective MacKinnon is a good guy. He's not gonna give you a hard time."

"Maybe not, but I still would rather you were there. Mom's gonna be no help. She'll be a basket case. I need someone I can count on."

"If you insist." I followed him to the living room.

Mrs. T and Sam sat facing each other, her on the tweedy sofa, him on a matching armchair. Lee eased down next to his mom, while I sat in the second chair.

Sam looked at me. "What are you doing here? This doesn't concern you."

"I asked her to stay," Lee said, voice curt. "How can we help you?"

Sam seemed like he was gonna say something but didn't. He took out his notebook and focused on the Tillotsons. "I understand your husband has been missing for some time, Mrs. Tillotson."

She clasped her hands together, face pale, but composed. "Yes. He has."

"How long? Meaning, when did you last see him?"

"Almost two weeks ago. Monday, March second."

"What time?"

"It must have been about four o'clock. No, that can't be right." She checked with her son. "Lee wasn't home yet and the girls weren't home from school, so it was earlier. Maybe two? I don't remember exactly. Is it important?"

"He didn't go to work that day?"

"No, he said he was sick."

"You didn't report him missing?"

She flushed. "No, I...no."

Sam turned to Lee. "What about you?"

"I left early 'cause I was on first shift that day," Lee said. His voice was wooden and he might have been talkin' about the weather judging by the look on his face. "That would have been five-thirty in the morning."

"He was still asleep or was he not home?"

Lee's shoulders twitched. "I s'pose he coulda been in bed. But like as not, he wasn't even home. He would often go tie one on after work. Sometimes he didn't get home until the early hours of the morning. Other times, he didn't come home."

"You didn't see him at all that day?"

Lee shot a quick look at his mom. "No."

"The times he didn't come home, did you know where he went? Was he at a friend's house?"

"I don't know. To be honest, I didn't care."

Sam's gaze sharpened. "Oh? Why's that?"

Uh oh. Be careful, Lee. I threw the thought in his direction and hoped he got the silent message.

"You asked if we said anything about him not coming home. My father was a difficult man, Detective," Lee said. "He drank quite a bit and he was a nasty drunk. We didn't do anything because our lives are quieter when he isn't around."

Sam murmured and jotted some notes.

"You wouldn't be here for a missing person, Detective," I said. "Did you find him?"

He glared at me and spoke to Lee. "His body washed up in the Buffalo River, down at the foot of Child Street. Judging by the...damage, it's been in the water for some time."

Mrs. T blinked. "Child Street? That's nowhere near the plant. Why would he be there?"

Sam turned to her. "We're still investigating. It's possible he fell in the water somewhere else and floated downstream. If he hadn't washed up where he did, it's likely he would have continued until he went over Niagara Falls and he might never have been found." He waited, studying her face.

She paled.

"Was it an accident?" Lee's voice sounded harsh, almost accusatory.

Sam slowly turned his head. "Again, we aren't sure. There will be an autopsy, of course. That will tell us more. Did your father have any enemies?"

"Besides me?" Lee bit off the words.

"Yes, but now that you mention it, I have to ask. Did you dislike him that much?"

Don't say it, Lee. Keep your trap shut, I silently urged.

Lee swallowed. "When he was home, I spent a lot of time putting myself in between him and Mom. We wanted different things, so I guess we were enemies in that way, but prob'ly not like you're thinking."

I relaxed a smidge. *Good job.*

Sam's expression didn't change. "Anyone else?"

"I bet some of the guys at GM are glad to be shot of him," Lee said. "He wasn't the most reliable worker. In fact, I've always been kinda surprised they didn't fire him ages ago. I guess they must have needed the bodies. He knew his job, when he was sober enough to show up and do it properly. He just didn't."

Something about Lee's words troubled me, but before I could figure out what, Sam spoke again.

"How about you, Mrs. Tillotson?" He looked at Mrs. T. "Did you get along with your husband?"

Lee's hand spasmed, but he stayed quiet.

"Oh, I...well, I can't pretend it wasn't stressful in the house, as Lee told you," she said, stuttering. "I mostly tried to stay out of his way. For my girls' sake, you know."

"You have daughters?" Sam asked.

"Yes, two. Anna and Emma. They're in the kitchen. I'd prefer they didn't know anything just yet."

I spoke up. "Are you sure it's Mr. Tillotson, Detective?"

"We found a wallet in his pocket with a driver's license inside in the name of John Patrick Tillotson," Sam replied. "The description matches the one of the missing man you gave me."

Lee shot me a dirty look, which I ignored.

Sam went back to studying Lee. "Is there anything else you want to say?"

"No, should there be?" Lee said. He lifted his chin in defiance and it was clear he thought the detective was challenging him.

"I suppose not." Sam stood and took a card from his pocket. "If you think of something, please call me at this number. One of you will need to come downtown and provide a formal identification."

Mrs. T took the card with shaking fingers. "Oh, I, uh, well, I'd rather not."

Lee gripped her shoulder. "Don't worry, Mom. I'll take care of it." He fixed Sam with a steady gaze. "If it is him, when can we have the body? We'll have to arrange for a funeral and stuff."

Sam's face didn't betray his thoughts. "As I said, there will be an autopsy. But we'll release him as soon as we can. If possible, I'd like you to accompany me to the morgue now so we can complete the identification."

A muscle in Lee's cheek flinched. "I want Betty to come with me."

For the first time, a flicker of annoyance flashed across Sam's face. "If you insist."

"I do." Lee stood and crossed the room. "I'll be back with our coats, Betty."

Mrs. Tillotson murmured something and left the room.

I faced Sam. "You aren't gettin' rid of me. I don't know why you even tried."

His expression soured. "I don't know why I did either."

Chapter Four

Sam drove Lee and me to the morgue, which was downtown in a nondescript stone building. After we signed in, a white-coated worker led us to a room with a big walk-in cooler, which was filled with stainless-steel tables on wheels. Every table had a body draped in a sheet on it. He checked the number on the file and pulled one out. A white tag was attached to the big toe and I could read the name "Tillotson, J" on it.

Lee watched with clenched fists and an expression that made his face look frozen as the attendant pulled back the sheet.

"Do you recognize him?" Sam asked.

Lee barely moved. "That's my dad all right."

I steeled myself and took a gander. Mr. Tillotson was blue, his face distorted and damaged. I couldn't tell if the marks were bruises or scrapes from any objects he bumped against as he floated downstream. Some of 'em looked suspiciously like nibbles, maybe where fish or other water-dwellers had gone in for a snack. "Is all that from being in the river?" I asked, pointing.

The white-coated guy shrugged. "Some of it, yeah. Others we won't know until the autopsy. The coroner and the pathologist will tell you. Want me to cover him up?"

"Let me see the rest of him," Lee said in an emotionless tone.

"I really don't think—"

"I want to see it."

I put my hand on his shoulder. "Lee, you don't need to do that. You know it's him. Anything else, well, it can't look good." I'd seen plenty to know it had to be a grotesque parody of a human body. The face alone looked like the skin had been filled with water or blown up like a cheap balloon.

"Put him away," Sam said.

The attendant yanked the sheet back up and rolled the body back into the cooler. He slammed the door. He faced us, hands in his coat pockets and a ghoulish expression on his face. "Hard to believe that was a living guy, isn't it? Death'll do that to ya, make you all gross and goofy looking."

"That's enough," Sam said, throwing the guy a dirty look.

I pulled Lee's hand. "Let's get outta here."

"Just a moment," Sam said. "Mr. Tillotson, I need you to sign off on the identification."

Lee didn't budge. I bumped his shoulder. "The detective is talkin' to you."

My friend snapped his gaze toward Sam. "I'm not used to being called mister."

"You are the man of the house now." Sam gestured for us to go through a door. "After you. Can I get you a glass of water?"

"Yeah, sure."

While Lee signed some papers, Sam watched him. "Is there anything you want to add to your statement from earlier?"

Lee tossed down the pen. "Like what? The old man is dead. I didn't see him before I went to work. I haven't seen hide nor hair of him since March second. I didn't like him. I suppose I loved him 'cause he was my dad, but honestly I'm glad he's dead and I don't have to put up with his garbage. Anything else?"

Sam appraised the younger man in front of him, his gaze cool and professional, not betraying a single thought. "Not right now. I'll be in touch as the investigation progresses, including when the autopsy is finished and we have an official cause of death."

That brought me up short. "Wait, didn't he drown? You said he was pulled out of the river at the foot of Child Street."

Sam spoke to me, but his eyes never left Lee's face. "He was, but until the coroner finishes, we won't know if he drowned or if there were other factors involved."

The men stared at each other for a long moment. Then Lee turned to me.

19

"Let's blow this joint."

"I'll get you a ride home," Sam said.

Lee didn't break his stride to the door. "Don't bother, we'll manage. C'mon, Betty."

I hung back to talk to Sam. "Was it an accident or not?"

His steady look gave no hint of his thoughts. He was prob'ly a great poker player. "We'll see what the autopsy tells us. Have a good night."

I emerged into the fresh night air to see Lee standing at the curb, staring at the ground. A few people bustled through downtown, along with a couple of cabs and the occasional bus. Overhead, threads of clouds streaked the sky, but stars twinkled down like points of ice. "Are you okay?" I asked.

Lee didn't look at me. He pulled a deck of cigarettes from his pocket and tapped one out. "Why wouldn't I be?" He lit up and exhaled, blowing a cloud of smoke. "I wasn't kidding, Betty. I'm glad he's dead."

"Lee, cut it out. You'll get in trouble."

"Why? When he was home, he was either drunk or lookin' to get plastered. He used my mother for a punching bag. I kept my sisters as far away from him as possible. He fought with me, and I don't mean just words, either. Remember that shiner I had last month?"

I nodded. It had been a big, ugly purple bruise down Lee's left cheek. A work accident, he'd said.

"That wasn't from banging against anything at GM. My father sucker-punched me after I told him I'd dumped his precious whiskey and he better never bring another bottle into the house." Lee's eyes sparkled in the glow of the lamplight. "Nobody who knew the whole story would blame me for feeling like I do. If you do, we aren't as good friends as I thought." He walked down the street to the bus stop. His limp seemed worse than it usually was.

I watched him go. I knew things hadn't been good at the Tillotson house for a while, but I also remembered better times. Mr. Tillotson fixing Sean's bike. Taking me and Lee to the park and pushing us on the swings. Going for ice cream afterward. I couldn't believe Lee didn't miss that, or that the memories didn't make him sad. Had things really been so bad that all Lee had left was his anger?

As I made my way toward the stop, another thought crossed my mind. Detective MacKinnon's cool, professional expression as he studied Lee, asking questions. I hoped the autopsy proved Mr. Tillotson's death had been an accident. Because if that wasn't the case, things were gonna get tight for my best friend.

Chapter Five

Dot pounced on me as soon as I got to the bus stop the next morning. "What happened at the morgue? Lee wouldn't say anything other than it was his father. He thanked me for watching the girls and told me to scram. Nicely, of course."

I told her everything, including my conversation with Lee. "He doesn't understand how serious this is."

"I dunno. I'm on his side. You know how it was at the Tillotsons. I don't see how anyone would hold it against him that he's glad his dad was dead."

"Dot, don't be a sap." The bus arrived and we got on. I went to the back and grabbed a seat next to a guy who was obviously coming home from working the night shift and grabbing a few Zs before he got there. I sat and pulled her down next to me. "What if the autopsy shows Mr. Tillotson's death wasn't an accident?"

"Oh, come on." Dot rolled her peepers. "Who in his right mind would want to kill an old drunk?"

"How 'bout the son who's tired of seeing his mother get whaled on when the 'old drunk' comes home?"

It took a second, but I could see the realization dawn in Dot's eyes. "Come off it," she said. "Lee wouldn't kill someone."

"Not on purpose, but what if things got outta hand?"

Dot bit her lip. "You said Mr. Tillotson's body was found at the foot of Child Street."

"That's what Detective MacKinnon told us."

"Then how did it get there? We don't live anywhere near that spot. I can't see Lee dragging his dad's body blocks and blocks to pitch it in the river down there. What, he got on a bus with it? You don't think that would make people talk?"

She had a point. "Maybe he didn't go in the river there. He coulda fallen in further upstream and that's just where he washed up."

She snorted. "Like where?"

"I don't know, but I'm gonna find out." Before my best friend took the rap for something he didn't do.

* * *

After work, I hightailed it over to the Tillotson house. "Afternoon, Mrs. T. May I come in?"

She pulled open the door. "Of course, Betty. Lee isn't home yet."

"That's okay. I didn't want to talk to him." I pulled off my mittens and unwound my muffler.

"It's pretty windy out there." She closed the door and waved toward the kitchen. "I have a little tea if you want something to warm you up."

Sharing a drink might make the conversation seem more normal. "That'd be swell, thanks." I followed her and took the offered seat at the table.

She bustled around the kitchen, getting cups and filling the kettle. "If you aren't looking for Lee, who do you want to talk to?"

"You. Say, where are Anna and Emma?" I didn't want the girls busting in on the conversation.

"In their rooms doing schoolwork. I hope Lee is home on time tonight. Emma has more math and I'm no good at that kind of thing." She put down a sugar bowl with so little in it I could see the bottom. Likewise, the tiny milk pitcher held maybe three drops. I'd be drinking my tea black. "I'm sorry I don't have anything else to offer you. Unless you want slightly stale birthday cake," she said.

"No, thank you."

She sat and smoothed her dress. "What on earth do you want to talk to me for?"

"Has Detective MacKinnon been to see you today?"

"No. Of course, I went to the market earlier, so I might have missed him."

"If he'd been here, he woulda left a note or something behind, I'm sure of it." So either the autopsy wasn't done yet, or Sam had other things to do before he followed up with the Tillotsons. "How have things been around the house?"

"Fine, Betty, just fine."

The forced note of cheerfulness in her voice didn't fool me. "Mrs. T, that's not even close to the truth and you know it. Lee has told me about his dad's drinking, so I know it's not been easy."

"Then why ask?" The kettle started to whistle, and she went to get it.

"Because I wanna hear it from you."

She fussed with the cups, pouring water. "I hope there's enough milk and sugar." She set my tea in front of me.

"You're avoiding my question." I blew on the tea, sending steam over the table.

She dropped into the seat opposite and stared at her cup. "It's been... difficult, if you must know. John is a good man. But that accident last summer, it was worse than anyone knew. He didn't mean for any of this to happen."

"But it did."

"He's never been a good drunk, I knew that before I married him. So did he, which is why he rarely drank. Oh, he might have a beer with the guys after work, but that was all. Then he hurt his back and the whiskey was the only way he could keep the pain away." She took a sip, averting her face.

"It got out of hand."

She paused and nodded. "When he was sober, he hated it. He'd say all the time how he'd give up the bottle, and this time he meant it. Then he'd go off, to work I thought, but when he came home, he'd be so drunk." She closed her eyes. "I could handle him taking out his anger on me. But it broke my heart seeing him fight with Lee."

While all along, her son felt just the opposite. "Mr. Tillotson never hit the girls?"

Her eyes flew open. "Oh, no. I don't think Lee or I would have tolerated that. No, they learned to stay away when their dad was in a mood. Lee and I were the only ones he fought with, either with words or his fists."

This was where it got tricky. "Did you ever wish he was gone? Or did Lee? Did you talk about it?"

"Sometimes." Her voice was only a little louder than a whisper. "One evening, Lee came home and found me in the bathroom, crying. John had been the worst I'd ever seen him. Fortunately, he passed out before he could really hurt me. I called my mother to get the girls and locked myself in so if he woke up he wouldn't find me."

"What did Lee say?" I took a drink.

She hesitated, staring at her hands. "That he'd kill his father if he ever laid a hand on me again." She looked up. Her eyes glimmered wetly in the kitchen light. "But this was an accident, John dying. Why are you even asking these questions?"

I fiddled with my cup. There was no good way to put it. "The reason I asked if Detective MacKinnon had been back is 'cause they're doing an autopsy. That'll tell the cops whether it's a real accident or not."

"If John was in the water, didn't he drown?"

"It could be he was dead before he went in the river. Or maybe there are injuries that meant he wasn't awake when he fell in, like being hit on the head or something. If that's the case," I paused, taking in her expression, "it would be murder."

She gasped.

"If Lee hated his dad that much, and actually threatened him, that's bad. The cops will be wondering if he killed Mr. Tillotson."

She put a trembling hand to her mouth. "I won't tell them, then. What he said, Lee. That way the police will never know."

"'Cept Lee has already said he's not sorry his father is dead. I'm afraid the damage is done."

She tried to pick up her tea, but her hand was so wobbly she knocked it over, sending brown liquid everywhere. She jumped up and grabbed a towel. "What am I going to do? I can't let them arrest my boy." She swabbed

25

at the table, but all she did was make a bigger mess.

"Believe me, I'm not too keen on that happening, either." I took the cloth from her and wiped up properly. "Tell me, did your husband have any enemies? People he argued with? Maybe someone at work?"

"John didn't talk much about his job. Or anything else. And the only people I know he fought regularly with were Lee and me."

That wasn't gonna help. "Where did he go to drink?"

She wrung her hands. "I don't know, wait, yes. He used to go to O'Malley's. He'd go straight there after work." Her eyes were huge. "Betty, Lee said you're a detective, is that right?"

"Yeah. I am."

She grabbed my hand. "Find out what happened, for Lee's sake. I'll pay you anything."

I patted her wrist. "Don't worry about the money, Mrs. T. I planned on poking around anyway. I know he's innocent and I'm gonna prove it."

Chapter Six

When Pop got home at six-thirty, I met him in the hallway. "Do you know anything about the bar called O'Malley's?"

He put his lunch pail on the hall table and hung his coat in the closet. He faced me. "Very little and what I know isn't good. Why?"

"I need to visit. If it's a bad place, I hoped you'd go with me."

"Betty, I don't think—"

We were interrupted by a frantic pounding on the door. Pop opened it to show Mrs. Tillotson, hand raised to knock again. Her face looked a mess, tear-streaked, pale, and her eyes were red from crying. "Betty, have you seen Lee?"

"No, ma'am. What's wrong?"

Pop stood aside. "Come in, Nora. Where are the girls?"

"I asked Mrs. Lennox to watch them for a few minutes." She stood in our entryway, wringing her hands. Her hair was wild, strands pulled out of her bun and stuck to her face. "You sure you haven't seen Lee?"

Mom came into the hall. "Nora? What on earth is the matter?"

"It's getting awful crowded. Let's go to the kitchen," Pop said and led the way.

Once there, Mom automatically started making tea. I guess she took one look at our visitor in the light and decided steps had to be taken. "What's the fuss, Nora? Something about Lee?"

I had an idea of what had happened. "Did Detective MacKinnon come to see you?"

Mrs. T nodded and more hair came loose from the force. "Yes. It was about half an hour after you left, Betty. He said, oh, goodness, I can barely repeat it."

"Was it about John?" Mom asked.

"Yes." The word came out in a wail and Mrs. T buried her face in her hands. We all let her sit a moment. Eventually, she pulled herself together, kind of at least, and looked at us. "They did that aw, aught—"

"Autopsy?" I asked.

"Yes, that." She dabbed her nose with her sleeve. Pop passed her his handkerchief. "He said John drowned, but he also had a cracked skull. The detective said he was probably hit before he fell in the water."

Pop, Mom, and I exchanged a dark look. "They're sayin' it's murder," I said.

Mrs. T burst into tears.

Mom set a steaming mug of tea in front of her, then moved to rub her shoulders. "What does this all have to do with Lee?"

Pop shot me a look out of the corner of his eye. He knew exactly what it meant.

"I don't know, the detective wouldn't say much, only that he wanted to talk to Lee," Mrs. T said. She hiccupped and took a sip of tea. "I said he wasn't home yet, I don't know where he is. That's the truth. The detective gave me a number and said it was very important Lee call him as soon as possible." She gripped her mug. "Betty, he's usually home by now. You don't think…you don't think he's run off, do you?"

"He wouldn't do that." But he was in big trouble. I knew he shouldn't have run his yap.

"I still don't understand," Mom said. "Why do they want to talk to Lee?"

"Because he's a suspect," Pop said. He was a lot blunter than I woulda been. Then again, he was older.

Mom slapped her hands over her mouth.

Mrs. T slurped her tea. Pop's hand twitched and I wondered if maybe he wanted to take it away and put a shot of whiskey in it, "for medicinal purposes." 'Cause she sure did look like she needed a bit of a pick-me-up, as my grandfather used to say. Eventually, she spoke again. "What I don't

28

understand is why Lee isn't home yet. His shift ended at three."

"He coulda gotten held up at work, right, Pop?" I said.

"Doing what?" she asked.

He reached over and patted her arm. "There's lots of reasons they could have asked him to stay late, Nora. It could be they got a big order of Allison engines and need men to work overtime. Maybe one of the machines broke down and they needed Lee to stay and help with repairs."

"Wouldn't he have called?"

"He might not have had time." He stood. "I wouldn't worry until it gets late and by that, I mean at least ten. Mary, would you take Nora home and sit with her? Mary Kate can watch the boys."

"Certainly." Mom knew when her husband didn't want to argue, that's for sure. Normally, she would have been full of questions or reasons why she couldn't. But Pop's tone said loud and clear that this was not a request.

"Good. Betty, I believe you wanted to go somewhere."

I blinked. O'Malley's had slipped my mind in all the hullabaloo with Mrs. T. "Yes, sir. I did."

Ever the gentleman, he stepped back and held out his arm. "Then get your coat and let's go."

* * *

Pop and I walked at a brisk pace, our breath glittering in the evening air. O'Malley's was only a couple blocks away, an easy walking distance, which was prob'ly why Mr. Tillotson had chosen it as his watering hole. He could save on bus fare and have more money for alcohol.

Pop's profile looked chiseled from granite in the glow of the streetlamps. He strode beside me, jaw clenched and his hands in his pockets. His expression, sterner and darker than I'd ever seen, discouraged talk.

But after a while, I broke the silence. "Pop? You were gonna tell me it wasn't a good idea for me to go to this place, weren't you?"

"I was."

"What changed your mind?"

A muscle twitched in his jaw. "Nora Tillotson is a good woman. She's put up with a lot over the last several months." His eyes flicked to me, then he looked straight ahead. "Yes, Betty, I know what's been going on behind closed doors."

"You did? Then how come you didn't say anything?"

"Not to you, I didn't. I've talked to your mother. And I've had several conversations with John. He was in a bad way. But he couldn't seem to help himself. Now it's too late."

"I wouldn't think it would be so hard to dry out. It's not like he'd been drinking for years."

"I'm not sure that was the whole problem." Pop halted at a corner, looked both ways, then hustled across the street.

I hurried to follow. "I don't understand."

"The last time I talked to him, I told him he needed to lay off the whiskey and get sober. He had a good wife, a nice family, and he wouldn't want to lose it. He said, 'Joe, it's more than that. I'm in a hole and I can't see a way out.' I told him the first step to getting out of a spot like that was to put down the shovel and stop digging."

"What'd he say to that?"

"He told me he would try, but the people supervising the work probably wouldn't let him. O'Malley's is that way." He turned left.

I trailed by a couple steps, mulling over the words. What he'd said to Pop made me think he was in bad trouble with the wrong people. I jogged to catch up. "When did he tell you this?"

"Two weeks ago, right before he disappeared. Here we are." Pop stopped in front of a dirty brick building, with a peeling beer sign and a faded metal placard on the wall that said "O—alley's." Judging by the dirt, the M had gone AWOL a long time ago.

"That doesn't fully explain why you came along. Sure, you admire Mrs. Tillotson and you feel bad for her. But normally you'd offer sympathy, tell Mom to take care of it, and stay out of the way. Why are you standing here instead of sitting in your cozy living room smoking your evening pipe and listening to the radio?"

"Because Lee Tillotson is on the way to being a fine man," Pop said. "When war came, and he couldn't enlist because of that leg injury, he didn't whine or moan. He didn't go off to drown his sorrows in the nearest bottle. He bucked up, got a job at General Motors, and pitched in as best he could by building the engines America needs. He stepped up to take care of his mother and his sisters. I'll be damned if I'll sit by and let a boy like that be railroaded for a crime he would not, could not, commit."

I'd never heard such a fierce tone in his voice. It was almost like he was talkin' about one of his own sons. "I had no idea you cared about Lee so much."

Pop's cheeks were red. It mighta been from the cold, but the color was a little too deep for it all to be from the weather. "This is important, so listen. O'Malley's isn't just a working man's bar. I can't be sure, but I've heard some shady characters come here. Gambling, some minor black-market deals, maybe more. You stay next to me and let me do the talking, unless I say it's okay for you to speak. If you can't follow those rules, I'll leave and drag you out. You got that?"

"Yes, sir." We went inside.

To call O'Malley's dingy would be kind. Cigarette smoke choked the air. The lights were low, putting much of the main room into a shadow that bordered on darkness. The brands of beer were unfamiliar and a thick layer of dust lay on the few whiskey bottles behind the bar, where the grimy mirror barely reflected the room. Men in worn work clothes stopped what they were doing to look at us. The air was close and unpleasant, a mixture of smoke and stale sweat. The low murmur of voices stopped when we came in, but picked up again almost immediately. The bartender leaned over to whisper to a couple of men and they laughed, a coarse, crude sound. A couple of characters in the corner paused their game of pool, but went back to it after giving us a quick once-over.

"Excuse me." Pop used his "big" voice, the one sure to call Michael or Jimmy from whatever they were doing, or that he prob'ly used while working at Bethlehem Steel. "This young lady is looking for someone. It would be nice if one of you can help her."

A seedy man, unsteady on his feet, wove over to us. A little of the beer in his mug slopped onto his hand and dripped onto the floor. "Hey, girlie," he said, words slurring. "Why doncha ditch Pops there and come over? I'll show you a good time." He reached out to touch my shoulder.

Pop grabbed the man's wrist before the hand got within six inches of me. "Don't touch my daughter."

Not even the drunk could miss the veiled threat in Pop's words, a steel fist in a velvet glove. The man stepped back and blinked like an owl. "I don't mean nuthin'. She's a looker though. You're a lucky man."

Pop folded his arms and stared.

The drunk wilted and slunk away.

Pop raised his voice. "Anyone else?"

Most of the drinkers turned back to their booze. The bartender resumed wiping his glass. I decided we'd struck out, when another man, wearing well-worn but clean, or at least cleaner, clothes came over. "Who are you looking for?"

Pop nodded to me.

I wanted to sag with relief and not just 'cause Pop was at my side. This guy seemed a whole lot neater, more sober, and more respectable. "I'm lookin' for anyone who knew John Tillotson. I've been told he drank here a lot."

"Still does, as far as I know," the man said.

I glanced at Pop, who nodded again. "Not anymore," I said to my new source. "He's dead. Police fished him outta the Buffalo River yesterday."

"Is that so?" The man's expression didn't change. He mighta just learned there was snow expected in the morning. Did he not care or was he not surprised?

"Yep." Emboldened by his manner, I continued. "Did you know him?"

A canny look came over his face. "What's it worth to you?"

Next to me, a deep rumbling sound came from Pop's throat. The man backed up a pace.

I didn't want to lose a source. "You tell me your price, I'll tell you if it's worth that much."

The man licked his lips. "Buy me a beer and I'll tell you what I know."

"Okay. But nothing fancy. Pop, would you stay with him?"

He gave a brisk nod and I went off to the bar, where I ordered a beer. I tried to ignore the looks from the other men seated there and said a silent prayer of thanksgiving I'd had the sense to ask my father to come with me. The bartender slid over a streaky glass filled with amber liquid that barely smelled like beer. Whatever it was, it couldn't be quality stuff.

I went back to my newfound friend and handed him the glass. "Let's sit over there, where we can talk." I pointed at a booth.

"Sure." He followed me, Pop close on his heels.

After we settled into our seats, Pop and I facing the other guy, I pulled out my notebook and a pencil stub. "Now tell me what you know about John Tillotson."

"I didn't know him that well, so it isn't much," the man said. "Oh, I used to see him when he came in, but I didn't talk to him. Too loud and obnoxious for my taste."

Having seen Mr. Tillotson when he was drunk, I could well imagine how he'd behave in a bar. "Who'd he drink with? Or was he mostly a loner?"

The man scratched his chin and thought a moment. "Danny Howley and Ned McDougal," he finally said. "I saw them together a lot. 'Specially Ned. I think…"

When the man didn't say anything else, Pop leaned closer. "What?"

The man dropped his voice. "You didn't hear this from me, 'kay?"

"I don't even know your name," I said. "What is it, anyway?"

"No, I ain't gonna tell you that. You don't know my name, you can't say who you heard it from."

"Okay. What's the dope?"

He shot a glance around the bar, but no one was lookin' at us. "I think they ran numbers. I don't know who for. I stay away from that. But I know some of the guys in here are elbow-deep in various shenanigans. Everything from numbers to loans, to horse racing, even a little black-market action and smuggling from Canada. Given the amount of time the three of them spent together, well, it wouldn't surprise me if they were all in it."

"You think they were in charge or did they work for someone?"

"I wouldn't put them in charge of garbage collection. Danny and Ned are smart, but not that smart. John drank too much." The man wrinkled his nose. "No, they woulda been working for someone, but don't ask who 'cause I don't know."

"Thanks," I said. "I don't suppose either Mr. Howley or Mr. McDougal is here tonight, are they?"

"Nope. They might come in later, but honestly, I wouldn't recommend you coming back or sticking around. Not even with the big guy next to you. Take care." He wandered off.

No one else looked like he wanted to gab, so Pop and I left. Once we were outside, I blew out a breath. "I sure am glad you were there, Pop."

He gave the place the once over and walked away. "I wasn't going to let my darlin' girl go into that hole by herself."

I matched his stride. "I don't s'pose you know either of those characters."

"McDougal or Howley? No. They don't sound like men who would hold honest jobs." He paused to wait for a truck to rumble by and crossed the street. "I don't recommend you going back to O'Malley's either. Not with me, not with Lee. Even if he has his knife."

"Oh, c'mon, Pop. Lee doesn't get into those kinds of jams."

"He's a First Ward boy." The knowing look in Pop's eyes said it all. "Oh, I don't think Lee goes looking for trouble or wants to start a fight. But just like Sean, I'm sure he can finish one if it comes to him."

Since that was the plain truth, I let it go. "Then how am I gonna find these two guys? They prob'ly aren't listed in the society pages of the *Courier-Express*."

Pop stopped outside an all-night diner. "A detective like you doesn't have contacts?"

He was right. I could ask Sam if he'd heard of Howley or McDougal. He might even offer to come along to talk to 'em. Surely nobody would tangle with a cop packing heat. I doubted Mr. Tillotson would have brought his so-called friends home, but I could ask Mrs. T and Lee all the same.

As if Pop had read my mind, he nodded. "Now you're thinking." He glanced at the window. "Want to grab a cup of joe? I hear it's a popular drink with private detectives. I'd rather you partake of that than whiskey."

"You buyin'?"

"Is that any way to treat the man who just provided you with protection services?"

I laughed and hooked my arm through his, and we went inside.

Chapter Seven

In the morning, I told Mom I might be late for dinner. "Did Lee make it home?" I asked as I pulled on my coat.

She nodded. "It was very late."

"Did he say where he'd been?"

Her eyes shone with worry. "He only said he'd been at work. Then he went to his room and slammed the door." She paused. "To tell you the truth, it wasn't like him at all. He didn't ask how I was doing, or about the family… just an abrupt good night and he left."

I had a sneaking suspicion that whatever had him on edge it had little to nothing to do with work.

I had to wait until after work to try and talk to Sam. Dot rode the bus with me downtown. "I'm jealous," she said. "Since when do your folks let you do whatever you want?"

"Believe me, it's not quite like that." I gathered my things. "But I laid it out for Pop last December. I was gonna be a detective, whether he liked it or not. So he could either cut me a little slack when it came to hours, 'cause it's not like I can investigate when I'm s'posed to be at Bell, or I'd move out. I guess he didn't want to lose my company."

"I'm still jealous." Dot's parents were rigid in their discipline. Until she married or moved out, nothin' would sway them. "You'll let me know what Detective MacKinnon says, right?"

"You bet." The bus stopped and I alighted on the sidewalk outside police headquarters. The weather had changed and it was warm for March. Business folks had left their offices, and stood on corners or flagged down

36

taxis in the failing afternoon light. I stopped to consider my approach. I knew from past dealings Sam was unlikely to give me the skinny on an investigation just 'cause I batted my eyes and said "please." In this case, it was doubly unlikely he would cut me in on the action. I was best friends with Lee, who had to be the prime suspect. In fact, I'd have to be careful not to trip up and give Sam any more ammunition than he already had.

I entered and asked the sergeant at the desk if I could speak to Detective MacKinnon. After taking my name, the man pointed at a bench where I could sit and wait.

Sam appeared a couple of minutes later. "I knew it was only a matter of time before you came to see me."

I stood. "The father of one of my close friends murdered? Of course, I was gonna come." I paused. "Have you talked to Lee?"

Sam crooked his finger and we headed for the elevator. "Let's talk about this upstairs." The car arrived and we got in. He pushed a button and the elevator began its climb.

I'd never been to a police office, but it looked exactly like the ones I'd seen in the movies. Men with ties loosened, shirtsleeves rolled, and jackets slung over the back of their chairs sat at the desks. Some smoked and talked on the phone, others pounded the keys of typewriters. A couple looked up as I followed Sam through the maze of desks.

He led me to a small room with a scarred wooden table that took up most of the space. He gestured at one chair and he pulled out the other for himself.

I sat. "Mrs. Tillotson came by my house last night, so I know her husband was murdered. I know you're lookin' for Lee. Have you talked to him?"

"No." Sam leaned back and pulled out a deck of cigarettes. He offered me one, but I remembered the taste of his brand, not at all like my favorite Lucky Strike Green, and shook my head. After he lit up and inhaled, he said, "I stopped again this morning, but he'd already left for work." Smoke escaped his mouth as he talked.

"You didn't go to General Motors to look for him?"

"Right now there's not enough urgency."

"After the way he yammered when we were here to identify the body, I was sure he'd be at the top of your list."

"He's near it." Sam tapped ash into the tray on the table. "You're right about that. But I'm not ready to slap the cuffs on him and I don't think he's going to skip town. His family will keep him here."

I revised my questions. "Mrs. T said he, Mr. Tillotson I mean, was bashed on the head. Did he die from that or did he drown?"

"He drowned. Considering the nature of the fractured skull and the location of the injury, the pathologist is pretty sure he was unconscious, but alive, when he went into the water." He inhaled on his smoke and the end glowed bright orange.

I drummed my fingers. "You found him at the foot of Child Street, you said."

Sam nodded.

"Is that where he went in? Can you tell when he died?"

He said nothing.

"Oh, come on, Sam. He's been missing for almost two weeks." I shook my head. "He was either coshed somewhere else and floated to Child Street, or he had been lurking around for a couple of weeks and was killed recently. I know the river, same as you. No way he was gonna float in that spot for so long. Somebody woulda seen him. There's too much barge traffic. Not only that, he prob'ly would have broken free and would be over Niagara Falls by now anyway. And I saw the body, remember? I'll bet you a cup of coffee he's been in the water for a good bit of time. That much I know from the movies."

He studied me and then grinned. "You are too smart by half, you know that?" He tapped ash off his cigarette again. "Obviously, I can't tell you everything. One, it's an ongoing investigation, and two, as you said, you're close to a major suspect. But you'll get this much out of your friend once I talk to him, so I might as well tell you now." He leaned forward. "You're right. The victim had been in the water for a while. Our best guess is that he was killed farther upstream, floated down, and got tangled up near Child."

I drummed my fingers. "You think he was dumped in the lake?"

"Not precisely." He didn't elaborate.

Where else would a body float from 'cept Lake Erie? I thought about all the times Tom and I had walked the shore, all the little nooks and crannies from here to Hamburg. Then it hit me. The canals to the grain elevators. Those fed into the Buffalo River. Boats and barges tied up there all the time, but late at night, under the cover of darkness, would be a good time to dump someone. That left the question of why Mr. Tillotson would be down near the grain elevators in the first place, if that was indeed where he'd been killed, but I could answer that later.

Sam watched me. "You have an idea, don't you? What is it?"

I grinned. "If you're not gonna tell me where you think he went in, I don't have to tell you my thoughts. We're not exactly on the same page on this one."

"You know how it is, Betty. I can't tell you everything. Not on an open case."

"I get it. Frankly, I'm not sure what my idea is yet. I wanna think about it some more." I paused. "One more thing. Can you tell me when this happened?"

"That's also something you'll most likely get out of young Mr. Tillotson when you talk to him, so I might as well tell you. The pathologist's best guess is this all happened around the time he disappeared. In other words, he didn't go somewhere, hang out for a few days, then encounter whoever killed him. We can't be too precise, but I think a safe bet is he was killed within twenty-four hours of his disappearance."

From the night of the second through the third, then. True, as Sam said it was a guess, but I knew he was good enough at his job that he was prob'ly not far off the mark. I stood. "Thank you for the information, Detective."

He followed suit. "You're not going to help me out on this one, are you?"

I opened the door. "If your intention is to put my childhood friend in jail, no, I won't." I paused. "Have you found Howley and McDougal yet?"

He blinked. "Who are they?"

"They're people you should talk to. That's all I'm at liberty to say. Good afternoon, Detective." I strode through the desks, garnering a few looks as I went. I had no doubt Sam would sniff out all the information on Howley and McDougal eventually. So would I. Hopefully whatever they said would lead away from Lee, not toward him.

* * *

By the time I made it back to the First Ward, it was five o'clock. I paused outside my house. I could go inside, eat, and then talk to Lee. But for all I knew, Sam had left HQ hot on my heels. He wouldn't have to wait for a bus, he had a car. I headed for Lee's place.

When I knocked on the door, Lee answered.

I didn't bother with a greeting. "Is Detective MacKinnon here?" I brushed past him and looked in the living room. Anna and Emma sat in front of the radio, listening to one of the afternoon programs.

"Hello," Lee said. "Nice to see you. Take off your coat."

"I haven't got time for that." I turned to him. "The detective could be here any minute."

"So?"

"He wants to talk to you."

"I don't have anything more to say about my old man."

I gave him a gentle push. "Don't be stupid. Did you talk to your mother?"

"Let's go to the kitchen. Dot's in there." He led the way.

Dot sat at the table, chewing away on her lip, her eyes big as saucers. "Betty. What's the news?"

I took off my coat and hung it on the back of the chair. "Just a minute, Dot." I fixed Lee with a stare. "Did you talk to your mom?"

"Yeah." He sat next to Dot and stretched his bum leg out under the table. "Who knew someone hated the old man enough to kill him?"

"Lee, I gotta ask." I hesitated. "Did you?"

"What?"

"Kill your dad?"

Dot yelped. "Betty! How could you ask that?"

"The fact is the police are gonna be lookin' at you, Lee," I said, ignoring her. "I'm surprised they aren't here already. I left HQ less than two hours ago and MacKinnon got awfully tight-lipped when I brought the subject around to you. You went on record as sayin' you hated your father and you wanted him gone. So did you do it?"

"What do you think?" Lee's voice and expression were flat and gave no hint to what was goin' on behind his eyes.

"Doggone it, don't play games with me. I'm on your side, but I gotta have facts to work with."

Our conversation was interrupted by the doorbell. Without a word, Lee rose and went to answer it. I heard men's voices and exchanged a look with Dot. *Police*, I mouthed.

She squeaked.

Moments later, Lee and Detective MacKinnon appeared in the doorway. "I expect you remember Dot Kilbride," Lee said. "And I know you're familiar with Betty here." He leaned against the fridge, arms crossed.

Sam tipped his fedora in our direction. "Ladies." He didn't seem surprised to see us. "Can we speak in private?"

"Anything you have to tell me can be said in front of them," Lee answered in a stony voice.

If the answer bothered Sam, he hid it well. "I'm glad I finally caught up to you, Mr. Tillotson. I've been trying since yesterday."

"My name's Lee," he said in clipped tones. "Mr. Tillotson is my father, even if he is dead."

"Have it your way, Lee," Sam said. "Where have you been?"

"Work."

"Your mother expected you home last night around five. When I saw her, she was surprised you weren't."

"We had a problem at the plant." Lee didn't offer any further explanation.

Sam didn't ask for one. Maybe he already knew. "I gather you've spoken with your mother by now, so you know the situation with your father."

Lee jerked his head in a nod.

Dot opened her mouth, but I laid my hand on her arm. We didn't need to be busting in on things. Yet.

41

Sam cast a look in my direction. Then he focused on Lee. "May I ask you a few more questions?" Judging by Sam's tone, it wasn't really a request.

Lee's brain had to be humming like a well-tuned Allison, but you couldn't tell from looking at him. "Sure."

Likewise, if the curt answers angered Sam, he gave no hint of it. He took out his notepad. "When you came down to the morgue for the identification, you expressed, shall we say, a satisfaction your father wasn't going to be around. Is that true?"

"Yeah."

"Why is that?"

For the first time, a hint of annoyance showed on Lee's face. "I already told you. He made this house a nightmare."

"I see." Sam paused to check his notes. "He ever hit your sisters?"

"No, thank God. I kept him from doin' that."

"And you said the last time you saw him was...?"

"March second, that afternoon."

"Ah." Another glance at the page. "You said previously you hadn't seen him that day."

My skin prickled. I'd seen enough detective flicks to know people changing their stories wasn't a good sign.

A flash of confusion crossed Lee's face. "I forgot. I did see him briefly when I got home."

"Oh?"

"Yeah. He was half outta his mind. He couldn't find his booze and he was ranting about something. I'd thrown the whiskey out. I told him, he got even angrier, and stormed outta the house."

"You said he was ranting. About what?"

I wondered if Sam had already learned who Howley and MacDougal were. Prob'ly so. Sam was no slouch when it came to detecting.

Lee's shoulders moved up and down. "Dunno. Like I said, he was drunk. He was slurring his words, staggering around, bellowing. Half of what he said was nonsense. Something about a dame, and the guys, and he would do whatever he needed to."

I wished I could write all this down 'cause I had a feeling it was important. But it wasn't the time to whip out pen and paper. I'd have to commit as much as I could to memory and ask Lee to repeat it later.

"I see." Sam jotted a note. "The night of March second, where were you?"

Lee raised his eyebrows. "Huh? I was here, didn't I just say that?"

Sam waved his hand in a circle. "I mean after you talked to your father. Did you stay home? Did you leave?"

Lee licked his lips. "I…I went out. I had to clear my mind."

"Did you go alone?"

Dot jumped up and spoke before I could do anything to stop her. "He was with me."

Sam turned oh so slowly to face her. "Is that so?"

"Yeah, we…we met up and went to the pictures. Just Lee and me."

I stuffed down a groan. *Oh, Dot, don't do it.*

Sam didn't flinch. "What did you see?"

She shot a look at Lee, who didn't move, then at me. "The…we saw the new Bogie flick. With Ingrid Bergman."

"*Casablanca?*"

"Yeah, that's it. *Casablanca.*" She lifted her chin, daring Sam to challenge her.

He didn't, simply wrote another note in his book. "I think that's all for now. I'd appreciate it if you wouldn't leave Buffalo for a while, but of course, I can't make you do anything. I might have more questions later. As the investigation progresses."

Lee remained frozen in place. "I got a job, a family to take care of, and a father to bury. I ain't going nowhere."

He may have been doing his best statue impression, but his bad grammar was a dead giveaway for me. Lee was upset. But whether it was 'cause of Sam's questions or his new situation as head of household, I couldn't tell.

The two men stared at each other. When it became obvious neither of them was gonna move, I stood. "If you're all done, Detective, I'll show you out."

"Thank you, Miss Ahern." He didn't break eye contact with Lee for a long second, then followed me out of the kitchen.

I opened the front door. "He didn't do it."

"Do what?" Sam buttoned his trenchcoat and pulled the belt tight.

"He didn't kill his father. Lee wouldn't do that. Punch his lights out, yeah. He might even throw Mr. Tillotson out and tell him to not come back. But not murder."

"You seem very sure."

I drew myself up. "I've known Lee Tillotson since I was in pigtails. He's loyal, caring, a good son and brother, and he'd never abandon a friend in need. But he wouldn't kill."

"Not even by accident?"

I had no response to that. I felt like Sam had Superman's powers, able to see right through me into my head and read my thoughts.

Sam tugged the brim of his fedora. "Good night, Miss Ahern. I'll be seeing you."

Chapter Eight

I closed the door behind Sam and returned to the kitchen. Dot and Lee were seated at the table. She had her hand over his and spoke in a low voice.

I put my hands on my hips and did my best imitation of my mother. "What was that about?"

Dot blinked. "What?"

"Telling Detective MacKinnon you were at the movies."

"I needed to give Lee an alibi, didn't I? It's plain to me that detective has it out for him."

"But it's a lie." I turned my frustration on Lee. "How could you clam up and let her fib for you?"

He didn't say anything and a familiar stubborn expression came over his face.

Dot turned on her best innocent look. "It's the truth." She wilted a little under my silent stare. "Well, it could be."

"*Casablanca* came out in January. This is March. It hasn't been in theaters in a couple of weeks. At least not local ones that you would go to. I know that and so do you. If you don't think Sam MacKinnon knows, well, think again." I couldn't believe her. Yes, I could. Dot, loyal as the day was long, would go to any lengths to cover for a friend. I knew that and I'd benefitted from it a time or two. I thought Lee cared enough to keep her from doin' something this stupid, though.

"Maybe we went to a different theater," she said.

I threw up my hands. "You don't lie to the cops! Hasn't watching all those

45

detective pictures with me taught you anything?"

She scowled.

Lee spoke up. "Lay off. She's doin' a lot more than you are, Betty. I thought you'd be all over covering for me."

"Lee, when it's your mom asking who ate the last cookie, sure. I'll lie through my teeth and say it was me. But this is different."

His mulish look deepened. "I don't see how."

"Because, you ninny." I swatted his shoulder. "You're a suspect. You get caught in a lie, you look worse. I don't know whose brainchild this idea was, but it stinks."

Dot shot to her feet. "It was mine. I'm tryin' to keep him outta trouble. It sounds an awful lot like you're trying to do the exact opposite."

I covered my face with my hands. *Deep breath, girl.* After a moment, I lowered them. "I don't think Lee had anything to do with his dad's death and I told Detective MacKinnon exactly that. I'm not sure he believes me, but I told him."

"So what's the problem?" Lee crossed his arms over his chest.

"You start lying and the next thing you know, the cops will be expecting you to take a powder or something." I ran my hands through my hair. "I know you two weren't at the movies. Lee, where were you?"

He glanced at Dot.

"Don't look at her," I said. "Your best shot at stayin' out of jail is to be straight with me—and with Sam. Where were you?" I laid a bit more force on each word this time. "After you argued with your dad and left?"

If looks could kill, I'd be dead based on the glower he sent my way. "Out."

"Out where?"

"Walking."

"Where?"

"Around."

Sam must have been a better investigator, or at least a more patient one, than me 'cause the one-word answers really grated my nerves. I was tryin' to help him, for goodness sake, and he was treating me like the enemy. "Were you down by the grain elevators?"

He hesitated. "No. I went wandering through the neighborhood and wound up at Conway Park. I smoked a cigarette, calmed down, and came home."

Finally, a real answer. "When?"

"I dunno. Maybe around ten? No, closer to eleven. I heard the bells at Our Lady of Perpetual Help sound the hour."

"You were alone?"

He nodded.

"Did anyone see you?"

He snorted. "What part of 'alone' didn't you understand?"

"Don't be a fathead." I reached out to swat him again, but he pulled out of my reach. "Did you stop to buy a deck of smokes, or did you see anyone in the street? Anything like that?"

"No." He pushed away from the table and rubbed his bad leg. "You don't believe me, do you?"

"As a matter of fact, I do. After a blow-up with your old man, that's exactly what you'd be about. You'd go somewhere quiet to cool your heels." I turned away from the both of them, but it wasn't lost on me that he'd chosen to stand near Dot, about as far away from me as he could get in the small room. I nibbled my thumbnail. His story still wasn't right. He said he'd argued with his dad that afternoon, maybe around four. There was no way Lee had spent seven hours hanging out in Conway Park. I decided to let it go until I knew more. "Pop and I went to O'Malley's last night."

Dot broke in. "Your dad let you?"

I waved her off. "He was with me. It's not a place I'd go alone, that's for sure." I turned to Lee. "Did your dad ever mention guys named Danny Howley or Ned McDougal?"

Lee thought a moment. "No, I don't think I ever heard him talk about them. Who are they?"

"The man I talked to at O'Malley's thinks they're numbers runners. He said your dad might be one, too." I grabbed a sheet of paper and a pencil. "Lee, after your dad left the house that night would he have gone to see a friend from work?"

47

"Betty…Dad lost his job months ago. Before Thanksgiving." One look at Lee's face and it was clear the admission cost him, in pride if nothing else. "He didn't say much, but I know it was 'cause of his drinking. He'd leave here in the morning, say he was goin' to GM, but I'm pretty sure he would be at the bar, either O'Malley's or a place over in Tonawanda near the plant."

That's why Lee's statement when Sam had first come to the house bugged me. The way Lee talked made it sound like the others at GM knew about the murder when they couldn't have. It wasn't that they knew about his death, it was 'cause he didn't work there any longer.

Dot laid her hand on his shoulder. "Gosh, Lee. Why didn't you say anything?"

He shrugged it off. "What, you wanted me to admit my dad was a bum who couldn't take care of his family?" The bitterness in his words cut the air between us like a knife. "I wasn't gonna tell you, or anyone in this neighborhood, that. What would they think?"

I recalled Pop's words from yesterday. "They knew," I said, softening my voice. "At least the men did."

"Bet they had a laugh at that. John Tillotson, neighborhood drunk." He stalked to the other side of the table.

Dot looked like he'd slapped her.

I wrapped my arm around her shoulders. "If most of 'em thought like Pop, no, they didn't. Pop admires you, how you've handled it all."

"He feels sorry for me?" Lee showed us his back. It didn't look like he found my words very comforting.

"That's not it. I don't think Pop spends much time thinkin' about your dad, but he sure admires you. He wouldn't want to see you stuck with a murder rap. That's why he went with me to O'Malley's."

Lee didn't turn around.

Dot bit her lip and looked up at me.

"Lee, I already told your mom I'd get to the bottom of this. But you gotta help me." I took a deep breath. "Who was his best friend at GM? Someone who would know the skinny on why and how he lost his job."

For a minute, I didn't think Lee would answer me. But then the starch went out of his spine and he slumped. He turned around. "He used to have lots of friends. But at the end, I think only one guy really stood by him. Steve Daletzki. I think he lives over on Fillmore, in Polonia."

I scribbled down the name. It wasn't a lot to go on, but I figured I'd ask Emmie Brewka, a co-worker who I'd helped on my last case, if she knew of a family named Daletzki in her neighborhood. "Got it. I'll see if I can find him."

"I didn't hurt him, Betty. I swear. Sure, there were lots of times I wanted to, and I'm not sorry he's gone, but I never would have killed him." A few moments ago, Lee had been a sullen young man. Now he looked like a frightened little boy, eyes wide and voice pleading.

I went over and hugged him tight. It wasn't a very Sam Spade type of move, but who said I always had to be tough?

Chapter Nine

The next morning at Bell, I tracked down Emmie Brewka and found her as she walked across the yard to the paint building. "Hey, Emmie!"

She turned, her Shirley Temple dimples on full display. "Morning, Betty. What's shakin'?"

"Not a lot. I have a question for you."

"Can we walk and talk? Mr. Satterwaite told me I have to get over to paint on the double. Something about filling in for someone before the whole works get jammed up." She resumed her brisk walk.

I fell in step beside her. A weak March sun shone down on us, giving a pale light and not a lot of warmth. "I'm looking for a guy and hoped you could help me."

"I'm no detective, Betty. Not like you." She grinned. "Why don't you ask Dot?"

"I was thinkin' you might know this person. He lives in your neighborhood."

"Oh, that's different. Who?"

"His name is Steve, prob'ly Steven, Daletzki. He works at General Motors. Does the name sound familiar?"

"Daletzki." Her mouth puckered as she thought. "Let's see. There's a bunch of Daletzkis who live over on Reed Street. Oh, and old Mr. and Mrs. Daletzki on Strauss."

I fumbled in my pockets for the tiny notebook I'd started carrying. "This guy wouldn't be a grandpa, he's maybe around my pop's age, could be younger. I don't think the older folks are who I'm looking for."

"They might have a son, though."

She had a point. I jotted down the address. "Anyone else?"

We reached the paint building. Emmie stopped, hand on the door. "Talk to Mrs. Wiese. She lives on Woltz Avenue, number 148. I'm almost positive her maiden name was Daletzki, so she might know a Steven."

"Got it." I looked over my addresses. Three leads. Living in a close-knit community could be a pain 'cause everybody knew everything. But other times, like these, it was pure gold, 'specially for a detective. "Thanks for the help, Emmie."

"Sure thing." She opened the door. "After all the help you gave me in December with my grandma, it's the least I could do."

* * *

Dot had been unusually cold, bordering on distant, toward me all day. I figured she hadn't forgiven me for my perceived betrayal of Lee the previous night because I hadn't immediately put Sam MacKinnon in his place. "Dot, what's eating you?"

"Nothing."

"Oh, baloney." I nudged her. "You've barely talked to me all day. Are you still steamed about what happened with Detective MacKinnon?"

Her voice was icier than Lake Erie in January. "I have no problems with *him*. Your behavior after he left is completely different. How could you do that to Lee?"

I wondered if Lee felt the same. I needed to talk to him and make sure things were square between us. "I explained that, didn't I?"

"Hmph." Clearly, she didn't agree with my reasoning.

"I guess that means you don't want to go with me over to Polonia and look for this friend of Mr. Tillotson's. I'm gonna see if he knows anything that could help."

I half-expected a refusal, but it turned out wild horses couldn't keep her away. "You better not even think of going without me," she said, a note of warning in her voice.

"Are you sure you won't get in trouble with your parents?"

"I'll deal with it." Her eyes had an unusual flinty look to them. "What's our first stop?"

I gave up and consulted my notes. "I think we should start with the Daletzkis on Reed, then talk to the older couple. Let's save Mrs. Wiese for last."

"Why?"

"I dunno. It seems more sensible somehow. I get the feeling she's the most unlikely to be our girl. Plus if we hit all the stops in that order, it's almost a big circle. When we're finished, we should be right near a bus stop and we can head home."

She didn't say anything in reply and faced out the window, studying the dreary late-winter landscape as though it was the most interesting thing on earth.

I wondered what it would take to get back in her good graces. Scratch that. I knew exactly what it would take.

My plan, however, hit a snag from the very first. There were indeed a bunch of Daletzkis living on Reed, but none of them was named Steve. Of course, it couldn't be a quick conversation. I had not counted on folks yakkin' for almost half an hour while they discussed all of their relatives, where they lived, and whether any of the guys had the right name. A simple "no" would have been sufficient, but before Dot and I left, I knew the history of at least four families, none of whom were the people I wanted to talk to.

Our next stop was the elderly Daletzki couple. They answered my question quick enough. No, they didn't have any male relatives named Steve or Steven, but wouldn't we like some tea? Or some *kolache* cookies left over from Christmas? We endured three photo albums full of snaps of children, grandchildren, and even a couple of great-grandchildren before we escaped.

"Jiminy," Dot said when we reached the safety of the sidewalk. Her frostiness had melted under the onslaught of Polish hospitality. "These people sure do like to talk. If I'd had to oooh and ah over one more set of photos, I was gonna scream."

I chuckled as I drew a line through the addresses we'd visited. "I'm pretty sure it's not a trait that is exclusive to the Polish. We Irish can chat it up when we want to. My grandma told me stories about living in Ireland, all the men in the pub."

"I s'pose," Dot said. "I'm sure every grandparent alive thinks their grandkids are the most amazing ones ever, too. 'Cept mine, of course."

That diverted my attention. "They don't? But you go over to your grandparents' house all the time, including every major holiday, don't you? Both sets?"

"Mom's folks are okay, I guess. They don't think she married as well as her sisters. They never miss an opportunity to remind Mom that she's only got me, and her sisters have an entire baseball team between them. But Dad's parents, well, they don't like Mom, which means they don't like me. I think Dad's cousin or something back in Ireland is one step away from landed gentry. They're always needling Dad that he married a common woman and now he pays for it by working with his hands. When he told them I was goin' to work at Bell, saying they snapped their caps is an understatement."

I didn't talk much to Mr. and Mrs. Kilbride, but I'd never heard any of this. "Why?"

Her cheeks were pink and I didn't think it was 'cause of the cold. "They said real ladies didn't work in factories. It was a lot like what Mom said, but worse. They understand housewives, you know, homemakers. That's woman's work. But they figured I ruined my chances of a good marriage the moment I put on pants."

"What a lot of crap."

"Yeah, I know." She fiddled with her mittens. "Also…Dad doesn't like Lee." Seeing my expression, she hurried on. "Oh, don't get me wrong. He likes Lee enough as a person, you know as a guy to hit the bar with. Dad would stand Lee a drink any time. But he doesn't like Lee as a, well, as a man I should be involved with, if you take my meaning."

I heard the inflection of her words and knew exactly what she was talking about. "They don't think he's husband material. Why not?"

She stopped at a bench and flopped down. "It's 'cause of his leg, the limp. Dad said," she gulped and her eyes shone, "he said marrying a cripple would doom me to a life of poverty 'cause I'd always be working. And Lee was more likely to drink since he'd never get a good job, and maybe he'd turn out like his old man. Mr. Tillotson, I mean. You know, start drinking 'cause he's in pain from his leg and, well..." Her voice trailed off and she looked at the sidewalk. "This situation doesn't help."

If Dot's parents weren't keen on Lee 'cause of his limp and his dad's drinking, a murder in the Tillotson family wasn't gonna change their minds. If anything, it'd make them even more determined to keep their daughter far away. For a long moment, the power of speech left me. Finally, I got my voice back. "Do you love him? Lee, I mean."

She swung her feet and looked away. After a moment, she turned back, and her eyes shone. "More than anything, Betty. I envied you and Tom for a long time. I wondered if I'd ever find a guy. That's why I tried to meet as many boys as I could. Then last December I realized I already had. I don't know if he feels the same, though. He seems to like me well enough, like at the birthday party. Other times he's so...reserved. It's almost as though he doesn't want to encourage me. However he feels, though, I can't lose him, not now. Not before we find out if we can make something out of whatever it is we've got."

She finally had wised up. I sat next to her. "You listen to me, Dorothy Kilbride."

She sniffed.

"Liam Tillotson is the second-best guy in the world. I say second-best only 'cause of Tom. Heck, maybe they're tied. Anyway, Lee loves you. He might not say anything, but I can tell. If he's holding back, it's 'cause he isn't sure how *you* feel and that's gotta stop. Tell him straight up how it is. He's not gonna do anything to hurt you and if you do wind up getting married, he'll work his tail off to see you get the best of everything. Whatever Mr. Tillotson did or didn't do that led to his murder has nothing to do with Lee. I'll get Pop to talk to your folks and put 'em straight if they don't figure it out themselves." I took off a mitten so I could pull my handkerchief out of my purse. I handed to her and said, "Now wipe your eyes. On your feet. We're gonna find Steve Daletzki and get to the bottom of this mess."

She didn't say anything, but her answering smile was as brilliant as a Lake Erie sunset.

Chapter Ten

The last stop on our list, the Wiese home, looked like mine, right down to the gold star in the window. Two bikes were leaned up against the front step. A wilted Victory garden took up space under the front window. The curtains had been pulled aside to let in the weak winter sunshine.

I went up to the door and knocked. Dot stayed behind me. I didn't hear any sounds, no voices or footsteps. I leaned aside to peer in the window. I could see the corner of the radio on the table, but it was dark. Perhaps the family had gone out for the evening. I knocked again. No answer.

I'd decided the visit was a bust and we'd have to come back later when the front door opened. "I'm so sorry, I had to finish wringing out the wash. How can I help you?" The woman, slightly breathless, looked about the same age as my mother. Her plain blue housedress was clean but wrinkled, her white apron spotted with water, prob'ly from the laundry she'd been doing. Her brown hair, liberally sprinkled with gray, was held back by a blue bandanna. Her face looked a bit harried and tired, but her eyes were kind. "I don't have any money to buy anything and we're already church-going folk, so if that's why you're here, you can save your breath."

"We, my friend Dot and I, are looking for Mrs. Wiese." I'd forgotten to ask Emmie for the woman's first name. Stupid of me.

"That's me. Who are you?"

"I'm Betty Ahern, this is my friend Dot Kilbride. We live over in the First Ward. We're looking for a man named Steve Daletzki and we were told you might know him."

At the mention of Daletzki's name, Mrs. Wiese's eyes turned wary. "What do you want with Steve?"

She knew *someone* named Steve Daletzki. The question was whether it was the right guy. "To ask him about a former co-worker of his at GM. Does Mr. Daletzki live here? Is he a boarder or something?"

Mrs. Wiese pursed her lips, maybe pondering what to say. "Steve, that's my brother, moved in with us last December. He's at work."

"Then he's at GM now?"

She hesitated. "No. He lost the job at the plant late last fall, that's why he had to move in with me." She pushed the door to close it.

I stopped it with my hand. "Please, we aren't looking to get him in trouble, honest. It's just…" I looked at Dot, who merely shrugged. No help there. I turned back to Mrs. Wiese. "It's our friend's dad. He died recently and there's some question about how. He used to work at GM. I'm tryin' to find some of his friends and find out what happened so I can help *my* friend get some answers." *And keep him outta jail.*

Mrs. Wiese bit her lip, clearly torn between her desire to be friendly and loyalty to her brother.

"I swear, I don't think Steve had anything to do with…well, anything. But there seem to be so few people who knew Mr. Tillotson. That's my friend's father. I only need to talk to Steve, that's all."

"You think Steve was friendly with that man? After what he did to my brother? Steve never did anything except work hard and John Tillotson—" Suddenly, she seemed to realize she'd let her anger get the better of her because she snapped her mouth shut. "You need to leave."

"Mrs. Wiese, I'm sorry about your brother, really I am." I had the feeling she'd been about to drop something important, but had clammed up at the last minute. "Lee, that's my friend, is in a tight spot. I need to know what happened between Steve and Mr. Tillotson."

Nothing.

"Look, how about I talk to him, huh? You tell me where he's working and we'll scram. This way it's his decision and you haven't ratted him out in any way. Please."

Her silence dragged on and finally she sighed. "Steve's working at Clifton's Auto Repair on Sycamore. Do you know where that is?"

"I'm not really familiar with this neighborhood."

She gave us directions. We thanked her and left. "Left, then right, then left," I said as I hurried along, Dot in my wake.

"Mrs. Wiese shut up pretty quick, don't you think?" Dot sounded breathless as she tried to keep up with me.

"Do you blame her?" I looked both ways, then crossed Broadway to take the turn on Lathrop. "Two strange young women showing up and wanting to gab with your brother about a dead guy is bad enough. It sounds like there was bad blood between 'em and my guess is it's because of the lost job. Mr. Daletzki prob'ly told her not to talk about it. We're lucky the mention of John Tillotson got her mad or else she might not have said anything."

We walked at a brisk pace. Eventually, we reached Sycamore, turned, and I slowed. "Here we are."

A white sign proclaimed the building in front of us to be Clifton's Auto Repair. The yard was choked with brown and wilting weeds. A bunch of vehicles were parked behind the fence, an assortment of trucks most likely owned by area businesses. The office door was shut, but banging and clanking could be heard from the garage across the yard.

"You think he's in there?" Dot asked, worrying her lip.

"How many times do I have to tell you to quit chewing your lips?" I batted her shoulder. "There's only one way we're gonna find out. C'mon." We crossed to the battered gray door marked "Customers" and entered. The waiting area was a tiny space with a big counter. Letter-box cubbies lined the wall above a peg-board holding sets of keys. I guessed they belonged to the vehicles currently in the shop. A cash register took up most of the desk space behind the counter. A beat-up metal chair with a torn green seat had been pushed away from the desk, but we were the only people in the office.

"Should we yell?" Dot's expression matched her voice, dubious. She pointed at a buzzer. "Or do we use that?"

"I'm gonna say we ring. There's no way anyone is gonna hear us above that racket." I depressed the silver button and could barely hear a buzz in the shop.

We waited for a couple of minutes, but no one appeared. As I pushed the buzzer again, a man came through the door. "I'm coming, keep your shirt on." His dark brown hair boasted a pronounced widow's peak and thinned at the temples. His blue coveralls showed liberal grease marks and the rag he used to wipe his hands had to leave behind as much dirt as it removed. "Can I help you, ladies? Are you lost? You don't look much like our regular type of customer."

"We're not lost, but we're not customers, either. I'm Betty Ahern and this is Dot Kilbride." I gestured at my friend, who wiggled her fingers in greeting. "We're looking for Steve Daletzki."

The man shot us a quizzical look. "What for?"

"His sister sent us."

The dark eyebrows pulled together. "Is something wrong? Is she in trouble?"

"No, nothing like that."

"Then why d'ya need Steve?"

I weighed how much to say. "He's friends with our friend's father, John Tillotson. I want to talk to him."

At the mention of Mr. Tillotson's name, the man's face, up until now a mix of friendliness and curiosity. became wooden. "Steve don't want to talk about that jerk." He turned to leave.

"Wait." Was this Mr. Daletzki or someone else? "It's important. Mr. Tillotson is dead. If I don't talk to Mr. Daletzki and pronto, our friend, Lee, could be in a lotta hot water."

The man stopped and half-turned. "Dead? How?"

"Technically he drowned. His body washed up in the Buffalo River a couple of days ago. But he was hit over the head first. The cops say it's murder."

"What does that have to do with your friend?"

"Lee didn't like his father," said Dot.

"Smart boy." The man had stopped wiping his hands with the rag.

I decided to play a hunch. "He wasn't quiet about it either. Problem is, now the cops think Lee might've killed his dad. You're Mr. Daletzki, aren't you?"

The man ran a hand over his head and left tiny streaks of dirt on the exposed skin. "Yeah, I'm Steve Daletzki. But I don't know what you want with me. I can't tell you much."

I glanced at Dot. It didn't seem like Mr. Daletzki was gonna ask us to sit. Then again, there was only the one chair. "You were friends with Mr. Tillotson."

Mr. Daletzki spat. "Were, past tense. And that goes way back before his dying."

"I thought you worked at General Motors," I said. "At least, that's where Lee told us his dad knew you from."

"I did. Now I work here."

"I'm surprised you left GM. You must've had a good job there."

He spat again. "I didn't leave because I wanted to."

"What happened?"

Mr. Daletzki clamped his mouth shut. After a moment he said, "I ain't gonna talk about it. I have work to do."

"Mr. Daletzki, your sister already told us about your fight with John Tillotson." His face turned red and I hurried on. "Now, don't get steamed at her, I don't think it was on purpose. I mentioned his name and I could tell from her response it was a sore subject. Our only goal is to keep Lee outta trouble. Honest."

He threw the rag onto the chair. For a moment it seemed he was gonna storm back into the garage, but then he looked at me. "Lee Tillotson works at GM too, don't he? John mentioned him once or twice."

Out of the corner of my eye, I could see Dot's nod. "Yeah," I said.

"Young guy, walks with a limp?"

"That's him."

"Nice kid. The opposite of his old man, or at least what he became. I'd hate to see Lee take the rap for this. I know there are two little girls at home, too." Mr. Daletzki blew out a breath. "John and I were buddies. Not only did we work together, we'd go out for a beer after the shift. I'm not married, but my sister has kids. We traded stories, that kind of thing. When he injured his back last summer and couldn't work, I gave him a couple of bucks to help the family. I knew he hurt bad and I knew he was hitting the bottle kind of hard. I told him he needed to stop. Get his back fixed up proper. He told me he tried, but nothing had worked. He couldn't afford a specialist."

He paused and I wanted to fill the silence, but instinct told me to keep my mouth shut.

Mr. Daletzki dropped into the chair. "I covered for him at work more than once, when he either turned up drunk or didn't show at all. I told him I couldn't keep doin' it, I'd lose my job. He told me he had something goin' on the side, but I needed to give him some time. He'd get it squared away, cut the booze, and be in a position to pay me back. Damn fool that I was, I believed him."

I leaned on the counter. "How'd you lose your job?"

He glared at me for a moment. "John came to work one day completely out of his mind, barely able to stand. I shouldn't have let him on the line, but I told him to go soak his head and get to his place. The foreman came up after John left, asked me if John was drunk. I lied and said no, he didn't feel well, but he was good to go. I'd sent him to the bathroom to splash water on his face, but he'd be back in a minute."

I knew this story wasn't gonna end well. It was written all over Mr. Daletzki's puss.

"John came back all right, still stinkin' drunk. I sent him to his spot. I thought we were gonna pull it off, then…all hell broke loose. I didn't know exactly what happened, still don't, but it ended with three wrecked engines and two guys sent to the infirmary. John was sacked, of course, and I got my walking papers at the same time."

Dot's mouth fell open. "Why? You didn't have anything to do with the accident, did you?"

Mr. Daletzki's lips twisted. "No, but I'd lied. I knew John shouldn't have been on that line, and I let it happen. Management held me almost as responsible as him and they were right. But that's not why I hated him."

What he'd said was bad, but I knew there had to be something else, 'specially if Mr. Daletzki held himself partly responsible for the accident. "Then what was it?"

"I asked John to cut me in on whatever he had goin' on. Losing that job… I lost my apartment. I had been helping my sister out. She's a widow, her husband died in North Africa a few months ago. Suddenly, not only could I not help, I was living in her basement, just another mouth to feed. Do you know what that does to a man?"

I didn't, but I could guess. After all, Mr. Daletzki came across as the proud type. He wouldn't like to be on the receiving end of charity.

"I felt John owed me, so I asked him for help." He banged his fist on the desk. "He told me to pound salt."

I looked at the desk. Mr. Daletzki had hit it so hard, there was a dent in the cheap blotter. "Did you see him again?"

He looked at his feet, a swift, furtive movement. "No."

I studied him, the stubborn set of his jaw, the grease streaks on his scalp. Yeah, he got a job in this auto shop, but the pay prob'ly wasn't a patch on what he'd made at GM. My eyes strayed to the dent. "One last question. Did Mr. Tillotson mention what it was he was involved with? The side job?"

He abruptly got to his feet. "No, he didn't. That all? I got a truck on the lift and I gotta finish before five-thirty."

I considered. "Yes, thank you for your time. I know you must be busy."

He opened his mouth. Then he bent, grabbed the rag from its spot on the floor, and shoved his way through the door, letting it bang behind him.

Chapter Eleven

After Dot and I left the shop, we wandered down Sycamore toward the bus stop. "Mr. Daletzki doesn't like Mr. Tillotson very much does he?" Dot asked as she pulled out her mittens. As the sun went down, so did the temperature.

I tapped a smoke out of my pack of Luckys. I lit it and gazed at the sun, a huge orange ball off over what I knew was Lake Erie, even if I couldn't see it. "No. Least not anymore."

"Do you think he was tellin' us the truth?"

"I'm pretty sure he came clean about what happened at GM. He knew his buddy was in trouble, tried to cover for him, and got burned. I also believed him when he said Mr. Tillotson refused to let him in on whatever the side hustle was."

"What don't you believe?"

I flicked away some ash. "That he didn't know what the job was. He knew, or had a pretty good idea. I also don't buy his story that he never saw Mr. Tillotson again after they argued. Something about the way he wouldn't meet my eyes bothers me."

Dot worried at her lip. "He's got quite a temper, doesn't he? Mr. Daletzki I mean. Did you see that dent he made in the desk blotter?"

"Yep."

"So if he did see Mr. Tillotson again, and they argued a second time…"

"Mr. Daletzki coulda been the one who bashed Mr. Tillotson over the head and pushed him in the water." I blew out a stream of smoke. Where had the victim gone in? It didn't appear that Sam was gonna tell me. I'd ask

Pop. He'd know, or at least tell me where I could find out.

We walked along without talking, while around us the neighborhood went through the motions of shutting up for the night. A few cars passed. Almost every shop was flipping the Open signs to Closed, with the exception of the local drugstore and an all-night diner. After a moment, Dot spoke again. "Betty, this side job. What do you think it was?"

I ashed my gasper. "I don't think it was anything legal, that's for sure."

"What makes you say that?"

We'd reached the bus stop, but our ride wouldn't be along for a few minutes. I leaned against a streetlight. "That bar, O'Malleys? It's not a place where honest men hang out, at least not very many. If Mr. Tillotson's job had anything to do with that place, it was shady."

"Numbers running, like that man at O'Malley's said?"

"Possibly. Or something worse than run-of-the-mill gambling." I looked down the street. No bus in sight.

"Mr. Tillotson also said the share was getting small. I guess that's another bad sign."

"Not necessarily. I mean, lots of legal ventures could have a limited amount of money to share. More people would mean a smaller cut." I exhaled a cloud of smoke. "I don't like how secretive Mr. Tillotson was. If the job is above board, the logical thing to say is here's what it is and sorry, but there's no room for more people."

She cocked her head. "I suppose that makes sense."

"What's more, I think Mr. Daletzki took another shot at asking Mr. Tillotson for a piece of the action. When Mom asks Michael or Jimmy if they've been up to something, they're always careful not to look at her, just like Mr. Daletzki wouldn't look at me."

She humphed, crossed her arms over her chest, and stuck her hands in her armpits. "People sure do lie to you a lot when you're a private dick, don't they?"

I took a long drag off my cigarette to give myself time to think. I needed to be careful about what I said next. It could make Dot mad at me again. "Don't snap your cap, but I think Lee is still lying to us, Dot."

64

She sighed. "I think so too."

That made me stand up straight. "You do?"

"Yes." She looked up at me, peepers wide in the fading light, most of the color sapped out of 'em. "That story he told us, about goin' to Conway Park? That's a load of baloney. He doesn't go to the park, not even in the daytime. Oh, maybe to take the girls to the swings, but not at night and not for hours. No, he went somewhere he shouldn't have and he's too ashamed, embarrassed, or scared, to tell us. Even me. I asked again the other night after you left. He didn't change his tale, not one little bit."

I stamped my foot. "Why is he doin' this? He's gotta know it won't look good, being caught in a fib."

Her shoulders twitched in a tiny shrug. "I don't know. I suspect he thinks if he just ignores it, the whole situation will go away."

"That's not gonna happen." I turned to see the lights of the bus as it approached our stop. "What do you know about currents in the lake?"

"Hardly anything. Why?"

The bus screeched to a stop and the doors opened. I got on and paid my nickel. "I gotta find out exactly where Mr. Tillotson was killed and why it took him so long to wash up by Child Street. Something tells me it's a big part of unraveling this mess."

* * *

I waited until after supper, when we'd retired to the living room, to ask Pop my question. "What do you know about the currents in Lake Erie?"

He puffed his pipe and leaned back. "That all depends. What do you want to know?"

"How something, or someone, gets from one point to another on the water." I shifted on the floor, tucking my legs up under me. "Mr. Tillotson's body was found at the foot of Child Street in the Buffalo River."

"All right."

"I don't think he floated there for two weeks and neither do the cops. And he was too beat up to have fallen in down there. I saw his body at the morgue, well some of it, and he looked pretty bad."

Mom, who was seated on the couch sewing, made a *tsk* sound. "Really, Betty. What on earth were you doing at the morgue?"

"I was with Lee when he went to identify his dad's body." I glanced at her. "I think he asked me to go with him to provide moral support."

She sniffed but didn't say anything.

I turned back to Pop. "I'm sure someone studies how the water flows, so they'd know where he got thrown in, right?"

Pop sucked his pipestem, eyes thoughtful. "Or they'd have a good guess." He blew out a smoke ring. "Yes, with all the boats and shipping around Buffalo, someone knows. That person isn't me, though."

I deflated a little. I had been sure Pop would have the answer.

"Have you asked your police friend, the detective?"

I pulled my knees up and rested my chin on them. "I'm not speaking to him right now."

"Oh? Why not?"

I hesitated. "Detective MacKinnon is determined to pin this on Lee."

Pop shot me a disapproving stare. "Betty, aren't you being a little unfair? You've always said this MacKinnon fellow was a good guy."

"I thought he was, but I guess I was wrong."

"Isn't it more likely he's doing his job? The police have to look at the whole picture. They can't afford to jump to conclusions."

I squirmed. Trust Pop to poke holes in my righteous anger. At the same time, Pop told me the reason he went to O'Malley's with me was 'cause he refused to let Lee take the rap. "Have you changed your mind? Do you think Lee's guilty?"

"I didn't say that." He stretched out his legs. "I already told you, I think he's innocent and I think Detective MacKinnon will come to that conclusion eventually. But look at it from his end. He can't take our word for it. A good detective looks at all the facts, even when the facts don't match what her ideas are."

I didn't think we were talking about Sam anymore. "You think I'm wrong? Believing Lee?"

"I didn't say that either. Would you say Lee has a motive?"

"Yes."

"Do you think he's physically capable of killing his father? I mean, is he strong enough to have done what the police say was done?"

"Of course he is. He works at GM. Heck, at this point I could prob'ly have done it, what with my work at Bell. That's 'specially true if Mr. Tillotson was drunk at the time."

Pop shook his pipestem at me. "Then why don't you consider Lee a good suspect?"

"'Cause I know him. He'd never do that. He might get into a fistfight, to protect himself or someone else. But murder? No, I can't see it. Sam oughta know that, too. He knows Lee."

"People can surprise you." Pop studied his pipe. "I grew up with a boy, Tommy Sweeney. Scrawny lad, frightened of his own shadow. One day, he stopped coming to school. When I got home, I learned he'd beaten his father so badly, using a hammer, the man almost died. Mr. Sweeney liked to hit his son with a strap and one day Tommy'd had enough."

I swallowed hard.

"If Detective MacKinnon considers Lee a suspect, you have to believe he has information you don't. Does he normally share everything with you?"

I shook my head.

"You see? What you really should be wondering is not why the detective doesn't believe you but what he knows that you don't. Maybe you should ask him." Pop reached for the radio knob.

"I have. He won't tell me 'cause he says I'm too close on this one." I traced patterns in the carpet. "Maybe that's true. I know Detective MacKinnon must have evidence, but that's why I want to know where this whole thing started. To do that, I have to figure out how his body coulda drifted down to where they pulled him out. If I can do that, and prove Lee wasn't there, I can tell Sam and clear Lee's name."

Pop clicked on the radio. "That makes sense. Is that all?"

I hadn't intended to tell Pop about my suspicions, that Lee was lying to me. But suddenly I realized I needed to. "No, there's one more thing. Pop…

I don't think Lee's being truthful. Well, not completely."

His hand froze on the radio volume dial. "Why do you say that?"

I told Pop about Lee's story of going to the park and my suspicions. "He's being too vague. And that worries me."

"How come?"

"If he wasn't up to something, why not tell me? He's gotta know I'm on his side. I've told him enough times. But he won't confide in me. Or in Dot for that matter. He's hiding something and I don't know why."

Pop was silent for a moment as he puffed away. Finally, he said, "I think you're asking the wrong question, Betty."

"What d'you mean?"

"Your first step shouldn't be discovering *what* Lee is lying about, but *why* he is lying in the first place."

Chapter Twelve

I awoke Saturday morning knowing what I needed to do, but with no idea of where I would start. Usually, on my day off, I'd hit the movie theater with Dot or Lee. But I'd gone to bed disheartened by the idea that Detective MacKinnon could show up at any minute to put one of my best friends in handcuffs, and I didn't have any evidence to prevent that from happening.

I swung my feet out of bed and grabbed my bathrobe and slippers. Then I shuffled to the kitchen. Any plans I might have had were brushed aside when I entered.

"Stalin can go dance a jig and sing for his supper as far as I'm concerned," Pop said as he slapped down the morning paper.

Mom murmured in response.

"What's the old Soviet up to now?" I sat and grabbed the paper.

"He wants a second front in Europe. We're already engaged with the Nazis in Africa and Greece. And I wouldn't be surprised if we were in Italy soon. That sounds like two fronts to me. Plus there's the whole Pacific theater." Pop grabbed his lunch pail and coat. "He's saying Roosevelt and Churchill have betrayed him."

"That's nuts." I scanned the headlines. "I mean, I don't think they trust him much, but they wouldn't sell out an ally, would they?"

Pop scowled. "No, but I bet Stalin wouldn't hesitate to do the same."

The news from Europe was all bad. America continued to suffer staggering losses in the Atlantic because of the German U-boats. I said a silent prayer of thanks that Sean was in the Pacific aboard the *USS Washington*. 'Course that started me thinking about Tom and where he might be. The 1st Armored Division wasn't part of Patton's II Corps, now on its way to Tunisia, but I knew they'd been in North Africa in February. *Wherever you are, stay safe, Tom*, I prayed and made the sign of the cross.

Pop leaned over to kiss Mom goodbye. "Oh, Betty. You have the day off today, don't you?"

His words jolted me out of my war thoughts. "I do. Why?"

"I remembered this morning that a buddy of mine is with the Coast Guard down at the Buffalo station. Are you still interested in water currents?"

"You bet I am."

He nodded. "They do a lot of search and rescue operations out of there. I called them and he's on duty. If you're looking for something to do today, go down and ask to talk to Petty Officer Tim Douglas. Tell him you're my daughter. He'll help you out." He left.

I hurried through the rest of breakfast. Then I dressed, finished my chores, put out a saucer for Cat, and went down the street to the Kilbrides' house. Dot came out the front door as I arrived.

"Hey, Betty," she said. "Are we going to the pictures today? I'm not sure what's playin' but there's a new comedy out, *It Ain't Hay*, that might be good. It'll take our mind off things. And we might get some good news from the reels."

"Not today, I have a plan. Pop gave me a lead on a guy in the Coast Guard who might be able to help me with the Tillotson case. You wanna come?"

"Lead the way."

The bus dropped us close to the Buffalo Coast Guard station and we walked the last couple of blocks. The building was on Fuhrmann Boulevard, where you could still detect the faint smell of CheeriOats from the General Mills plant a little upriver. We entered and stopped at the front desk, which was manned by a young man with close-cut hair wearing a brilliant white uniform. I didn't know anything about Coast Guard ranks, but he had three stripes on his sleeve. "Excuse me, Sergeant."

He smiled. "Seaman."

"Sorry?"

"Sergeants are in the army. I'm a seaman. What can I help you ladies with?"

His explanation threw me off my game. Dot nudged me to bring me back on course. "Sorry. I'm looking for Petty Officer Tim Douglas. I understand he's on duty this morning and I'd like to speak with him."

"I'll check. Your name please?"

"Betty Ahern. You can tell him I'm Joe Ahern's daughter."

The seaman smiled again and went through a door. Dot wandered over to read the flyers and maps on the wall. "They're lookin' for recruits."

"Isn't everybody?"

She scanned the wall. "It would be a swell assignment, though. I bet you could live at home, catch a movie in your off-duty hours, and hey, no Germans or Japanese to worry about."

"Maybe, but something tells me they keep these guys plenty busy." While we waited, I checked out the lobby. It held a lot of information about the Coast Guard. They might not have a lot of Japanese fighter planes or German U-boats to deal with on Lake Erie, but I figured rescue missions and policing any black-market trade between the United States and Canada prob'ly kept them on their toes. Pop had told me stories about Prohibition, and how some folks he knew would smuggle whiskey across the border and sell it out of their homes for a nickel a shot.

It seemed like it took forever, but was most likely only a couple of minutes before the seaman reappeared with an older man behind him. The new guy couldn't have been much older than Pop, but he was in better shape. His salt-and-pepper hair was close-cut and the friendly light in his brown eyes matched his smile. "Good morning," he said, holding out a hand. "I'm Petty Officer Douglas. Which one of you is Joe's daughter?" He sized up each of us in a snap. "Never mind, must be you. You've got your dad's chin. Pleased to meet you, Miss Ahern."

I shook his hand. It was callused and firm. There must be a lot of manual labor in the Coast Guard. Petty Officer Douglas didn't look like an officer though. "Good afternoon, Officer."

"Petty Officer. First Class, if you want to be technical. It's not really an officer's rank. I'm the Coast Guard's equivalent of an Army staff sergeant. But you didn't come all the way down here to talk the trivialities of rank." He held out his hand to Dot. "Who is this young lady?"

Dot blushed. "Dorothy Kilbride, sir. They call me Dot."

Petty Officer Douglas laughed, a warm Santa Claus-style sound. "Good gracious, Miss Kilbride, don't call me sir. As the joke goes, I work for a living." He winked. "Did Joe send you down here? I hope everything's okay with him."

"Sort of, s—I mean Petty Officer." That was a mouthful. "That is, everything's fine with Pop. He suggested you as an expert resource for a problem I'm trying to solve."

He led us to a couple of seats at a table near the window. "What kind of problem are you working on that you could possibly need my help?"

"Well, have you read about the man's body found in the Buffalo River, down near Child Street?" The story had made the *Courier-Express*. Not a big piece, but a couple of paragraphs. If the petty officer was a man who worked the lake, it might have snagged his interest.

"Hmm. I seem to remember reading something along those lines. It was earlier this week, yes?"

"That's right. The man turned out to be the father of a friend of mine." I hesitated. Should I tell him Mr. Tillotson had been murdered? Why not. It was public knowledge. "When they did an autopsy, they found out he'd been hit over the head, most likely before he was pushed into the water."

"Murder, huh? Did your friend have anything to do with it?"

"I don't think so. 'Course Lee, that's my friend's name, didn't much like his dad so the cops haven't ruled him out."

Petty Officer Douglas lifted an eyebrow. "What does all that have to do with you? Or me, for that matter?"

"Well, I'm a private detective." I waited for the laugh that usually followed that statement, but he just motioned for me to continue. "I'm tryin' to prove Lee's innocent."

"Because he's your friend?"

Dot piped up. "Yes, but also because he *is* innocent. Lee would never do such a thing." I could tell her glare dared Petty Officer Douglas to argue. *Don't make things difficult, Dot.*

He must have been too smart for that because he didn't even try. "All right. I still don't see why you would come down and talk to me."

"I know, or at least I'm pretty sure, Mr. Tillotson, that's Lee's dad, didn't fall in the Buffalo River where he was found." I shifted on my chair. "I think he was killed somewhere else and that's where he went in the river. Or maybe he was dumped. Either way, I need to know where that spot is."

"I think I understand. You want to know if the Coast Guard could backtrack from the location where the body was found and determine the point of entry." He rubbed his chin.

"Exactly." I waited. When he didn't say anything, but continued to stare at the wall, I kept talkin'. "Well, can you?"

He shook himself as if coming back to reality. "Of course. When we do search and rescue, we often only have an entry point. Based on currents and other factors, we can guess where the person, or object, will end up. You want to do the same thing, but in reverse." He rose and showed us to a small room with a table, maybe where they met with recruits. "I'll fetch some maps. Can I get you some coffee or water while I'm at it? The coffee isn't that great, I warn you."

I shrugged out of my coat. "All we get is chicory at home, so coffee of any kind is swell."

Dot murmured her agreement.

"Two coffees," he said. "I'll be right back."

Dot draped her coat over a chair. "He's awful nice. What's the catch?"

"I hope there isn't one." I sat. "He knows Pop and the Coast Guard is all about helping. Here's hoping it pans out."

A couple of minutes later, Petty Officer Douglas returned carrying two steaming mugs and a pile of maps. "Do either of you want milk or sugar?"

For a moment I couldn't say anything. Milk? Sugar? Was he hoarding? But then I realized the service prob'ly had different rules than civilians. "No, thank you. I can drink it black."

Dot could only mumble a response and declined the offer. Maybe she was also dazed by the idea of milk and sugar.

"These maps." I waved at the papers. "What do they mean?"

He spread out the first one, which showed Lake Erie, the coastline, and all the tributaries, including streams and the various canals, all marked with lines and numbers. "This is a map of the currents. Based on this, if I know where an object, in your case, a human body, ended up, I can backtrack to where it entered the water system. Now, tell me again. Where, and exactly when, was this gentleman found? And about how big is he?"

I tried to study the blue blobs and squiggles, but it didn't make much sense, even though my map-reading skills were better than the average person's thanks to Pop. "In the Buffalo River at the foot of Child Street. I don't know the exact time. The paper only said they found him the morning of March sixteenth." I gave him my best guess at Mr. Tillotson's height and weight.

He leaned over and placed his finger at a spot. "Here. Okay, let's work back from that." He traced a path with his other finger. "This here is the current of the river. See, this is where it meets up with the lake. You can see where the water empties from the lake to the Niagara and Buffalo rivers, then how they go down around Grand Island and over Niagara Falls."

I followed his finger. It didn't make much sense, but I trusted him.

"Do you know how long Mr. Tillotson's body was in the water?"

"The cops won't tell us," Dot said. She hadn't bothered to study the maps, but sat sipping her joe.

"However," I put my mug aside and leaned forward. "The last time he was seen was the afternoon of March second. So we know it wasn't longer than two weeks."

"That helps." He traced some more lines. Then he pulled a pair of metal tweezer-looking things from his pocket and measured off some distances. All the while, he muttered what sounded like calculations. It was mumbo-jumbo to me. Lee would've loved it. Whether it was history or math, he could get into this kind of stuff.

Finally, Petty Officer Douglas marked off a couple of spots on the map using a thick pencil he'd also had in his pocket. "There's no way to be absolutely certain, at least not from this. But based on the body's size, its final destination, the speed of the water this time of year, seasonal conditions, and the current patterns, these are what I'd say are the most likely points of entry."

I grabbed the map. "May I turn this around?"

He nodded.

I rotated it and looked. One spot was up on the lakeshore on the other side of Lackawanna. If I was right, the only thing there was a park and a beach. But Woodlawn Beach was a popular spot. Even now, during the winter, there was the hotel, restaurant, dance hall, and other recreational facilities. No, the area was too visible for an illicit meet. Plus, if the illegal racket were being run out of the First Ward, why would they go to a whole other city to flap their gums?

The second was a bit closer, near Bethlehem Steel. Pop could confirm for me, but I didn't think it likely someone would be able to get right down on the water line from there.

"None of these are very far away from where the body was found," I said.

"No, but there are lots of points along any of these routes where it could have gotten tangled up in, well, anything. Debris, vegetation, all kinds of things. All of that would slow the journey down. It's not unlikely it would take almost two weeks for the body to surface near Child Street." He tapped his tweezers on his palm.

The third point was not on the lake, but one of the canals that went inward. This one butted up near General Mills. "Dot, when Detective MacKinnon came to talk to Lee that last time, to ask where he was, didn't Sam say something about the grain elevators?"

Dot pursed her lips. "Maybe. Yeah, I think he did. He wanted to know if Lee had been down there after he fought with his dad. Why do you ask?"

I pushed the map toward her and tapped Petty Officer Douglas's mark. "See that? If you were lookin' to get rid of a dead body, that's a mighty nice spot, don't you agree?"

Her eyes widened. "Down by the grain elevators on the canals?"

"Yep. 'Specially at night. Few lights, few people." I grabbed my mug. "It's the perfect spot to commit a murder. Or to cover up one."

Chapter Thirteen

We stepped out of the Coast Guard building into bright, but still chilly, sunshine. A brisk wind came off the lake, making it feel even colder. A few hardy gulls wheeled above the whitecaps that speckled the water.

"Where to now?" Dot asked.

I held back the hair whipping across my face. "I wanna go to the grain elevators. But I think we'll have to detour home. It isn't much use to go looking for someone if you don't have a picture to show around. I might have a snap of Lee we can use."

"Hold on." Dot stepped around the corner of the building, where she'd be partially protected from the wind. She reached into her purse, pulled out a wallet, and flipped through some pictures inside. She held one out. "Will this do?"

In the picture, Lee wore a t-shirt, a cigarette between his lips. He smiled at the camera, a half-assembled dollhouse on the floor in front of him. It must have been taken around Christmas because there was a small tree in the background. "Where'd you get this?"

"My dad got a Kodak 35 camera as a present for his birthday last year. He's always been fascinated with taking pictures. But he got real frustrated with it. His shots kept coming out blurry." She blushed. "After he gave up, I started playing around with it and I'm pretty good, at least I think so."

I studied the photo as we walked to the nearby bus stop. "I'm no expert, but it'll work just fine for what we want. Why do you have a photo of Lee in your pocketbook?"

Her cheeks got redder. "You have a picture of Tom, don't you?"

"That's different."

"How so?"

The fierceness of her voice and the spark in her eyes startled me. Was it different? Just because she didn't have a ring on her finger and I did? I handed back the picture. "You're right, it's not. Sorry. Here, hold on to this. I wouldn't want to walk off with it."

She tucked it away in her purse again. Then she sat on the bench and chewed her lip. "Betty, I'm scared."

I stuffed my mittened hands in my pockets. "Why?"

"The night Detective MacKinnon came, you know, the same night he asked about the grain elevators. Do you remember what Lee said?"

I exhaled. "Yeah. 'My father *was* a difficult man.' Or something like that."

"Exactly. He said *was*. And he said it before Detective MacKinnon told us Mr. Tillotson was dead. Betty, why would he do that?"

I knew what she meant. The same thing had been eating me, even though I tried to ignore it. Lee's evasiveness coupled with his use of words. "I know. It's like he already knew his dad was dead when the detective showed up."

She blinked rapidly, her eyes shiny. "I can't believe I'm saying this, but what if he did, you know, kill him? His dad?"

"Stop that." I held my hair out of my face. Too bad I hadn't been thinking or I'd have grabbed the bandanna I used at work. "It doesn't mean anything, well, not necessarily. It could have been a slip of the tongue. Or maybe he knew his father was dead, but that doesn't mean he was involved."

"You think he doesn't know who the murderer is? Or he does know and he's protecting someone?"

"Either of those could be true."

We huddled together against the wind, not saying a word. I didn't want to think of the second option. The list of people who Lee would go to jail for, once you removed Dot and me, was small. In fact, I could only think of one person, Mrs. T. And I didn't want her to be a killer, either.

* * *

It was around nine-thirty by the time the bus dropped us off near the grain elevators and we walked to the canals. The scent of cereal was stronger here than it had been at the Coast Guard station. A few puffy clouds had moved in, but the wind hadn't died down much. My cheeks felt dry and tight by the time we reached our destination.

Dot looked around. "Now what?"

Not many people were there. A few men in coveralls worked on a barge that was tied to the edge of the canal. Another couple toted sacks toward the metal buildings in the distance. I could see the doors at the lowest level and metal ladders climbing the side of the elevators. I didn't want to think about what it felt like at the top. I was level with the lake and the wind sliced through my clothes like a knife. I'd prob'ly feel like I was being flayed alive if I was at the top of the building.

"C'mon, we gotta talk to some people, see if they saw anything. You have the picture?"

She patted her pocketbook. "We're interested in March second, right?"

I nodded. "Late afternoon through, oh, I don't know, nine or ten at night? Lee said he got home at about eleven o'clock. How long do you think it would take to get to the First Ward from here?"

Dot scrunched her face in thought. "No more than an hour, and that's if you had to wait for a bus."

"Then we're interested in about four in the afternoon through ten at night. Come on."

We questioned the men at the barge. They didn't remember seeing anything out of the ordinary that night. From there, we moved on to a couple of guys toting sacks, but still came up empty. Most of 'em barely glanced at the picture. We asked a guy coming out of one of the elevators. "Excuse me. Have you ever seen this person here at the canals? Specifically, we're wondering if he was here the night of March second."

Dot dutifully held out the photo.

The man studied it for a long minute. "Maybe. Hard to say. I was here that night. A barge came in late and we were unloading. There was a guy around, but I can't say whether it was this one. He was tall and skinny, I can

78

tell you that. He wore a long coat and one of those squashy caps, and he was smoking 'cause I saw the burning end. But it was dark and blustery. The coat collar was turned up, so I didn't get a clear look at his face. Sorry."

"Did he limp?"

"When I saw him, he was standing still." He walked away. Then he turned back. "You should ask over in the office." He pointed toward a smallish cement building. "Someone's there nearly all the time, twenty-four hours a day. If anybody was here who shouldn't have been, they might know. I think Ray, the guy who's on duty now, was working that night." He left.

Dot faced me, eyes wide and anxious. "You think he saw Lee?"

"I don't know. Remember, Mr. Tillotson and Lee were pretty much the same height and both were thin. They both smoked. Mr. Tillotson had a long coat. In fact, I think he was wearing it when he went missing. Come on. Let's see if this Ray can tell us anything."

We headed to the office building. Inside felt twenty degrees warmer, but that was most likely 'cause we were out of the stiff wind. "Excuse me, are you Ray?"

A man who looked like a bulldog in coveralls looked up at me. "Who wants to know?" He wore a knit cap, but I could tell his hair was shaved close to his head. A heavy blue jacket covered powerful shoulders. His hands were the size of hams, dirty and calloused from manual labor.

I introduced myself and Dot.

"I'm Ray Thatcher. What are you doing down here? This is no place for dames, especially young ones like yourselves."

"I'm a private detective." Again, I waited for the normal jokes, but Ray must not have thought that was a strange idea, 'cause he didn't say anything. I continued. "We're looking for someone. Not right this minute, but we want to know if he was down here the night of March second. A man outside told us you worked that night. Did you see this guy?"

Dot held out the picture.

Ray stood and held out his hand. "The second you said? That was a crazy night."

"Oh? Why d'you say that?"

"Normally it's quiet down here, well, as quiet as a place like this gets. But most of the time, I don't see anyone who doesn't work here, not that late at night. One day runs into another. But I remember the second 'cause you might have thought we was running a tourist show, from the number of people I saw."

My pulse quickened. "Like who?"

Ray tilted the picture to get better light. "I don't remember this guy. But I don't know, there were three or four of 'em. Nuts I tell you. Who hangs out at the grain elevator canals at night?"

I handed the picture back to Dot. "What did they look like?"

"I told you, guys. One of 'em walked like he had a limp. That's about all I remember."

"Tall or short? Young or old? Do you remember what they were wearing?"

"Heck, I don't know. I was busy. I didn't stop everyone and demand to see an ID."

Despite the assurances from the man we'd met outside, Ray didn't seem inclined to be helpful. "What did their voices sound like? Did any of 'em have any scars or other marks that stood out?"

Ray lifted an eyebrow. "Lady, you're killing me. I told you, it was a busy night. There were people around. I'm not the cops, I didn't question them. Now get outta here before I call security."

"Thanks for your time." I tried to keep the sarcasm out of my voice. I turned to go. Dot looked like she was gonna keep talkin' but I shook my head and nudged her toward the door.

"Hey, before you go," Ray said.

I stopped and turned. "Yeah?"

He looked at me, then Dot, then back again. "Tell me, who put you up to this? I gotta know."

"Excuse me?"

"You said you were a private detective. There ain't no girl detectives. Is Charlie playing a joke on me again? Where is he?"

Dot huffed, but I grabbed her coat and gently pulled her toward the door. "Get with the times, Ray. Women are everywhere these days. With all the men off to war, who else is gonna solve the crimes?"

Chapter Fourteen

Dot waited until we were on the bus to break down. "Betty, Lee was there, I just know it. That guy, Ray? Why didn't he tell us?"

Better question, why was Lee at the grain elevators at all? I gnawed my thumbnail. "Cool it, Dot. There are lots of Joes in this city who walk with a limp. Heck, the first worker we spoke to couldn't even tell us that much. The only thing I know is it's gonna take someone more intimidating to get Ray to spill the beans."

"You think he knows more than he said?"

"I'm not sure. But we aren't gonna get anything out of him if he thinks this is all a joke." I needed someone at my back. That used to be Lee. Who was I gonna ask now?

"But it could be Lee. Admit it." She bit her lip until it bled.

For once, I didn't reprimand her. Heck, she had a right to be upset. Lee had promised to me, not on a stack of Bibles but pretty solemnly, that he hadn't killed his dad. So what was up? Maybe Pop would come with me. But he had to work and following what could be a wild goose chase wasn't enough to justify him taking time off.

I tried to reassure myself. Buffalo was a big town. There had to be other guys who wore newsboy caps and who walked with limps around. On the other hand, most of the fighting-age men were gone off to war. Anyone left was gonna be older, like Pop, or a 4F like Lee. My gut told me I wasn't gonna be so lucky and find out it was some schmo instead of one of my best friends.

After a long moment of silence, Dot spoke up. The anguish in her voice cut like a knife. "What are we going to do? About Lee?"

"There are too many unknowns. Ray barely told us anything, except there were a bunch of strangers around that night. It could have been anybody."

"There are only three other people in this. Howley, McDougal, and Mr. Daletzki."

"Only three that we know of, although that's plenty if you ask me. We have to talk to Lee, pronto." I glanced at her. "Is he working today?"

"No, I think he took the day off. He said something about making funeral arrangements." She swallowed hard. "He ought to be at home."

If he hasn't been arrested already. But I didn't give voice to my thought. The mere sight of Dot's face crushed my heart, making it hard to keep that legendary stiff upper lip. I knew that she'd crumble at the mere mention of Lee getting sent to the pokey. I had to stay strong for her sake.

The bus reached the stop at the corner of Louisiana and we ran down the street, heedless of the wind off the lake. We reached Mackinaw and proceeded to the Tillotsons' house, brushing by my brothers.

"Hey, Betty, where's the fire?" Michael asked.

"Tell you later." I leaped up the stairs and pounded on the Tillotson front door.

Lee answered, a cigarette clamped between his lips and his shirtsleeves rolled up. He wore trousers that looked almost part of a suit, but no shoes, just socks with a hole that had been darned over the big toe of his right foot. "What's the emergency?" he asked as we pushed through the door.

I wheeled around. "You gotta be straight with me. Where were you the night your dad went missing? That's March second, in case you need a refresher."

His face went wooden. "I told you. I was out walking around at Conway Park."

"Don't give me that b...malarkey." I held myself back from cussing by sheer force of will. "You were seen, Lee. There's a witness."

"To what?" If the news bothered him, I couldn't tell by his voice, which stayed deadpan.

"I don't know. That's what you have to tell me. But we, Dot and I, just spoke to a guy who said he saw you down at the canals by the grain elevators that night. We also talked to a Coast Guard petty officer who says that's definitely a place your dad could have been dumped into the water." I fought against the burning sensation in my chest to keep my words calm. "Lee, enough is enough. You gotta tell us the truth."

Dot spoke up. She clearly either wasn't fighting or had lost the battle against panic and fear. Her eyes shone with tears and her voice cracked. "Please, Lee. We'll understand, whatever it was. But we can't help unless you come clean."

His jaw moved, like he was chewing his words. "You won't get it," he said.

"We will, cross our hearts." I made an X over my chest. "Why were you at the canals?"

Before he could say anything, there was another knock on the door. It was firm and purposeful. Not a random visitor. None of us moved. Maybe we all hoped the person would move on. I know I did.

If that was the case, our wishes were thwarted by Emma. "Just a second," her voice trilled as she skipped to the door. Dot made a grab for her but missed. A second later, Emma opened the door to reveal Detective MacKinnon and a uniformed Buffalo cop.

The grim expression on the detective's face told me all I needed to know. He stepped inside, ignoring the child. "Liam John Tillotson?"

"That's me," Lee said, without a flicker of emotion. "Emma, go upstairs."

"Why? Lee, why did this man use your full name? Are you in trouble? When Mom says it, you're in trouble." Her peepers were wide, her voice puzzled.

"I said get upstairs, now!" Lee snapped.

Emma's face scrunched. She wailed and tore upstairs, crying her heart out. She was prob'ly more upset at Lee. Her adored big brother never spoke to the girls in that tone of voice.

Sam cleared his throat. "Thank you. I was going to ask one of the ladies to take the little girl away. No sense doing this in front of her."

Lee said nothing.

"Liam Tillotson, you are under arrest for the murder of John Patrick

Tillotson. Officer, cuff him."

Dot shrieked and darted in front of Lee. "No, you can't!"

I pulled her back. Lee refused to meet my eye. I turned my attention to Sam. He shot me a look of…I wasn't sure. Sympathy? Frustration? Anger? I couldn't read it. For a long moment, I stared at him while Dot sobbed. I'd talk to him later. Hopefully he'd agree to that.

I pulled Dot to me and wrapped my arms around her. She was shaking, tears streaming down her plump cheeks. "Shhh, Dot. It'll be okay. This is all a mistake." I lifted my eyes to Sam's. "Right?"

He didn't blink.

I kept staring at Sam, but spoke to my friend. "Lee, we'll talk to your mom and get you the best lawyer we can. In the meantime, just keep your trap shut." I switched my focus to him.

His gaze flickered to Dot and me. "I know the Fifth Amendment, Betty. I paid attention in school."

The implication was I hadn't. Normally that would make me mad, but I brushed aside the words. The situation was too serious for joking. I patted Dot's shoulder and faced the detective. "Now what happens?"

"Mr. Tillotson will be taken to the city jail, where he'll be held for arraignment. That will most likely happen Monday or Tuesday. At that time, he'll go before a judge for a bail hearing and enter his plea." Sam glanced at Lee, who stared straight ahead. "If you're going to have an attorney present, that would be the time." He held up his hand to the uniformed officer. "Wait, get his coat. It's freezing out there."

As the officer undid the cuffs so Lee could slip on his coat, he finally turned to me. "Betty. Tell…tell my mom, would you? Tell her, well, you know."

"I'll take care of it. I told you I'd talk to her, me or Dot. Don't worry."

He opened his mouth to say something, but shut it without a word. Then the officer secured the handcuffs again and marched Lee out of the door to the waiting police car.

Sam paused on the doorstep. "Miss Ahern, Betty…I wish this hadn't happened. I truly do."

Dot gulped air. "You, you…I don't know what you are. You're wrong, that's for sure. Lee didn't do anything." She broke away and ran after Emma.

I crossed my arms. "You and I have to talk, Sam. I'll be down to see you later, after I take care of the girls and Mrs. T."

He tugged the brim of his fedora. "You know where to find me." He left, closing the door behind him.

Chapter Fifteen

I took a little—okay, a lot—of talking to convince Dot to stay with Anna and Emma. Dot wanted to barrel right over to the jail to start haranguing someone about how wrong they were. "Besides, someone will need to be here when Mrs. T shows up. Someone who can give her the straight dope. I thought about doin' it, but I think I'd be better off doing something else."

"You'll call if you need me?"

I grabbed my coat. "You betcha." I hustled home, busted through the door, and grabbed the phone book. "Mom. You know any lawyers? Specifically, ones who are defense attorneys?" I paged through the thin sheets. I flipped aside the white pages and went straight to the yellow ones to look under "L."

Mom followed me into the kitchen. "What on earth would you need a defense lawyer for?"

"I don't need one for myself. Lee's been arrested for the murder of Mr. Tillotson."

Mom gasped and covered her mouth with her hands. After a moment, she said, "Does Nora know?"

"She wasn't home. I left Dot watching Lee's sisters." My fingers trembled and I tore a page. *Slow down.* The listings wouldn't do me any good if I ripped them to shreds.

Mom took deep breaths, then went to the hall closet. She came back with her coat. "I have to go over and be there for Nora. I don't know any lawyers, defense or otherwise. Maybe your father—"

Pop stormed into the kitchen, pulling his suspenders over a white T-shirt.

"What's all the commotion? Betty, you know I worked overnight and I'm trying to get some sleep. I can't do that with all this racket."

"Sorry, Pop. But this is an emergency. Do you know any defense lawyers?"

He blinked, all the air let out of his lecture. "What for?"

I told them the story, how the police had shown up and hustled Lee downtown. "I need to find him some help, pronto."

Pop's face reddened. "This is the same police detective who's been here before? There isn't more than one named MacKinnon?"

"Only one that I know of," I said. I'd finally reached the section listing all the lawyers, but jeepers there were a lot of 'em. I wanted a good one. A bunch of names wouldn't help me figure out who that was.

"Did he tell you what evidence he has?" Pop settled his suspenders. "You said you didn't think he'd railroad Lee, didn't you?"

I paused in my reading. Would Sam do that? "He didn't say anything about the evidence. Detective MacKinnon has always played fair with me. You were right the last time we talked. If he arrested Lee, it's bad. That means the police have real reason to think Lee's guilty." I looked up. "I know there are cops who'd play fast and loose with the rules, but I truly don't think Sam MacKinnon is one of them."

Pop held my gaze for a second. Then he nodded. "One of the guys at the plant, his brother is an attorney. I remember because he recommended his brother to Bud Miller when Bud's son got in a tight spot before he shipped out. I'll call him." Pop left. I heard him dial the phone and speak.

"Betty." Mom fastened her coat. "Is there anything I should tell Nora when she gets home? She's going to be frantic."

I tried to remember everything Sam had said and told it to Mom. "Just be there for her. Dot is there now, but Dot's hardly more than a kid in Mrs. T's eyes."

"What if she wants to visit Lee?"

"She could go to city jail, that's where Detective MacKinnon said Lee would be. I'm not sure he'll want to talk to his mom, though. He might try to keep her as far away as he can until the trial." *Assuming it gets to trial.* "The detective said Lee would be arraigned Monday or Tuesday. Our priority right now has to be to get him a good lawyer for when that happens."

She tugged on her gloves. "How bad is it, Betty?"

I paused. Pop came back from the hallway. "I told you. I don't know what evidence the cops have, but I'm sure it's pretty solid. Detective MacKinnon is no slouch." I turned to Pop. "You get in touch with your buddy?"

"Yes. Here's his brother's phone number." He held out a slip of paper.

I copied the number into my notebook, then waved the scrap toward Mom. "Take that to Mrs. T. I've seen plenty of movies, but I don't know how it works in real life. In case Lee doesn't get a chance to call anyone, she should."

Mom grabbed the paper and put it in her pocket. She faced me. "I assume you're going to the jail."

"After I talk to Detective MacKinnon, yeah. I'll try to have this done in time to be home for supper."

Mom and Pop exchanged a look. He turned to me. "Do you still believe Lee is innocent?"

"Yes. He's never lied to me, not about anything important. He's gotten in a lot of scrapes, but nothing like this."

Pop gave a small, quick nod, like I'd said what he expected. "Then don't you worry about supper. You go do what you have to do."

* * *

Every nerve in my body screamed at me to rush to Lee's side. But I needed information first. As I boarded a bus for the short trip downtown, I thought about Lee, who was prob'ly sitting in a cold jail cell by now, either alone or with some oversized mook from the streets. Lee didn't belong there. He should be with his sisters, or Dot, or a dozen other places. It was up to me to figure out what was really goin' on. If Tom were here, he'd say the same thing.

It occurred to me that the tables had turned. Lee had promised to look after me and here I was, lookin' after him.

At police headquarters, I went straight to the desk sergeant and asked, as nicely as possible, to see Detective MacKinnon. Judging from the sergeant's expression, somewhere between indignation and amusement, I hadn't been all that polite.

I didn't wait long, though. Sam came off the elevator only a couple of minutes after the sergeant phoned upstairs. "Miss Ahern. Why am I not surprised to see you?" He guided me to a far corner. "I expected Miss Kilbride to be with you."

"She's watching the Tillotson girls until their mother gets home. If I were you, I'd be glad she isn't here. You're not one of her favorite people at the moment."

Sam actually flinched a little and a look of chagrin crossed his face. "I'm truly sorry about earlier. Arresting Lee, I mean."

"It's a little late for apologies, Detective." I didn't try to stop the scorn as it dripped from my lips. Across the lobby, the sergeant looked over at us, then picked up a ringing phone. "I don't know what kind of evidence you have, but this whole thing stinks. Let's go upstairs and talk." I took a step toward the elevator.

Sam grabbed my shoulder, his grip firm, but not harsh. "Wait."

The move stopped me in my tracks. He'd never touched me like that before. "Please take your hand off me."

He maneuvered so his back was to the sergeant, who was studying us again. "I'm sorry, Miss Ahern. I can't talk to you any longer. Have a nice afternoon." He shook my right hand with both of his and I felt something poke my palm. Then Sam released me and walked away. As he got on the elevator, the sergeant smirked and returned to his duties.

I shielded my hand from the sergeant's vision and looked down. Sam had pressed a folded note into my hand. I turned around to face the corner and read it, careful not to let anyone see what I was doin'. If Sam had gone to such lengths to slip me a secret message, I wasn't gonna trumpet it all over the police HQ lobby.

Moe's Diner on Main. Fifteen minutes. I'm buying. SM

What on earth was goin' on?

Chapter Sixteen

I grabbed a booth at Moe's and ordered two cups of coffee, black. As I waited, my thoughts raced. Why hadn't Sam wanted to meet at HQ? Why had he been so secretive? He'd never hidden his association with me, even when I'd visited him a few days ago. It must be serious if he was watching his step now.

He came into the diner almost exactly fifteen minutes after we'd spoken. I'd left the facing seat in the booth open. He shot a quick glance at the door. "Switch places with me."

Now I knew something was goin' on. But I obliged. "Why all the sneaking around?"

"It's just better this way." He slid into his seat and slugged back some java. "I don't have a lot of time, so first thing's first."

"You were awful quick to arrest Lee, Detective. I'm kinda surprised."

"Believe me, it wasn't my first choice." He checked out the passersby through the glass. No one gave us a second look.

The cloak-and-dagger stuff had my nerves jumpy. Was that woman at the counter studying us? No, it was my imagination. *Cut it out.* "Have you found Howley and McDougal yet?"

"No, and that's one of the reasons I wasn't keen on arresting your pal. Captain Finley, that's my boss, ordered me to make the collar."

"Why would he do that?"

"Oh come on, Betty. You aren't dumb so don't play games with me," he snapped. "Lee Tillotson hasn't acted like an innocent man. He lied about his whereabouts on the night of his father's death. I have a witness who saw him down at the grain elevator canals. I'm sure you've discovered that by now, as well as the fact that Mr. Tillotson senior was most likely killed down there."

I bought time by taking a sip from my mug. "Then you think there's only one scene? He wasn't killed somewhere else and taken to the canals?"

"It's hard to transport a half-conscious man unseen through this city. Remember, he drowned. Also." Sam paused to scope out the diner. Then he lowered his voice. "We found a pile of pipe lengths down at the canals. The victim's head wound was consistent with that type of weapon, so we took a few for evidence. Your buddy's fingerprints were all over them."

I swallowed against a lump in my throat. "Lee admitted he was glad his old man was dead. That the family was better off without him."

"Now you see why I can't dismiss Lee as a suspect." Sam's voice returned to something near normal. "But, I haven't found the other two men either. Nor have I been able to definitively determine what Mr. Tillotson was mixed up in before he died. I have a strong suspicion it was tied to illegal gambling or numbers."

I thought about what Pop had told me. Mr. Tillotson had said something about being in a hole. Getting on the wrong side of the head of a racket would not be good for your health.

Sam drummed his fingers. "Then there's the woman."

I snapped back to reality. "Excuse me?"

"I finally know something you don't." He grinned. "My witness at the canals said he saw her. I don't know who she is, where she came from, or where she went."

"Then I don't get it." I stared into the inky liquid in my white ceramic mug. "With all these unknowns, why'd your captain make you arrest Lee? It's a bum rap and you know it."

He narrowed his peepers and jabbed a finger at me. "No, I *don't* know it and that's the point. I wanted time to gather more evidence. My captain saw a suspect with means, motive, and opportunity. Case closed."

"But what if Lee's innocent? I mean, he is innocent. Doesn't that matter?"

"The captain thinks that's for the courts to decide. The police make the arrests, we don't determine guilt." Sam leaned back. "Let's just say the captain has political ambitions, reasons he wants a swift end."

I shouldn't have been shocked that cops could be politicians, but I was. "What do you mean?"

"He wants to be mayor."

I chuckled. "A police captain thinks he'll be more popular than Mayor Kelly? Your captain is gonna lose the Irish vote if he puts a First Ward boy in jail without making sure he's guilty."

"You don't go directly from captain to mayor. First, you get yourself appointed chief of police. How do you think you do that?"

I thought. "Prove you're tough on crime?"

He pointed at me. "Got it in one. You do that by closing cases. Or more precisely, by running a department that closes cases. Now you see why the pressure was on me to get this one off the open list. I had a crime and a solid suspect. Close it, give it to the DA's office, and move on to the next one. If the DA doesn't prosecute or fluffs it in court, well, that's not my problem and, therefore, not Captain Finley's. Unless it becomes a trend, I suppose. But that hasn't happened yet."

My coffee had gone lukewarm, but I didn't care. Drinking it helped me think. If I forced myself to be objective, I could understand the police captain's actions, 'specially after Sam explained it that way. Lee sure did look like he was the guy, or could be, at least to someone who didn't know him. "Now what are you gonna do?"

"Nothing." Sam spread his hands. "I've made my collar. I move on to the next case."

I blinked. "Just like that?"

"Just like that." He smirked. "You, however...that's something different. You're a private individual. No one's breathing down your neck wanting to wipe a case off the board."

I got his meaning. Sam wouldn't be looking for Howley, McDougal, or this mystery woman. But I could. "Where do I start?"

He pulled a slip of paper from his pocket. "Here. This is a list of known racketeers and gambling dens in the city. I got it from our Vice guys. I didn't have a chance to interview them, but if John Tillotson was involved in the numbers game, these would be the guys who would know. In addition, if Howley and McDougal are part of it, this is where you'd find them."

I studied the names. A couple of the groups were in the First Ward, others were dotted over Kaisertown, Polonia, and even a few downtown. Without Lee to back me up, though, I didn't know how smart it would be for me to visit. Dot wouldn't be much help here. "What about the woman?"

"She's a ghost." Sam drained his mug. "But my gut says you'll find her when you locate the other two suspects."

I folded the paper and put it in my purse. "I gotta talk to Lee. Can I do that?"

Sam's puss sobered. "Yes, but it's tricky. He's in jail."

"Tell me something I don't know."

"You don't understand. You can visit him. But anything you say, well, they'll be listening."

Sam was right, I didn't get the drift. "Listening to what, our conversation? Whatever for?"

"Yes. There will be guards standing around when you're there and someone is always monitoring incoming phone calls. Whatever he says is fair game when the prosecutor starts building his case."

Now I caught his meaning. "They, the cops or the district attorney, could use whatever we talk about to prove Lee is guilty."

Sam nodded, face solemn.

It would be hard, but I'd figure it out. If Tom and I could beat the censors of the U.S. Army, I could have a meaningless conversation with my friend. At least it would seem that way to anyone eavesdropping. "Understood. How much time do I have?"

"If you want to be safe, I'd try to get to the bottom of this before he goes in front of the judge." He pushed back his coat sleeve to check the time. "I gotta go before I'm missed. Good luck, Betty. Remember, Tuesday at the latest. If I find out anything more, I'll try to get in touch." He doffed his fedora, tugged it back on, and left.

I stared at my now-ice cold coffee. No pressure.

Chapter Seventeen

Before I left the diner, I dropped a nickel in the payphone and called Dot. "Is Mrs. T home yet?"

"No, and the girls are getting antsy. I don't know what to tell 'em."

I didn't want Dot to lie, but I didn't think they needed to hear the truth, either. "Just say their brother might be away for a couple of days and they have to be good for their mom."

Dot huffed. "What about for me?"

"That too."

She paused. "Have you found anything out?"

I told her everything I'd learned from Sam. "Given all that, I'm not surprised they arrested Lee. I'm not happy with Sam, and I told him so, but sounds like he got read the riot act from above. He didn't have a choice."

"You always have a choice," Dot snapped. She didn't sound as willing to give Sam a pass as I was. "You talked to Lee yet?"

"I'm heading to the jail now."

"I wish I was there."

"I know, but Sam tells me it could get dicey." I relayed what he'd said about privacy. "I'm thinking it's not a bad thing to keep the group small."

"It's easier to hide a conversation between two people. I get it." She pulled away from the phone to yell at the girls. Then she returned. "I'll go later. Tell him...well, you know."

"I will. I promise."

I hung up. Mom and Pop had given me a pass for the day, so I didn't have to worry about keeping in touch with them. Except for one thing. I fished around for another nickel and called home. "Pop, remember O'Malley's?"

"How could I forget?"

"Would you be willing to do me a favor?"

"Is it to help Lee?"

"Yes."

"What do you need?"

I thought. I didn't need either Howley or McDougal showing up at the house, not if they were thugs. "Go to the bar and see if Howley or McDougal is there. If they are, just tell 'em that a detective you know needs to talk to 'em about the numbers game and they should be at Moe's Diner downtown at one o'clock."

"I was afraid you were going to ask something like that." He hesitated a beat. "I would, my darling girl, but I've been called in to work. I can't."

Rats. "Thanks anyway."

"I don't want you going in that place. Not by yourself."

"I gotta get in there somehow. But I promise, until I can do it safely, all I'll do is snoop around the outside."

He sighed. "Betty, you know to be careful, don't you?"

"Right now I'm goin' to visit Lee, Pop. I don't think anyone will hurt me around a bunch of cops or prison guards."

I hung up and went over to the jail. At the front desk, I said I was a friend of Lee Tillotson's and asked if he was available to talk. The guard, a pot-bellied man with close-cropped gray hair, nodded in the direction of a bench. "Take a seat and I'll find out."

After about ten minutes, another guard came through the door. "Betty Ahern for Liam Tillotson?"

I stood. "That's me."

"This way, please."

I followed him into a dingy gray hallway, all plain walls and worn linoleum floor, to an equally sad-looking room. In the middle of the space were booths, I guess you'd call 'em. A sheet of glass ran down lengthwise on top a wooden desk that stretched from one end of the room to the other, one chair on either side. A dividing wall separated each pair of chairs. A few of the pairs were occupied, mostly women on the visitors' side and grim-faced men on the other. Guards were stationed all around the room within easy listening of everybody. Sam had been right about no privacy.

The guard who'd escorted me in led me to an empty seat. "He'll be out in a minute," he said, motioning to the chair. I sat and clutched my purse. If the visiting area of the jail was this bleak, I didn't want to see the inside.

It wasn't long until a guard led Lee out to see me. His hands and feet were shackled and his limp was worse than ever. He wore a shapeless gray jumpsuit. The guard guided him over to me, not unkindly, and left us as alone as the situation allowed. "Are you okay?" I asked.

Lee's face was already sallow and a bit pale, even though he'd only been inside for a few hours. What would years do to him if I failed? "Okay, I guess. I haven't been here long. Nobody's really talked to me. They tell me lunch is in half an hour, so I'll find out what prison chow tastes like." He licked his lips. "Does Mom know I'm here? What about Anna and Emma?"

"Dot's at your house with them. She only said you'd be gone for a while. Your mom isn't home yet, not when I called and that was only fifteen minutes ago or so."

"Good." He stared straight at me, like he was working up the courage to tell me something.

"Listen, Lee. I'm gonna get you out of here. Pop knows a guy whose brother is a lawyer. You gotta be patient."

"I'm gonna plead guilty."

It took a moment for my brain to unravel what he'd said. "What?"

"They explained how it went when they booked me. I'm gonna tell 'em I did it."

I knew Lee was the kind of guy to cover for a friend. But this was ridiculous. "Why on earth would you say that?"

"I lied. I was at the grain elevator canals that night. I saw my dad, picked up a pipe, and hit him over the head. He fell in the water and I didn't bother to do anything about it. Detective MacKinnon said they have the murder weapon with my fingerprints. The end."

The scene was all wrong. The Lee Tillotson I knew did not go around banging people's heads with a length of pipe. And yet Sam had told me the cops confiscated multiple lengths of pipe with Lee's fingerprints on them. There had to be a reason. I'd ask Sam if they found the exact weapon later. "Let's leave that for a moment. Did you see anyone else?"

"A couple of guys. Dad argued with them, but I didn't recognize either one."

"What about a woman?"

He twitched. "No."

"Lee, this isn't the time to fib. If you saw a woman—"

"I didn't see no woman, all right? If this is all you're gonna yap about, I'm outta here." He pushed away from the desk.

"Lee, stop it. I'm tryin' to help." My mind raced. He'd seen a dame, I was sure of it. Why would he lie? The answer came almost instantly. He thought he recognized her. What woman would follow his dad? His mother. That had to be it. He thought he'd seen Mrs. T. Why? I had to find out. But how was I gonna ask him questions without tipping off the guards? "Mom said somethin' about goin' over to your place to sit with your mom. I haven't asked lately, is she working? Your mom?"

He stared at me, an intense, harsh look. "Here and there. In fact, she's been doing a lot of late-night cleaning jobs. She goes out who knows where and I don't see her sometimes until morning."

"Every night? Wow, that's a lot."

"Often enough." Still, that piercing gaze. "Lots of times it was just me and the girls. Pop would be out drinkin' or whatever. Mom was workin'. See, she has a lot of factory or business jobs. Offices, like those at General Mills or Bethlehem. The big guys go home, Mom comes to clean."

Now I had to be real careful. None of the guards seemed to be payin' attention to us, but still, I lowered my voice. "Lee, I know you said things were tough at home. And the relationship between your folks hasn't been great. Tell me straight. Was she home that night?"

His lips barely moved. "No. Like I said, she works late a lot. But that night..." He glanced around and leaned in. "I don't think she was workin'.

She left all dressed up and said she was goin' out, but didn't say nothing else about it."

"Dressed up how?"

"She had one of her nicer dresses on, and she'd put on makeup and done her hair. She has one pair of those stupid shoes women wear."

"High heels? Pumps?"

"Those. She hardly ever wears them so she can barely walk straight. She wore her good coat, too. The one with the big collar."

I took all this in. "When did she come home?"

"Late, real late. I heard the chimes at Our Lady of Perpetual Help strike twelve."

The picture snapped into focus. Lee was afraid his mother had been at the canals on that night. But why would she get all dressed up to go there? Had she been out, seen her husband, followed and confronted him?

My mind raced. If Lee had been at the canals, for whatever reason, maybe he'd seen the mystery woman with the pipe, or watched her murder his dad. No wonder he was so intent on takin' the fall. I didn't believe for a moment it had been Nora Tillotson. But Lee did, and that's all that mattered. I had to get Ray to cough up more details. "I wonder if any of your dad's friends will be at the funeral. Especially any of the guys from O'Malley's. They might bring wives or girlfriends."

A cautious light came into his peepers. "Oh, uh, maybe. I don't know about any of that. Dad didn't bring his friends to the house."

"None of the guys he went to games with?"

"I didn't even know he gambled. He had a lot of faults, but hanging with racketeers wasn't one of 'em."

Lee didn't know Howley or McDougal or anything about a numbers racket.

The guard came over and touched his shoulder. "Time's up, Tillotson."

With the guard's help, Lee stood. "Thanks for coming to see me, Betty. Tell Dot...tell her I wish we'd had more time."

"Tell her yourself when she visits. And Lee?"

The guard had pulled him away, but he stopped and looked back.

I rose and shouldered my purse. "Don't do anything stupid."

Chapter Eighteen

As soon as I left the jail, I found the closest payphone and used another nickel to call Dot at the Tillotson's. "Is Mrs. T home yet?"

"She got here a little while ago," Dot said. "She's a wreck, as you might expect. Thank goodness your mom was here 'cause I don't think I coulda handled it. Your mom gave Mrs. T a cup of tea with a big shot of whiskey and she's resting."

"What about the girls?"

"I got Emma calmed down. Anna doesn't seem to know what's happening. I'm playing Chutes and Ladders with them." She made a *hmph* sound. "I hate that stupid game. It makes no sense whatsoever, do you know that?"

Her words brought on a memory of Lee making the same complaint. I pushed it aside.

"Did they let you talk to Lee?"

"Yes, and you're not gonna like it." I related my conversation with him.

As expected, Dot's anger was obvious. "What does he think he's doin'? How can he even think of pleading guilty to a crime he didn't commit? Does he want to spend the rest of his life in prison, or worse, get the chair?"

"I would hope they wouldn't execute him." But I hadn't thought of that possibility. Something else I needed to push outta my mind.

"Did he say anything about me?"

I couldn't miss the hopeful note. "Only that he was sorry he didn't get more time with you. I told him not to be a dope, he'd be free in no time flat."

Dot didn't respond, but from the sniffing, I knew she was holding back tears.

I tried to divert her attention. "I need you to do something for me."

She paused. "What is it?"

"Lee said his mother has a coat with a big collar and a pair of pumps. I want you to check and see if she still has 'em." A smart woman who had just killed a man would get rid of clothing that could identify her and whatever else Mrs. T was, she was smart.

"What, I should look now?"

"I'm not comin' back to the First Ward to find out and I need the info. Just go look, please and call me back at this number. I don't want to waste the coins waiting."

"Fine." She hung up and I imagined her slamming home the receiver with a little more force than necessary. I hoped like heck no one was on the party line for this conversation or else it'd be all over the neighborhood by dinner, if it wasn't already.

A few minutes later the phone rang and I picked up the blower. "What's the answer?"

"Yes, she has a navy blue one in the closet with a big fluffy collar," Dot said, her snappy tone sayin' she was still peeved at Lee's decision. "It looks almost brand new, not a speck of dirt on it."

That was good. A coat that had been down to the docks would almost certainly be dirty. "What about the shoes?"

"She's lyin' down in her room, so I couldn't go rummaging through her closet. But she was awake, so I asked if she needed nice shoes for the funeral 'cause I'd loan her a pair. She said she has one pair of black pumps, but she doesn't wear them a lot because she can't walk well in them and they pinch her toes. I asked if she wanted me to polish them up, but she said they didn't need cleaning." Dot hesitated and I could envision her chewing her plump bottom lip. "He can't really think his mother is a murderer, can he?"

Even if the coat had managed to stay clean, the shoes wouldn't have. Again, Mrs. T was too smart not to remove traces of a murder scene from her clothes. Then again, she mighta cleaned them herself or maybe she didn't want Dot to know they were dirty. "It's what he's afraid of that counts. He didn't say it outright, but how could he with the guards listening?"

"You want me to talk to her, see if she'll tell me anything?"

"That'd be swell."

"What's your next move?"

"I'm gonna try and find this Howley and McDougal. I'll call later, or at least stop at the house. Will you be at Tillotson's or your place?"

"I told your mom I'd stay until dinner to watch the girls." She paused again. "Do *you* think Mrs. T coulda done it?"

"I don't want to, but I don't know, Dot. I just don't know."

* * *

It didn't take more than thirty minutes, to get to O'Malley's. I stood outside, staring at the dingy white space where the "M" used to be, and weighed my options. I didn't particularly want to go inside. My last visit had convinced me that nice young girls didn't belong in a place like this, even if they were tryin' to be private detectives. It was worse than any other bar I'd ever visited in the Ward.

I pulled out a Lucky, lit it, and leaned against a lamp post. It was only mid-day. Maybe there weren't many people there. Maybe the toughs only came out at night. Maybe I could spot my quarry and get out quick.

Maybe I was askin' for trouble.

For a brief moment, I wished I really *was* Sam Spade, or at least that I was a guy. Men like Spade wouldn't have a second thought about barging through that door and hunting down their quarry. I could see the scene play out in front of my eyes. Spade or Marlowe dominating the space, getting the job done with their force of character and power.

That wasn't my style. Then I thought of Nick Charles. He would never be caught in a place like O'Malley's. But he'd get the answers. He'd charm someone into working for him. I might admire the tough guys, but in this case channeling my inner smooth talker would be much more effective.

Who could I get to do the job for me? I scanned the street. There weren't many people around at lunchtime, at least not anyone who'd go into a bar. I didn't need an average drinker, someone who went out for a beer after work.

I needed a *serious* boozer, like Mr. Tillotson. A guy who needed a drink so badly he'd do anything for alcohol, no matter the quality. I immediately sharpened my focus.

I started thinking of the few folks on the sidewalk as potential targets, people I could bribe. There was a mother with a baby carriage. She was out. Two guys dressed in worn, but clean, coveralls. No, prob'ly not. They were more likely to be working stiffs on a lunch break than alcoholics looking for their next shot. An old man with a cane strolled down the opposite side of the street. He wasn't gonna be a good mark. I'd feel guilty if he got hurt. Not that I was expecting violence, but Howley and McDougal were unknown quantities. They might have been involved in Mr. Tillotson's death. I couldn't send someone's grandpa into a bar to ferret out the information I looked for.

I smoked another two cigarettes while I loitered, trying to find a good mark. I was about to give up, grind out my gasper, and move on, when a man ambled around the corner. His dark blue pants didn't only need a wash, they needed a seamstress to fix the gaping holes and frayed hems. The shirt was beyond help, stained and torn, not even fit for rags. Even from five yards away, I could see the broken veins in his nose and bleary eyes. Just what I was looking for. I went over to him. "Excuse me, sir?"

He scratched his stomach and looked around. "You talkin' to me?"

"Yeah, you. There's no one else around." Ten steps took me close enough to catch his smell, a mixture of unwashed body, booze, and stale water from the lake. Unfortunately, I was downwind, so the stench smacked me in the face. I stopped and tried to angle myself so I inhaled as little of the odor as possible. "You look like you could use a drink."

A desperate light came into his eyes. "You're singing my song, sweetheart. You got a bottle?"

"Not on me, no."

A crestfallen look stole over his puss.

"But." I unclasped my pocketbook, pulled out my change purse, and took out two bits. "I do have some coin."

He reached out his hand and licked his lips in greed.

"Not so fast." I held the quarter just out of reach. "You gotta do something for me in return."

"Anything."

Exactly what I wanted to hear. This could go south. He might disappear into the bar with my dough and never come out. But it was the only play I could see that had a chance of success and kept my skin whole. "See that bar over there, O'Malley's?"

He turned around. "Uh huh."

"The job is simple. You go in, buy a drink or two, and find out if either one of two guys is in there. Their names are Howley and McDougal."

"How'm I gonna do that?" He grabbed at the money, but I jerked it away.

"Heck, I don't know. You can ask, you can listen, eavesdrop, whatever. I just need to know if either of those two Joes are inside."

"What if they are?"

"Finish your drink, come out, and tell me. And make sure to get a half-decent description." I waved the silver in front of him. "We got a deal?"

He didn't hesitate. "Deal." He snatched the money and headed toward the bar.

Chapter Nineteen

I pulled an empty milk bottle crate out onto the sidewalk so I could sit, seeing as there wasn't any other place to go, no coffee shops or steps where I could park my keister and get off my feet. I made a deal that I'd wait no more than an hour. Much longer and I'd have to come up with a plan B. I didn't have the time to waste sitting around outside a run-down bar waiting for a guy who might not show his mug again.

Turns out, I didn't wait that long, not more than twenty minutes. My guy must have guzzled that booze. He staggered out of the door, brushing his shirt. "I don't sell on credit and I ain't no bank. You want another drink, you come back with your own coin," a snarly male voice said. The speaker yanked the door shut with such force the resulting breeze ruffled my drunk's greasy hair.

He pivoted, rubbing his mouth, obviously looking for me.

"Over here." I hauled myself to my feet. "They in there?"

"If you'd see fit to give me a little more dough, I'd have more information for you."

I didn't know how much liquor a quarter bought. Enough so this guy's pupils were dilated and he swayed on his feet, the scent of beer mixing with his previous odors. It wasn't a pleasant result. I took a step back. "Oh, no. I'm not paying for you to get sloshed, at least not more'n you are already. Did you see Howley and McDougal or not?"

"It's gonna cost you another two bits."

"We had a deal." I wished I'd brought Sean's switchblade. Not that I planned to use it, but the sight would probably have this dope peeing his pants and telling me his life story. "If you're gonna welch now, we have nothing further to talk about."

"What about if I not only tell you about those guys and give a description, but add some information I overheard that might be valuable?"

I wavered. I had doubts about what this lush thought valuable information was, but I didn't want to say no and spite myself. "I'm listening. Tell me what you know and I'll decide if it's worth it."

"Well." He staggered to the wall and leaned against it. "Howley is in there. He's a tall fellow, at least six inches taller than you. He has dark hair and eyes and is on the skinny side. But the most interesting thing about him is the scar on his face." My drunk dragged a finger down his cheek. "It turns a plain face into something unforgettable."

Six inches taller than me put the guy at about six-two. "What else?"

"He was talking to another man in there. This guy, not Howley, the other, was shorter, looked like a weasel. Nice suit, shiny shoes, oily hair. Smoked cigars. Honestly, while this is a fine establishment," he waved his arm wildly, "I would expect him to be more at home in one of the bars on Main Street, not in what is clearly a place for honest working men."

I suppressed a snort. There prob'ly wasn't an "honest working man" within twenty feet of O'Malley's and that included the bartender. "Is that all?"

The drunk held up a finger. "I heard Howley say, 'It's best you don't know the details. The important thing is everything's been taken care of.'"

"What was taken care of?"

"I don't know." His face turned mournful. "They were sitting at a table, talking. I'd taken a seat nearby to listen in. But at that moment, the barkeep tossed me out. Something about taking up valuable space when I couldn't buy another round." His slurred words combined with indignation would have been comical under other circumstances. "If I'm not mistaken, that is worth at least another quarter."

I fished another one out of my change purse and flipped it to him. "Here. You can scram now."

He grabbed for the coin, but missed. He spun about wildly, looking for his treasure.

"It's at your feet."

He lunged for the quarter, picked it up, kissed it, and headed into O'Malley's.

If Scar Face was Howley, the other man had to be his boss, maybe the guy who ran the numbers game. It sounded like he wanted details on some situation, and my gut told me they'd been talking about what had happened at the grain elevators. If he'd sent Howley and McDougal to talk to Mr. Tillotson, maybe he was concerned the murder would be traced back to him.

Only one way to find out.

* * *

I chafed at the delay, but I had to wait. Not on my milk crate, but somewhere less conspicuous. I couldn't barge into O'Malley's and demand the answers I needed. Sooner or later Weasel Man or Howley would come out of the bar. Then I'd be able to tail them to their next stop.

Unless they got into a car.

I was wasting time. It was already one o'clock. What if neither man came out of the bar? I'd spend hours sitting here like a dope when I could be doin' other things, like tracing down this mystery woman.

There was no way out of it. I had to call Sam. I went into a soda shop a block away to use the phone. "I need your help," I said when I reached him at his office.

"With what?"

"Can you meet me near O'Malley's on South Street and I'll explain? It's gotta be fast, though."

"I'll be there in ten."

Sam was as good as his word. He walked up to me as I stood across the street from the bar, drinking a Coke I'd gone and purchased, hopefully looking like I was up to nothing more sinister than whiling away a Saturday afternoon. "You aren't gonna get in trouble with your captain, are you?" I asked. "I shoulda asked that before."

"Don't worry. I made my collar, so he's happy. As of noon, it's my weekend off. I was about to leave when you phoned. My time is my own, unless there's an emergency and I get called in. What's the situation?"

I explained what I'd done so far and described Weasel Man and Howley. "Neither of 'em have come out of O'Malley's. I need to talk to at least one of 'em, but I've been in that place with my pop."

"It's not a good situation for an unaccompanied young woman of principle. The description of the one you call Weasel Man sounds familiar. If it's who I think it is, you'd best stay clear." He took off his fedora and jacket, and slipped his badge in the front pocket of his trousers. "Wait here. They'll probably still make me for a cop, but I'll do what I can." He paused and ran his hands through his hair. "I'm impressed you bribed a drunk. That's a professional trick."

"Thanks."

I watched him trot across the street and into the bar. Barely five minutes later, he came back out, but alone. Once back at my side, he fixed his hair then put on both hat and jacket. "They're gone."

"What do you mean? I didn't see anyone come out."

"You must have been spotted or your drunk raised suspicions. There's a back exit. The bartender said both men slipped out nearly ten minutes ago."

Words that were not meant for nice young ladies ran through my head, but all I said was, "Darn it."

He guided me to his car. "Don't worry. I convinced the barman it was better for everybody if he told me as much as he could. The man with the scar is indeed Danny Howley. The other man is Blackie Thomas. He's the head of one of the bigger numbers rackets in the city. Blackie runs his business out of a social club over on Abbot Road. I have the address."

"How did you get the bartender to tell you all this?"

"I think it best you don't know." Sam walked around the car and got in. "I want to make a stop first."

I slid into the passenger seat. "Where?"

"We're going back to the grain elevators. What's the name of the guy you talked to?"

"Ray Thatcher. He wasn't all that helpful when I was down there earlier." Sam pulled away from the curb. "I think we'll find him a bit more cooperative this time. I have something you don't and it can be very persuasive."

I thought a beat. "A badge? What is this, good cop, bad cop?"

He shot me a look and his lips slanted in a grin. "I think we're going to have a lot of fun together, Miss Ahern. Don't you?"

Chapter Twenty

I'd forgotten how nice it was to work with Sam. He was a good investigator and a smart guy to boot. Also, there was no waiting for the bus. We arrived back at the grain elevator canals a lot faster in his car. "This way," I said and led Sam to the office building.

Ray was still inside. He looked up at the sound of the door. "Okay, miss. Enough's enough. I don't have time for games."

"Mr. Thatcher, I want to introduce you to another friend of mine. This is Detective Sam MacKinnon from the Buffalo Police Department's Homicide Division."

Ray slapped down a book he held. "Listen. I don't know who put you up to this or where you got some joker to play cop. I got work to do. Scram before I call security."

With one hand Sam showed his badge, while he reached out the other one and grabbed Ray's shirt. Sam pulled him in real close to the badge, so close the other man had to cross his eyes to see the shiny gold. "Now tell me. Does this look like a piece of costume paraphernalia to you?"

Ray swallowed. "No, sir."

"I'm glad to hear you say that. Now. Nothing about this is acting. The young lady is a professional private investigator and I'm a quite-real police detective. You don't want any trouble, do you?"

I'd heard this voice out of Sam before, smooth-talking over an iron core. But I'd never seen him get physical with a suspect. It made me very happy I'd decided to bring him.

"You're going to answer Miss Ahern's questions. Quickly, thoroughly, and politely. Understand?" Sam said in a friendly voice that made it clear he wasn't asking.

"Yes, sir."

Sam let go of Ray's shirt. "Miss Ahern, ask away. I think you'll find Mr. Thatcher here more forthcoming than you did this morning."

"Thanks." I wished I had the picture of Lee, but I'd make this work. "Earlier, you said you hadn't seen the guy in the picture I showed you. Is that right?"

Ray gave Sam a wary look before answering. "Yes."

"But there were other people here. Tell me about them."

"I only spoke to one of 'em. He was an older gent who looked like the guy in your picture. I was coming in from my rounds. He stopped me and asked if anybody else was there. I could tell from looking at his nose he was a drinker, but I didn't see a bottle. He said he was meeting a business associate. My foot. What kind of business needs to be done by the grain elevator canals at nine at night?"

"What did you tell him?"

"That I hadn't seen anyone and that was the truth. He thanked me, left, and walked off that way, toward where the canal opens onto the lake." Ray waved in the general direction.

I took out my notepad and jotted down the info. "You mentioned other men. When did they show?"

Ray thought a moment. "I dunno. It didn't seem like very long after I talked to the first guy, but I guess it coulda been as much as fifteen or twenty minutes. I was reviewing the books for the day. I looked up as they were standing under the light over there, near the water. Seemed to me like they were looking for someone."

Sam broke in. "What did they look like?"

Ray sidled toward me, maybe nervous about Sam grabbing him again. "I didn't see them real good, I swear. One was kind of tall, the other shorter. They had on dark clothes. I'm pretty sure the tall guy had a scar on his cheek. A big one." He drew a line on his own face.

"Sounds to me like you saw plenty." Sam crossed his arms. "What makes you say that?"

"It's what, five yards away? I know it don't seem like it, but those lights are pretty bright, they gotta be in case there's a barge that needs loading or unloading at night. It ain't like there are curtains at the window. It's a straight view from here to there and my eyesight's pretty sharp." Ray shrugged. "I didn't see 'em good enough to draw a picture, no hair or eye color, nothing like that. But the guy's face looked funny and the first thought that crossed my mind was a scar. Guess I sorta assumed it."

Based on what Sam had said earlier, I figured the man with the scarred face was Howley. Maybe the short fellow was McDougal. "What did they do?" I asked.

"Stood around for a minute. I went back to work. Next time I looked up, they were gone." Ray paused. "But a few minutes later, I heard voices, down from where the first guy had gone."

"Is that all?"

"No, there was a woman, too. She came a little bit after the others."

I looked up. "Are you sure it was a lady?"

Ray laughed. "I know the difference between a guy and a dame, sweetheart. She definitely wasn't no dock worker's missus, either."

"How can you tell?"

"She stopped under one of the lights. Seemed to me her face was all made up, but I guess that coulda been 'cause of the way the light fell on her. She stood a minute and looked around as she clutched her coat. That was the real giveaway. Fur trim at the collar and sleeves. Nobody around here can afford to put their women in duds like that." He arched his eyebrows. "I think she was definitely a woman used to the finer things in life, if you get my meaning. Something in the way she stood. She reminded me of a mobster's moll, like from a Cagney flick. She tottered off the way the guys went."

"Tottered?"

"Yeah. She was wearing those crazy shoes dames wear, with the high heels. She was wobbling around like she was drunk." He spat.

I knew exactly the type of woman Ray was talking about. No wonder Lee thought it might have been his mother. This woman was wearing the same kind of coat and pumps. She couldn't walk in the shoes. If I didn't know Mrs. T better, I'd have thought it was her. "All these people. Did you see any of 'em leave?"

"No, and that's the funny bit." Ray leaned on the counter. He had apparently forgotten about Sam and focused on me. "I finished the books and realized I hadn't seen any of them again. So I walked off in the direction they'd all gone. Not a one of 'em was there. Almost as if a hand had reached down and picked them all up. Not a crate was out of place, though."

"Is there another way off the dock?" I asked.

"This is the last canal in the row, so yeah, they coulda scaled the fence and gone off the back way, toward Fuhrman. Or legged it when I went out to do my hourly patrol. They left somehow, 'cause I didn't see no one when I was out."

"One last question." I glanced at Sam. "What about in the canal? Did you see anything, or anyone, there?"

Ray's eyebrows climbed toward his hairline. "Sweetheart, are you kidding me? The water is freezing. And no one goes into the canals if he can help it. It's dirty as sin in there."

The key phrase was "if he can help it," but I didn't say anything. Mr. Tillotson definitely couldn't have helped himself, not that night.

"Did you see anything on your way back here?" Sam asked. "You know, after you went down the dock."

"No, sir, nothing." Ray furrowed his forehead in thought. "I did notice a lot of slips of paper around."

"What kind of paper?" Sam asked.

Ray shrugged. "Betting slips of some kind. I did wonder where they all came from, but it was cold and I wanted to get back into my warm office."

"Anything else?"

Ray's forehead puckered. "There was a car. It was smokin' and burnin' oil like anything. They don't fix that pronto, they're gonna go up in flames in the middle of Buffalo. And I ain't exaggerating. But that disappeared, too. Come to think of it, the woman might have gotten out of it, but I'm not sure. It wasn't there when the men showed up."

Sam thought a second. "Mind if we take a stroll down the dock?"

It looked like Ray wanted to object, but his gaze flicked to where Sam's badge was and he said, "No. Just be careful so you don't get hurt."

"Thanks," I said. Sam and I left and headed toward the lake. "What are we looking for? Any paper is long gone."

"You're right, but it's worth searching. We did a canvass of the area before, but a second look never hurts."

We reached a spot near the middle of the canal. A bunch of wooden crates had been piled to the right. Multiple columns led from where we stood to the end of the canal near the main office. They offered plenty of hiding spaces for someone who wanted to spy on the action. "You said you found pipes. Where was that?"

Sam waved. "Over there."

The wind had come up again now that we were close to the water and I tucked my hair behind my ears.

Sam fished in his pocket and held out a rubber band. "Here. It's not great, but it's the best I can offer."

I gathered my hair and snapped the elastic around it. It would prob'ly snarl, but it was better than constantly brushing it out of my face. In between two of the towers of crates, I spied a neat pile of metal piping, tucked away so it wouldn't be obvious. Lengths of about three feet formed a flat-top pyramid. "There looks to be some missing. Are those the ones you took away?"

"Yes." Sam came over. "We're pretty sure the actual murder weapon is at the bottom of the canal."

That answered one of my questions from earlier.

"But we took a couple as evidence, to compare to the injury on the back of Mr. Tillotson's head, and two of them had Lee Tillotson's prints, that's been confirmed."

"You said that before. How'd you get Lee's fingerprints before he'd been arrested?" And why, for the love of Mike, didn't he wear gloves that night?

Sam's cheeks reddened, but whether from the wind chill or a blush I couldn't tell. "The water glass from when he came to identify his father's body. I lifted them after you left, just in case."

I made a mental note to never accept anything from a police detective. "I thought you were lookin' to clear him."

"Then you were mistaken."

"You said you didn't want to arrest him."

"I didn't want to arrest him *yet*." Sam stuffed his hands in his coat pockets. "Betty, don't misunderstand. I'm not here because I'm convinced your friend is innocent. I'm here because I'm not convinced he's guilty. If you think about it, I'm sure you'll see the difference."

I rolled the words around in my head. I saw the logic. Sam hadn't cleared Lee as a suspect, but he also hadn't eliminated anyone else. At the same moment, I realized I had to do the same. Believing Lee to be innocent was a heck of a lot different than proving it. If I wanted to be a professional, I had to put emotions aside. The last thing I wanted to do, however, was admit that. Not to Sam, not yet. "Let's keep looking before I freeze in place."

We crawled all over the dock. I inspected every crate, thinking maybe someone had hidden behind them. My meticulous search was rewarded by a tiny scrap of heavy blue wool snagged on a nail sticking out of a crate. "Sam, over here." He came over and held out a pair of tweezers. I used them to detach the fabric. "I s'pose this coulda come from a dock worker's coat."

Sam peered at the wool and held out an envelope. "Maybe. It looks like it might have come off a man's winter coat, like a pea coat." He sealed the evidence and marked it.

"Lee has a dark blue coat like that," I said, my soul shriveling a bit more. "But why would he hide behind the crates? Unless he didn't want to be seen 'cause he'd just dumped his dad."

"Don't sound so glum." Sam slipped the envelope into a pocket. "All this scrap tells me is he might have been here and I already knew that from the prints. Hell, even those aren't conclusive evidence of guilt."

"What do you mean?"

"He could have straightened the pile, he could have seen the bloody pipe and threw it away, he could even have knocked over the pile and put it back together to disguise the fact someone had been here." Sam ticked points off on his fingers. "Yes, he'd hide if he had just killed his father, but also what if he was spying on the other men? Or that woman? If he knew who they were, he might not have wanted to be seen either because he feared for himself or because he was covering for someone."

The last sentence made me remember the results of Dot's search. "I didn't tell you, this earlier. When I talked to Lee, he said he was gonna plead guilty." I swallowed.

"Why would he do that?"

I told Sam about Mrs. T's coat and how in the dark, it might be taken for a fancier garment. "I think Lee believes he saw his mother. He'd do anything for her, even go to jail."

Sam paused. "Surely Mrs. Tillotson has an alibi."

"I don't know." I gazed out over the steel-colored waves, then turned back to Sam. "The night her husband died, Lee told me she left and said she was goin' out and didn't come back until after midnight. She didn't say with who and Lee didn't ask." *What kind of friend are you?* But if I was gonna be professional, I had to keep all my options open.

Sam's forehead creased. "Let's keep looking."

We scoured the canal in silence for another fifteen minutes. All I could think about was the scrap of wool, Lee's fingerprints, and his intention to plead guilty. I tried to reconstruct any scenario that made sense. He'd followed...*someone* down to the canal docks. His mom? His dad? My money was on Mr. Tillotson. After the fight at home, Lee would've wanted to see what his father was up to.

Sam's voice cut the frigid air. "Betty! Over here."

I ran to where he crouched next to another pile of crates. He'd used his handkerchief to pick up an object and was tilting it to study the side. As I got closer, I could see it was a pocketknife. "Where'd you find that?"

"Next to these boxes. Somebody is missing a very nice utility knife. Not a switchblade, but one that'd be handy in a machine shop. Looks like it might have been a gift." He held it out. "It's engraved 'To Steve with love.' Know anyone involved in this with that name?"

Oh boy, did I ever.

Chapter Twenty-One

While Sam and I drove to Polonia, I told him everything I knew about Steve Daletzki and his relationship with Mr. Tillotson. "This Daletzki, he lost a good job because of John Tillotson?" Sam asked.

"Yeah, but I don't think that was the sticking point." I braced myself as we turned. I wasn't watching the speedometer, but I had a funny feeling Sam wasn't strictly obeying the city speed limit. "It was the racket, specifically Mr. Tillotson's refusal to give his friend a piece of the action. If you ask me, that's what really got Mr. Daletzki steamed. He thought Mr. Tillotson owed him for what happened at GM."

"Daletzki doesn't sound like a shady character. Not based on what you've said."

"No, but when a guy loses a good job and feels he needs dough, especially to support a family, who's to say what he'd do?"

"You have a point. It'll be interesting to talk to him and see what he has to say about his knife being at a murder scene."

We arrived at Mrs. Wiese's house. I let Sam go ahead of me. He had the badge and I didn't think she would be keen to talk to me, not after what had happened when Dot and I were last here and especially not after she heard why Sam and I were there.

"What are you doing back?" Mrs. Wiese snapped when she opened the door. "I have nothing to say to you. I sent you to talk to Steve and you've done nothing but cause trouble for him. Get out." She started to shut the door.

Sam put out a hand and flashed his badge. "Mrs. Wiese, I understand you might be upset with Miss Ahern. But I would like a few moments of your time."

"I'm not more inclined to speak with the police. I'm not going to get my brother in trouble."

"A conversation with me now may keep him out of trouble."

She sniffed and grasped the door. "All right. But I'll shut this the moment I don't like what you're saying."

"Fair enough." Sam glanced at me. "When was the last time you saw Steve?"

"This morning, when he went to work at that god-awful job he had to take because of that drunkard John Tillotson."

A boy about six years old came around the corner. "Mom, what's for dinner?"

Mrs. Wiese chased him away. "You just had lunch. Go play with your brother."

Sam continued as though he'd never seen the child. "When do you expect him home?"

"I don't usually see him until at least six. The shop closes at five and then he has to clean up."

"He's there now?"

An angry light flashed in her eyes. "Are you deaf? I said he was at work, where else would he be?"

Sam smoothly changed the direction of the conversation. "What about the night of March second? Do you remember where he was then?"

"I don't recall. He went to work and he must have come home because that's what he does every night. Now excuse me, Detective. I have things to do. Goodbye." She shot me a frosty look and slammed the door.

"That went well," I said as we got back into the car.

"It's about what I expected, to be honest." Sam started the engine. "Families rarely want to talk to the cops. Especially when they think talking would get their loved ones in hot water. Mrs. Wiese is clearly one of those people. Where is this garage?"

I directed Sam to Clifton's Auto Repair. But when we arrived, the man there, who said he was the other mechanic, told us Mr. Daletzki hadn't come to work that morning.

"Not really like him," the guy said. "I can count on one hand the number of times he's been late or absent and still have four fingers left. I hope nothing is wrong. But if he don't call or show up Monday, Mr. Peyton is gonna have to let him go. There are too many good mechanics out there who need the work and who will come in steady for Mr. Peyton to play around with a guy who only works when it suits him."

Sam handed over a card. "I'd very much like to talk to Mr. Daletzki. Would you please have him call me at this number if you see him?"

"Is Steve in trouble?"

"No, but I have a few questions. Tell me, do you have any idea of where he'd be if he wasn't at work?"

"Only place I'd know of would be his sister's house. That's where he lives. We don't pal around when we aren't here working, so I don't know much about his social activities."

We thanked him and left. "Mrs. Wiese says her brother is at work," I said. "That guy said if he isn't at work, he'd be at home. That's not much help."

"Not unusual." Sam leaned on his car. "Did you ever visit those places I gave you earlier today, the numbers games?"

"I haven't had time. You think Mr. Daletzki is following up with those guys to see if there are any openings now that his friend is dead?"

Sam pushed off the car. "I don't know, but I think it's worth a shot. Don't you?"

"Why not? But I gotta make a call first." I pulled out my purse and hunted out a nickel. "I'm running out of change."

"Here." Sam tossed me a coin. "Until you can get more."

"Thanks." I hot-footed it across Sycamore to a payphone where I called Dot at home. "Any news?"

"Not much," she said. "Your mom said if you called, I'm s'posed to tell you that your dad got a hold of his friend, the one with the lawyer. He's gonna meet with Lee up at the jail at two-thirty, maybe three o'clock."

I looked at my watch. It was two-twenty-five now. "Okay. Thanks for the tip, Dot. Mrs. Tillotson say anything before you left?"

"Nah. All she could do was wail about Lee and how she couldn't believe her husband would do this to the family. She kept sayin' 'But he was a good man at heart, how could he have done this?' It was awful to have to sit through."

Mr. Tillotson may have been a good man once, but he'd taken a bad turn somewhere. "Thanks, Dot. I'm with Detective MacKinnon now. If I need you for anything, I'll call."

"Why is *he* there? Didn't he get his man?" The bitterness in Dot's voice came through loud and clear.

"He didn't want to arrest Lee, not at this moment. Say, that's what you can do." I looked over at Sam and held up a finger to tell him one more minute. "According to Sam, his captain has ambitions. He wants to be mayor. Your dad gets the *Courier*, right?"

"Yeah."

"Go through any issues you have lying around and see if you can scare up any dope about a Captain Finley from the Buffalo PD." I heard a drawer open.

"Spell the name," Dot said. "F-I-N-L-E-Y, got it. What kind of information?"

"I'm interested in any activities he may have been involved with that could help him get elected."

"I thought he'd have to be chief of police first."

"He would and he seems to be working on that. But running a mayoral campaign costs a lot of lettuce. He could be saving up for when he needs it. See if there are any stories of donations or people he might be hanging around who could help him out."

"Got it." She paused. "What are you gonna do with anything I find?"

I drummed my fingers on the phone booth wall. "Ask me again when you find it."

* * *

"Change of plans," I said when I jogged back to Sam's car. "I need you to take me to the city jail."

"Why?" he asked as he slid inside.

I got into the passenger seat. "Lee's lawyer is showing up soon. I gotta be there when he does." I said a quick Hail Mary, crossed myself, then braced my feet against the floor and my arm against the door.

"What was that for?"

"Your driving leaves a lot to be desired." I didn't risk looking at him.

He chuckled and pulled away from the curb. "I'll take you to the jail, but remember what I said. Attorney-client privilege will protect Lee once the lawyer arrives, but be careful what you say or do before that."

"Gotcha."

Sam dropped me off in front of the jail building. "I'll be back in an hour. Will that be enough time?"

I put my hand on the handle. "I think so. What are you gonna do?"

"I'll be checking out those names I gave you. Someone on that list worked with, or knows of, Howley, McDougal, or John Tillotson."

Once inside the jail, I said I was there to meet with Lee and his lawyer. A guard led me to a smallish room with a table and a few chairs that looked the worse for wear. Lee sat across from a middle-aged man in a dark blue suit. Black glasses perched on a beaked nose below slate-blue eyes. The part in his hair was so sharp it coulda been made with a ruler. "Sorry I'm late."

The man looked up. "Who are you?"

Lee stood and gave me a hug. "This is Betty Ahern. You can say anything in front of her." He tugged my hand and I sat in the chair next to him. "This is Mr. Williams. He's representing me."

I held out my hand.

Mr. Williams peered at it as though it was a dead fish. "I'm sorry, Miss Ahern. You have to leave."

I glanced at Lee.

He gaped a moment and said, "I told you, she's a-okay. She's my best friend. I want her to know what's goin' on."

Mr. Williams removed his glasses, set them on the table, and folded his hands. "It's not that simple. The presence of any person other than the two of us could jeopardize the attorney-client privilege."

I could tell Lee was as confused as I was. "How so?" I asked. "If Lee said I could be here, isn't that enough?"

"I'm afraid it isn't." Mr. Williams straightened his papers. "The prosecution could argue that since people other than Mr. Tillotson and I were party to the conversation, privilege doesn't apply. If that argument was upheld, anything we talk about in this meeting could be used in court."

"There's no way around that?"

"I'd have to employ you. Privilege extends to any member of my defense team, inclusive of other lawyers and staff."

Lee waved in my direction. "So hire her."

Mr. Williams unbent enough to permit a small smile. He replaced his specs. "I have a secretary, Mr. Tillotson. I don't need another."

"I didn't say as a secretary." Lee slapped the table. "Betty is a private detective and a darn good one. I want her on my team. If you don't, you can walk out that door and I'll find myself another lawyer."

Mr. Williams turned his head slowly to face me. "You are a private detective, miss?"

My face warmed and I hoped I wasn't blushing. "Yes, I am. I've solved murders, too. Three of 'em as a matter of fact. Plus other cases."

He paused. His face coulda been carved from the stone under Niagara Falls. "You won't find another attorney, Mr. Tillotson. Not one you can pay for. Is it important to you that this young lady be involved?"

Lee crossed his arms, that familiar mulish expression firmly in place. "It is."

"Very well." Mr. Williams turned to a fresh sheet of paper on his pad. "You said your name is Betty Ahern? Could you spell that, please?"

I did.

"And what is your daily rate?"

The question brought me up short. I'd never thought about that. I'd always charged by the job, not the day. "Um." I glanced at Lee, who shrugged. I wasn't gonna get any help from him. "When do you expect Lee to be arraigned?"

"On Monday. Tuesday at the latest," Mr. Williams said.

This case might require me to take time off at Bell. I had to assume it would. I made a little over three dollars an hour there. I'd be losing at least one and possibly two eight-hour shifts. I did some quick math. "Twenty-five dollars a day. Plus expenses." That would more than cover my lost wages at Bell. I waited for Mr. Williams to haggle.

"Very well." He made some notes on the pad. "I'll have my secretary draw up a contract when I return to the office. You'll have to come in to sign it. I assume you're a legal adult and can do that?"

I lifted my chin. "I'll be nineteen in April."

He nodded and pushed over a business card. "Come to that address on Monday morning to take care of things."

I took it. "Do I have to leave until I do?"

"No. You are officially an employee." He gave me a stern look over his glasses. "If you do not sign the contract, however, you'll be breaking privilege and you'll put your friend's defense in jeopardy. Do I make myself clear?"

I swallowed. "Yes, sir."

"Good." He transferred his attention to Lee. "Before we were interrupted, you were telling me about that night."

"Right." Lee dusted his hands on his legs. "I saw Dad the afternoon of March second. I'd just gotten home from GM. He came home, drunk as usual, and was looking for his bottle. I'd thrown it out. We fought and he left." He paused. "After that, I went out like I said, but I only walked around the block."

I knew he hadn't hung out for seven hours at Conway Park. But I held my tongue.

"As I was comin' up the street, I saw him outside the house again. I thought he'd gone, but clearly he came back. Anyway, he looked...I don't know, odd. Almost as if he was tryin' not to be seen. I decided to follow him."

"Quick question, did you have mittens or gloves?" Mr. Williams asked.

"No. I was so mad when I left, I forgot 'em. I didn't want to go inside to get 'em 'cause I didn't want to lose sight of Dad."

That explained the fingerprints on the pipe.

Mr. Williams didn't look up as he wrote. "Where did he go?"

"At first, just a couple of bars. I didn't go inside any of 'em 'cause I didn't want him to see me." Lee rubbed his bum leg. "Round about eight, maybe a little later, he jumped on a bus and I managed to get on without him noticing me. The bus dropped us off about two blocks from the grain elevator canals. I remember I thought it was strange. He didn't have any business down there during the day. I couldn't even begin to imagine what he'd be doin' there at night."

"You continued to follow him. What happened?"

Lee hesitated. "He spoke to some guy in the office then headed toward the lake. I went after him. I ducked behind some crates so he wouldn't see me. He paced for a while and eventually I heard footsteps. I risked a peek and two other Joes had joined them."

"What did they look like?" I asked.

"The light wasn't good. One was tall, one was short. I think the tall one mighta had a scar on his face, but that coulda been a trick of the light." Lee's forehead wrinkled as he thought. "I thought they mighta been workers 'cause their clothes were, you know, like a dockworker's. I didn't see much. I didn't want to be noticed."

I thought of my search earlier. Lee musta been hiding where I found the scrap of wool. He'd caught his coat on the crates. "What coat were you wearin'?"

"My blue wool one. Why?"

"You snagged it. I found a scrap."

Lee cussed.

"Go on," Mr. Williams said.

"They were keeping their voices low, so I didn't hear everything they said," Lee continued, absently rubbing his leg. "I heard Dad say something and one of the others said, 'Don't even think about it, pal. You're already in it up to your neck.' Or something like that. Next thing I know, I heard a car. I risked another glance around the crate. It was parked a ways off, but there was a woman walking up." He shot a nervous look at me.

"What about a driver?" I asked.

"I didn't notice one, but I s'pose he might've stayed in the car. Or she drove herself."

"This woman. Did you get a good look at her?" Mr. Williams asked as he looked up.

Lee hesitated.

"Mr. Tillotson, you need to be completely honest with me if I am going to help you." Mr. Williams's gaze pierced me. "Did you recognize the woman?"

"I didn't see her clear, but I thought...I thought it might be my mother."

I knew it. "Lee, you told me she went out with friends."

"That's what she said, but it's not like I tailed her to make sure." His voice took on a miserable note. "And earlier that day...you know Mom, Betty. She doesn't complain much. But when I got home, she and the old man were at it hammer and tongs. She told him to clean up and get sober or get out of the house. And if she needed to take matters into her own hands to protect the girls, so be it."

I sensed that wasn't all. "Okay, but what made you think it was your mom down at the canals?"

"She was wearing her good coat when she left the house." Lee's voice cracked. "And those high heels. It looked like she was off to somewhere other than work." He dashed his hand across his eyes. "I thought she was goin'...somewhere special."

The pieces snapped together. "You thought she was steppin' out on your dad and she was all dressed up for a date. And the car?"

"She could've borrowed it from...someone."

The sight of Lee near tears broke my heart. I'd never seen him cry, not even when he'd broken his leg as a kid on that tire swing dare. It was the most horrible thing I'd ever experienced. "Lee, I don't think she'd do that. Never." Not to mention it was completely illogical that she'd leave a date to confront her husband at the grain elevators.

"The woman at the dock." Lee hung his head and his voice sounded thick. "She was wearin' the same kind of coat, least it looked that way. And she was wobblin' around as though she didn't wear heels often."

"Just like your mom." I laid my hand on his shoulder.

Mr. Williams had the grace to let Lee collect himself. "What happened after that?"

Lee exhaled, scrubbed at his face, and lifted his head. "The other guys, they weren't happy to see the woman either. 'The boss ain't gonna like it,' one of 'em said. The other one mostly swore. They all moved down to the end of the canal where I couldn't see 'em. I waited for a bit, then decided I'd follow. But just when I stood, I heard a thwack and a grunt. Then two splashes. The men were cursing. I heard footsteps, I think it was the woman, judging by the clicking sound. I ducked back behind the crates. Then I heard the tires of the car squeal as it left."

"Did you see any of the men again?"

Lee frowned, and shook his head. "No. They didn't come back up the canal. I gave it another couple of minutes and when I was pretty sure no one was comin' I crept down the dock. No one was there, just a few scattered pipes. I put them back in their pile, 'cause I thought maybe then no one would know anyone had been there and scrammed."

Mr. Williams and I exchanged a look. I was dead certain Lee had heard his dad being murdered.

Chapter Twenty-Two

I snuck a quick look around when I left the jail with Mr. Williams. I didn't see Sam, which was a good thing. I doubted Mr. Williams would keep me on the payroll if he saw me in the company of a cop. "Penny for your thoughts," I said.

Mr. Williams fussed with his briefcase. "I've heard worse stories. Mr. Tillotson is very honest about disliking his father and he admits to being on the scene. That doesn't help. I'll have to interview the mother. If I like what I hear, I may have to call her as a witness and have her say where she was that night. She has just as much motive and it doesn't sound like she's a weak woman."

"Hardly. She's had to put up with a lot and she works as a cleaner. She has a lot of strength, physically and mentally. But Tillotsons don't have a car." I slipped a Lucky from the pack and held it out.

He shook his head. "Thanks, but I don't smoke. Not having a car doesn't mean anything. She could have borrowed one or had someone drive her, especially if she was meeting a man."

"She wasn't having an affair. And even if she was, why would she go out with the new man, then follow her husband to the docks?"

"Perhaps the date was over, she saw him, and got curious."

"No, I don't buy it."

He gave me a dubious look. "Mrs. Tillotson could be a good witness for us though. She'd provide reasonable doubt."

"Lee isn't gonna let you cast any suspicion on his mother. If your strategy is to offer Mrs. T as a potential killer, you'd better think of something else.

Did you get him to plead not guilty?"

"I at least got him to think about things. And he may not have a choice regarding his mother. If he ties my hands, there will be very little I can do." He pushed up his glasses. "What are your plans?"

"I have a few leads on the men who were there, or who we think were there. The ones Lee described."

"We?"

Oops. "My friend Dot and I. I had been askin' questions earlier with her."

"Remember, you can't share information with anyone who isn't on the defense team."

"Right. Anyway, from what I've learned, Mr. Tillotson may have been involved with a numbers racket. If he sold them out, he'd be in trouble." I told him about Howley and McDougal, and about finding Mr. Daletzki's knife at the canals.

Mr. Williams raised his eyebrows and his glasses slipped a little. "The numbers game is a good angle. You think this Daletzki could be involved?"

"It's something I want to pursue." I ashed my cigarette. "Looks like I need to find this woman and tie up that loose end. I'd bet my next paycheck it wasn't Mrs. T."

"You get paychecks?"

"It's a figure of speech." I didn't want to tell Mr. Williams that private investigating was a side job. I needed him to look at me as a pro. "If I come to your office at eight o'clock Monday would that be too early?"

"Not at all. I'll have my secretary draw up the contract. She's usually there at seven." He peered at me over his glasses. "You'd better take this seriously, Miss Ahern. I will not take it kindly if you jeopardize my client's defense."

"You got it."

He nodded and strode off down the street.

There was still no sign of Sam, so I decided to call Dot. "What have you found?"

"First things first. How'd it go at the jail?" she asked.

Jeepers. Right off the bat, I had to start fudging. "I can't tell you exactly. Mr. Williams, that's the lawyer, said it could violate the attorney-client relationship. I guess if I blab and the prosecution gets wind of it, they could make me testify against Lee and use whatever was in that conversation to convict him."

Dot's voice was anguished. "You can't tell me anything?"

"Let's put it this way. Lee told us where he was that night. It makes more sense than him hanging at Conway Park for seven hours. You and I were right about that being a load of baloney. And we were right about why Lee decided to plead guilty." She'd remember that conversation for sure.

"We...oh. Was she really there?"

"I don't know for sure. Somehow I doubt it. That's on my list of things to check up on. What did you find out about Captain Finley?" I checked out the cars whizzing by, but none of 'em were Sam's. Over the line, I heard the rustle of paper.

"I got lucky. Mom still had a huge stash of papers in the basement. Your police captain has been a busy guy," Dot said. "I found a couple stories where he was talking about the murder rate in the city and his tactics for bringing it down. It sounded like he was criticizing the mayor without saying so, if you know what I mean."

"The way Mr. Satterwaite jabs at us?"

"More subtle. Captain Finley doesn't come out and name Mayor Kelly. Instead he says things like, 'Decisions have been made, blah, blah.' But the types of decisions he's talkin' about can only have come from the mayor's office. It's pretty clear to me he's settin' himself up as a problem-solver and a guy who's tough on crime."

"Which will help him accomplish step one, get appointed chief. As long as he doesn't criticize his boss outright." I clamped my gasper between my lips, pulled out my notebook and a pen, and took notes. "What else?"

"He's been at a lot of parties. Not fundraisers exactly, but not places I'd expect to see a homicide police captain. He's definitely glad-handing people with dough. But the funny thing is there's often a guy in the pictures standing right behind him. A real Jimmy Cagney type, if you catch my drift. And not *Yankee Doodle Dandy* either."

A mobster. "Is he named?"

"No. But he's in three pictures that I saw. The latest is a snap from a Christmas party this past December. If you come to the house, I'll show you."

"I'll try. What's the date?"

"December twenty-third."

A car horn sounded behind me. I looked over my shoulder and saw Sam waving at me. "Great work, Dot. I gotta go. Sam and I will be by to see that paper if we can, but if not, at least I have the date."

Dot was silent and I could imagine her chewing away at her lip. "Do you really think Detective MacKinnon wants to prove Lee innocent?"

"I think Sam wants to find a killer, Dot." I leaned my forehead against the cold phone box. "Right now, that's the best we can ask for."

* * *

I got into Sam's car on the passenger side, mulling over what I'd say when he asked about my talk with Lee. I didn't wait long.

"How'd it go?" He narrowed his peepers, as if trying to pull the answer from my thoughts.

"Fine. I got some info outta Lee."

"Like what?"

I blew out a breath. "Uh, I can't tell you. Not word for word."

"Why not?"

"I sorta work for his lawyer now." I shot a look from the corner of my eye. I expected Sam to look outraged, but instead he had a grin on his face like he enjoyed seeing me squirm. "You rat, you knew that would happen."

"I guessed." He took one last puff on his cigarette and flicked the butt out of his window. "He must have cited attorney-client privilege. Tell me, do you have a private investigator's license?"

My silence was answer enough.

"I thought so. You'd better hope this doesn't go to trial. Without a license, you aren't a professional and the district attorney will have a field day arguing there is no privilege."

"Don't remind me." I rubbed my face and, in general terms, told him what had gone down in the meeting. "The good news is I've got a real, honest-to-God, private detective job now. Bad news—"

"You can't share any detailed information with me, even if we ignore the license issue," Sam said. "I get it. Tell me this, did Lee's story make sense?"

"Yes." Saying that much couldn't hurt, right? I ran over the rest of the conversation. "I think we're on the right track trying to find out about the numbers guys. Plus, the woman. I was right about Lee's fear, but I think he's barking up the wrong tree."

"Who else could she be?"

"I don't know."

Sam took out his notebook and reviewed his writing. "I'm certain that dock is where John Tillotson was killed."

"Can you send someone to dredge the canal, try to find the pipe?"

"Probably, but no one is going to want to spend that kind of dough, not when we have a suspect in custody and enough evidence to convict. At least that's what Captain Finley will say." He put the car in gear. "Who were you talking to on the phone?"

"That was Dot." I told him about the newspaper pictures.

"Yep, sounds like the captain is laying the foundation of a mayoral run. He might not toss his hat in the ring right away, not before he gets his promotion, but he's looking to make the connections now." He pulled away into the meager traffic. "Did she describe the man in the photo?"

"No, and I didn't think to ask. Can you guess who he is?"

"Not from that description, but it would be interesting if it's your Weasel Man. That would go along with one of my hunches."

"We need to stop by Dot's house and get the paper."

"I have a better idea. Let's go to the library and check the archives." He hung a right and headed that way.

I'd been in the main branch of the Buffalo and Erie County Public Library exactly once. That had been last December when I'd been tracking a Polish immigrant family, trying to discover if they'd come to Buffalo. I hoped this trip would be as successful as that one.

Once there, Sam and I went to the front desk. He showed his badge and asked to see the copies of the *Courier-Express* for the last six months.

"Isn't that overkill?" I asked in a hushed whisper as we trailed the librarian. "Dot told me to look at the issue from December twenty-third of last year."

"The more information we have, the better."

The librarian showed us into a room full of shelves containing stacks of newspapers, all arranged by date. After telling us to let her know if we needed anything else, she left.

"Grab the stack over there," Sam said, as he pulled November's papers from their place.

"Got it." I hauled down the issues from December 1942. "She didn't ask who I was."

"You're with a member of the Buffalo PD. I doubt she even wondered." He flipped through his stack. "Let's start with the issue Miss Kilbride mentioned and see if I know our mystery man."

I rifled through the stack until I found the morning and evening editions from December twenty-third. I found the picture we wanted in the morning edition. "I think this is it. There was a party the previous night hosted by some bigwig. Yeah, here's a snap of him and some guests. And here's your captain. He's in this one, too." I spread out the pages.

Sam pored over them. "This guy, right here." He tapped the page. "Look, he's in the background of this shot, too. That's Blackie Thomas. Ten to one that's your Weasel Man from O'Malley's."

"This is the second time you've mentioned him. Who exactly is Blackie Thomas?"

"Publicly, he's a successful local businessman. In reality, he's head of one of the biggest numbers rackets in the city." Sam glanced at me. "While you were at the jail, I started visiting those names I gave you. None of them employ Howley, McDougal, or Tillotson. Blackie was the last name on my list." He set aside the paper. "Let's look at the others."

We searched old copies for about twenty minutes and found at least four other shots of Captain Finley at social events. Blackie Thomas was in the background of all of them. Once, he posed with the host couple and Captain

Finley. I could see he had a small gap in his front teeth. Maybe that's why he didn't smile much in the other pictures. "Mr. Thomas sure gets around, doesn't he?"

"That he does." Sam stretched his back. "If Finley does indeed run for mayor someday, he needs, or at least he'll want, the backing of every one of these families. Their endorsements will go a long way toward a successful campaign."

"It still doesn't make any sense. What would he want from a criminal? He must know the businessman thing is a front." My neck was sore from bending over sheets of newsprint, so I twisted it until I felt a welcome pop.

"Of course he does. You mean to say you can't think of why? I'm surprised at you, Betty."

I paused. "You said Thomas is in charge of a numbers racket. Gangsters hang out with the swells all the time. I mean look at Capone, Lansky, and Luciano. They had money and sometimes that's all you need, right? You mentioned Captain Finley would need cash for a mayoral campaign. Could Mr. Thomas donate?"

"That he could." Sam stacked the papers into neat piles by date. "And he'd most certainly expect something in return."

Chapter Twenty-Three

A little more than twenty minutes after we left the library, Sam pulled up in front of a social club on Abbott Road, near the intersection with Dorrance Avenue. The windows were dark and there weren't any flags or other signs the club was associated with a particular group. A hulking figure in a decent-fitting suit lounged against the wall. He looked like any other guy outside for a smoke break. But as soon as Sam and I approached, he threw away the cigarette and came to attention. I immediately figured he was a guard for whoever was inside.

"Can I help you?" he asked in a low voice as he straightened his jacket.

I spotted the grip of a handgun tucked into a shoulder holster. What kind of shooter did criminals carry? It didn't matter. A small hole would kill me as dead as a big one. I scooted closer to Sam.

He reached behind his back to grab my hand and gave it a brief, comforting squeeze while showing his badge with his right. "Detective Sam MacKinnon, Buffalo PD. I'm here to talk to Mr. Thomas."

If possible, the guard swelled bigger. "What about?"

"Because I want to."

The lug scowled. "Wait here." He came back minutes later. "Mr. Thomas says if you can't say what it's about, you can shove off."

Sam only smiled. "It's about an employee of his named John Tillotson."

I noticed Sam didn't ask if Mr. Tillotson worked for Mr. Thomas or refer to him as a "former" employee. Then again, maybe the doorman wouldn't know anything about the murder.

"Don't move," the guard said and disappeared.

I shivered and not from the coolness in the air. "My folks would snap their caps if they knew I was here." The sun was on the way down and long shadows spread from the buildings. I caught the faintest whiff of rotting garbage, but the streets held no more debris than the average city neighborhood. There were no people on the sidewalks, no housewives heading home to make dinner, no kids playing stickball or pulling wagons of paper. It was as though everybody knew to avoid this little corner of Buffalo at night. "Are you sure we'll be safe? You seem pretty calm."

Sam replaced his badge, but removed his revolver and checked to make sure it was loaded. "Pretty sure," he said and replaced the gun. "I don't think Blackie wants a shoot-out at a place where he does business. If he takes us somewhere else, that's when we get nervous."

The door opened and the guard returned. "Mr. Thomas says you and the girl can come in. But you have to leave your piece with me."

"I don't want to do that," Sam replied.

"The only way you get to see him is if you hand it over." The man held out a meaty paw. "Otherwise, you can beat it."

"How do I know Mr. Thomas isn't going to drag us somewhere to work us over?" Sam sounded relaxed, but I saw the twitch at his mouth. He wasn't as cool as he looked.

The man grinned, but it wasn't friendly. More leering. "Mr. Thomas says if you and the girl promise to behave, so does he. That's as good as you're gonna get. Now hand over the gun or scram."

Sam hesitated for a fraction of a second, then slapped his revolver into the guy's hand. I was gonna object, but then I stopped. Didn't cops carry a second gun? They did in the pictures. I had to hope Sam did as well.

"Hold out your arms," the guard said. He patted Sam's coat, and I held my breath. But he didn't search beneath the waist. On the one hand, the guy was doing a bad job. On the other, it worked for us, so I kept my trap shut. He took a step toward me.

"Touch the lady and I'll break your fingers," Sam said as casually as if he were discussing the weather.

The guard hesitated, then beckoned. We followed him as he led us through the main room. Smoke swirled thick in the air and the only smells were cigarettes, cigars, and sweat. A few patrons paused to look at us. The bartender leaned over and said something to another man, who laughed as his gaze traveled up and down my body. I wasn't wearing anything revealing, but I felt as though he could see right through my clothes. The back of my neck itched and I walked so close to Sam that I nearly mashed my puss into his back when he stopped in front of a table tucked so far in the back corner it was practically invisible.

"Mr. Thomas," Sam said. "Nice of you to see me."

I don't know what I expected. A pudgy man like Al Capone, or well-dressed gangster like Lucky Luciano. Mr. Thomas was neither. Even seated, I could tell he'd be short, maybe even barely as tall as Dot, who stood five-foot-six. He had dark hair that was slicked back and gleamed in the light hanging over his table. He had a medium build, not as rangy as Lee, nor as muscular as Tom the last time I'd seen him. His eyes were dark pools that barely reflected the light. Smoke from his long, thin cigar leaked out of his sharp nose and narrow-lipped mouth. His clothes, however, were impeccable. The white shirt was blinding and the tie had to be made of silk from the way it shone.

"Detective MacKinnon," Thomas said, his voice thin and unimpressive. "I must admit, I was curious. Just a moment." He turned to the man standing next to him. "And get that oil pan fixed. I'm tired of smelling burnt smoke and we're leaving a trail all over Buffalo."

"Yes, sir." The man hurried away.

Mr. Thomas refocused on us. "Please, sit down. You too, miss. What is your name?"

The voice was absolutely not what I expected out of the man in front of me. I opened my mouth.

"Her name isn't important," Sam said, cutting me off. "All you need to know is she's with me."

"Very well." Thomas tapped his cigar against a silver and stone ashtray. "Nelson said you were asking after John Tillotson. What makes you think he works for me?"

"I've talked to all the other major players in Buffalo's numbers scene and came up empty. You're the last, best game in town. I know he works for someone."

They were talking about Mr. Tillotson like he was still alive. Either Mr. Thomas didn't know what had happened or he was playing a game. If it was the first, I knew Sam wasn't gonna be the one to enlighten him.

The numbers boss blew out a thin stream of smoke. "John Tillotson is one of my employees. Or rather, he was."

"Was? How so?"

At that moment, a woman came over. She wore an expensive dress and a rope of pearls. Her makeup was perfect and her honey-blonde hair curled beside a heart-shaped face. Her eyes were the feature that struck me. They shone like emeralds. Pop always said a green-eyed blonde was a rarity. The woman was average-looking otherwise, but with that combination of hair and eyes she'd draw the attention of any man she passed. She leaned over Mr. Thomas. "Baby, I want to go out. You said you'd take me to dinner tonight, someplace nice." Her voice was sweet, but there was a note of petulance there.

"In a minute, Frances," Thomas said, a slightly annoyed look coming over his face. "These people have come to talk business."

Frances straightened and stumbled as she stepped back. "How long is *that* going to take? You're always talking about work."

The irritated look deepened. "Not long. Why do you insist on wearing those ridiculous shoes? You can't walk in them."

I glanced at Frances's feet. She wore shiny black heels, but I could detect small scuffs on the toes, like she tripped over them a lot. I remembered Lee's description: a woman who wasn't comfortable in pumps. I wondered if Frances had a fur-trimmed coat. I got the feeling she did.

"I won't get any better if I don't. Besides, they're all the rage." Frances fluffed her hair. "What kind of business?"

"Do you know a guy named John Tillotson?" I blurted.

Frances's eyes widened just a fraction, so slightly I almost missed it. But I was sure the name caused her a flicker of unease.

Before she could answer, Mr. Thomas cut in. "It's nothing important. Now sit down at the bar like a nice girl and wait. Nelson, get Frances a gin." His eyes narrowed.

She fingered her pearls as she studied Sam and me. "Okay, baby. But don't take too long." She sashayed away, the stride marred only once by a wobble.

"Dames." Mr. Thomas ground out his smoke. "She'll break an ankle in those things."

Sam shot me a look. "As fascinating as the conversation about women's shoes is, can we get back to John Tillotson?"

"Certainly." Mr. Thomas settled back. "John and I parted company a few weeks ago. I'm sure you understand. I can't have employees I don't trust."

"Have you seen him since then?"

"No. I don't hobnob with former workers."

Tired of sitting on the sidelines, I spoke up. "He was okay then? The last time you saw him?"

"Of course." Lines appeared on Mr. Thomas's forehead. "Poor, but otherwise the bloom of health. Well, as blooming as you get when you drink as much as John did. Why do you ask?"

Sam replied before I had a chance to say anything. "When exactly was that?"

"I told you, earlier this month." Mr. Thomas pulled out another cigar, but didn't light it. "The night we went our separate ways, as a matter of fact."

"Why did you?" I asked. "Part ways, that is."

He leaned back and appraised me. "He had his fingers where they didn't belong."

"He was filching from the cookie jar?"

"Among other things." From his voice you'd have thought he was discussing the weather, but the dark eyes gleamed colder than the depths of Lake Erie in January.

Other things. What other things? I glanced behind me. Frances leaned against the bar, running the pearls through her fingers, watching us. "The kind of things with blonde hair and green eyes?"

As if Frances knew I mentioned her, she transferred her attention to the bartender, tossed her hair, and smiled.

Mr. Thomas didn't move. Then he grinned, revealing the slight gap in his front teeth. "You've got moxie, girl. I'll give you that."

I let out my breath slowly. I'd unconsciously crossed a line.

He shook his glass, setting the ice cubes rattling, and downed his remaining liquor. "Why all the questions about John Tillotson? I wouldn't think he'd be worthy of the attention of Buffalo's finest."

"Not usually," Sam said in a pleasant voice, "except for the fact his body turned up in the Buffalo River a few days ago, with lungs full of water and a cracked skull. Naturally, we're looking into it."

"You don't know anything about that, do you?" I asked.

This time, there was no answering smile. "Moxie is good, kid, but it'll get you into trouble if you aren't careful." Mr. Thomas held up his glass and one of his bodyguards took it from him. "Now why would I know anything about a two-bit runner?"

I countered him. "It's good business?"

Once again, the smile. "You're definitely a pistol. Yes, as you say, it's good business. But I don't have anything to say about John Tillotson that hasn't already been said."

Sam reached over and squeezed my hand. "Duly noted. One more thing."

"You both are trying my patience, Detective." Mr. Thomas took out a silver lighter and flicked it to light the cigar. The scent of the smoke made me think of burning socks. "Just one."

"What's your relationship to Captain Finley?"

Mr. Thomas's smile widened. "I've seen him at social engagements. Good man. I understand he has his sights on a promotion, and perhaps the mayor's office in a few years. I wish him well."

Although Mr. Thomas had been clear that he'd only answer one more question, I opened my mouth. I didn't get a chance to say anything.

"Thanks for your time. We can see ourselves out." Sam tugged my hand and I followed.

"Be seeing you," Mr. Thomas said and laughed.

But halfway across the room, I stopped and turned. I couldn't help myself.

"Oh, Mr. Thomas. I apologize, but I've gotta ask you one more thing."

"Moxie." He drew on his cigar. "I like you, kid. But I've got a business to run. So be snappy."

"Does the name Steven Daletzki mean anything to you?"

His gaze was dark and cold. "Nothing whatsoever." He gave another low laugh.

I felt a cold shiver run down my spine. That laugh was enough to raise the fur on Cat's back. I rejoined Sam and we headed for the exit.

On our way, we passed Frances. "Terrible shame about Johnnie," she said.

"Yes, it is," Sam said, not bothering to slow his stride.

I wanted to stop, but given the fact that Sam had grabbed my hand again, I had no choice but to follow. Frances had been a good ten feet away. We'd been talking quietly and there had been enough noise that it wasn't likely she'd have overheard our conversation. How'd she know about Mr. Tillotson?

Chapter Twenty-Four

Sam let go of my hand once we were outside. He holstered his gun, which he'd retrieved from the doorman. "For God's sake, Betty. Warn me next time." He put on his fedora and tugged down the brim.

"Sorry, it sorta came over me." I tapped out a Lucky and lit it. My hand shook a bit. Had I just challenged a major player in the Buffalo numbers racket? "I wanted to see his reaction. Are you mad?"

"That's not it. When you work with a partner, you have to coordinate." He glanced back at the door. "It was a good play. But for a moment, I thought he was going to have his goons take us out back."

"The thought crossed my mind." I blew out a long stream of smoke. "You didn't stop to question Frances."

"It would have been a waste of time." He walked down Abbott toward his car. "She wouldn't say anything with her sugar-daddy sitting ten feet away."

"But Mr. Thomas's crack about fingers. He wasn't just talkin' about money, was he?"

"If Frances wasn't the woman on the docks that night, I'm a monkey's uncle." He opened the car door for me. "I'll take you home. Your folks will want you back for dinner."

"Don't bother. They know I'll be out late tonight. I cleared it with Pop." I got in and wished I could tie myself to the seat.

Sam followed and started the car. "Then how about we get some grub? My treat."

Hopefully, his driving would be better when we weren't racing to question a suspect. "I never pass up free food."

The diner was also on Abbott, but a couple blocks away, down toward Ridge Road. It was clean and well-lit, with a delicious smell of fresh apple pie mingling with the fried grease coming from the grill. As usual, Sam grabbed an empty booth near the back, where he could watch all the comings and goings. He handed me a menu. "I highly recommend the meatloaf."

I ran my gaze down the listings. Holy smokes. Did Sam eat like this all the time? "I just need a fried baloney sandwich and a glass of water."

Sam stared, then cracked a grin. "If you're going to be a professional, you need to keep up your energy. How long has it been since you ate lunch?"

Had I eaten at noon? My stomach rumbled, reminding me I had not.

He must have heard the noise, 'cause his smile widened. "I thought so. Get the meatloaf, potatoes, and gravy, with a slice of apple pie for dessert. This one's on me."

"Sam, I can't."

He waved me off. "If you're half as successful as I think you're going to be at this job, you'll be paying me back before you know it."

We placed our orders with a gum-snapping waitress. I added a Coke to mine, instead of the water. After she left, I took out my notebook. "We need to figure out how to question Frances on her own. You're right, I don't think we'll get anything outta her in front of Mr. Thomas."

"That's for sure." He unfolded his napkin. "What made you ask about Daletzki?"

"It was a hunch. We found that knife at the docks. Mr. Daletzki is gone. We know, or at least suspect, Mr. Tillotson met a couple of guys from Mr. Thomas's outfit down there. I wanted to see his, Mr. Thomas's, face when I dropped the name."

The waitress returned with our drinks. Sam sipped his coffee. "What did you think of his answer?"

"I don't know. But that laugh, it gave me the willies." I played with my glass. "I think he wasn't bein' quite truthful."

"You're learning."

The food arrived. The scent of the meatloaf and gravy was heavenly. The first bite sent me back a few years. The meat was moist, the potatoes creamy, and the gravy tied it all together. There were actual green beans. I closed my eyes and savored the flavors. I hadn't eaten like this since before the war.

Sam chuckled. "Now, aren't you glad you didn't settle for fried baloney? Wait until you taste the pie."

"Do you eat like this every night?" He was too slim for that.

"No, only when I'm working after hours." He cut a slice of his chicken, chewed, and washed it down with another swallow of coffee. "What do you want to do next?"

He asked as if I were a real partner. "Frances is a bust, at least for now. As long as she's around Mr. Thomas, she'll keep her yap shut."

"Agreed."

"We've no idea where Mr. Daletzki is. I don't think his sister would welcome us back with open arms."

"Also agreed."

"That leaves us with Howley and McDougal. You said you didn't find them at any of those other places." I scraped up a forkful of potatoes and dragged it through a pool of gravy. "We didn't see 'em when we visited the club."

"True, but that's only Blackie's office. The numbers games themselves move around. They do that to outwit the Vice squad. But the boys are wise to the rotation. I have a friend I can call and get the location of tonight's action. Saturday night, I bet a lot of players are out."

"What good will that do?"

Sam picked a chicken bone clean and tossed it aside. "How do you feel about going on a raid?"

* * *

After Sam called his Vice friend, I checked in with Dot. "What's the scoop?"

"Not much," she said. "I went over to your house to talk to your mom. Mrs. T has locked herself in her room and won't come out. I don't know what's gonna happen with the girls. Your mom said she'd take care of it.

That meant I couldn't get in Mrs. T's closet, but I ransacked the one in the hall."

"Did you find anything?"

"Not me personally, but your mom said she talked to Mrs. T. I guess she didn't go to work that night. She and some girlfriends went out to a social club. But she got very evasive when your mom asked for details. Lots of 'I don't know' and 'I can't remember.' Not at all like the Mrs. T we know."

"Thanks, Dot."

"Are you making progress?"

"I think so. It's hard to tell. Sam isn't worried, so I guess everything is normal. We're gonna try and find Howley and McDougal next."

"How?"

I figured telling her the truth would terrify her, so I said, "Sam has some contacts. Say, can you do me another favor? Tomorrow, go see Mrs. T. Try and get her to talk about her husband, any suspicious activities or money he had that didn't come from his job at GM."

Dot agreed. I called home quick, just to let them know I was okay and I didn't know exactly when I'd be back, but I was with Sam. He came over just as I was hanging up.

"I have the location of tonight's game. Do you still want to do this?"

To be honest, I was more than a little twitchy. But this was part of the job. Sam would keep me as safe as he could. "Let's go."

Sam drove us back toward the social club, but this time he passed it to park opposite a small grocery store called Jasper and Sons a few doors down.

"We're not going to the club?" I asked

"I told you. That's the business office." Sam put the car in park and turned it off. "This store is one of the locations for the games. It keeps a little distance between the various parts of the operation. If the game is busted, the cops only get the money on site at the time, plus the players and the low-level criminals. Not all the books, cash reserves, and big fish."

I guessed it was a sensible setup, if you were looking to break the law and protect your assets. "So what are we gonna do now?"

Sam pulled back into the shadow of a building and lit a smoke. "We're waiting for the high sign from my Vice contact to say it's safe to enter."

I lit my own cigarette. "You don't wanna take me into an active den of iniquity?"

He gave me a lopsided grin. "I don't want to go busting in on my own, either. Blackie may not be there, but there will still be guards and they're all armed. One cop against all of them would be like Jim Bowie trying to defend the Alamo. No thanks. I like my skin in one piece."

I wasn't the history buff Lee was, but I knew things had not ended well for Colonel Bowie and his troops that day. 'Course in our situation, we'd be playing the role of Santa Anna, but Sam's point was understood. It was better to hold tight.

We didn't wait long. Maybe ten or fifteen minutes after the Vice guys moved in, a uniformed officer came out of the front of the store and waved in our direction.

"That's our signal," Sam said. He threw down his cigarette and jogged across the street.

I followed him and he led me to the back of the store. Inside, a number of uniformed cops watched over a group of downtrodden men. I gathered they were having a bad night. They'd prob'ly lost money and now they'd been busted in an illegal gambling den. I scanned the room. There seemed to be two groups, one more sullen than the other. I guessed those in coveralls or patched work pants were the customers. The ones in dress shirts, slacks, and ties, both bow and neck, were the employees. One cop stood guard over a pile of revolvers. But I didn't see hide nor hair of our targets.

A man in a brown suit and fedora gestured to us. "Sam, over here."

Sam threaded his way through the crowd with me in his wake. "Dave, you got them?"

He hoisted his thumb over his shoulder. "I hope these are who you are looking for. They're the only two who match the descriptions you gave me. I gotta go supervise the rest of the bust. Will you be okay if I leave you with two uniforms?" He caught sight of me. "You didn't tell me you were bringing a civilian. Who's the girl?"

"She's with me. Betty Ahern, Dave Trip." He made the introductions.

"We'll be fine."

"If you say so." Detective Trip looked me over, but didn't add anything and ambled away.

I turned to the two men under guard. One of 'em was the tall guy with the scar. The other was shorter with a lazy eye. Both had their hands cuffed behind their backs. "I think these are the guys, Detective."

"I believe you might be right." Sam tilted back his hat. "Which one of you is Howley and which is McDougal?"

Neither man said anything.

I wasn't sure why Sam was askin', since we knew already. Maybe he wanted to hear it from them.

"I'm not in the mood to play games, fellas." Sam eyed them.

Still no answer.

He sighed. "Officer, if you please."

The cop on the left, a young red-head who mighta played football at some point in his short life, grabbed hold of Scar Face's hand, or so I assumed. It looked like he was applying pressure of some kind. Scar Face gritted his teeth and held out for a few seconds, but finally gasped, "I'm Danny Howley, he's Ned McDougal."

Sam nodded at the young cop, who relaxed his hold. "See how easy that was? Just answer the questions and this'll all be over. I know you work for Blackie Thomas. How do you know John Tillotson?"

"We don't know no mook named Tillotson," McDougal said, voice low and rough.

Sam reached over and slapped his head. "Wrong answer."

"Look guys," I said. I didn't know these two from Adam and I cared even less, but I didn't want to stand around and watch them get roughed up. More importantly, I didn't have time. "Here's the facts. You know John Tillotson. You met him the night of March second down at the docks by the grain elevator canals. You all argued. You left, he didn't. Someone hit him over the head with a length of pipe and dumped him in the canal. We can flap our gums for the next few hours, but that's what happened."

Both men got wary expressions on their faces, but kept their traps shut.

I glanced at Sam, who tilted his head indicating I should continue. "We also know John Tillotson worked for Blackie Thomas as a runner. Or used to, to be more accurate. We've talked to Mr. Thomas. Oh, and we know there was a woman down there with you. What we don't know is whether you two did the deed, if it was the woman, or someone else. These gentlemen," I nodded at the cops, including Sam, "would love to entertain you all night, but I'm on a schedule. Save us all a bunch of trouble, and yourselves some pain, and spill."

The red-headed cop took a blackjack out and slapped it on his palm.

Sam smothered a grin. "I don't know. Seems like you might want to talk to the lady. Otherwise, things aren't looking too good for you."

Howley maintained his stubborn silence, but McDougal looked at me for a long moment with his good eye. He flexed against the cuffs. "Okay, fine. Tillotson was a runner, like you said."

"Jesus, Mary, and Joseph, shut up, Ned," Howley said, his voice a hiss that didn't mask the heavy Irish brogue.

"She's right, Danny. We ain't telling 'em what they don't know, well, not much." McDougal arched his back, maybe trying to relieve the pressure on his shoulders from being cuffed. "Anyways, Johnnie was pretty good at the job. He had the drunk look down, so no one paid attention to him."

He had the look down because he was one. "What went wrong?" I asked.

"Same thing as happens with a lot of guys." McDougal gave me a knowing look. "He got greedy."

It was hard to tell if he was looking straight at me 'cause of his left eye, which gazed off in another direction. Which one did I look at? "Greedy as in money?"

"Among other things."

Howley bumped his partner with his shoulder. "That's enough. Shut it. We ain't saying nothing more until we get lawyers."

Sam scuffed his shoe along the floor. "Are you sure that's the way you want it? Once the suits come into the picture, it'll get more difficult to help you guys out."

"Help us how?" Howley asked.

Sam pointed at me. "Keep talking to the lady and we'll see."

I must've been doing a good job if Sam was willing to let me take the lead. "What other things do you mean?"

McDougal snickered. "You said you talked to Blackie. Down at the social club, I'm guessing. That's where he holds court. Did you see Frances while you were there?"

"Maybe." Instinct told me to hedge. "Who's she?"

"Frances Corbett, that's Blackie's dame. At least she's the current one. She's not much to look at, but blonde hair and green eyes, well, that's unusual. But women take effort and Blackie's often got his mind on his business." McDougal paused. "Eventually, he gets bored with them all."

"And? What does that have to do with Mr. Tillotson?"

He rolled his eyes. It was an interesting effect with the lazy one. "Geez, do I gotta spell it out for you? I'm not sure which was worse. Finding Johnnie's bag short three times in a row, or coming up on him and Frannie all cozy together in a corner booth at the club."

Mr. Tillotson had a lot of flaws it seemed. I never imagined him cheatin' on his wife. "You're putting me on," I said. "He was married."

"Right, because married men don't do such things," McDougal sneered. "Tell me another, doll face. Rumor has it, Frances was gonna run off with someone. I thought she had better taste than Johnnie. But he must've gotten cold feet 'cause they didn't leave. Literally, I guess, seeing as the lake ain't that warm this time of year."

Sam must have seen my anger in my expression because he cut me off. "That night at the docks. What happened?"

Howley exchanged a look with his buddy. "You said you could help us out. Like how?"

Sam crossed his arms. "I still haven't heard anything worth my time."

"Okay, we met Johnnie like you said." Howley's desire to avoid jail clearly outweighed his fear of his boss. "We told him that Mr. Thomas no longer needed his services and he was out. We may have roughed him up a little in the process."

"With a lead pipe?" Sam asked.

"Just our fists," McDougal chimed in. "We'd only started to talk when Frances showed up, mad as a wet cat and cussin' Johnnie out something fierce. All about how he'd messed with her for the last time. Guess the bloom had come off the rose. He told her to beat it. She spat at him and stormed off. We finished our conversation and left. He wasn't in great shape, but he was still breathin' when we walked away."

It felt like half a story. I glanced at Sam. I could tell from his expression he felt the same way. "That's it? You didn't see another man?"

"We picked that spot 'cause it was private," Howley said, voice full of scorn. "We weren't puttin' on no show. We walked away from the office in case anybody was workin' late."

I thought of Mr. Daletzki's knife. "And you didn't see anybody else. No one at all."

"No one at the time," McDougal said. This time it wasn't just his lazy eye that didn't look at me. "Just us, Frances, and Johnnie."

It was a bald-faced lie. But the mulish looks on both men's faces didn't make me hopeful they'd crack and tell us anything else.

"We talked," Howley said. "You gonna help us or not?"

"Oh, I'll help you all right," Sam said. He looked over at the red-haired cop. "Take them downtown. Make sure they get the finest beds available."

The uniforms pulled at the prisoners, who struggled. "What kinda help is that?" Howley's heels scraped as the cop dragged him across the floor.

Sam rocked back and forth. "I'm helping you get a good night's sleep. Isn't that enough?"

Chapter Twenty-Five

I t was after eight by the time Sam and I departed and left the Vice cops to complete their work. "They'll be at it most of the night," Sam said, taking a deep breath. He took out his cigarettes, inspected the pack, and put it back.

"What, are you quittin' or something?" I asked, nodding toward his breast pocket.

"No, I only have one left and I'm not going to get a chance to go to the corner store for more until tomorrow at this rate." He checked his watch. "Instinct tells me to hang onto the one I've got."

I pulled out my pack. "Want one?" With most of the smokes going to the boys overseas, I rationed myself, but courtesy demanded I offer.

"Nah, it's not my brand."

I put away the deck before he could change his mind. "Howley and McDougal." I pointed behind us. "What do you think of their story?"

"It's a load of hooey."

"Then why didn't you say so?"

"Because it wouldn't have done any good." He opened the car door. "I misspoke. I don't think the entire story is bunk. But I think they're leaving parts out. The problem is I don't know what and I don't have enough information to call them on it." He got into the car.

I slid in beside him. "I don't understand."

He turned to me. "Think about it. How did we get them to talk just now?"

"We told 'em we already knew they were there when Mr. Tillotson got killed. Which we did."

"But we only knew they'd been on the docks. That was just enough information to make it sound as though we already had the whole story. We didn't. We knew from Blackie that Tillotson was involved in the racket, but we didn't have anything else. Why'd you let him jabber on about Frances?"

"I dunno, I just did."

He gave me a flat stare.

I squirmed in my seat. I hadn't really believed Mr. Tillotson would have an affair, even when he was drinkin' and fightin' with his wife. But Sam's question made me think back on past events. Mr. Tillotson always paid women compliments, noticed their hats, or had a cheerful hello. Not exactly *flirting*, but on at least one occasion, the other husband had gotten short with him. "I...she's a good-looking woman. Mr. Tillotson, he had an eye for that. Then there was Mr. Thomas's suggestion and Frances's behavior at the club. I mentioned Mr. Tillotson's name and her eyes about bugged out. McDougal confirmed it. Mr. Tillotson was involved with Frances. I never thought he'd step out on Mrs. T, but I figured one of those two would either confirm the story or shoot it down flat."

"That's what I meant. You knew enough about the victim that it was likely there had been some interaction. I heard you. You might not have done it intentionally, but your tone of voice was begging those two, McDougal especially, to spill the minute you made it sound as though there couldn't possibly be anything between Frances and the victim." He turned the key. "In fact, I'd have to say you're rather a natural at interrogation, Betty. And I mean that as a good thing. Some detectives never are able to question someone effectively."

I should be pleased. On the other hand, Sam was pretty much saying I was a good enough liar to get people to tell me the truth. "They didn't mention Mr. Daletzki."

"No, they didn't." He pulled away. "But they let something slip."

I replayed the conversation. "They didn't see someone *at the time*. That makes it sound like they found out later, either heard it somewhere or saw someone leave. We know Mr. Daletzki was there 'cause we have his pocket knife."

"Correct."

"Then what do we do?"

"We see if Mr. Daletzki has come back home."

＊ ＊ ＊

We drove back across the city to Mrs. Wiese's house on Woltz. But not only was Mr. Daletzki not there, Mrs. Wiese didn't have any trouble lettin' us know why, at least according to her.

The minute the door opened she took a look at me and stormed out, hands outstretched like claws. "You! It's all your fault. Where is he?"

I backed up. "Where is who?" But I knew.

"My brother, that's who. He left for work at seven this morning and now he's gone. It's all your fault!"

Sam stepped in between us in the nick of time. "Calm down, ma'am. I'm sure this has nothing to do with Miss Ahern."

"Don't think I'm letting you off the hook, mister." She writhed in his grasp. "A cop shows up looking for Steve and now he's gone. He hasn't done anything, I tell you. Nothing!"

Sam's ability to keep Mrs. Wiese contained, while keeping her fingernails away from his face, impressed me. Maybe they taught you that when you became a cop. "Mrs. Wiese, you need to take a deep breath and settle down," he said.

"I will not!"

Sam didn't bother asking any more questions while she squirmed in his arms, ranting and raving about dishonest cops hassling poor working folk. Eventually, she lost steam and sagged a bit. "Are you done?" Sam asked.

She said nothing, but gave him an evil-eyed stare.

"Whatever has happened to your brother, I assure you it has nothing to do with us. At least not directly. We left your house earlier today, went to see him at work, and the other mechanic said he never showed. That means he was gone before we came to your door." He glanced at me. "If I let you go, will you behave?"

"Yes," she said, voice sullen.

He released her, but stayed ready to grab her again if she made a move.

But she didn't. "You said he never showed up at work?" she asked, brushing her hair back. She still wouldn't look at me. That was okay. I'd taken the brunt of her anger last time. It was Sam's turn.

"Not according to the man we spoke to. Tell me," he removed his notepad from his pocket, "do you know where he might go? Aside from work. Especially if he was nervous about anything."

She frowned. "Why would he be nervous?"

"No special reason. It's a standard question."

I took a step forward. Despite my intentions, I couldn't stay quiet. "Does he have any friends he might stay with if he were trying to lay low?"

That comment earned me another dirty look. But Mrs. Wiese answered. "I don't know. As far as I'm concerned, Steve didn't have a reason to lay low, as you call it. You obviously think differently. Why? What's he done?"

Sam spoke up before I could. "It's not so much what he's done, but what he might have seen. We found this at a murder scene earlier today." He took out the knife and showed it to her. "Do you recognize it?"

"It's Steve's work knife." Her hand pressed to her mouth. "I gave it to him for his birthday a couple years ago, so he'd always have a blade handy when he was on the job. You said you found this where someone had been murdered? Is he dead?" Her voice climbed as she spoke the last words.

"No ma'am, nothing like that." He put away the knife. "Are you aware that John Tillotson was killed?"

"I read something about it in the paper. And Steve mentioned it to me a few days ago."

Sam studied her. "We think your brother may know something about it."

"You think he did it?" Her voice climbed the register again. She was gonna start all the dogs in Polonia howling if she kept it up.

"Not necessarily, but we would like to talk to him." Sam put away the notebook and knife and handed her a business card. "When he gets home, it is extremely important he call me. Would you have him do that, please?"

She took the card with trembling fingers. "I'll try. If you find anything, you'll let me know, won't you?"

He tipped his fedora. "Yes, ma'am. Leave it to me. You try and have a good night."

She shut the door and we walked back to his car.

"Mr. Daletzki seems to have disappeared." I got into the car. "That's suspicious, isn't it?"

He followed and started the engine. "It's something, that's for sure."

"Now what? Nine o'clock, not much is gonna be open."

"I don't think we can do anything more tonight. Our two low-level gangsters are in custody, we don't have a clue where Steve Daletzki is, and I'm not sure we know enough to go back to Blackie Thomas and rattle his cage." He pulled away.

"We could talk to Frances."

He thought a moment. "We don't know where she lives. We agreed talking to her in front of her boyfriend is a lost cause." He turned and I could tell he was headed back to the First Ward. "I'm taking you home. We'll start again tomorrow, early. Seven o'clock okay?"

"You'd better make it eight. No, eight-thirty." At his quizzical look, I explained. "My folks gave me a pass for today. But we go to early Mass every Sunday and there's no way they're gonna let me outta that."

Chapter Twenty-Six

At Mass on Sunday, I lit three candles. One for Tom and one for Sean, as always. The war news was mixed. On the one hand, General Patton was on the move in Tunisia. On the other, German U-boats were having a field day in the Atlantic with Allied convoys. I felt a stab of selfish joy that Sean was in the Pacific.

The third candle was for Lee. Sam and I had spent all day yesterday driving around Buffalo, yet it didn't seem like we were any closer to finding our killer. And now we had a missing person on our hands in Steve Daletzki.

As I walked down Mackinaw and approached our house, I saw Dot sitting on the step. Cat was in her lap, enjoying the weak March sun and the chin scratches from his current human slave. "What's shakin'?" I asked.

She didn't look up. "He's fatter than he used to be."

"Regular meals, even scraps, will do that for you." I narrowed my peepers. "You didn't answer my question."

"What are you gonna do today?"

"Same as I did yesterday, I s'pose. Sam will be here any minute and I expect we'll spend the day chasing down information. And that's still not an answer."

She gave Cat one final stroke, then picked him up and deposited him beside her. He meowed in obvious feline discontent and stalked away, tail swishing. She stood. "Take me with you. I want, I *need*, to help and I don't mean by babysitting. It's Sunday and not only will Mrs. T be home, your mom will prob'ly be over there most of the day. I'll go nuts waitin' around and wonderin' what's happening."

I lit a Lucky and thought. "Have you visited Lee?"

"I can't." She wrung her hands. "I don't think I can bear seein' him in that place. Please, Betty. There has to be something I can do."

I blew out a long stream of smoke. "Dot, Sam and I were out all day yesterday, almost until ten at night. What are your parents gonna say?"

"Phooey on them." She stamped her foot. "I'm an adult, eighteen years old. I work and I only live at home because I haven't bothered to find my own place. If they can't accept that, well, it's their problem. I love Lee and I'm not gonna sit around and do nothin' while he rots in jail."

Her indignation amused me, if only 'cause I didn't see it often. But it also touched my heart. I'd be sayin' the same things if roles were reversed and it was Tom in the clink. "Let me go inside and change. Sam isn't here yet, although he should be any minute. I want to talk to Mrs. T before he arrives." I carefully put out my cigarette and dropped it back into the box so I could finish it later. Then I went inside and switched my church clothes for sensible slacks, flats, a plain button-down, and a cardigan. I stopped in the kitchen on the way out. "Mom, I'm off with Dot to the Tillotsons' house. I'm pretty sure Detective MacKinnon will be here soon. If I'm not back, can you give him a cup of coffee or something?"

She stood at the sink, washing the breakfast dishes, and turned her head to look at me. "Are you going to be out all day again?"

"I don't know. I s'pose it depends on what we learn and how fast. Is there anything I can get for you while I'm out? Maybe from the Broadway Market?"

"No. I'm going to go sit with Nora as soon as I'm finished here." She pursed her lips. "Be careful, Betty. I wish you luck."

Boy, what a long way she'd come from my first case. I stepped over to give her a quick hug. "Promise."

Outside, I finished buttoning my coat and slipped on my mittens. The clouds had once again given way to bright sunshine that promised warmth, but didn't deliver. I heard the cry of gulls in the distance, a mournful sound. Since I hadn't freed Lee, it seemed fitting. The neighborhood was quiet, as though everyone held their breath, waitin' on the end of the story. I nodded

THE LESSONS WE LEARN

at Dot. "Let's go."

A few minutes later, Dot rapped on the Tillotsons' front door. "Mrs. T, it's Dot and Betty. May we come in?"

The door swung open, but it was Anna who stood there, not her mother. "Ma is upstairs," she said, her little girl voice missing its usual bounce. "She won't come down, not even for church. All she does is cry. Emma and I don't know what to do."

Dot and I went in and I knelt before the girl. "Don't you fret. Your brother will be home before you know it. My mom is gonna come as soon as she can. Don't worry about goin' to church today. I think God will understand. Can you read a book or something to pass the time?" She nodded and I stood. I looked at Dot. "Let's go upstairs."

We found Mrs. T still in bed, surrounded by sodden handkerchiefs and a nearly-empty box of Kleenex paper hankies. Her face was blotchy and her eyes swollen, mute evidence of her misery. She mumbled a greeting as we entered the room.

"Hey," I said. "I won't ask how you're feeling. I can guess it isn't that great."

Dot wordlessly swept up the used tissues and deposited them in the small trash can by the door. The worst of the handkerchiefs went in the laundry hamper.

"I know you're miserable, but I need to ask you a couple of questions." I perched on the edge of the bed. I ignored the stone that had taken up residence in my stomach. If I were gonna be a detective, unpleasant conversations were part of the job.

She twisted a tissue into a ball and said something I didn't catch.

I took it that I was okay to proceed. "The night Mr. Tillotson disappeared, you went out. Lee said you were wearing your nice coat and he thinks you had heels on. He thought it was unusual and figured you were going out somewhere special. You told my mother you did, but wouldn't say anything else. Where did you go?"

No answer.

I glanced at Dot, who shrugged. "Mrs. Tillotson, this is really important. I don't care what you did, where you did it, or who you did it with." Unless

158

I was wrong and she had clocked her husband down at the grain elevator canals. "But to help Lee, I gotta know the truth."

There was a pause and the breath went out of her in a long sigh. "Some friends and I went to one of the social clubs down on Abbott Road. We didn't intend to do anything other than have a couple of drinks, maybe a nice dinner. There was a little band. They had a dance floor. I…"

"Yes?"

It seemed like she struggled a moment with how much to say. "There was a man there. We danced. He…he kissed me at the end of the night and told me I was a lovely dance partner. He wanted to see me again. You don't understand." She lifted her face and her eyes shone. "It's been a long time, so long, since a man made me feel beautiful. I had a bit too much to drink and I'm afraid I may have encouraged him a little. He saw my wedding ring, but it didn't seem to bother him."

I ignored the tiny gasp from Dot. "Did you leave the club with him?"

Mrs. T fixed me with a wide-eyed stare. "I didn't, I swear. I told him at the beginning of the night I was married. He asked if my husband was overseas. I said no, he was too old to serve and was ill. I didn't want to admit John was, well, what he was."

"A drunk."

She bit her lip and nodded. "Anyway, this man, Gary, said my husband couldn't be much if he was letting such a beautiful woman out without him. He asked to take me home. I…oh, Lord help me, Betty. I wanted to say yes." She buried her face in her hands.

Lee had been right to be suspicious and no wonder he was worried the woman on the dock was his mother. 'Course I didn't blame Mrs. T in the least. She'd put up with a lot from her husband in the past year. "But you didn't."

She sobbed, but eventually answered. "No, Martha saved me. Martha Connor. She lives over on Alabama Street. She was one of the friends I was out with. She swept in and said how we had to get along and pulled me out of the club."

"When was this?" Dot asked

"I don't know." Mrs. T dabbed at her eyes. "It was late, I know that. I was quiet when I came home. I knew John wouldn't be here, or if he was he'd be passed out. But I didn't want to wake Lee or the girls."

She looked so guilty, like a little girl with her hand caught in the cookie jar. I believed her. I figured she'd be so relieved to spill the beans to a sympathetic ear, she'd have told me if anything else had happened. After all, who was a better shoulder to cry on than your son's best friend? I moved on. "Lee told me you'd argued with Mr. Tillotson. Right before he disappeared, I mean. Is that true?"

Mrs. T took a steadying breath and wiped her eyes with her hand, having used up all the Kleenex and now bereft of a clean hankie. "It is. I, oh, I got so mad. I couldn't take it anymore. John had come home drunk, like he usually did. That very morning he'd promised to stop. He had a new black eye and his pants were ripped at the knee. I'd mended them not a week ago. I said if he couldn't straighten up and get sober for the sake of his family, he could pack his bags and leave. And if he didn't, I'd chase him out with the broom. And then he disappeared." She dissolved into tears and I searched for something to give her.

Dot tugged my sleeve and held out her own hankie. "It's okay, Mrs. T," she said. "We understand, really. We know you were just mad. Heck, I don't blame you in the slightest."

My mind had caught on the details. "The black eye and ripped pants," I said. "Did he say where he'd gotten them?"

I waited while Mrs. T gathered herself enough to speak. "No," she said. "In fact, that was part of the reason I was so angry. I knew darn well he'd gone on a binge again, probably fell down in some alley, ruined his clothes, and banged his head off something. But he wouldn't tell me. All he said was I shouldn't worry, he was taking care of things, and it wouldn't happen again." She clucked her tongue. "Like I didn't know it would happen the very next week."

I exchanged a look with Dot. I could tell by the look on her face, she didn't believe Mr. Tillotson's explanation any more than I did. Neither of us said anything, though. It wouldn't have helped.

I heard the front door open and my mother's voice called up. "Betty? Dot? Are you girls upstairs?"

I patted Mrs. T's hand. "Mom is here. She'll tend you, get you anything you need. Thanks for talkin' to me. Oh, one more thing. Do you have a photo of your husband I can borrow?"

She gave me a watery smile. "As long as it helps my boy. There are a couple of albums in the living room. You can take something out of there."

Dot and I found Mom in the kitchen, the girls at the table, the radio playing soft music. Mom looked up from a pot of tea and plate of toast in front of her. "How is Nora?"

"Still pretty down," I said. "Thanks for coming, Mom. Is Detective MacKinnon here yet?"

"Yes, I left him at the house in the kitchen with a sorry excuse for a cup of coffee and the last of the toast." Her smile was a bit rueful. "He offered to help dry the dishes. I may have been too hard on the poor man in the past. For a police officer, he's very polite."

I smothered a grin. Mom would not appreciate what she'd see as smugness. "You're the best. I'm glad you're here. I think Mrs. T is a bit fragile."

"A bit?" Dot shook her head. "That's an understatement if ever there was one."

"I'm just gonna grab a photo Mrs. T said I could borrow and then we're off, Mom. I'll see you...I don't know when. If I have news, I'll call the Tillotsons' house."

She put the toast and a pot of tea on the tray. "I'll keep praying that the news is good."

Chapter Twenty-Seven

My plan to include Dot hit a bump as soon as I got home and talked to Sam.

"She can't come." He took his empty cup to the sink, washed it, and set it on the drainboard. He faced us.

Dot reddened. "Watch me. Haven't you learned by now that I'm more than a pretty face?"

He held up a hand. "Miss Kilbride, that's unfair and you know it. This has nothing to do with your abilities and everything to do with young Mr. Tillotson's case." He aimed a finger at me. "You're already on thin ice. The minute you show up to sign that contract tomorrow, and Williams finds out you don't have a PI license, this whole game is over."

I crossed my arms over my chest. "Then what does it matter if Dot is there?"

"Because Williams might be able to finagle something if the story is you're working on a license or something is in progress. If we bring another unlicensed person in, who knows what will happen?"

I glanced at Dot. Her face was redder than a tomato. "Why can't we just say she's my employee?"

Sam threw up his hands. "How can a PI without credentials have an employee? The DA will blow this out of the water if we don't play our cards right. Is that what you want?"

I closed my eyes and said a quick prayer for strength. Then I turned to her. "I can't put Lee in danger. I'm sorry."

She spun toward me and jabbed me in the chest. "You can't shut me out,

Betty. I need to help him."

I flashed to that heavy feeling in my stomach when Mr. Williams had told me I couldn't be in the room when he talked to Lee. "Dot, listen." I put my hands on her shoulders. "Sam is right. The more people we bring in, the more the DA can challenge the whole client confidentiality thing. Now, if I can get this wrapped up before Lee even goes before a judge, maybe that doesn't happen. But in case I can't, we gotta keep the circle as small as possible."

Her brown eyes welled with tears. "I have to do something, Betty. Isn't there anything, some job you can give me that doesn't break the rules?"

I looked at Sam. He frowned in thought. "Mrs. Ahern said you two were talking to Mrs. Tillotson. What did you learn?"

I quickly told him about Mrs. T's outing and her final disagreement with her husband.

"We need to confirm that alibi." Sam pushed off the counter. "Miss Kilbride, that's your task. Go back to Mrs. Tillotson. Get the names of her friends."

"Martha Connor is one," Dot said.

"Good. See if there were others. Talk to them and see if they corroborate her story. Where was this club?"

I handed Dot a clean towel to wipe her face. "Down on Abbott Road, I think that's what Mrs. T said." There sure were a lot of 'em down there.

"Double-check that. Go and see if they remember seeing these women, Mrs. Tillotson in particular, and the man she danced with. If you can get his full name, terrific." He paused. "How long do you think that will take you?"

Dot blew her nose. "Noon at least, I think. It's Sunday. This place may not even be open."

"That's okay. Get as much information as you can. Then go home. We'll call you around twelve to check on your progress." He grabbed his jacket off a chair.

I continued to rub Dot's shoulder and reminded myself to thank Sam later. Poor Dot. She'd been my right-hand girl on all my previous cases. Here was the most important one to date and she was shut out by some legal rules. "Where are we goin' if Dot is gonna check all that?"

"We know Howley and McDougal were arrested at the grocery store. If John Tillotson was one of their runners, someone at the store might have seen him around the games. We need to corroborate that. His wife said he showed up at home looking like he'd been in a fight. Where and with who?"

"We start with Jasper and Sons and Blackie Thomas's club?"

"Yes, to the store, no to the club. With Blackie there, everyone will stay mum. The store owners also may not tell us anything, but we should talk to them anyway." He grabbed his fedora off of the table. "Second, Steven Daletzki said, or at least intimated, that Tillotson had been involved in something shady for a while. Your father, Betty, said much the same thing and McDougal mentioned light money bags. If Blackie suspected him of skimming money, he'd have his men harass him everywhere. His home, his job."

Dot piped up. "He got fired from GM last Thanksgiving, that's what Lee said."

"They might have tried to corner him after work before that happened," Sam said. "We should also go back to the Tillotson's. Find out if either Howley or McDougal ever visited." He nodded at me. "Are you ready to go now?"

"Yeah, I s'pose." I faced Dot. "Remember. We'll call you at lunchtime. Get as much dope as you can."

Her fierce look was a little out of place next to her pinup girl dimples. "Don't worry. I'll get all the details. Remember, I've been working at Bell for a while. I may not look like much, but I've learned how to swing a hammer. Figuratively speaking, of course."

Too bad determination alone couldn't get Lee out of this jam. Based on the gleam in Dot's eyes, he'd have been out of jail yesterday.

* * *

Sam and I made a quick stop at the Tillotson house, but Mrs. T wasn't helpful. She'd never seen a man lurking around that fit either Howley or McDougal's descriptions and neither had her daughters. We thanked them and left.

"Where to first?" I asked as I got into the car.

"Let's start with his old employer," Sam said. "It could be that someone spotted Howley or McDougal around GM, maybe waiting for Tillotson to get off work."

I nibbled a fingernail. "Sam, I had a thought."

"Yes?"

"Frances Corbett. How serious would it be if she and Mr. Tillotson really were carryin' on?"

"Blackie would take someone moving in on his woman personally, although it wouldn't be as bad as the money." He shot me a look out of the corner of his eye. "Does the idea of the two of them make you uncomfortable?"

"As a matter of fact, it does." I stuffed my hands under my armpits, mostly so I didn't make them bleed with all my nail-biting. "So far, I've learned a lot of things about my friends and their families I didn't know, most of which I wish I hadn't. I don't want to add one more sin to the pile." I blew out a breath. "But if that's the case, should we focus on pinning down Frances and find out what she knows?"

"To be honest, I'm not sure how. Remember, we need to get her on her own."

I mulled it over. "You're sure you don't have any idea where she lives?"

"No. But if she truly was running around on her man, that *is* information they may give up down at the club. Especially if they are more loyal to him than her, which I'm betting is the case."

We pulled into the main parking lot at GM around nine-thirty. Like Bethlehem, GM ran around the clock, seven days a week for war production, churning out vehicles like jeeps, but also the Allison engines used at Bell and other companies. With the help of some signs and a passing maintenance man, we found the main office.

Inside, Sam produced his badge. "I'd like to speak to a manager, please,"

Sam said.

"The only management here right now is our Sunday day-shift supervisor, Adam Campbell," the young woman behind the desk said.

"He'll do just fine."

She laid her hand on a telephone receiver. "Certainly. Can I tell him what this is about?"

"The murder of a former employee, John Tillotson."

The woman paled, but she made her call. A few minutes later, Mr. Campbell appeared. He was a wiry man with dark beady eyes and thinning gray hair. I guessed he was several years older than Pop, maybe in his early fifties. He might work in an office now, but I'd bet anything he'd climbed up from a regular line grunt to management. "Are you the police detective?" He held out his hand.

Sam shook. "Detective Sam MacKinnon, Buffalo Police, Homicide Division. This is my associate, Betty Ahern."

Mr. Campbell did not reach out to shake with me and I ignored the insult. "Pleased to meet you."

"Is there somewhere a bit more private we can talk?" Sam asked.

Mr. Campbell studied me a bit, then said, "Sure, there's an empty conference room. Your—associate did you call her? She can wait here."

"She goes where I go." Sam's voice didn't lose its polite tone, but again I heard the underlying steel.

Mr. Campbell hesitated a moment, then twitched his shoulders. "Suit yourself." He turned to the receptionist. "Send up a pot of coffee and some cups. Make sure it's fresh. Last time you tried to foist off some swill from the previous day."

"Yes, Mr. Campbell," she said, eyes downcast.

The insults to me I could tolerate. But there was no need to talk down to the staff. I almost offered to help her, but that would demean me in Mr. Campbell's eyes and I was already not high in his estimation. "Anything you bring will be fine," I said and gave the girl an encouraging smile. *We both know who really runs things, don't we?* I tried to telegraph.

Her answering smile was broad. "It's no problem. I'll be in momentarily."

I followed the men into a room bare of any decorations except a picture of the General Motors logo on the wall. A rectangular table surrounded by chairs took up most of the space. Sam seated himself at the corner and I grabbed the chair next to him, which forced Mr. Campbell to move to the other side of the table. The conversation would be conducted interview style, not a casual chat between the menfolk.

I think Mr. Campbell came to the same conclusion because he scowled as he took his seat. "You said you wanted to talk about John Tillotson? Whatever for? Word on the floor has it he drowned."

"As I said to your receptionist, this is a murder investigation," Sam said as he removed notepad and pen from his jacket pocket. "Did you know Mr. Tillotson?"

"He did a regular Sunday shift for us for years," Mr. Campbell said, leaning back. "I knew him as well as any other employee, I guess."

"What was he like, as a worker?"

"Before or after his accident?"

"Both." Sam paused, pen hovering over the paper.

"Aw, shoot." Mr. Campbell stared at the ceiling for a long moment before returning his focus to Sam. "Before he hurt his back, John was a good one. Never complained. Always early, a lot of times he stayed late. He'd pick up shifts from other guys without a second thought. I often said if I had a roster full of men like John, we'd increase our production by fifty percent."

"And after?"

"It wasn't too bad at first." Mr. Campbell ran his fingers over the table. "Oh, he moved slower. Couldn't lift as much. Things like that. But he didn't complain."

"It didn't stay that way, though, did it?" I asked.

He gave me a dirty look. "You don't have any idea what it's like to work a production line, missy. I'm surprised things didn't go south for him sooner."

I s'pose I should have ignored the patronizing tone and insolent looks. I could see Sam's face out of the corner of my eye. His lips twitched as he fought off a grin. He knew what was coming. "For the record, I work at Bell Airplane up in Wheatfield. I know all about machinery, production, assembly lines, long hours, and dirty work. I'm pretty sure there's nothing you could say about manufacturing that would surprise me, Mr. Campbell." I folded my hands on the table. "I'm also not sure what you're thinking when Detective MacKinnon here calls me his 'associate,' but believe me. I've done my share of investigating, too. I'm not some prissy secretary who is afraid to get her clothes messy."

At that moment, the young woman from outside came in with a tray holding a coffee pot, some cups, milk, and sugar.

"You made it fresh, like I told you, right Delores?" Mr. Campbell waved at the tray. "Well don't just stand there gawping, pour it out."

I held up my hand. "Delores, that's a pretty name."

She colored. "Thank you. It was my gram's."

Sam cottoned on fast, because he said, "Miss...I'm sorry, I didn't catch your last name."

Her cheeks turned even redder. "Nally, sir."

"Miss Nally. If you would be so kind as to pass me a cup. No milk, thanks."

She poured out the coffee. I noticed she took greater care with Sam's joe and mine than she did with her boss's.

Sam said, "Thank you, Miss Nally. If I need anything else, I'll call."

She bobbed a curtsy and left.

Sam sipped his drink. "Mr. Campbell, I don't know if you've noticed, but a lot of our boys aren't around right now. The way I see it, we menfolk are at the mercy of our women. If I were you, I'd rethink your approach."

Mr. Campbell blinked. He added milk and sugar to his coffee, all the while muttering under his breath.

Sam set aside his drink. "Now, I believe Miss Ahern had asked about Mr. Tillotson's attitude post-injury."

Mr. Campbell stalled while he drank, but he finally answered. "I started to notice a change about a month after he returned to the line. His clothes were sloppy and so was his work. First he reeked of beer, then whiskey. He staggered when he walked and sometimes his voice sounded slurred. I pulled him aside after a shift, asked how much he was drinking. He admitted more than usual, but said he had things under control."

"Was that the end of it?" I asked.

"No. The tipping point was when he started coming in late. He even missed a shift or two completely. When I pressed him for a reason, he got cagey. Said he had some things in the works, couldn't talk about them, but it was temporary. As soon as he got rid of his obligations, he'd be fine."

"What obligations?" Sam asked.

Mr. Campbell shook his head. "I never found out. Before I could, there was an accident after he showed up flat drunk. He got another man fired in the process, Steve Daletzki. I wasn't the manager the day it happened, but I heard about it afterward." He studied us. "Are you sure John was murdered?"

"Quite sure," Sam said. "Why do you ask?"

"I dunno. I never thought much about it, but now I'm wondering if John got himself caught up in something with these 'obligations' he talked about. At the time, I thought it was odd he wouldn't be more specific, but I brushed it off. I hope they aren't connected. Are they?"

"We don't know." Sam pushed aside his cup. "Did Mr. Tillotson ever get visitors while he worked? You know, people who showed up at the main office and said they had to talk to him, that sort of thing?"

"Not to my knowledge."

"Did you ever see strangers around at quitting time? We're specifically looking for a man with a scar on his face or another one with a lazy eye."

Mr. Campbell thought and shook his head. "Nope. I mean, lots of guys here are scarred in some way from things that happen in the plant, but I know all of them. I never saw anybody I didn't know like you describe."

'Course, that didn't mean Howley or McDougal hadn't caught Mr. Tillotson at work, only that Mr. Campbell hadn't seen 'em. "Anybody here we could talk to who was close to Mr. Tillotson?" I asked.

Mr. Campbell looked at Sam, who crossed his arms and stared.

Whatever message had been sent, Mr. Campbell had gotten it. "John's drinking cost him a lot of friends. Most guys, well, they'd backed way off by the time he was fired. If you're asking if anyone else would have known what John was up to or if either of those guys had been seen around here, the only person I'd say to talk to is Steve Daletzki. He was John's best friend here and the one who stood by him to the end."

Sam stood. "Thank you for your time. We can see ourselves out."

Mr. Campbell shook the detective's hand, mumbled something in my direction that might have been "good-bye" and left us.

Chapter Twenty-Eight

We wandered back to the reception area, where Delores was back at her desk.

"Thanks for letting me take the lead for once," Sam said, not bothering to hide his sarcasm.

I lifted my hands, palms up. "I had questions."

Delores flagged us down. "Excuse me, Detective MacKinnon? I'm so sorry for eavesdropping, but are you here about Mr. Tillotson?"

"We are. Did you know him?" Sam leaned on the desk.

"A little. Not well, mind you, but he often attended meetings on behalf of the workers, at least he did before his injury. He always had a smile and a joke when he came in. Not like most of the others, who barely acknowledge me or worse, are a little too free with their hands, if you know what I mean." She bit her lip and folded her hands in her lap.

"I do," I said. "Can you tell us anything about Mr. Tillotson? Do you know what he was up to?"

"Oh no, nothing like that." Delores looked up. "Only, I heard you just now, asking about a man with a lazy eye? I left one night and on my way to the bus stop, a man like that stopped me. He said he'd seen me come out of GM and did I know if John Tillotson was still on the grounds. I said, no, I worked in the office and I wasn't likely to see the men as they came and went."

Sam and I exchanged a look. "Did you see him again anywhere? Maybe with the scarred man?" I asked.

"I don't know if it was the same man, but right before Mr. Tillotson was fired, I saw him outside the fence. He was arguing with someone. I didn't see the other man's face, but Mr. Tillotson didn't seem happy. I heard him say, 'I got it, lay off. Don't worry. And stop hounding me about the money.' Then he stalked off. He was let go not long after that, so I never had the chance to ask him if he was okay. He seemed so sad and angry."

"Thank you, Delores. That helps." Sam tipped his fedora at her.

Outside, I faced him. "Aside from learning that Mr. Tillotson was a good worker, then he wasn't, and he prob'ly got a visit from McDougal, and possibly someone else, did we learn anything?"

Sam tapped out a cigarette and cupped his hand around it while he flicked his lighter. I noticed it was the one I'd given him for Christmas, the Zippo with the shamrock on it. "We learned that his problems started long before his body turned up floating near Child Street."

"We still don't know what those problems were, though." I pulled my pack of Lucky's from my purse and slipped one out.

Sam held out his lighter to me. "No, but you're smart enough to do the math. He was running numbers for Blackie Thomas. If all Tillotson had done was play patty-cake with Blackie's woman, he'd have been roughed up, maybe shown the door, but not killed. Not in my opinion. No, my money is on theft. Tillotson was losing it at work, maybe bringing home less in the paycheck. Then he's fired. There's cash at hand. Maybe he considered it a loan and thought Blackie would give him the opportunity to pay it back." He strolled toward his car. "Plus, I don't see a young woman like Frances Corbett falling for a drunk like John Tillotson, no matter how many compliments he paid her."

"I can't believe Mr. Thomas would kill him first," I said as I trailed behind. "He'd want his money back, wouldn't he?"

"Who said it was the first reaction? Remember, McDougal said Tillotson's 'bag had been light' three times in a row. Blackie might have already tried the talking approach and had stepped up his response. He'd also want to set an example for anyone else who got the same idea." Sam reached the car. "Howley knows, McDougal knows. Count on it."

"They aren't gonna talk to us, not more than they have already."

"No." Sam opened the door. "But Steve Daletzki might. If we can find him."

* * *

We went back to Mrs. Wiese's house. Not only was her brother still not home, now she was hysterical. "He's not here, I don't know where he is and it's all your fault!" The words burst out of her mouth as soon as she opened the door.

Sam switched into what I assumed was his "calm down the witness" cop style. "Mrs. Wiese. Clearly you're upset. May we come in?"

Wordlessly she turned, leaving the door open. Sam entered, and I followed hot on his heels and closed the door behind us.

Mrs. Wiese led us to the kitchen, although I'm not sure she intended to. It seemed to be more where she ended up. She sat at the table, clutching a hankie. Sam and I sat to either side.

"Now, take a deep breath," he said as he moved a heavy glass ashtray full of loose change out of the way. "When was the last time you saw your brother?"

She thought a moment. "I told you before, Saturday morning. No, that's not right. He wasn't here when I got up, so I figured he'd gone to work. I saw, or rather heard, him Friday night when he got home."

"What time would that have been?" I asked.

She gave me a scathing look. "Don't you know? You went and hounded him at the garage." She pressed the cloth to her mouth. "He's gone and I don't know what to do." As soon as she finished talkin', she let loose a banshee wail that raised the hairs on the back of my neck.

"Mrs. Wiese, I'm very sorry. I didn't mean to upset you or him." I studied her. "Do you, um, want me to make you some tea or somethin'?"

Sam said nothing, but his raised eyebrows telegraphed his surprise.

"It's what Mom does when someone's upset." I spread my hands. "It couldn't hurt, right?"

My offer must have bled the anger out of her, or maybe she was just worn out, because she said, "That would be lovely, thank you." Mrs. Wiese hiccupped and waved a limp hand in the general direction of the corner. "The tea things are over there."

Having said it, I had no choice but to get up, fetch the teabags, and set the kettle boiling. Behind me, Sam continued his talking.

"I'm very sorry to hear Mr. Daletzki isn't home. Have you called the police?"

"No. Can't you do something? You're a police detective, aren't you?"

"Ma'am, I work Homicide, not Missing Persons. Not to be rude, but you don't want me working on your brother's disappearance."

"I can't involve the police, I just can't. It would upset my children. And what if the neighbors found out? If Steve is up to something, it would be mortifying if it got around the neighborhood."

"Where are your boys?"

"I sent them to their grandmother's house for the afternoon."

"I see." He paused. "Well, if you won't call the police, I suggest you talk to a private detective."

"Where do I find one of those?"

"There happens to be a very fine one over there, making your tea."

I whipped around. "Me?"

Sam's eyes twinkled, but his voice was somber. "Yes, Miss Ahern."

"Detective, may I speak with you in private a moment? Maybe in the living room?" I headed for the door. Once in the front room, I faced him. "What in heaven's name are you doin'?"

"Getting you another job."

"What about the whole license thing? As in, I don't have one?"

He held up his hands. "This is a completely different situation. All you're trying to do here is find Steve Daletzki."

"And what happens if I find him dead?"

"You call me, I take your statement, and the Buffalo PD takes over the investigation."

I fumed. I had my hands full helping Lee. I couldn't allow a missing man to sidetrack me, even if that person could be a witness in Mr. Tillotson's murder.

"Think of it this way. If you're serious about becoming a PI, helping Mrs. Wiese can only bolster your reputation. You'll need that. And we *have* to find Daletzki...sooner rather than later."

I hated it when Sam was logical and it was even worse when he was right. "Fine, I'll do it. But you don't have to help me get any more cases, okay? Two at once is enough."

We returned to the kitchen, where the kettle was whistling. I took it off the flame, poured hot water in the teapot, and took the pot, a teacup, and a bowl containing maybe a couple of tablespoons of sugar to the table. I set them in front of Mrs. Wiese. "I've talked to Detective MacKinnon. Do you want to hire me or not?"

She gave me a watery stare. "I want you or someone to find Steve. But I can't spare a lot of money."

"How much do you have?" Part of me wanted to waive any fee, but Sam was right. If I intended to build a reputation, I needed to charge something, even if it was only a small amount.

"I might have five dollars set aside for my pin money," she said, stirring a tiny amount of sugar into her tea. "Is that enough?"

"It'll be fine. Now." I scooted my chair closer and pulled out my notepad and pen. "You said you heard your brother two days ago, on Friday night when he came home. You didn't see him?"

"No, I was in the living room, listening to the radio. I heard the door open, asked if he was hungry, and he said he wasn't. Or something like that. I didn't listen to him all that carefully. Most of my attention was on the program." A round of fresh sobs escaped her.

I waited with what I thought was infinite patience. At the next break, I said, "You're positive you didn't hear or see him the next morning?"

"No, like I said, he was gone when I got up."

"Then how do you know he left at seven like you told us earlier?"

"It's when he usually goes to work. But now that we're talking, I might have heard him again later Friday night."

I suppressed a sigh. All the backtracking was making it hard to keep the timeline straight. "When would that have been?"

"Oh, I don't know, after ten? I'd gone to bed. It sounded like someone opened and closed the door, trying not to be heard. At first, I thought it might be one of the children. They are never as sneaky as they think they are."

I knew what she meant. The last time Michael and Jimmy tried to go through their window late at night and fool Mom, it had sounded more like a troop of elephants getting out than two young boys. "You didn't get up to check?"

"I only looked in on the boys. Steve's door was closed." She took a sip of tea. "He gets up so early, I didn't want to wake him."

That made sense. "Let's go back to earlier Friday night for a moment. Do you know exactly what time it was when you talked to him?"

She thought a moment. "Yes. The radio show I was listening to is on between seven and seven-thirty at night."

"After seven, before seven-thirty, got it." I scribbled a note. *Daletzki last seen March 19 between seven and seven-thirty.* "Now, think hard. Has Mr. Daletzki argued with anyone lately? Anyone you can remember? Have any strangers come lookin' for him at home?"

To her credit, she did stop and ponder a moment. "No. Steve is so mild-mannered. He gets along with all of our neighbors. He mows the grass for old Mrs. Wasniewski across the street. This is a close-knit neighborhood. If any strangers had been around, I'd know it."

I glanced at Sam, who mouthed "the knife." I nodded. "We, Detective MacKinnon and I, told you about finding your brother's knife at Mr. Tillotson's murder scene. Would he have given it to anyone? Say, Mr. Tillotson?"

"Never." Her chin lifted. "He treasured it. He'd never loan it out, especially to a rat like John Tillotson."

Sam broke in. "You don't like Mr. Tillotson, do you?"

"No, I don't." Her eyes flashed, grief forgotten for a moment. "Steve was never anything but kind to John. Even when it was clear he had a problem with the bottle. Steve always made excuses for him, gave him 'one more chance.' And look where it got him. Fired from a good job at GM, one where he could have made shift manager in a year or two."

"After that happened, did Mr. Tillotson come to the house? Try to explain or make amends?" Sam asked.

"Not to the house, no. I gathered he did visit Steve at the garage once. They argued, I think. About what, I can't imagine. I told Steve he was well shut of such a poor friend." She paused. "His response, it was so funny."

I leaned forward. "Funny how?"

She studied her hands, then looked up. "Steve said, 'He's into something big, sis. More money than I'd ever make at GM. And I'm gonna find out what if it kills me.'"

Chapter Twenty-Nine

As Sam and I left, I tucked the four crumpled dollar bills and collection of coins Mrs. Wiese had paid me into my wallet. I caught up to him near his car. "You do know that if finding Mr. Daletzki wasn't directly connected to helping Lee, I'd have passed on this job."

"But it is, so there you go. Two birds, one stone, two fees, and you're done." He drummed his fingers on the roof of the car. "At least if you're lucky."

"What do you mean?"

"If Steve Daletzki was poking his nose into the same business that got John Tillotson killed, the search could end in another dead body."

I'd been trying not to dwell on that, but Sam's words made that impossible. "Thanks a lot."

"Don't mention it." He stared off into space.

There weren't any people on the sidewalk and it was quiet as a church, so I knew he had to be deep in thought. "What're you thinkin'?"

"How best to proceed." He faced me. "Our tasks are multiplying, but our time isn't."

I worried my nail, which was almost down to the quick. Sam was right. We could divide up the tasks, but if we split up, it would make it more difficult to stay in touch. I didn't have the number for every payphone in the city and I couldn't wait at each one for a call. "I s'pose I could go back to the club or Jasper's grocery to find out about what happened to give Mr. Tillotson a shiner and ripped pants before he died."

"Out of the question. You are not going to talk to Blackie Thomas alone."

"Or I could try and pin down Frances, while you take on the others." A crow squawked somewhere nearby, letting me know what he thought of that idea.

Sam scowled. "I'm not letting you go talk to a potential killer without me along for backup either."

I didn't think he'd go along with the plan, but I had to try. "For cripe's sake, Sam. I know how to take care of myself." Although I should prob'ly stop home and get Sean's pocketknife before I went. It wouldn't be much, but more than what I had right now.

"It's not about you taking care of yourself. One of these people had no qualms about killing John Tillotson. You think they'd give a second thought to getting rid of you? And this is not the time to bring a knife to a gunfight." He arched his eyebrow, as though he knew what I was thinkin'.

"But Sam, they might be more willing to talk to me. I'm not a cop."

"True, but you're not doing it without me nearby to help out if something goes south." He tapped his foot. "Forget it, we're not splitting up. I'm finally in your mother's good graces. I'm not putting her daughter in danger. We'll simply have to work faster."

"How about this?" I leaned on the car. Bits of sleet spit from the sky and I felt a cold bite on my cheek. "Let's go to Jasper and Sons. I'll go in and talk to the folks inside. If I don't come out in, say, fifteen minutes, you can wander in and make like you're buying a pop or a box of Cracker Jack."

"Why the grocery?"

"I know people like those." I snugged my coat closed against a gust of wind. "They're good folks who don't want trouble. Sure, they let low-level gangsters like Blackie Thomas and his goons ride over them, but it's because they don't have much of a choice. Or they go along because in exchange for putting up with a weekly numbers game, they get protection from some other gang in the neighborhood."

"I never heard Blackie was in the protection business."

"He might not be, it could be a sideline. Also, I think it more likely Mr. Tillotson was roughed up close to home, as it were. Not his home, mind, but where the games happen. I don't think Mr. Thomas would run the risk of going outside his turf. He'd play it safe, stay in his own neighborhood."

Sam pointed at me. "And yet, John Tillotson was killed down at the canals."

"Yeah, and the more I think about it, the more that doesn't make sense. Why go down there? No, listen." I held up my hand to stop Sam from interrupting. "I admit it, the grain elevators are mostly deserted at that time of night. It was pure luck that Ray Thatcher happened to see the gathering. But if Mr. Thomas was gonna tell his guys to kill Mr. Tillotson, why do it in a place where they might be seen by someone not under Mr. Thomas's thumb?"

Sam frowned. "What are you saying?"

"I don't think Mr. Thomas, or anyone who worked for him, set up that meeting. It's more likely Mr. Tillotson picked the place, hoping a neutral site would work to his benefit. He'd be able to control the discussion."

"If that's the case, it didn't work."

"No, it didn't." I was outta nail to chew, so I ran my thumb over the ragged edge.

"Two enforcers, Daletzki, and a woman who could either be Frances Corbett or Mrs. Tillotson. Quite the party."

It was, but, somehow I didn't think it had been planned that way.

* * *

It took a little more cajoling, but I got Sam to go along with my plan. When he pulled up outside of Jasper and Sons, I grabbed the door handle, but he spoke before I could pull it. "I thought of something on our way over. It's Sunday. The store is going to be closed."

"Rats." I scanned the empty street. The fact that it was the Lord's day had every business in view shuttered, threatening to ruin my plans. But then I saw a new possibility. "I bet they live above the store."

"What makes you say that?"

I pointed toward the sidewalk and an older lady with gray hair held back in a neat bun who was heading our way, apparently making a beeline for the closed-up store. She was dressed in a long black coat, sensible shoes, and wore a black hat with a white bow on it. "I'll bet you anything that's Mrs. Jasper. She's prob'ly on her way home from church. Maybe she'll let me inside, we'll flap our gums, and I'll learn something."

He sighed. "You get fifteen minutes. Any longer and I'm coming after you."

I opened the door. "Don't flip your wig, Sam. I'll be fine." Before he could answer, I was outta the car and over to the sidewalk. "Hello, Mrs. Jasper."

She stopped and clutched her purse. "Goodness. You scared the daylights out of me."

"Sorry about that. My name is Betty Ahern. I hoped you'd give me a little bit of your time."

"It's Sunday, young lady. I don't appreciate door-to-door sales on the Sabbath."

I held up my palms. "I'm not selling anything. I want to talk to you about Blackie Thomas."

She paled. "I don't know who you're talking about. Good day." She pushed past me.

But I wasn't gonna give up. "Ma'am, you know exactly what I mean."

She threw a frightened look in my direction.

It hit me. She didn't want any of Mr. Thomas's men to see her. "Why don't we go inside? I promise I'll be in and out. No one'll ever know."

For a moment it looked like she would blow me off, but she gave a sharp nod. "Fine. Quickly, come on." She opened the door and we entered.

Inside the store looked like any other mom-and-pop grocery in Buffalo. The shelves held an assortment of canned goods, a few loaves of Wonder bread, boxes of Cracker Jack, and bottles of Coke. The aisle holding bakery items was nearly bare. They hadn't restocked for the week. Of course, this might be all they had to put on the shelves. In which case, I wondered how they stayed in business, but it could be this was the neighborhood store, so it was where folks did their shopping.

She shooed me to the back, out of sight of the windows. "What do you want?"

I glanced around, but we appeared to be the only two in the place. "I know Blackie Thomas runs a numbers game out of the back of your store on occasion." I didn't mention I knew this 'cause I'd been at the last raid. "I don't really care about that. I am lookin' for information on the father of a friend of mine. See, I think the father is in trouble and I wanna get my friend some information so he can help out his old man." I neglected to add that my friend was in jail for the murder of his father. I had a feeling that detail would not endear me to this woman.

From the icy look in her faded blue eyes, my instinct was on the money. "I have no idea what you're talking about."

"C'mon, Mrs. Jasper." I paused. "I know a lot of people like you down in the First Ward. That's where I live. They just wanna earn a living. No fuss, no cops, no trouble. But they don't know how to stand up to thugs like Blackie Thomas, so they gotta go along with stuff they'd rather not be a part of."

She narrowed her peepers. "What's your point?"

"You help me with this. Give me the straight dope on Mr. Thomas and his enterprise. I have a friend in the Buffalo PD. Five'll get you ten that if I pass what you tell me to my friend, he can get your unwanted guests out of your back room." I waited. Instinct told me this woman wouldn't be swayed by pleas to help an innocent man or see justice done. She just wanted to be shot of the crooks taking up space in her store.

After a long minute, she said, "You can do that? Get those no-good ruffians off my property?"

"I think I can."

She ran her tongue over her lips and straightened some cans of soup on a nearby shelf. "You're right. Mr. Thomas uses our storeroom the third Saturday of every month. Mr. Jasper, he objected the first time one of those goons made the offer. The very next day, some young man in dirty clothes came in, took all the money out of our till, and swiped a bunch of our stock. Mr. Thomas's people came back. Mr. Jasper turned them down again and this time, some hoodlum threw a brick through our front window." She waved at one of the glass openings, where the paint on the frame looked a little newer. "We got the message. It's only once a month. In return, Mr.

Thomas keeps the riffraff out. At least when the cops show up, as they did this past Saturday, they don't bother us. I think they know we don't have any choice in the matter."

"I bet they do." I took the borrowed picture of Mr. Tillotson out of my purse. "Did you ever see this man?"

Mrs. Jasper took the snap and studied it. "He looks sort of familiar. I think he might have been a messenger of some kind. Yes, I noticed him a couple of times. They'd give him the bag at the end of the night and he'd take it. I don't know where." She handed back the photo.

"Do you remember when you saw him last?"

"Oh gosh, I have no idea. Not last Saturday, I can tell you that. But before then? Sorry, I don't know."

"Did you ever see him with two other men? One has a scar on his face and one has a lazy eye."

She pursed her lips as though she'd bitten a lemon. "I never saw the three of them together, but I know the two you're talking about. They come in a couple of days before the scheduled game night to make sure 'everything is copacetic.' Hmph. They usually help themselves to a bag of chips and a bottle of Coke, too."

"What about earlier this month? Before the second. You sure you didn't see them together?"

"No, sorry."

Rats. I'd been hoping this had been where Mr. Tillotson had the run-in that had left him with ruined clothes and a black eye. I took a look at the clock on the wall, plain but clean. Five minutes before Sam busted in on my conversation. "The only time you saw the other two was to set up before the gambling night?" I wondered if I should buy a box of Cracker Jack off her for her troubles, but although the shelf where the snacks would be was clean as a whistle, it was also as bare as Old Mother Hubbard's cupboard.

"Yes, although now that you mention it, I do think my husband might have seen them."

"When?"

"Right around when you asked about, early this month, could have been the last of February. Max, that's my husband, took out the trash. When he came in, he said he'd seen the two setup men in the alley behind the store, even though it wasn't a game night. They said they were talking to a third man, but Max doubted it was a casual conversation. The third man was bent over, hugging himself, and his face was all blotchy. 'He's gonna have one heck of a shiner. You oughta go out in about five minutes and offer him a bag of ice for his eye.' But Max was very adamant I not go out immediately."

Hope blossomed in my chest. "Did you? Go out with the ice?"

"I did, but the injured man was gone. All of them were." She paused. "Are you sure this is going to help? I don't want to get into trouble with Mr. Thomas if he finds out I've been telling tales."

"Don't worry, Mrs. Jasper. He'll never know." Wait until Sam heard about this.

Chapter Thirty

I rushed outside and trotted over to Sam's car. "Get a load of this," I said when I got in.

"I was about to come in after you."

"Good thing you didn't 'cause I'm pretty sure Mrs. Jasper woulda clammed up." I told him everything I'd learned from the store owner's wife.

"Your ability to wheedle information out of people never fails to amaze me." He tapped the steering wheel. "Howley and McDougal roughed someone up in the alley, huh?"

"Then Mr. Tillotson turns up at home with a shiner and ripped pants." I scribbled down notes from the conversation before I forgot anything. "D'you think either of 'em would talk to us now?"

"Maybe, but let's try Frances Corbett first. She might know what went on, especially if she was the reason behind the beating."

"But we still don't have her address. Unless you know something I don't."

"I've got an idea. Let's ask around the club. We're in the neighborhood, and like I said, the people there might give her up if they are loyal to Blackie."

"There's something else goin' on there. The more I think about it, the more I can't see her involved with Mr. Tillotson, not romantically. You were right. He doesn't have anything to offer her, not like Mr. Thomas."

Sam leaned on the car. "McDougal said Blackie saw Frances and Tillotson together in a booth."

"Right, but maybe it wasn't sweet nothings they were talkin'. Mr. Thomas may have assumed that, along with everyone else, but that doesn't mean he was right."

Sam rubbed his chin. "You might be on to something with that. I guess we'll find out if and when we talk to Frances. Let's go."

I stashed my notebook in my purse and we walked the two blocks down Abbott Road to the club. No guard lounged outside today. I assumed that meant Blackie Thomas wasn't on the premises.

At the door, Sam turned to me. "Leave this one up to me. And I mean it this time."

I laid a hand on his arm. "I just thought of something. Won't the bar be closed? You can't sell booze on the Lord's day."

Sam lifted an eyebrow. "Betty. Do you really think Blackie Thomas is concerned about the blue laws?" He pulled the door open and we went inside.

He had a point. Maybe the absence of a guard was to make it look like the joint was closed. There were even fewer people around now than there had been before, maybe 'cause only the die-hards had come for a drink. A quick look at the corner told me I'd been right about Mr. Thomas. His booth was empty. I also didn't see a trace of Frances.

Sam strode up to the bar and showed his badge. "I'm looking for Frances Corbett."

"She ain't here," the bartender said, not looking up from the gin he was pouring.

"I can see that. Any clue where I could find her?"

The bartender set down the glass and slid it across the gleaming wood surface of the bar to its destination. He reached behind him for a beer mug. "Nope."

"None whatsoever? I find that hard to believe."

"Why's that? I'm not interested in some floozy, especially if she's with Mr. Thomas."

Sam leaned forward. "Then she and Mr. Thomas are still involved? I'd heard otherwise."

That got the barman's attention. "You heard wrong."

"The way I understood it, she'd moved on." Sam pushed back his fedora and made a seemingly casual study of the various bottles behind the bar. "A little birdie told me she'd taken up with one of the gang."

The bartender slammed the beer glass onto the wood, slopping a little foam over the top. With a swish of his towel, he wiped it up. "Your birdie is singin' the wrong song, mister." He pushed the glass forward. "Here, on the house, since you made me spill it. Drink it and get lost." He pulled the tap to fill another glass and walked away.

Sam sipped his beer. I punched him in the arm. "What about me? Don't I get a drink? And it's Sunday!"

"As a Catholic, I personally don't believe in blue laws and I'm not interested in the paperwork that would result from me citing this place, especially on my day off. I have more important things to do." He looked around the dim interior. "I also don't think they serve Coke in this joint and you don't seem the beer or whiskey type." His mouth slanted in a lopsided grin. "Or is this another unknown facet of your life?"

"You coulda asked for a glass of water."

He laughed and took another drink.

I turned to survey the space. It looked a little cleaner than last time, but the scent of cigarette and cigar smoke was just as thick. Someone in here liked stogies. Most of the patrons didn't spare us a second glance, even if they'd made Sam for a cop. Maybe they figured he was just as entitled to an illicit drink as they were. He wasn't gonna bother them, they wouldn't fuss.

After a moment, I noticed a man in the back. He looked up, made a small waving motion, then turned his attention to his drink. I nudged Sam. "Don't look now, but I think the guy in the back wants to talk. Second booth from the door, the working stiff."

Sam turned, holding his glass, putting on the act of a casual drinker. "Got him."

The man threw a glance over his shoulder and made another furtive wave.

"Let's go see what he wants." Carrying his glass, Sam made for the table, me hot on his heels.

"Afternoon, friend," I said as we slid in. "You look like you could use a refill." I nodded at his mostly empty glass of whiskey.

"Mighty neighborly of you," he said. "I stick to one an afternoon, but I used my last dime today."

I didn't miss the meaning and fished one out of my purse. "For tomorrow. You don't care about the blue laws?"

"This is one of the few places in the city where a man can get a drink on a Sunday." He swept up the coin. "You're a very understanding young lady." He focused on Sam. "I couldn't help but overhear your conversation with Larry at the bar. You're a police detective?"

Sam showed his badge.

"What do you want with Miss Corbett?"

"Just to talk," Sam said and wiped foam from his upper lip. "Do you know anything about her?"

"I might."

Sam arched an eyebrow. "You already got your payoff from the lady."

The man shrugged. "Can't blame a guy for trying. You know Frances is Blackie's girl, I assume."

"That's the word on the street." Sam took another sip of his beer. "At least for now."

"I feel sorry for the poor lass. Pretty thing like that and Blackie treats her like trash."

I leaned forward. "He hits her? By the way, I didn't get your name."

"Oh, I'd rather keep names out of it. Except for yours, sir, which you announced to the entire room." The man nodded toward Sam and tossed back the rest of his whiskey. "To answer your question, no, Blackie never raised a finger to Frannie. But he never paid her the attention she was due. I s'pose that's why she went looking elsewhere. You can hardly blame her. Women like to be noticed."

For all the world, it looked like the only thing Sam was interested in was the golden liquid in his glass, but I knew better. "Did anyone notice her?" he asked.

The man threw a glance over his shoulder, but no one paid us any mind. "The name John Tillotson was mentioned. He had a way with women. Beautiful manners and he always knew what to say. A true ladies' man, despite his drinking. In fact," he dropped his voice, "rumor had it they'd been spending a lot of time together lately."

Sam abandoned his casual air and focused on our source. "Who knew about this rumor?"

"Let's put it this way, if I knew, Blackie Thomas knew."

"And how would Blackie take the news his dame was on the arm of another guy?"

"Not well." The man slowly rotated his glass. "You should talk to Frannie about it. Get the story."

"Too bad we can't find her to ask," I said.

He paused a moment. "Blackie puts her up at a nice boarding house, 437 Ramona Avenue. Ask for Miss Corbett. Make sure the house mistress knows you're police or send the young lady in. No men allowed." He pushed away the glass, stood, and grabbed a threadbare overcoat.

"Thanks for the tip." I eyed him. "What's in it for you?"

He shrugged on the coat. "I beg your pardon?"

"You gave up the address and the skinny awfully easy," I said. "Why?"

His answering smile was tinged with sadness. "Frannie is a good girl. She got in over her head. She'd never admit that, but a big brother has an obligation to look after his sister. Lord knows she hasn't listened to me before. You two might be my last chance to bail her out." He fastened the coat and left without another word.

Chapter Thirty-One

As soon as we left the club, I fumbled around in my purse for change. "I better check in with Dot. There's a payphone across the street." Sam nodded. "Meet me at the car when you're done."

I jogged across to the booth and dialed Dot's number. "It's me. What have you learned?"

"Mrs. T's telling the truth," she said. "I checked up with her friend, the one who dragged her off the dance floor that night. I also called the club. Not only did the manager remember the group of women, he's familiar with this Gary. The manager says he's a real swinger. He's too old to go to war, so he haunts all the local hangouts, hittin' on the women. Young, old, doesn't matter. He sounds disgusting, if you ask me."

I wrote all this down in my notebook. "Thanks, Dot. As always, you're a pal."

"This means the woman at the docks that night was Frances, right?"

"That's my guess. Sam and I are goin' to see her."

Dot paused. "What else can I do?"

"Nothing right now, but sit tight. If I think of anything, I'll call and let you know." I hung up. Mrs. T was out of the running, not that I'd ever really believed she was in it.

I went back over to Sam. "I talked to Dot." I gave him the scoop on Mrs. T's alibi. "That leaves Frances Corbett. I refuse to believe there's a third woman in this."

"Then I guess we better go talk to her."

* * *

We drove to the boarding house on Ramona in silence. The sky was iron gray, promising snow. It was like the sun didn't want to shine, not when we were on such serious business. After we arrived, Sam parked and turned to me. "You're up."

"Alone? Don't you think we'd have more luck working together?"

He shook his head. "You heard Frances's brother. The landlady doesn't like men. This is your show."

I couldn't argue with his logic. "What do I say?"

Sam reached in the back seat for a copy of the morning *Courier-Express*. He shook it out. "You'll think of something."

"She might be a killer. What happened to that worry?"

He didn't look up. "I'm quite sure a good First Ward girl like yourself can handle anything Blackie Thomas's lady of the moment can throw at her." He paused. "I'll be right here and the housemother is inside. If something happens, make a lot of noise."

I huffed, ignored the bold lettering of the front-page headline, and got out. The story was prob'ly something about the war, but I couldn't be distracted, not if I was about to interview a murder suspect. I also knew Sam was only teasing. If I didn't reappear in a reasonable amount of time, he'd barge in after me, man-hating landlady be darned.

I approached the house, thoughts whirling. Everybody assumed Mr. Tillotson and Frances had been romantically involved. But as much as my illusions had been stripped away over the past week, I didn't buy it. Not that I thought Frances would stay loyal if she was ignored. Everyone swore, however, that she and Mr. Tillotson were spending a lot of time together. I didn't doubt the stories. So what else could be up?

I rang the bell. The door was answered by a short, stout woman with dark hair and a face both red and wrinkled, like one of last fall's apples. "I don't have any rooms."

German, and not long off the boat, judging by her accent. I put my hand on the door to stop it from closing. "I'm not looking for a place to stay. Is

Miss Corbett in?"

"What do you want with her?" The woman's eyes narrowed.

"I'm an old friend of her brother's." If you counted half an hour ago as old. "He gave me a message to pass on to her. He knew men weren't encouraged here, so he asked me to come."

The landlady looked me up and down with as much caution as if she was buying a side of meat at the Broadway Market. "Wait in the hallway." She closed the door and bolted it behind me. "I go get her."

Once she was gone, I slid the bolt back. If I had to make a quick getaway, I didn't want to be fumbling with the lock.

Frances appeared a couple of minutes later. When she saw me, she frowned. "You're the girl from the club. You don't know my brother."

"As a matter of fact, I do. I met him earlier today. He's the one who gave me this address and suggested I drop by."

"Whatever for?"

"Girl talk."

She crossed her arms.

"How'd you know John Tillotson was dead?"

Her eyebrows pulled together and she plucked at her sleeve.

"Your brother says the two of you were an item."

She stamped her foot. "That's a lie. I'd never betray Blackie. Never."

There was too much denial in her voice. Maybe she hadn't cheated on Mr. Thomas with Mr. Tillotson, but there was some other Joe in the mix. "That's not what I've heard."

"Get out. Right now."

"Look, lady." I held up my hands. "I don't really care who you're carryin' on with. Here's the deal. My friend is sittin' in the city jail ready to plead guilty to a crime he didn't commit. On the night of March second, John Tillotson, you, and two men who work for Mr. Thomas were down at the grain elevator canals." I didn't mention Mr. Daletzki. "Three of you walked away. Mr. Tillotson landed in the water. I'm gonna find out which one of you killed him and when I do, I have a friend in the Buffalo Police who'll be interested in the information."

She tossed her head. "I wasn't there. You can't prove it."

"Oh, yes, I can. And if you don't talk to me right this minute, I'm gonna assume it's because you're the culprit. There's a phone on that table." I pointed. "How long do you think it'll take the cops to get here?"

She paled and touched the pearls at her neck.

"You get the picture? You wanna talk here or somewhere we can sit down?"

Frances bit her lip between perfect white teeth. "Come into the sitting room." She led me to a long room that held two chintz couches, a dark wood coffee table littered with women's magazines, and a couple of chairs in matching upholstery. She sat on one of them, legs crossed at the ankles.

I dropped onto the couch nearest her. I did not cross my ankles. "Talk or I'm makin' a phone call."

She played with her pearls, running them through her fingers. "Johnnie and I weren't a couple."

I could barely hear her. "Speak up. You weren't running off together?"

"No. That wasn't it."

I waited. "Well?"

"Blackie is good with the gifts, but not so good with the attention, if you know what I mean." She darted a glance in my direction. "It's like the night you and your cop friend showed up. I always take second place to business."

Considering the condition of her clothes and the nature of the boarding house, which was pretty darn nice, I didn't feel inclined to spare much sympathy. On the other hand, stuff is great, but if you don't get the emotion, what good is it? I twisted my engagement ring. I'd bet if Frances got a rock from her beau, it'd be a lot flashier and she'd treasure it a lot less. "Let me guess, John Tillotson made you feel good."

"Not him." Frances dropped her hands to her lap and stared at them.

"Who then?"

"One of Blackie's lieutenants, a guy named Walt. You don't need to know his last name. He had enough dough to give me nice things, but more importantly, he *saw* me, if that makes any sense." She clenched her hands.

Funny thing is, it did. And the minute she said it, I knew what she and Mr. Tillotson had been talkin' about in that booth. "Mr. Tillotson found out," I said. "He threatened to go to Blackie unless you, or Walt, gave him something, prob'ly cash."

She nodded and wiped her nose with her hand. "The first time was twenty-five dollars. I paid him. What else was I gonna do? If Blackie found out, he'd toss me to the curb on the spot and who knows what he'd do to Walt. I thought that was the end of it."

I reached over to the box of tissues on the table, pulled one, and handed it to her. "Lemme guess, it wasn't."

"Not by a long shot." She blew her nose, a decidedly unladylike sound. "Two weeks later Johnnie wanted another twenty-five. I couldn't get it, so Walt paid. Johnnie found out about that. This last time, he wanted fifty."

"Why'd you go to the grain elevators that night?"

She looked away. After a long pause, she turned her head and lifted her chin. "I heard Ned McDougal tell Blackie that Johnnie wanted a meet to discuss business. Blackie instructed his boys to meet Johnnie and set the record straight. 'I want this done, even if he winds up taking a bath,' Blackie said. I overheard the conversation and decided to follow them."

I longed to find out more about that threat, but I didn't want Frances to be diverted, either. "When you got there, who'd you see?"

"Johnnie, of course. Danny Howley and Ned. Whatever Johnnie had said hadn't done him much good. They were working him over pretty hard."

"You didn't see anyone else?"

"I think there might have been a worker in that little booth I passed up at the top of the canal."

"That's it?"

"I didn't see your friend. I read about him in the paper."

"No one else, you're sure?"

She frowned. "Yes. Who else should I have seen?"

I waved a hand. "Then what happened?"

"Blackie's guys got pretty mad when they saw me. One of 'em, I don't remember which, called me a dumb broad. I'll say this for Johnnie, he stood up for me. He said that was no way to talk to a lady. That earned him a punch in the gut. I don't know why, he was just bein' nice."

I marveled at her stupidity. "You two were seen together, you and Mr. Tillotson. People assumed he was the one you were cheatin' on Blackie with. When you showed up, it confirmed it. Howley and McDougal were standing up for their boss."

"Oh." She didn't sound particularly upset. Then again, Mr. Tillotson was puttin' the squeeze on her and her lover. "Anyway, I left soon after that. I didn't want to see a man being turned into hamburger."

Her story was off. "Mr. Tillotson was alive when you beat it?"

"Yes."

"You didn't hear a splash or see any scattered pipe lying around?"

"No, I went back to the car and told the driver to leave." Her gaze remained fixed on her hands.

I was pretty sure Lee had heard a splash before everybody, including Frances, had vamoosed. "You're sure?"

"How many times do I have to say it?"

I chewed my thumb. "Back up a sec. Blackie definitely said he didn't care if Mr. Tillotson wound up in the canal? I mean, with the bath comment."

This time she looked at me. She blinked, the picture of innocence. Why did it remind me of Cat, standing over a spilled garbage can and lookin' for all the world like he hadn't played a part in the mess? "That's what he said. I...I didn't really think about it. I was focused on the fact I knew where Johnnie would be and could talk to him. I wanted to get him off our backs, me and Walt."

"Did you know what Howley and McDougal were s'posed to be takin' care of?"

Again, that wide-eyed expression. "No, I didn't know anything about Blackie's business."

Baloney. Frances might not be the sharpest knife in the drawer, but she'd been smart enough to listen in. She knew where her bread was buttered, which meant she had a clue what the disagreement was about. And her sequence of events definitely didn't match what I knew. I needed to check with Lee. I stood. "Thanks for bein' honest with me."

"Did I have a choice?"

"Not really." I shouldered my purse and turned to leave.

"Wait." She stood.

I pivoted to face her. "What now?"

Her pretty eyes gleamed and her bottom lip trembled. "Are you gonna tell Blackie? He doesn't need to know all this, right?"

I thought a moment. "It's Sunday afternoon. Do you normally see him, maybe for dinner?"

"He canceled today. He said not to bother coming around until he asked for me."

Despite her cluelessness, or maybe because of it, I felt a stab of pity. "Sounds to me like he already knows."

Chapter Thirty-Two

I returned to Sam's car to find him finished with his newspaper. He stared down the street, fingers tapping the steering wheel. He didn't move when I got in. "What's wrong with you?"

He didn't move. "Captain Finley is looking for me."

"Is that unusual?"

"On a Sunday when I'm not working an active case? Yes. He's apparently called headquarters, my house, and sent a patrol officer to see me." He spared me a glance. "While I was sitting here, a friend of mine on the beat passed. He's the one who told me all this. He said I needed to keep my head down. Finley is of the opinion that the Tillotson case is closed and I'm not to quote, 'muck it up with a lot of unnecessary trouble with Blackie Thomas.'"

I ran over the statement. "You didn't start workin' with me until yesterday, after you left for the weekend. How'd Finley know you'd been to see Mr. Thomas?"

Sam started the engine. "You caught that too, huh? Someone tipped him, someone at that club if not Blackie himself. I'll tell you one thing, though. It makes me more convinced that Liam Tillotson is not our man. If Captain Finley is taking a bribe from Blackie, some unsolved cases we currently have on the books suddenly make a lot more sense."

"What cases?"

"I'll tell you later. What did you learn from Frances?"

I was so caught up in wonderin' about the relationship between a criminal and the head of a police department it took a minute for Sam's question to sink in. "Oh, yeah, get a load of this." I relayed all the dope from my conversation with Frances.

"You don't say." He put his hand on the gear shift. "Never mind cutting her off, I'm surprised this Walt character is still walking around. Unless he isn't and we don't know about it yet. Sounds like John Tillotson tried his hand at a spot of blackmail. We should check on Walt's whereabouts on March second."

The thought hit me like a thunderclap. "He said *did*."

"Come again?"

"Blackie Thomas." I turned to Sam. "When we talked to him at the club, remember? He said, 'when you drink as much as John Tillotson did' or something like that. The point is, he said *did*, past tense. And he said it *before* you mentioned anything about Mr. Tillotson's death."

It only took Sam a second to catch my drift. "He already knew."

"Then who's blowing smoke? I mean, I can't see Mr. Daletzki spilling the beans to him, or Lee, but any of the others would. Heck, maybe Howley and McDougal weren't just roughing up Mr. Tillotson over the money. It could be Blackie didn't appreciate his lady being blackmailed, even if she was soon to be his ex-moll. It's an extra insult, on top of the stealing."

"You're cutting Daletzki out? I'm not."

"I don't see it."

"He might have created that employment opportunity he wanted. He killed Tillotson, went to Blackie and told him as part of the interview."

Sam had a point. "Then why is Mr. Daletzki missing?" I asked.

"I don't know." Sam pulled away from the curb. "I see a few possibilities. He failed his interview, is one. Another is Daletzki witnessed the murder and tried to wheedle money out of Blackie. In either of those cases, a body should turn up."

I mulled this over. "Or he saw the murder and he's hiding 'cause he's scared they'll ice him before he can tell anyone."

Sam dipped his head in agreement.

I thought again about Frances's story. "Say, does the jail have visiting hours on Sunday?"

"Of course. It's a popular day for visitors, in fact. Especially mothers and sweethearts. Why?"

"I gotta talk to Lee. Part of Frances's tale doesn't mesh with what he said and I want to go over it."

Sam shot a glance in my direction. "I don't suppose you'll tell me which part."

"Her order of events. But I can't tell you why it doesn't agree with Lee's account."

"Fair enough."

* * *

We pulled up outside the jail shortly before twelve-thirty. "I'm going to leave you here. I'll be back at one."

I paused, my hand on the door. "Where are you goin'?"

"To talk to a few people. I want to know where Captain Finley's information came from. I'll see you in half an hour."

I got out. Blackmail, theft, cheatin' girlfriends, murder, and now a crooked cop. It was almost enough to make me rethink my career as a private investigator.

Chapter Thirty-Three

I met with Lee in the same room I had before. I tried to argue that I worked for Mr. Williams and deserved the same privacy, but the guards refused since I couldn't produce either a PI license or a copy of my contract. It was annoying, but no matter. Maybe it was my imagination, or perhaps it was 'cause now I felt the increased pressure, but the place seemed more dismal than before, the colors more washed out. I swear it also smelled like my brothers' dirty socks, but that had to be a reflection of my mental state, not reality. Least I hoped it was.

It hadn't been more than twenty-four hours, but Lee looked even paler than he had previously, his prison clothes rumpled like he'd slept in 'em. Maybe he had. Prison prob'ly didn't provide pajamas and slippers. He leaned in, the bags under his eyes obvious. "Hey, Betty."

No sense lying to him. "You look awful. Are you okay? They aren't mistreatin' you are they?"

"Nah, I didn't sleep very well last night. I kept having nightmares of breakin' rocks at Attica or worse." He rubbed his bad leg.

"Dot sends her love."

"I saw her yesterday. We talked." He didn't meet my eyes. "What's the scoop on Dad's murder?"

She'd come after all. I wondered what they'd talked about, but if either of 'em had wanted me to know, they would have told me. "I'm workin' with Detective MacKinnon and we're makin' progress. At least he's not so sure you're the killer."

Lee sucked in his breath. "Betty, remember what Mr. Williams said. How can you be workin' with a cop, 'specially the one who put me here?"

I waved off the words. "You know Sam MacKinnon as well as I do. He's on the up and up. The fact is, he didn't want to arrest you, not that particular night anyway. He wasn't convinced then you did it and he's even less sure now. He's usin' his own time to help me figure this out. It's square."

"Maybe, but I don't have to like it. Or him."

"No, you don't. If he helps get you out, though, you might want to rethink your feelings."

Lee grunted. "What's goin' on?"

I considered how much to tell him, since jail guards were everywhere. No wrinkles on their uniforms. "I can't go into detail. But there are things that don't add up." How to phrase this next bit? "Turns out a lotta people like walking the docks by the canals at night. I wouldn't have thought it was a spot for romance."

"For..." He pulled his eyebrows together a moment, then his expression cleared. "Me, neither."

"And people throwin' things in the water. What do they think it is, a wishing well? At least they should stick around to make their wish. Couples walk away, then splash. I've always thought you should watch the coin fall through the water. Of course, if the woman leaves first, I guess that lets you know how things turned out."

He ran his hand over his thigh, the gray fabric rasping against his palm. "Nah, it's the ones who watch who interest me. They argue, then you hear the splashes, like they made the wish together and both threw something. But yeah, then the girl walks away. The guy leaves less than a minute later and bam, you know how it all ended."

I'd been right. Lee had heard the fight, then the sound of two objects hitting the water, then Frances had left, followed by the other two. "I can't stand peeping toms, either. You know, the folks who hide to watch all the action, then scurry away like rats."

His shoulders twitched. "Wouldn't know about them."

He hadn't seen Mr. Daletzki, either hiding or leaving the scene. I checked the position of the nearest guard. He stood over by the dingy wood door.

I pulled out my notebook and read my info from the interview with Ray. The dock manager hadn't seen anyone vamoose, but he admitted he hadn't been paying attention.

"Is that all you came to talk about?" Lee asked, jolting me back to the present.

"Pretty much." I flipped my pad shut and dropped it into my purse. "If Dot comes later, should she bring you anything?"

His answering smile was weak. "A get out of jail free card?"

"I don't think the city honors board game pieces." I studied my childhood friend. He'd aged ten years in two days, his face lined and gray. I wondered how much of the pain in his leg was real, and how much was brought on by realizing the situation he currently faced. The chairs we used were hard as rocks and this room was as depressing as a house stripped of Christmas decorations. His mattress and cell prob'ly weren't much better.

He looked at his hands, flexing them, and laid them on the flat surface in front of him. He looked up. "Then I guess you'd better bring me a real one. Before Tuesday morning would be good."

That must be when his arraignment was set. I pressed my hand to the glass. "Count on it."

Chapter Thirty-Four

After the guard led Lee away, I sat and thought. I put way more stock in his version of events than Frances's. I knew more than I did the night of the raid. Enough to get one of the toughs to flip? A guard walked over. "Miss, if you're done, you need to leave."

"Just a sec." I weighed my options. I still had a good ten minutes before Sam would be back. "I'd like to see Ned McDougal." He'd been the more cooperative of the two. Of course, I didn't have a red-headed beat cop with a blackjack at my side, but this was the jail. That had to count for something.

The guard hesitated. "Why would you want to see him?"

"I was there the night he was pinched." The guard remained unconvinced, so I added, "Just ask if he'll see me. Tell him the woman who was with the homicide detective would like a chat. He'll know who you mean."

For a moment, it looked like he was gonna argue, but he shrugged. "Fine. Wait here."

I watched the minute hand of the clock tick by. *C'mon. Gimme five minutes.*

The door opened and another guard led McDougal to my station, his walk more of a shuffle, hands cuffed at his waist. The guard pushed him down into the chair. "Be snappy."

McDougal faced me, expression carved from stone, except for the lazy eye. "What do you want?"

Once again, I wondered which eye to follow. Without Sam, I had to come off as confident. I picked the eye lookin' straight at me. "Talk to me about Frances Corbett."

"What about her?"

"I hear she was runnin' around on your boss. Some fella named Walt, one of Mr. Thomas's lieutenants."

"Yeah?"

I didn't move. "If that's the case, I'm surprised a stiff called Walt hasn't turned up in the morgue and that Frances is still walkin' around. I didn't think Mr. Thomas was the type to take his dame cheatin' on him lying down."

McDougal let loose a laugh that sounded more like a bark. "Frances is old news. Her time was over. Blackie had moved on, even if he hadn't gotten around to tellin' her yet. He gave Walt a black eye, just to keep up appearances, but he didn't really care."

If Frances had known, it would have saved her some dough. "You knew it was Walt all along, not John Tillotson?"

"After Walt showed up here to tell me not to worry, I'd make bail, and I saw the shiner, I did. Not before. He gave me the details. I hafta admit, I thought it odd she and Tillotson were together, whatever the scuttlebutt said. He's definitely a step down for Frances, if you know what I mean. But at the time? I wasn't the only one who believed Johnnie was steppin' out of bounds. He and Frances were spendin' a lot of time together."

Walt and Frances had covered their tracks well. "But Mr. Thomas wouldn't have cared? If she'd really been with Mr. Tillotson?"

"Not too much." McDougal rolled his shoulders. "Oh, there might have been the obligatory punch, like with Walt, to remind Johnnie who was boss. But the money was the real issue."

I leaned forward. "Tell me about that."

McDougal sneered. "Why?"

"You're in there, I'm out here."

"Who cares? I'll be out soon enough."

I rested my chin on my fist, trying to look casual. "Maybe."

"Don't play me, girlie. I ain't gonna spend serious time in the slammer over a two-bit gambling charge."

"What if I said I had a witness who saw you kill John Tillotson?"

That wiped the smirk off his face. "You're bluffing."

"No bluff."

"Tillotson's boy couldn't have seen squat. Not from where he was hidin'."

"Who said he was the witness?"

McDougal scoffed. "Ain't he takin' the rap? If I were him, I'd be blaming everybody, including my own mother."

Which proved how little he knew about Lee. "Are you sure you can beat the charge? Have you talked to Miss Corbett or your buddy Howley?"

He scowled. "I've seen Danny in the yard. We got our stories straight. Frances will keep her trap shut if she knows what's good for her."

"And the other witness?" Frances did know what really happened.

"I ain't worried about him."

Did he know about Steve Daletzki or not? I couldn't make up my mind. "Why're you so loyal to Miss Corbett if she's on the way out? What's she ever done for you?"

"It ain't about her. I don't—" He leaned back and wagged a finger at me. "Clever, girlie. Real clever. You almost had me." He clicked his fingers. "Guard. Take me back. I'm done here." He shoved his chair back and stood. "Blackie Thomas has been at this since you were in diapers, sweetheart. Give it up." He let the guard lead him out of the room.

* * *

I lit up a Lucky as soon as I left the jail. Lee hadn't seen Mr. Daletzki. McDougal, Howley, and Frances were playing coy. On one hand, they wouldn't admit it, but on the other, I couldn't rule it out. I needed to get my hands on a copy of the Sunday *Courier-Express* and see if any bodies had turned up. That was something Sam might know, even if he wasn't workin'. I scanned the cars idling at the curb. I spotted his and walked over.

He was inside, reading the paper.

I opened the door. "Hey, mister, would you give me a ride?"

"Get in before you let out all the heat." He tossed the paper in the back seat. "What did you learn?"

"I was right, Frances is lying. Whatever landed in the canal, she put it there—or saw it put there." I settled in and closed the door. "What about you?"

"Captain Finley came into headquarters this morning. He was in quite a state. Demanded to know where I was and what I thought I was doing." Sam pulled away from the curb. "He also had a visitor yesterday."

"Mr. Thomas?"

"No, Blackie wouldn't be that stupid. But the desk sergeant swears it was one of Blackie's lieutenants. The guy had a hell of a shiner."

Walt. "Your mystery man got the black eye from Mr. Thomas, or at least at his orders. He's also the guy who was actually running around with Frances." I told him about my talk with McDougal.

"I can't believe you talked to that goon. Never mind, yes I can. At least there were guards around." He drummed his fingers on the steering wheel. "Thomas was involved in whatever happened."

"He at least knows the details. Go back to Captain Finley. What did he and his guest talk about?"

"The sergeant doesn't know. According to my friend Fred, who was in the bullpen, Finley's interest in my whereabouts coincided with this guy's departure." Sam pulled away and merged into the light Sunday traffic.

I'd run out of nails to chew. "I got the feeling this whole thing hinges on Mr. Daletzki and learning what he saw." I reached back for the paper. The front-page headlines were full of war news, tanks and ships. I didn't want to read that. At least not at the moment. I thumbed to the local section. "How'd you avoid the captain?"

"Save your time, there's nothing there." He stopped at a light. "As for Finley, he'd left. Fred and the rest of the guys swore I'd never been anywhere near the office this weekend and they had no idea where I was." He grinned.

"It helps to have friends."

"That it does. I also asked at HQ whether there had been any fresh stiffs, John Does or otherwise, anywhere in the city in the last twenty-four hours. Nothing. Steve Daletzki is very good at hiding."

"Or he's dead because he tried to bargain his knowledge for a job and the people responsible are good at stashing the body." I tossed the paper aside.

"After all, it took two weeks for Mr. Tillotson to wash up."

"That could be true. Call it a gut feeling, but I don't think Daletzki is pushing daisies." He handed me a slip of paper.

I unfolded it to see an address. "Who lives here?"

"The owner of the shop where Daletzki works. We're going to pay him a visit."

It took fifteen minutes to reach 72 Rohr Street. The house was just north of Polonia. It showed streaks of winter grime. A limp American flag hung beside the front door. There were two stars in the front window, one blue, one gold. Someone in this family had paid the ultimate price in the war. I crossed myself and muttered a quick prayer. Then I joined Sam on the sidewalk. "How do we play this?"

"Technically, the search for Daletzki is your case."

"This guy isn't gonna talk to me."

"If he doesn't, I flash my badge and play backup. After you."

Chapter Thirty-Five

I knocked while I inspected the remains of a sad, wilted Victory garden. "What's the owner's name again?" I asked.

"Ralph Peyton. Yes, I know. Not Polish. I don't know why he set up shop in Polonia."

Sam took up a position behind me while I knocked again. I s'pose to reinforce that I was the one in charge.

A girl about Mary Kate's age answered the door. "Yes?"

"My name is Betty Ahern. I'd like to speak with Mr. Peyton, if he's here."

"Just a minute." She let us in to a clean but plain front room, then went off. "Pa! Someone to see you."

It wasn't long before a heavyset, balding man came out. His fingernails were permanently stained black, but his pants were clean and his shirt was pressed. Maybe he'd just gotten home from church. "Who are you? Not that it matters. I ain't interested in whatever you've got to say, so you can clear off."

"I'm a private investigator." I wished I had a badge or other identification to show. "I'm here about Mr. Steve Daletzki. Are you Mr. Ralph Peyton, owner of Clifton Auto Repair?"

"I am." His gaze flitted between me and Sam. "I've never heard of a woman private dick. Is she for real or is this a hoax?" The last question was directed at Sam.

He nodded. "Very real."

"You her assistant or something?"

"No, sir. Detective Sam MacKinnon, Buffalo PD." He showed his badge.

Mr. Peyton crossed his arms. "Well, I'll be. This war has everything topsy-turvy. Next thing you know, there'll be girl grease-monkeys."

I wanted to tell him that women were already building planes, tanks, and other vehicles, but it wasn't the time. "I understand Mr. Daletzki is one of your employees. At least, your second mechanic said he is unless he blows off work again tomorrow."

"That's right."

"But up until now, he's been working at your garage, yes?"

The shop owner hesitated and again looked to Sam, maybe for guidance.

Sam held up his hands. "She's running the show, not me. I'd answer the question if I were you."

Mr. Peyton cocked his head. "I don't want to get Steve in trouble. Firing him for not showing up is business. He's a decent guy."

Is this what the police went through? "I understand and I wouldn't ask you to do anything like that. The problem is, I think Mr. Daletzki is already in a bind. My goal is to get him out of it."

He stared at me for a good long minute. Finally, he said, "Steve's a good mechanic. Came to me from GM. I understand he got a bum rap there 'cause of some friend of his who is a drunk. Ex-friend, I guess I should say. I wouldn't stay buddies with a guy who shafted me like that. I didn't really need another guy, but I felt bad for him so I brought him on."

I held out the picture of Mr. Tillotson. "This the ex-friend?"

Mr. Peyton took it, looked, and handed it back. "No clue. I never saw him. But Steve talked about him, at least at first. I don't remember the name. Jack, Joe, something that started with J."

I shot a look at Sam, who motioned for me to continue. "When was the last time you saw Mr. Daletzki?"

"Lemme see." Mr. Peyton's forehead wrinkled. "It had to be Friday night before I left around four. I don't go in on Saturdays and the mechanics close for me. Gotta get home to the missus. Steve was workin' on a truck up on the lift. I said good night, I'd see him Monday, and that was all. My other guy called yesterday to say Steve hadn't shown and asked if I had heard anything."

"I take it he hadn't been in touch. Mr. Daletzki, that is." I took out my pad and jotted notes.

"Nope."

"It's kind of rough, isn't it, to fire a guy over one missed day?"

Mr. Peyton lifted an eyebrow. "You obviously have never worked machinery, young lady. It's not like detecting. I need reliable people. Those who skedaddle without an explanation aren't welcome in my shop."

Sam must have noted my expression because he broke in. "Did anyone come around looking for Mr. Daletzki? Strangers? We're specifically interested in a tall man with a scar or one with a lazy eye."

"Don't ring a bell," Mr. Peyton said.

I'd gotten my temper back under control. "Had Mr. Daletzki been nervous at all? Especially these last few weeks. Did he mention seeing anything that, well, scared him?"

Mr. Peyton's confusion showed. "Steve scared? Never met a braver man in my life and that's a fact. He served in the Great War and he'd have gone back this time if recruiters hadn't told him he was too old."

"He never talked about a side job, or an opportunity he was after?"

"We only jabbered about shop business." Again, Mr. Peyton looked from me to Sam. "Say, what's this about?"

"Mr. Daletzki's sister is worried about her brother," I said. "She's hired me to look for him. Think carefully. Do you know of anywhere he would run if he thought he was in trouble? Somewhere safe where he could hide?"

"Why would he need to do that?"

"Never mind why, did he ever mention anything?"

Mr. Peyton ran his hand over his jaw. "Lemme see. Steve don't have kids, but his sister does, I'm pretty sure. We were talkin' about boys one day, the lengths they go to run from their mammas when they get into trouble. Steve said his nephews were pretty good, but they weren't a patch on him. He'd had a bolt hole as a kid no one could find."

I glanced at Sam. "Did he say where?"

"Not directly." Mr. Peyton stuck his hands in his pockets. "Just that it was a place where a good Catholic boy would normally never dream of going, so no one would ever think to look there."

Chapter Thirty-Six

Sam got back into the car. He hadn't stopped grumbling since we had left Mr. Peyton's house. "What a colossal waste of time."

"Maybe not." I stared off into the distance. "If you were looking for a, uh, certain kind of woman, where would you go?"

He turned to me, paused a moment, then a grin spread over his face. "What kind of woman?"

"A, um, you know."

"No, I haven't the foggiest clue," he said in an innocent voice.

My cheeks warmed. "A woman you could, you know, be intimate with for a single night in exchange for money."

His grin turned a little wicked. "You mean a prostitute?"

I folded my hands in my lap.

"Good God, Betty. Can't you even say the word?"

I shot a glare at him. "Don't take the Lord's name in vain. Anyway, what kind of girl do you take me for?" I fussed with my purse. "It's not like the boys in my life don't look at pictures or those kinds of things. Heck, I've seen the magazines that Sean, and Tom, and Lee passed around when they were growing up. But that's as far as it went, least I'm pretty sure."

"What's your point?"

I sighed. "They were talkin' one day, messin' around. I think some other kid they knew had gotten in trouble with the cops, tried to hide, and been found pretty quick. Sean said, 'If I was gonna hide from the police, I'd go to the red-light district. Nobody'd look for a guy who'd been a Catholic church altar-server there.' When you asked Mr. Peyton about where Mr.

Daletzki would hide, what did he say?"

"A place no one would think to look for a good Catholic boy."

I spread my hands. "It can't hurt, right?"

"Nope." Sam pulled away and made a quick left. "The best place for that is down at the foot of Main Street. There are a lot of flophouses and working girls in that area. They cater to the crews from the lake boats bringing grain and iron ore into the city." He slanted a look in my direction. "Your brother is wrong, you know."

"About what?"

"We would look there."

We didn't talk much as Sam drove. I didn't know what to expect to see once we got there. Scantily clad women beckoning to the men on the street, prob'ly. But when we reached our destination, the area was silent, the only sound the lonely cry of gulls and the skittering of trash as it tumbled down the sidewalk ahead of a stiff breeze.

I tugged my coat closer. "Where are all the people?"

Sam came around the car. "It's Sunday afternoon. I don't think there's a lot of action right about now. It's a trade that thrives at night." He swept the street with his gaze. "This way." He headed toward a bluish building with a white door and an empty flower pot on the window ledge.

A blowzy woman with frizzy blonde hair answered the knock. She clutched a bathrobe around her neck and fuzzy blue slippers covered her feet. "Well, hello, handsome. We don't open for business for a few hours, but I could make an exception."

Sam showed her his badge.

She pursed her lips in a pout, but her expression stayed slightly amused and coy. "Are you gonna bust me, sweetie?"

"Not my department." He pulled Mr. Daletzki's picture out and held it toward her. "Have you seen this man recently? By 'recently' I mean the last two days."

She studied it. "Who is he?"

"Someone we want to talk to."

For the first time, she realized I was standing behind and slightly to the left of Sam. "Pardon me for saying so, but you don't look like you belong down here."

While the thought of what could be goin' on inside the house scandalized me, I knew this was part of a private dick's life. "I'm a private investigator on a missing person case."

"Well, I'll be. Good for you." The woman winked. "Who's missing?"

"The man in the photograph. We'd be grateful for any information you can give us."

She took the picture and gave it another look. "No, he's not one of mine or any girls here." She handed it back.

Sam slipped it into his pocket. "What about one of the other houses? Maybe someone saw him on the street a couple of nights ago? It most likely would have been Friday."

She struck a pose and loosened her grip on the bathrobe, revealing a hint of creamy skin and a glimpse of a full bosom in a bright red bra. "Hmm, let me think."

I fought to keep my cool. The thought occurred to me that she was playing things up for Sam and maybe teasing me in the process.

As if she read my mind, she glanced at me and winked again. "Like I said, he's not one of ours. But if you want to ask around, I recommend talking to Shirley next door and Ruth in the green house across the street."

"Only them?"

She grinned. "Ruth and Shirley, they're building their clientele, if you take my meaning. Your missing man would've been more likely to find someone who was...available." She ran a foot up and down Sam's leg. The garters that held up her stockings matched her bra. "I don't usually take strangers myself, but, like I said, I could make an exception."

He lifted his fedora. "I appreciate the offer, but I don't think that would be wise. Good day, miss."

With a silvery laugh, the blonde closed the door.

Shirley-next-door was a short, curvy girl with jet black hair and striking blue eyes. She didn't bother holding her robe closed. I turned around and only with great effort could I keep myself from pressing my hands to my cheeks, which I'm sure were flaming red. After some banter with Sam, laced with naughty laughter, she denied recognizing Mr. Daletzki and shut her door.

Sam and I checked for traffic and crossed Main Street. "Are you sure you're cut out for this?" he asked. "You can't turn around and act the blushing maiden."

"How can you be so calm? That woman practically threw herself at you."

He shrugged. "I'm not here to arrest them and my personal opinion of their profession is irrelevant. They're sources of information. If you're gonna be an investigator, you have to go where the dirt is."

"I guess I'm surprised they're so willing to talk to you."

"I have been told I'm a handsome devil and quite the charmer." He chuckled. "I don't work Vice. I'm not asking them to give up names, just whether they've seen a man in a picture. I'm sure if I went after details, the results would be different. I'm also not demeaning them or their profession. They aren't just prostitutes and ways to find what you need, Betty. They're people. Remember that, treat them fairly, and you'll get farther."

I considered his words. He was right, of course. If Jesus could pardon an adulteress and let one of 'em wash his feet, the least I could do was ask a couple of questions.

Sam knocked on Ruth's door. We waited longer than at the other two houses. He knocked again, this time with a little more force. "This is Sam MacKinnon from the Buffalo PD. I'd like to talk to Ruth, if she's here."

The front windows were covered by dark, heavy curtains, but one of them twitched a little. Not enough to let me see inside, but enough to tell me someone was there. "Knock again. Tell 'em I'm here, too."

"Why?"

"I think someone else is in there."

Sam complied.

The front door cracked open, just enough to let us see a slender young woman with chestnut hair cut in a bob and big, dark eyes framed by impossibly thick, dark lashes. She wasn't wearing makeup, but she didn't need it. I could tell from the sliver of her face that was visible she had perfect

215

skin. "What do you want?"

I pushed my way forward. "We're looking for Steve Daletzki."

"He's not here." She slammed the door shut.

Sam and I exchanged a look. She hadn't even pretended not to know the name. I reached over and banged on the door. "Ruth, c'mon. I just wanna talk to you. I don't wanna cause you or Mr. Daletzki any trouble. But this is important. Open up."

"Are you sure he's inside?" Sam said in an undertone.

"Either that, or she knows where he is." I waited, hand raised. Right before I pounded again, the door opened.

Ruth didn't wear a bathrobe. She was clad in a plain blue dress, her feet bare. I'd been right about her perfect complexion, all roses and cream, with the faintest blush on her cheeks. She held the door open enough that we could see her, but not inside. "Why are you lookin' for Steve? He hasn't done nothing."

"We know." I heard a soft thud, maybe a footstep, from inside. "His sister sent me. She's worried about him. To tell the truth, so am I. 'Cause if I'm right, he's in deep water. I'm here to offer him a life jacket."

She bit her lip and threw a look over her shoulder. "Who'd you say you were?" she asked, looking at me.

"My name's Betty Ahern. I've met Mr. Daletzki before. At his work."

She nodded. "Wait a second." She closed the door. Voices rumbled, but no distinct words carried. Less than a minute later, Ruth reopened it. "Come in. Leave your shoes in the hall."

Sam and I entered and kicked off our shoes, lining them up on the mat. The interior of the house was dark and warm. I detected a spicy, flowery scent, something that struck me as exotic. The furniture was all dark wood and the wallpaper a deep maroon.

Ruth led us to a back room filled with furniture boasting tapestry fabrics. A few expensive knick-knacks were on the polished tables. At least they looked expensive, like the pictures I'd seen of those fancy eggs the Russian nobility had before the collapse of the monarchy. The lights were low and the exotic scent was stronger. I hadn't known what to expect of a house of ill repute, but this was definitely fancier than anything I'd thought of.

As my eyes adjusted to the low light, I noticed a figure sitting on a chair on the far side of the room. He didn't look like a Joe on the run. His clothes were clean and someone had been keepin' him fed. I crossed the room, my hand out. "Hello, Mr. Daletzki. I've been lookin' for you."

Chapter Thirty-Seven

After we sat down, Ruth disappeared and returned a few minutes later with a tray full of steaming porcelain cups decorated with delicate flowers. I took mine and sipped out of politeness. "Real coffee? How'd you get that?"

She smiled, slyly. "I have my sources."

Whether it was coupon-trading or black-market, I didn't want to know. The joe was too good. It warmed my hands, which had gotten chilled in our search. Before the silence could get awkward, I spoke. "How long have you been here, Mr. Daletzki?"

"Since Saturday morning. I never went to work. Maybe I should have let my sister know, but I couldn't risk it." He held his cup with shaky hands.

"How do you know Miss, uh, what's your name?" I asked.

She shook her head. "Just call me Ruth."

I didn't get the secrecy, but whatever she wanted. "How do you know Ruth?"

Mr. Daletzki set down his coffee. "She and I are cousins. Well, sort of. What is it, Ruthie, second cousins once removed?"

"It's all the same as far as I'm concerned," she replied.

"We've known each other since we were kids. She had a falling out with most of the family, but I stuck by her." He reached out and patted her arm. "To tell the truth, I always felt closer to Ruthie than my sister. We've helped each other out of any number of scrapes. When I needed to lay low, of course I came here. We don't have the same last name, see, so no one knows we're related."

"And as you told your boss, no one would look for a good Catholic in a house of ill repute." I looked at Ruth.

She didn't blush. "That was our logic, but it didn't work. You showed up, didn't you?"

"I'm Catholic myself and I have brothers. They may be altar boys, but that doesn't mean they're always pure as the driven snow." I turned back to Mr. Daletzki. "We found your knife down at the grain elevator canals. You were there the night John Tillotson got killed, weren't you?"

He stared at the carpet. His silence was answer enough.

"Why did you go down there?" Sam asked. "You might as well look up. You aren't going to find an answer in your socks. Did you arrange to meet John Tillotson?"

"No." Even in the silent room, Mr. Daletzki's voice was hardly able to be heard.

"Come again? A little louder this time. We're all friends here."

Mr. Daletzki cleared his throat. After a moment, he looked up. "I tailed John down there." He cracked his knuckles. "I warned him. I said unless he got me a piece of the action, it was gonna be ugly."

I studied him. No doubt he was angry. I remembered the dent in that desk blotter and I studied his fists. Strong hands, callused and chapped. The mitts of a man who could wrestle heavy machinery into place. He'd have no problem with a human, 'specially a drunk. "What kind of action?"

"I don't know."

"I find that hard to believe."

Mr. Daletzki glared at me, fire in his eyes. "I knew he had *something* goin' on, but not what, all right? No matter how bad things were, John always had money. Hard cash, not coupons or stuff like that. Even after he was fired from GM, we'd get together and he'd always pay for the first round. But no matter what I said, he wouldn't tell me where he got it. 'It's not a good racket, Steve. I'm lookin' for an escape hatch. You don't want a piece of this.' But I did!" He clenched his hands and Ruth got up to sit on the arm of his chair so she could be beside him. He took a deep breath. "It was shady, I figured that much. But when you gotta put food on the table, and your sister is pinching every penny she can to make ends meet, well, who cares?"

Sam put down his cup. "You thought you would meet Tillotson on the docks to talk. Did you think you could beat it out of him?"

Mr. Daletzki ran a hand over his face. "No, I swear it wasn't like that. I went over to talk to him at his house. I had to give it one more shot. This was earlier in the month, a few weeks ago."

"March second?" I asked.

"I guess it could have been. I don't remember the exact date. Anyway, when I got to the First Ward and John's street, I saw him come out of his house. He looked...twitchy. As though he didn't want anyone to see him. He'd flipped the collar of his coat up and he scurried down the street in the opposite direction. I decided to follow him. I was surprised as anyone would be when we ended up down at the grain elevators."

"You talked to him there," I said.

Mr. Daletzki shook his head. "I was gonna. But two other guys showed up before I could say or do anything, so I ducked outta sight. I wasn't more than five feet away, so I saw 'em pretty clear. They gave me the creeps. The way they carried themselves and the way they talked. I didn't see any weapons, but I was sure at least one of 'em had a piece."

He was silent for so long I thought Sam or I was gonna have to nag him again. Ruth beat me to it. "Out with it, Steve. Tell 'em what you told me. All of it."

He looked at her, then back to us. "I don't know why I didn't leave. But I followed 'em down the docks where I hid behind some crates. I didn't think they saw me. The two toughs were...not angry, but I got the feeling they weren't happy. Or more accurately, whoever had sent them was the angry one and they were the messengers. 'Three times, Johnnie. Three. You know that don't make the boss happy. When he ain't happy, none of us is.'"

Sam cut his eyes toward me. He leaned forward. "What did Tillotson say?"

"How he was sorry, it wouldn't happen again, he'd make it up. You know, the usual baloney a guy says in that situation. But you know it's just talk and nothing's gonna change." Mr. Daletzki paused. "Then the two others told him it wasn't just the money, John had horned in on the boss's dame.

John denied that, said it was some other guy, and anyway, the boss always said women were a dime a dozen, so why would he care? 'It's a matter of principle, Johnnie.' Then he punched John in the gut, hard. I crouched down real low, but they must've heard me 'cause one of 'em said, 'What's that? The night watch? I thought I saw someone earlier,' and the other said it wasn't important. Right about then, the woman showed up."

"Did you see her?" I asked.

Mr. Daletzki nodded. "She was blonde and wore a dark coat with a fur collar. There were a couple of swanky rings on her fingers and I thought maybe she had a manicure. She wore shoes with high heels, but I got the impression she wasn't real comfortable in 'em, 'cause she didn't walk too good. Boy, did she lay into Johnnie when she got there. All about him being a scum bucket for prying into her affairs, and how he wasn't gonna ruin it for her, and he'd better stop demanding money or she'd have her man take care of it. I gathered she meant the boss and this was the dame."

It wasn't exactly right, but I couldn't see a reason for setting Mr. Daletzki straight. "Then what happened?"

"One of the guys said to the woman, 'You need to get outta here." She said something about how she could protect herself and the same guy said, 'It ain't about you.' Then they worked John over, hard. I ducked down, but I could hear the punches and John gasping. The woman said he deserved it for putting his oar in where it didn't belong. I didn't watch. I wanted to get away, but they were blockin' the best exit. I figured I had to wait it out."

"But it didn't occur to you to help your friend," Sam said, voice dry.

Mr. Daletzki's peepers widened. "Are you kidding? I wasn't gonna get mixed up in that and get myself pounded to mincemeat. I'd gone there for dough, not a fight."

I shook my head. "Didn't it occur to you that these two toughs were exactly why Mr. Tillotson didn't want to get you involved? That he knew they were dangerous and was tryin' to keep you out of it?"

Mr. Daletzki gaped. Obviously, he hadn't, not then and not now.

"Go on," I said. "What happened next?"

He slugged back some coffee. "Got any whiskey, Ruthie?" He turned back to Sam and me. "The beating went on for a bit. I heard the dame egging them on. Then I heard a crunch, not like a fist hitting flesh, more like, I don't know, one hard surface hitting another. Then a splash. 'What the hell did you do?' one of the men said. 'The boss ain't gonna like that. He wanted him alive. Scram, now.' I heard a tumble of metal. Then a bunch of footsteps. I waited a few minutes and risked a look. Everybody was gone. I hot-footed it down the dock, but I could see someone was in the office, so I jumped the fence and beat it back home."

Sam and I exchanged a look. "Didn't you wonder where Tillotson had gone?" Sam asked.

Mr. Daletzki's face had a stupid, dazed expression. "I figured he left with the others."

"A man who takes the kind of beating you described doesn't just walk off on his own power," I said. "He'd have been lyin' in a heap. Didn't you wonder what made the splash?"

Mr. Daletzki didn't answer, but the expression remained. He was either dumber than he looked or he was a better actor than Bogart.

"Why'd you run to Ruth to hide?" Sam asked.

Mr. Daletzki blinked furiously. "Last Friday, one of them, a man with a scar, showed up at the garage. He said they'd knew I was a friend of Johnnie's, they'd seen us together before. They'd been lookin' for me. He said he'd seen me leave the docks that night. Anyway, he said if I knew what was good for me and my family, I'd keep my mouth shut unless I wanted trouble. The way the guy kept hitting his palm with his fist, I didn't have to ask what kind of trouble. It scared me so much I watched to see if I'd been followed home. I didn't see anyone, so I took off the next morning. If I had seen someone, I'd have called Ruthie sooner. I don't want any trouble for Margaret."

Ruth returned with a glass of whiskey, which she handed to Mr. Daletzki. "Are you gonna give him some protection? Can't you see he's in danger?"

"I'm sure he is." Sam stood. "I'm also not convinced the tale I heard was the truth, at least not all of it. The best thing you can do, Mr. Daletzki, is stay in your hole. No one knows you're here except Miss Ahern and me." He handed over a small white card. "If you have anything else you want to say, you can find me there. Good afternoon." He lifted his fedora.

I got up and prepared to follow Sam out.

"I didn't kill him, John, if that's what you're thinking," Mr. Daletzki said. "Yes, I wanted to beat him silly for everything he's done to me, but I didn't kill him. You gotta believe me."

I gave him a careful look. He looked like a desperate man, but I'd seen too many movies where men begging the cops to believe them turned out guilty as sin. "Just stay here, Mr. Daletzki. We'll be in touch."

As I exited the room, I could hear him, almost sobbing, and Ruthie's comforting whispers. When I thought of Mrs. Wiese and her sharp-toned voice, I figure he might not only be safer here, he'd get more sympathy, too. No matter how much she was worried about her brother, I suspected he was in for a tongue-lashing when he got home.

Chapter Thirty-Eight

I went outside, pulled out a Lucky, and waited for Sam. He met me on the snow-crusted sidewalk outside Ruth's house. "Do you believe him?" I asked.

He lit a cigarette and held out his lighter so I could do the same. "I'm not sure. What do you think?"

I blew out a cloud of smoke and started back to the car. "I feel good about the first part of the story. He went to talk to Mr. Tillotson, followed him to the grain elevators, and witnessed the beat-down. The part I'm not so sure about is the very end."

"If he heard the splash the way he said, how could he not know it was the sound of Tillotson falling, or being pushed, into the canal?"

"Right. Did the others leave their victim groaning on the dock and then Mr. Daletzki finished him off outta spite?" I ashed my smoke. "What do you make of the metal sound?"

"If a length of pipe was the murder weapon, he probably heard the pipe rolling around after one was grabbed, or possibly the pile was kicked around so no one would notice a missing piece." Sam exhaled a cloud of smoke. "Or it's a false trail and Tillotson was bashed with something else. The pipe is there to make us *think* that was the weapon so we'd stop looking. That's not the sound that interests me though."

"He only mentioned one splash. Lee was pretty clear he heard two."

Sam pointed his cigarette at me. "Your buddy would have heard two because he stuck around 'til the body was disposed of. If Steve Daletzki only heard one, maybe he *caused* the second splash."

"Which of course he wouldn't mention." I tapped my foot. "Was it just me, or was the bit about Howley catchin' up to him at the garage kinda thin?"

"A little. First Daletzki swore up and down he wasn't seen. But then magically this goon shows up at his job and threatens him? I think it more likely he got scared, ran off before everybody left, and was spotted. Or he wasn't as sneaky as he thought and they saw him leave."

"You think they stuck around? After all, they did mention hearing a noise."

"Maybe. When you've got that kind of muscle, you don't care if someone sees you. You'll just intimidate them later. It wasn't until the murder happened that they were motivated to find Daletzki."

I pulled my coat collar close against a sudden gust of wind. "Or Mr. Daletzki is just flat lying."

"There is that." He brushed a thin layer of snow from the windshield. "Let's go before I get a ticket."

I laid my hand on the door handle. "I don't s'pose we can dredge the canal for the length of pipe?"

"I don't think I could get the approval. Not just for the cost of a frogman, but I'm not supposed to be working this case." He flicked away his cigarette.

"What are we missin'?"

"I don't know, but it's right beyond my fingertips."

I stared off into the distance, my mind churning through the facts. "Captain Finley warned you off the case, you said."

"Yes. I told you, I think he got a visit from Blackie's lieutenant."

"You mean Walt? What's his story?"

"Walt Reynolds. He started as a foot soldier, you might say. He's worked his way up to be one of Blackie's junior right-hand men."

"He ran around with Mr. Thomas's girl, but he's still standing. You think it's 'cause Mr. Thomas was ready to ditch Frances and find himself another woman."

"That's right. I know Frances is still at that boarding house, but it could be Blackie hasn't gotten around to having her evicted yet."

An idea started to form. "You thought the higher-ups accepted Lee as the culprit pretty fast. If Mr. Thomas sent his boy to see Captain Finley after we talked, wouldn't you say it sounds like he was tryin' to protect someone? Why cut it off early? Why not let you keep investigating?"

Sam rubbed his chin and stared at the gulls swooping through the iron-gray sky. "Logical. Who on that dock is worth protecting? Two toughs? A woman he was cutting loose? It doesn't make sense. It sure wouldn't be Steven Daletzki. If anything, he'd be another patsy."

"Mr. Thomas could be covering for himself. After all, he sent Howley and McDougal." I dropped my cigarette butt and ground it underfoot. "That means he's just as guilty, right? What do you call it?"

"Conspiracy to commit murder. He didn't do it, but he gave the order." Sam thought a moment. "That could be it. Howley and McDougal weren't supposed to kill Tillotson, just rough him up. Given that Tillotson owed him money, that makes more sense. Things got out of hand, Tillotson ends up in the canal. Howley and McDougal had to have seen Daletzki arrive or leave. They told their boss there might be a witness. I'm not sure how they knew him."

"Like Mr. Daletzki said. They saw the two men together. Remember, Delores at GM said she'd seen a guy we know was Howley. He coulda recognized Mr. Daletzki from there."

"It's possible. Anyway, Blackie tracked Daletzki down, maybe through Captain Finley, and Blackie sent his guys to put the squeeze on him. We know what you saw, keep your yap shut or else. That kind of thing. Daletzki didn't hear the second splash because he left before the clean up, which was when the murder weapon was thrown in the water."

I could see it happening. "Why let his goons get picked up? Why not hand the cops Mr. Daletzki?"

"We already have Lee Tillotson," Sam said. "Remember, we got Howley and McDougal at a numbers raid. Vice, not Homicide. All Blackie has to do is keep pressure on Captain Finley to stall us until young Mr. Tillotson is safely convicted and out of the way. Blackie isn't protecting Frances, he's keeping his men, and by extension himself, out of a murder rap." He opened the car door and got in.

I slid into the passenger seat. "Back to the jail?"

"No." Sam started the engine. "How would you like to meet the head of the Buffalo Police Homicide Division?"

* * *

Captain Finley lived on Koester Street in South Buffalo. It was a slightly higher-class neighborhood than the First Ward, but not as swanky as Delaware Park. If the weather were better, the Finley place would be neat, with the bushes trimmed and the shutters washed. Right now, it was looking a little dirty and ragged. Around the back, I could see a fenced-in spot for a Victory garden. There were two blue stars in the front window, so I knew he had at least two sons.

"I'm guessing you want me to stay silent, huh?" I asked.

Sam gave me a tight grin. "As silent as you ever are. It's not every day a man gets to accuse his superior of colluding with a known criminal."

"Are you sure you want to do this?" I asked. "Seems to me you don't have a leg to stand on."

"I don't have hard evidence. But remember those open homicides I mentioned? They involve other local gang leaders, people who might have stood in the way of Blackie Thomas expanding his operations."

I thought about it. "The unsolved murders make a lot more sense if Mr. Thomas is paying off Captain Finley in exchange for the Homicide Department looking the other way."

"Right. I'm not the lead investigator, but it's been bugging me that no one seems to have any interest in pursuing these cases. Especially since the captain is so uptight about his close rate." He studied the house. "I'm willing to risk the bluff."

"Anything I should know about the captain before we see him?"

"He's married, two boys overseas. I believe he has a daughter, but she's got her own family and lives somewhere in the Southtowns. Mrs. Finley is a nice woman and I doubt she has any idea of what is going on. Finley himself is a bit of a coward. He's not fond of confrontation and he's ambitious. Definitely the kind of man to take the easy way out, as long as it didn't pose a threat to him."

"Or his family?"

Sam went up to the dark blue door. "No, to him personally. I think he'd throw his wife and children to the dogs if it would help him get ahead."

Great guy. I stood behind Sam as he knocked.

A kind-faced woman who reminded me of an older Joan Fontaine answered the door. "Detective MacKinnon, isn't it? I remember you from the Christmas party."

Sam doffed his fedora. "Yes, ma'am. Good to see you. Is the captain in by any chance?"

"He's in the den, reading the paper and listening to the radio. Who is the young lady?"

I held out my hand. "Betty Ahern. Pleased to meet you, Mrs. Finley."

Sam tilted his head in my direction. "Miss Ahern is a friend of mine. Do you think we could talk to Captain Finley for a bit?"

"I don't see why not." She bustled through a living room crammed with furniture and knick knacks. The floral pattern on the upholstery did not match the striped wallpaper. We went down a narrow hallway to a smallish room at the back of the house.

Bookshelves filled with thick volumes lined the walls. I noticed a layer of dust on the books. A roll-top desk occupied one corner. The captain sat in the leather chair that took up the other. Hanging over the chair was a brass standing lamp next to a table, the newspaper lying on it, still folded. A wood-cased radio broadcasting some talk program stood next to it. Whatever his wife said, Captain Finley didn't seem to be much of a reader. At the sight of us, he used the paper to cover a glass holding two fingers of whiskey.

"That nice Detective MacKinnon and a Miss Ahern are here to see you, dear." She turned to us. "Can I get you anything to drink? Coffee, water, tea?"

From my first look at Captain Finley, I wasn't impressed. Standing he'd be a little shorter than Pop. His hair was thinning and his face puffed at the jowls. It was as though someone had taken Orson Wells, ripped out half his hair, and made him pack on twenty pounds. He didn't have Wells's intense eyes, though.

"I'm busy, Helen, I can't..."

Mrs. Finley had disappeared, prob'ly to fetch a cup of everything she'd just offered.

A flash of annoyance crossed Captain Finley's face. "It's Sunday, Detective. There better be a good reason for you bothering me at home."

"Oh, there is, sir." Sam held out his arm toward me. "Where are my manners? This is Betty Ahern, a friend of mine. Miss Ahern, meet my boss, Captain Finley."

"Please to make your acquaintance." I offered my hand.

He ignored it. "What the devil do you want, MacKinnon? Did the men at the station tell you I've been looking for you?"

"They have, sir. That's the reason I'm here," Sam said.

"You aren't still causing problems with the Tillotson case, are you? That one's over and done. Leave it alone, Detective."

At that moment, Mrs. Finley came in with a tray holding three empty willow-patterned teacups with saucers and what were prob'ly milk and sugar. "We didn't have coffee, I'm afraid. Not enough for three. So I put on the kettle for tea. I hope that is all right. Unless you'd like a Coke, my dear? I might have one dusty bottle somewhere." She smiled at me.

"Tea will be swell, Mrs. Finley. Thank you," I said.

She frowned at her husband. "George, why don't you go into the front room to talk? It's rude, not being able to offer your guests a chair. I've always said—"

"They're just leaving, Helen." The captain snapped at his wife, but his gaze never left Sam's face.

"Why did you let me go and make tea? For heaven's sake—"

Captain Finley's face reddened. "Be quiet. Go do some knitting or something. Don't shove your nose in where it doesn't belong."

Mrs. Finley's face crumpled, so I rushed to soothe her. "Don't worry about us, ma'am. Sam...er, Detective MacKinnon and I don't mind standing. I really don't think we'll be here long."

"I'll leave you folks alone to talk." She still had an injured expression, but she managed a polite tone as she closed the door.

Captain Finley banged his fist on the chair arm. "For the last time, Detective. The Tillotson case is closed. I don't care what this hussy next to you has said. If it were up to me, I'd charge her with wasting police time. As for you, there are other cases...unless you'd like me to bust you back to patrol for insubordination."

"I think you want to hear what I have to say, sir." Sam faced his boss. "I don't think the Tillotson investigation is over at all. In fact, I think we're going to have egg all over our faces if we let the DA take Liam Tillotson to trial."

"Oh really?" Scorn dripped from the captain's words. "Then why'd you arrest him?"

"Because you ordered me to. I always thought the case was too flimsy. And now I've learned there were other people on the dock that night, all of whom had valid motives to kill John Tillotson."

I marveled at Sam's ability to keep his tone mild.

Captain Finley thrust out his chin. "Like who?"

"Frances Corbett, Blackie Thomas's soon-to-be-ex-girlfriend. Two of Thomas's enforcers, men named Danny Howley and Ned McDougal. The latter two are cooling their heels in the city jail. Vice nabbed them in a numbers sting this weekend. They beat Tillotson on Blackie's orders, trying to recover some money, and may have gone a little overboard."

Some of the red faded from Captain Finley's face.

"Oh, and a man named Steve Daletzki. He used to be friends with John Tillotson. Daletzki lost a good job at GM because of an incident where he covered for Tillotson's drunken behavior and he has quite the chip on his shoulder." Sam paused. "There's something else I'd like to know."

Captain Finley said nothing.

"The same people who told me you were looking for me said you had a visitor. Why'd Walt Reynolds come to see you?"

That did it. The captain's face went from red to the color of new milk. "I don't know what you're talking about."

I wanted to say something, but the drama in front of me was too intense.

A word from me could break Sam's rhythm and I could tell he had his boss exactly where he wanted him.

"Come on, sir. Yes, you do." Sam looked around. "Here's what I think. You want to be mayor. We all know that. But first, you need to be chief of police and to get there, you need a stellar record. After that, a mayoral campaign will cost money and lots of it. That's where Blackie Thomas comes in."

Finley tried to bluster. "Thomas can't help me close cases."

"No, sir, but he can give you cash." Sam clasped his hands in front of him, looking for all the world like my fifth-grade teacher, Miss Darnly, delivering a lecture. All he was missin' was her gray hair and spectacles. "You strike a deal. You let Blackie slide on some of the activities he needs to complete to get ahead in the criminal hierarchy or even direct attention away from him. In return, he promises to fund your campaign when the time comes. Maybe he's already given you money to sock away."

"What possible things could I give Thomas a pass on? That would be Vice, not Homicide." Again, there was a note of defiance in the captain's words, but also an unmistakable layer of fear.

"The murder of Clarence Biggins three months ago. He ran another numbers racket on the West Side. We found him in his car with a slug in his chest. I believe that one's still unsolved. The death of Eugene Trawley last month. Trawley ran protection and racketeering. The official word is he was mugged, but noon on a Sunday is a strange time for a mugging, wouldn't you say?"

I watched as Finley's face went from pale to slightly green. I wanted to take notes. Sam was giving a masterful performance.

"And, of course, there's John Tillotson. He worked for Thomas. I have reliable information that Tillotson was dipping into his employer's coffers. People also believed he was fooling around with Blackie's current mistress. That turned out to not be true, but it was worse. He was blackmailing her. I doubt Blackie cares much for the girl, but he wouldn't want to be embroiled in such an ugly situation. Knowing all this, you told Blackie not to worry about any of his people getting hauled in by Homicide. You'd make sure someone else took the rap, and Liam Tillotson made a perfect fall guy."

"You're...you're mad, completely out of your mind. I'll have you in front of a review board tomorrow," Captain Finley said in a hoarse voice.

Sam had described his superior officer as a coward and I could see why. Under the onslaught of facts, and left alone to face the music, he crumbled. He couldn't even muster enough bravado to talk his way out of the corner he was in.

Sam took a step toward him. "No, you won't. Because if you do, there's a chance I'll tell the board exactly what I've just said. And trust me, if you don't think they'll be all over this story, you're deluding yourself. Nothing Blackie Thomas can do will help you. But if you come clean right now, maybe—just maybe—I'll spin it to make you more of a victim and you might at least be able to save your pension. Either way, I think you can kiss promotion and the mayor's office good bye. What's it going to be...*sir?*" He tacked on that last word like he was driving the last nail into the captain's coffin.

I held my breath. I didn't expect Captain Finley to go down without at least a little fight, but Sam was clearly in control.

The police captain didn't disappoint. "See here, MacKinnon. You can't come into my own home, with some...civilian, and treat me like this. Who is she, anyway? Some tart from down Main Street? What did you do, pay her off to level some outlandish accusation if I don't go along with you?"

Sam motioned me to speak.

"My name is Betty Ahern, sir," I said. "I'm a private investigator. I asked Detective MacKinnon for help 'cause I'd uncovered information I thought the police should know." I straightened my shoulders and looked at Sam. "If you need me as a witness in front of that board, I'll be happy to tell 'em what I know."

Silence filled the room, broken only by the faint tick-tock of a grandfather clock somewhere in the house. Sam and I kept our stares on Captain Finley. I could see his thoughts, running around like rats scurrying back to their holes after the trash cans were put away.

He caved. "I didn't have a choice. I swear." He ran a hand over his face, which had aged ten years in ten seconds. "It started harmlessly enough. Yes, I was toying with the idea of running for mayor in a few years. I met

Thomas at a party, about a year ago. I told him my plans. I knew I'd need money, but I could deal with that later. 'I can help you,' he said. 'Always willing to back a good horse.' That night he wrote a check for five hundred dollars."

Sam hadn't budged. "Let me guess, you didn't see the strings."

"It was little things, at first. Could I tip him off when Vice was planning to raid one of his games? He passed on information on other gambling organizations. We were taking down criminals, what was one tip?"

"But it didn't stay small."

Captain Finley shook his head. "The first was the Biggins murder. One of our leads pointed to Blackie's organization, if not to him directly. His man, this Walt Reynolds, paid a call. He gave me a hundred dollars cash and said there'd be more if the trouble just faded away. It's not like Biggins was a Delaware Park notable." He swallowed. "Then Trawley, which was much the same situation."

Mrs. Finley had never come back with the tea, but I didn't care. "What about Mr. Tillotson?"

He leaned forward and held his head in his hands. "One morning, I stopped for coffee at Moe's diner across from headquarters and Reynolds was there. He said the Tillotson case could be inconvenient for Mr. Thomas. He'd heard a rumor Tillotson's son was on the scene. The boy hated his father. He slid a bunch of twenties across the counter and said how sad it would be to see a son arrested for patricide, but these things happened. I said the investigation hadn't been completed. Reynolds said that was too bad. I was such a good mayoral candidate. Mr. Thomas wouldn't be happy to have to pull his support. I got the hint. I told you to arrest the son."

I clenched my jaw. I'd never seen a more miserable-looking grown man, but that didn't dent my anger. "You were willing to sell a young man up the river to save your own career, is that it?"

He didn't respond for a moment, just looked at the dusty carpet on the floor. Finally, without lifting his head, he said, "I was sure the case would fall apart before it went to trial."

"And if it didn't?"

The hangdog look on Captain Finley's face was answer enough. Without another word, I stormed out of the house.

Chapter Thirty-Nine

I walked back and forth in front of the Finley house so many times while I waited for Sam, I expected to see a worn spot in the cement. The sun hung low in the sky and the air felt a bit colder. That weasel. He mighta thought the DA wouldn't get anywhere, but I knew in my heart he also wouldn't have raised a finger to help Lee if that had turned out to be wrong.

I wasn't sure how long it took for Sam to follow me, but it seemed like forever. I turned around in my pacing and suddenly, he was there. "Did you arrest him?"

"No, I didn't."

"Why not?"

"He didn't commit murder, Betty. A crime yes, but not homicide."

I balled my hands at my side. "That old coot would've sat back and not done a thing to prevent Lee from goin' to prison for life. You know that."

"I do and don't think I'm going to let him off the hook. But I can't do it myself. There's a process to follow. That might not be what you want to hear, but that's the way it is."

"But you're gonna get Lee outta jail now, right?"

He glanced at his watch. "Unfortunately, that also requires paperwork. I can't just march up to the door and tell the guards to let someone go. It's three-thirty on a Sunday. I can make some calls, but I don't know how much will happen today."

My blood boiled. "Are you tellin' me my best friend has to sit in a stinking jail cell another night because of a *formality*?"

Sam looked at me and raised his eyebrows.

I knew it wasn't right to take my anger out on him. He was doin' his job. But heck, he was the only one here. I stalked back and forth, feeling the bite of the March air on my cheeks. I whipped around. "Then if you can't spring Lee and we can't arrest Captain Finley, what *can* we do?" I didn't like the note of despair in my voice, but I couldn't help it. I was so close.

Sam patted my shoulder as though to telegraph his understanding. "Let's go back to Daletzki. We need to push Blackie on exactly what his guys did, but I want to grill Daletzki on those inconsistencies first. See if we can dig up additional ammunition."

But when we got back to Ruth's place, she told us Mr. Daletzki had left. "I didn't want him to, but he felt guilty."

Doggone it. We'd just found the guy. "About what?" I asked.

"He said he was going to the soda shop down the street to use the payphone and call his sister. He didn't want her worrying about him." She pointed in the direction of the shop. "Go a block that way. You can't miss it."

Sam and I hustled down the street. There was no sign of Mr. Daletzki inside, but I did see the payphone in the corner. "Excuse me," I said and walked up to the counter. "Did a man come in here and use that phone in the last couple of hours?"

The soda jerk shrugged. "I ain't paid to watch the phone, lady."

"But there's no one else here. You must have seen him if he came in. He woulda been your only customer. Maybe he bought a Coke?"

The boy, a freckled kid slightly older than Mary Kate, shrugged.

Sam joined me at the counter. "Listen, pal. Put down the dishtowel and answer the question. Did you see a man use that phone? He would have looked like this." He held out the picture of Mr. Daletzki.

The soda jerk didn't even look up. "I told ya, I don't know," he said in a tone of obvious boredom.

Sam flipped out his badge with one hand and slapped the counter with the other. "Do I have your attention, son?"

The soda jerk glanced up, saw the badge, and turned as dingy-pale as the towel he was usin' to dry glasses. "Yes, sir." He swallowed hard.

"Good. Look at the picture again. Did you see that man using the payphone?"

This time, he gave the picture a thorough study. "Um, I think so. I only had one adult customer this afternoon. He came in and used the blower. He grabbed a bottle of Coke and a bag of chips, paid, and left."

"How long was he here?" I asked.

"Golly, ten minutes, not even?" The kid wrung the towel. "He made the phone call, bought his stuff, and hit the bricks."

"Did you hear what he said?"

"Not much beyond 'Margaret, it's me.' That was at the beginning of the call. He turned around and lowered his voice. I don't think he wanted me to hear him. Like I said. Quick call, food, Coke, and he beat it."

We thanked him and left. Back at the car, I said, "We're gonna go talk to Mrs. Wiese, right?"

"You bet your life."

* * *

We parked in front of the Wiese house. As before, the curtains were drawn, but this time the bike was missing. Mrs. Wiese did not answer to Sam's authoritative knock.

I scanned the front of the house. It was silent, but not the kind I associated with an empty place. "Try again."

Sam complied.

I wandered around the building. A shadow passed in front of a side window. I returned to Sam. "I saw a figure. And I don't think it was a woman's shape."

Sam frowned. Once again, he banged on the door. "Mrs. Wiese, it's Detective MacKinnon and Miss Ahern. It's vitally important that we speak with you."

Another minute ticked by before she opened the door, barely a crack. "Steve's still not here. Now isn't a good time."

I stepped forward. "I have information about your brother."

"I don't want to hear it. Keep the money. I don't want you looking into it any further. Goodbye." She made to close the door.

Sam put his hand on it. "Ma'am, we aren't going away. You need to let us in. I promise we won't take long."

She gripped the door, face pale. She glanced behind her and a second later took a step back. "Two minutes."

The room looked as pristine as the last time we'd been there, but something was off. "Have you heard from your brother?" I asked.

She shook her head and some of her hair came loose from her bun. She looked a little haggard to me. Her dress was wrinkled and the shoes didn't match.

Sam studied her. "Has anyone else been in contact with you?" he asked.

Another violent head shake.

I knew what was different. The faint smell of cigarette smoke overlaid the scent of furniture polish. I hadn't noticed it the last time we'd been there. Armed with that realization, I scanned the room. A heavy glass ashtray graced the coffee table. It held two crushed butts and a mostly-smoked gasper. A thin wisp of smoke came from it. I'd seen that ashtray on a previous visit 'cept that time it had been in the kitchen and the only thing in it had been an assortment of nickels, dimes, and quarters. "That's a shame." I pulled out my deck of Luckys. "Mind if I smoke?"

Her shoulders twitched.

I patted my pockets as though I was looking for something. "Darn, I think I've lost my lighter. Got one I can use?"

"I don't s—" She caught herself and stared at me through eyes as big as Cat's milk saucer.

"No matter. C'mon, Sam, we gotta go." I tugged on his arm.

He scowled. "We just got here and we haven't talked about anything."

"No matter, Mr. Daletzki isn't here, just like the lady said. Sorry for disturbing you." I pushed Sam through the door, pulling it shut behind me.

Once we were outside and on the sidewalk he wheeled around. "What the hell do you think you're doing? She's hiding something and we need to get her to say what."

"Sam, I think your temper is still up from confronting your boss and it's getting in the way of you paying attention. There's someone else in the house." I told him about the ashtray and the scent of smoke. "She almost slipped when I asked for the lighter."

"Who says it isn't Daletzki?"

"I'm pretty sure he's not a smoker. She's scared stiff. I know you picked up on that. If it were her brother in the back room, she would say so." I shielded my eyes against the setting sun and swept the street with my gaze. It looked abandoned, but I couldn't shake the conviction there was a very unfriendly visitor in Mrs. Wiese's home.

He put his hands in his pockets. "Whoever is in there, it can't be Howley or McDougal."

"No, but I bet it's one of Blackie Thomas's goons." I tapped my foot. Then I moved to make sure my back was to the house. "You drive off that way." I jabbed my finger in the direction I wanted him to go. "Go around the block and park a ways from here, but still in sight of the house." I gave another sweeping, violent gesture with my right arm.

"Why are you waving your arms like a madwoman?"

"I'm tryin' to make it look like we're arguing. I want whoever is inside to think we've given up. Act annoyed."

For a moment it seemed he was gonna ruin everything by laughing, but his expression settled into the scowl that was often on Pop's face when the boys were up to their usual shenanigans. "Like this?"

"Perfect." I flung out my left arm. "I'll go off this way and meet you. If you drive away, he, or she, will think it's safe to leave Mrs. Wiese. After all, even if I stuck around, what can I do? This way, we can watch and see who comes outta this house and pinch him. Or her."

He threw up his hands. "Sounds good to me. Here's my contribution to the act." Then he stormed to the driver's side of the car, got in, slammed the door, and drove off with a squeal of rubber thrown in for good measure. Sam was a good actor.

I stalked down the street for the benefit of anybody who was watchin' from the Wiese house. I sure hoped they'd bought our charade. When I was about five houses away, I ducked behind a parked truck. I didn't wait long. Sam pulled up and parked just behind the truck. We were close enough to see, but still far enough down the street that the car prob'ly wouldn't be noticed by anyone leavin' the house. I hurried to the passenger side and got in.

"Did you see anyone?" he asked.

"Not yet." I slouched down in the seat, low enough that I wouldn't be noticed 'cept by someone passing the car, but not so much that I couldn't see over the dashboard.

"You're sure someone is in that house?"

"Positive."

Sam reached over the seat and retrieved a newspaper. He opened it up and arranged it so no one could see his face. "All right then. Welcome to your first stakeout."

Chapter Forty

Nothing happened for at least half an hour. As Sam finished sections of the newspaper, he passed them to me. I got caught up on the Buffalo sports scene, local politics, and the gossip column while we waited. I'd already heard the latest war news, the facts, that is. I wasn't particularly interested in opinion columns speculating on possible events in the two theaters. All I wanted was for my fiancé and my brother to come home safe.

I was scanning an article about gas-rationing when Sam slapped my arm. "Showtime."

I looked up to see a man standing on Mrs. Wiese's front step. From his profile, I could tell the unwanted visitor was Walt Reynolds. "What is he doin' at the Wiese house?"

"That is the question."

Walt jawed at Mrs. Wiese, punctuating his speech with a few pokes of his finger.

"Are we gonna follow him?" I asked.

"We could interview the sister again, but I doubt she'll tell us much. I think a tail is more productive."

"On foot or by car?"

"Neither is a great option." Sam paused. "There aren't enough people around for us to blend into a crowd. But if we roll behind him, he's going to get suspicious and turn around." He pointed. "Our best hope is he heads toward Sycamore. If he comes this way, not only will it be harder to follow him, we'll have to duck and hope he doesn't look in the car."

It seemed the saints were with us, because Walt gave one final jab with his finger and took off toward Sycamore, walking at what seemed to be a fast clip by how rapidly he moved away.

Sam tossed aside his paper. "Let's go."

We left the car behind and tried to match Walt's rate of speed as we followed, keeping a good fifty yards behind him. Our luck held. He didn't look back. When he reached Sycamore, he turned right.

Sycamore wasn't that much busier, it being almost dinner time on a Sunday evening, but there were at least a few more people around, allowing us to fill some of the empty space between us and our quarry. We followed him for three blocks until he turned right at Sobieski Street. We waited at the corner and watched him enter a blue house about twenty-five feet away. Then we approached.

There was nothing special about the building. No stars in the window, no Victory garden, no garage for a gas-starved car. It stood a scant few feet from its neighbors, a short length of chain-link fence lining the sidewalk on either side. The porch was bare of furniture, the windows covered by plain white curtains. It almost looked abandoned.

Except we'd seen Walt enter. So at least one person was there. "Are we gonna knock or bust in?" I asked, without looking at Sam.

"Two people don't bust into anything. We have no idea what's in there. He could have a dozen armed friends."

I studied the lot. I could tell there was a small yard in the back. I went up to the fence, shook it, then climbed up and over.

"What the h...heck do you think you're doing?" Sam sounded like someone was choking the words outta him.

"You knock on the front door to distract him. I'm gonna go around back. At least I will as long as I don't see anything. There isn't a guard dog. If we didn't hear one when Walt entered, he woulda come around when I hopped the fence, or at least barked, if he was chained up. If the back windows are clear, I'll look inside. I got a hunch, and it's just a hunch, mind you, that he's alone. I'll meet you back here in two minutes."

Sam grumbled, but headed toward the front door.

I tip-toed to the back. Despite my casual words, I wasn't positive there wasn't a guard dog, nor was I sure Walt was alone. But something about this place led me to believe I was right. I passed a couple of dented garbage cans. The back yard was as bare as the front, wilted brown winter grass crowding up to the side of the house. I went back to the cans and lifted the lids. Only one soggy paper bag of trash sat in one of 'em, leading me to think I was right about Walt living alone. Two or more people would make more garbage, I knew that from my own house.

I returned to the back. There were no signs of a dog, no chains, or bowls, or a doghouse. There were, however, two windows, and the curtains here weren't closed as tightly as the front. I peered in to see a kitchen with a fridge, stove, sink, and a wooden table with one chair.

Sam was tapping his foot when I returned to the fence and clambered over it. "What did you see?"

I brushed my hands together. "Not much. Dollars to doughnuts I'm right. Did you knock?"

"I didn't want to until you returned."

I mounted the front step. "Let's try now." I beat on the door with my fist. In a very short time, it opened.

When I'd learned Walt Reynolds had been runnin' around with his boss's girl, I'd doubted his intelligence. Today confirmed it. He didn't ask who was there, or look through a peephole, nothing. He opened up and stared at us, mouth hangin' like a landed fish, stupidity written all over his face. Then he did the only thing he could do.

He bolted for the back.

"Go in after him," I told Sam. Then I ran to the fence and scrambled over. I'd already been in the yard, so I knew that while the house had a back exit, I also was aware that the entire area was surrounded by a chain-link fence at least five feet tall, if not more, with no gate. Walt might get there before me, but he'd have nowhere to go and would be slowed by climbing the fence.

Sure enough, when I rounded the house, there was Walt, about halfway up the fence. It appeared his foot, or maybe his trousers, had snagged on the wire, 'cause he was tugging and swearing a blue streak. I heard Sam, but he hadn't come out yet. I grabbed Walt's suspenders and pulled. We tussled, but I didn't lose my grip. Finally, with a loud rip, he fell backwards onto the ground. I stepped back just in time to avoid getting squished. He rolled onto his front and tried to get up, but before he could do more than put his hands in front of him, I flopped onto his back.

I'd done enough wrestling with Sean that I could stay clear of his flailing feet and keep him pinned. If I'd been on my own, his strength would have eventually overcome me. Fortunately, Sam showed up a moment later, gun in hand.

"Walt Reynolds. Get up and put your hands on your head."

He spat out a mouthful of grass. "Tell your girl to get off me."

Sam nodded to me.

I pushed myself to a standing position and brushed dirt and grass from my slacks.

"She's off," Sam said. "Slowly now. Hands on your head."

Walt's glare looked all the more sullen 'cause of the bruise on his face. He stood and clasped his hands on top of his hair as instructed. "I didn't do nothing."

"Over there." Sam waved the gun at a rusty table surrounded by chairs that took up most of the space on a cement flat spot near the house. "Sit. Keep your hands where I can see them."

Walt complied. "I told ya. I didn't do nothing. This is harassment."

"Oh, yeah?" I said. "If you're so clean, why'd you run?" Up close, he looked to be in his late twenties, no more than thirty. He ought to have been overseas, but his boss had prob'ly helped him dodge the draft. I wondered how such a young guy got to be a lieutenant in a crime ring. It occurred to me that maybe it was like the Army's first lieutenants. Maybe a step above a common foot soldier, but way down the line when it came to seniority. "Here I've been expecting a man and you're nothin' but Blackie Thomas's errand boy, aren't you?"

He glared at me. "Mr. Thomas knows he can trust me."

"Really?" I crossed my arms. "Even after you stole his girl? Of course, she was old hat, wasn't she? He blacked your eye 'cause he had to, but he didn't really care. How's it feel to have the boss's cast-offs?"

He growled and started to rise from his chair.

"I didn't give you permission to stand," Sam snapped. To me, he said, "That's enough."

I held up my palms in surrender.

"Where've you been all day, Walt?" Sam asked.

Walt dropped back into his chair. "Here. By myself. It's Sunday."

Sam kept his revolver trained on the younger man. "Funny. I could have sworn I saw you coming out of the home of Margaret Wiese not more than an hour ago."

"Don't know who that is."

"If you've been home all day, what've you been up to?"

"Nothing. Listening to the radio."

"Oh? What program? Got a favorite?"

"I've been scanning the stations."

I noticed the bulge of a cigarette pack in his shirt pocket. "Mind if I smoke?" I reached out and plucked the deck out. "Same brand as I saw in the ashtray." I held it out for Sam to see and shook it. The remaining smokes rattled around.

"So?" Walt said. "Lots of people smoke Chesterfields. Just 'cause this broad had some doesn't mean I was there."

"One, Mrs. Wiese doesn't smoke." I tossed the pack in his lap. "Two, I didn't say *where* I saw 'em. I said they were in an ashtray. How'd you know a woman had 'em if you've never been there and don't know her?" He really was a fathead.

His face reddened, but whether it was from anger or embarrassment was hard to tell. Maybe both.

"Walt, we know you went to Margaret Wiese's house. We saw you." Sam relaxed a smidge since it seemed for all his bluster and bravado, Walt Reynolds was a chicken at heart. "All we want to know is why you were there and who sent you."

"Who said anyone told me to go to the dame's house?"

I snickered. "You went there on someone's orders. You're too stupid to have thought of it yourself. You didn't even check who was at the door before you opened it. Who was it?"

Walt's response would have had my mother reaching for her bar of soap.

"Betty, I told you that's enough," Sam said, this time his voice a bit sharper. "However, she has a point, Walt. You don't strike me as an eager beaver. Why'd you go see Mrs. Wiese?"

Walt's eyes darted back and forth. "I was lookin' for her brother," he finally said.

"Did someone ask you to do that?"

For the first time, a flash of fear came over the low-level mobster's face. "I...no. Yes. The hell with you."

"Watch your mouth," Sam said.

"Don't worry about it." I didn't blame Walt for not squealing. There was no doubt in my mind that he was there on Blackie Thomas's orders. If Walt didn't go to jail, whoever was fillin' in for Howley or McDougal would prob'ly pay him a visit as soon as Blackie heard about it. If Walt ended up in the slammer, well, Howley and McDougal were already there. Blackie could get them a message. "Did you find him?" I asked. I knew the answer was "no," but I wanted to hear Walt's story.

"Daletzki wasn't there and his sister didn't know where he was. But..."

"Go on."

Walt glanced at Sam, who still had his piece trained on the target. "While I was there, he called."

"Who called?" Sam asked.

"Daletzki. I couldn't hear him, but from what his sister said, he was checkin' up on her and lettin' her know he was okay."

Darn it. We'd told Mr. Daletzki to sit tight. "Mrs. Wiese looked awful scared when we visited her," I said. "What did you do to her?"

Walt paused, clearly unwilling to talk. "I...I convinced her to tell her brother she had to see him," he said, finally. "I had her younger boy in my grasp. She begged him, Daletzki. I don't think he wanted to, but she got him to agree." Sam growled and raised the revolver "I wouldn't have harmed the kid. I just needed her to put on a good act. You know, sound so frightened her brother would go along with the scheme."

I shivered at the thought of this jerk using a young boy to threaten his mother. But I tried not to let Walt see it.

"Where'd you send him?" Sam asked.

Walt eyed the gun. "The Fruit Belt."

"Where?"

I got out my notepad. When no answer came, I slapped it across Walt's chest. "The man asked for an address, you dope."

That earned me an evil eye. "Twenty-six Lemon Street."

"Final question," Sam said. "Who sent you to see Mrs. Wiese?"

The fear returned to Walt's face and he gave a shake of his head. "I ain't sayin' anything else. Cuff me or get out."

I could tell Sam wanted to put the cuffs on him, but we needed to get to the Fruit Belt. "C'mon, if we hurry we might catch 'em." I headed back through the house.

We walked much faster on our way back to the car. "Get in," Sam said.

I did. "You didn't say anything that last time, when I hit Walt with my pad. Why?"

Sam turned the key. "Because you hitting him with a notebook was better than me punching him in the face." He pulled away and we headed for the Fruit Belt to find Mr. Daletzki.

Chapter Forty-One

The building at 26 Lemon Street turned out to be a garage-type structure located next to a mature apple orchard. The entire area got its name from the many fruit trees planted by immigrants from Germany who settled down here when they arrived. Most of 'em had been farmers of some sort in the Old Country. I had no idea why they'd chosen to name the street after something that didn't grow in Buffalo. I didn't come here often, but if there were trees, there had to be buildings where they could collect the fruit, maybe press them for cider, or make other foodstuffs. The garage might have been something like that.

The neighborhood was quiet on a Sunday. My imagination provided the vision of people holding huge baskets, picking apples or pears in the fall, with the scent of fresh-made cider or applesauce on the air while children played tag. But on this cold day in March, only a few sad leaves lay on the ground while the barren trees reached fingers to the sky.

I held my hair back to keep it from blowing in my face. "Kinda open for a meeting, don't you think?"

"It is. Not a place I'd pick. But I don't see any bodies either."

I pointed at the building. "Did we miss them or are they in there?"

"Only one way to find out." Sam unholstered his gun and moved toward the darkened structure.

As we approached the door, the hairs on the back of my neck prickled. I couldn't put my finger on it, but I could tell something was off. Call it gut instinct, or women's intuition, but I knew in my heart of hearts going inside was a bad idea. I put my hand on Sam's shoulder. "Maybe you should get backup."

He hesitated. "I'm not sure I want to do that yet."

"Why not?"

"Look around." He turned in a circle. "If Steve Daletzki is meeting someone here, why don't we see something? Or hear any voices? All I see are empty streets with houses where people are most likely inside doing Sunday afternoon things. What do I say I want backup for?"

"Oh c'mon. This doesn't feel hinky to you?"

"How so?"

"I dunno. I get the creeps lookin' at the place. There aren't enough people around."

"It's March. Nobody's going to be out picking fruit."

He was right, but I couldn't shake that feeling. "Where's Mr. Daletzki? We haven't been all that quiet. Wouldn't he come out and greet us? Or give some other kind of sign?"

Sam glanced at the door. "He could be hurt or like I said, maybe he isn't here any longer. It could be he doesn't want to talk to us again."

"Humor me, please. Don't you know someone local to call? I know you're all fired up after confronting your boss, but I don't think goin' in there yourself is a good idea."

A grin flashed across his face. "I'm hardly alone."

"Dummy." I pushed him. "I'm unarmed. I don't even have my brother's switchblade."

"All right. The friend who gave me the tip about Walt's visit to Captain Finley lives in this neighborhood. I'll try radioing the station, see if they'll contact him and have him meet us." He stabbed a finger in my direction. "But don't you go in without me, understand?" He jogged back to the car.

I had no intention of goin' inside on my own. I circled the building. All the windows were shut and boarded over, which made sense given the season. As Sam said, no one would be around to pick apples or press cider. Not in a Buffalo winter. "Mr. Daletzki?" I called, keeping my voice soft. "It's me, Betty Ahern. Detective MacKinnon is with me. You can come out."

Silence.

Sam returned. "The friend I mentioned should be here soon."

Less than five minutes later, a grizzled man showed up, gray hair cut close, but he was still in good physical shape. "What's the situation, Sammy?"

I smothered a smile. I couldn't imagine anyone calling my friend "Sammy."

As if he read my mind, he shook his head. "Thanks for coming, Fred. We think there's a guy in there we've been hunting. Witness in a homicide."

Fred pulled a gun. Whether Sam had told him to or not, he'd come prepared. "Anyone else?"

"Not sure, but we don't think so."

"Is he armed?"

"No. At least he shouldn't be."

Fred shot a quizzical look in my direction.

"She's with me," Sam said. "She's the one who insisted I call for backup even though I think the place might be deserted."

The questioning glance turned respectful. "Smart cookie. You don't live as long as I have, Sammy, by being reckless," Fred said. "Let's see what we got. You knock, I'll cover you." He nodded toward the orchard. "You might want to stand over there, miss."

I hadn't seen a back door when I inspected the structure, so there was no chance of Mr. Daletzki, or anyone else, bolting that way. I took up position behind the tree, ready to trip up our suspect if he got past the two policemen.

Sam held up a hand and counted down from three on his fingers. He banged on the door. "Steve Daletzki, or anyone else in there. This is the Buffalo Police. Come out slowly with your hands up."

No sounds came, except the distant cry of a winter bird and the rustle of a breeze through the bare branches of the apple trees.

Sam pounded again. "This is the Buffalo Police. We have the building surrounded. Come out."

Still no movement.

Sam and Fred exchanged a glance, and Fred nodded at the door. Sam reached out and turned the handle.

The door opened.

I didn't expect that and judging from my companions' expressions neither

250

did they. Fred hoisted his gun a little higher. Sam darted in. And swore. Violently. "You shouldn't come in, Betty. Fred, go to my car and call for a meat wagon."

I shot a look at Fred, who shrugged and did as ordered.

"Is it bad?" I asked.

"No, but stay outside," Sam said.

Despite his order, I entered the building. The light was dim 'cause of the boarded windows. The whole place was dusty and smelled faintly of rotten apples. A cider press occupied most of the room, draped in a sheet, maybe to keep the dirt off during the winter. Bits of dried apple and scraps of skin were scattered on the floor and two big barrels, stacked one on top of another, took up the far corner. Once my eyes adjusted, I could make out a man's body lying on its side, head pillowed on the left arm. It was Mr. Daletzki.

"I told you to wait," Sam said.

"You said it wasn't a mess. Is he sleepin'?" I asked, but I knew the answer.

"He's dead."

Despite Sam's disapproving stare, I inched closer. Mr. Daletzki's eyes were half-closed and I could tell the pupils of his eyes were big, but the body was otherwise clean. No dust. The skin was pale, but not the bluish color I'd come to associate with a corpse, like when I'd seen my first body. I reached out a hand, then looked at Sam.

He nodded for me to continue, a resigned expression on his face.

I laid my palm on Mr. Daletzki's forehead. Cool, but not cold. He hadn't been laying here long. I didn't want to touch anything else, but I inspected as much as I could. A red stain spread on his chest, carrying the unmistakable coppery scent of blood.

"Stabbed or shot?" I asked.

"I don't know. We'll have to wait for the coroner." Sam holstered his gun. "There's no one else here. The place only has one room."

I stood and dusted my slacks. "I hope he hurries up."

"Steven Daletzki isn't going anywhere."

"No, but we have to." Sam cocked his head and I continued. "We gotta go back and talk to Walt. Find out who Mr. Daletzki was s'posed to be meetin'.'"

I didn't know exactly what had happened, but one thing was for darn sure. Mr. Daletzki wasn't gonna be able to tell us.

* * *

There wasn't much to do, even after the coroner showed up. He told us there were three holes in Mr. Daletzki's chest, but refused to make any other guesses, even though he found no other injuries on the body. Including any defensive wounds. Sam and Fred did a walk-through of nearby houses, but it bein' Sunday, they didn't turn up any clues. Families had been sittin' down to dinner or listenin' to the afternoon radio. No one had seen or heard anything suspicious. One man reported a sound that coulda been gunshots, a car backfirin', or a kid's pop-gun sometime between four and four-thirty, but he wouldn't bet his life on it. There weren't any bullets, which meant they were still in Mr. Daletzki. I pushed that idea to the back of my mind. I might be a budding PI, but that didn't mean I had to dwell on the messy details.

While the cops did their questioning, I prowled around the scene, careful to keep outta the way of the official folks. The dust on the floor was mussed enough that I couldn't make out prints. I didn't see anything on the ground outside either, since the dirt was still frozen solid and I'd done a pretty thorough job of trampling the grass while waiting for Sam.

On the street, however, I did find two things. One was a fresh spot of motor oil. A car had been parked there and not that long ago. The second was a white cambric handkerchief. Well, it used to be white. It had spots of dark brown from lyin' on the ground, and streaks of blackish gray.

Sam found me crouched over the spot. "What are you looking at?"

"There was a car parked here with a leaky oil pan." I straightened and waved at the street. "That's fresh. And there's this." I held out the hankie, which I'd picked up with a pair of tweezers I kept in my purse for pickin' up evidence. "Ten'll get you twenty someone used that to wipe off his hands, maybe after he shot Mr. Daletzki."

Sam inspected the scrap before dropping it in an evidence bag. "Wiping off gunshot residue?"

"Or oil or some other dirt. Looks like a man's handkerchief to me."

"What makes you say that?"

"A lady's would be more delicate." I looked up and down the quiet street. "No initials, I checked."

"Nice work." Sam slapped me on the shoulder. "You may not have a license, but you're a fine detective."

I knew I blushed and I hoped he would think the brisk evening air was the reason. "You done inside?"

"Yep. Fred will wrap things up. The coroner left with the body. Let's go see what Mr. Reynolds has to say for himself."

But when we arrived at Walt's place on Sobieski, he didn't have much to say. Mostly 'cause he wasn't there. That touched off another storm of profanity from Sam.

I shook my head. "Other people can't swear around me, but you can?"

He shot me a dirty look.

"You better not let my mother hear you talk like this. She'll never let you in the house again."

"I shouldn't have left him alone." He slapped his fedora against his leg. He jammed it back on. "Of the two, who is more talkative, Howley or McDougal?"

"In my opinion? Ned McDougal for sure. It's not like he's a blabbermouth, but he'll at least give you the time of day. Why?"

"We're going to the jail." He stormed back to the car.

"I thought you said that was a waste of time." I slid in.

He jammed the car into first gear and pulled away with a slight squelch of rubber. "I changed my mind."

Chapter Forty-Two

Visiting hours were over when we arrived at the city jail slightly before five-thirty, but that's the best part of workin' with a cop. The normal rules don't apply. Sam flashed his badge at the guards and said, "I need to see Ned McDougal. In private."

The guard paused, like he wasn't sure what to do. "What about her?" He pointed in my direction.

"Relax, she's with me. Just bring the prisoner to a private room."

The guard gave us directions and we went to what I took for an interrogation room to wait. Least it looked like a room for grilling suspects. Plain wooden chairs, a scarred table, and hooks for attaching handcuffs. I wasn't sittin' in the hot seat, but the stale air gave me the willies.

We didn't wait long before McDougal was ushered in. He took one look at Sam and turned to the guard. "I wanna go back."

"Tough." The guard pushed McDougal into a chair. "The detective wants to talk to you." He looked at Sam. "Let me know if you have any problems."

"Will do." Sam took off his hat and laid it on the table. He sat across from McDougal. "Tell me about Frances Corbett and Walt Reynolds."

I sat next to my friend and took out my notepad.

McDougal eyed us, at least with his good one. "I already did."

"Yeah, you said how you learned they were together, Frances cheating on Blackie, how he was tired of her, and gave Reynolds a black eye." Sam waved his hand. "What else?"

McDougal ran his hand over the table. "I don't know nothing else."

"Bull." Sam slapped the wood. "I just came from another stiff, one I found minutes after talking to Reynolds, who had also paid the dead man's sister a visit. Reynolds arranged for the victim to go to the place where he was killed. But Walt doesn't strike me as the ambitious, or clever, type so I'm guessing someone told him what to do. I have two candidates. The man he works for and the woman he's involved with. Tell me about Frances Corbett. Did she know Blackie was dumping her for someone new?"

McDougal ran his tongue over his lips. "As in did Blackie tell her? I'm not sure if she knew it for a fact. But although she's a dame and not the brightest, she had to have suspected it was comin'. Blackie had stopped takin' her out, he didn't buy her gifts, and he barely spoke to her when she was at his place. The writing was on the wall."

"How did she react?" I asked. I knew any girl of my acquaintance would be more than a little miffed. Frances had a guy, but if she was at risk of losing her sugar daddy, that might be completely different.

McDougal shrugged. "On the surface, she didn't seem to care, or didn't act like she did. But lookin' back, I think it was an act. Why else would she pay off Tillotson to keep his yap shut?"

"You think she coulda been tryin' to keep Mr. Thomas in the dark while she had her fling?"

McDougal tilted his head. "Maybe. Walt is younger than Mr. Thomas and better looking. Hell, look at their teeth. But Walt's way down the list in seniority. Frances, she likes the finer things. Walt may be better company, if you catch my drift, but Mr. Thomas is where the dough is. No matter how dim she is, she wouldn't lose sight of that. It wouldn't work, but she'd try."

An idea began to form in my mind. "So if she caught wind of someone threatening her situation, either Mr. Tillotson or someone else, you think she'd flip her wig?"

"At the very least."

Sam turned and held my gaze. He had to be thinkin' the same way I was. He faced the prisoner. "Who does Walt take orders from?"

McDougal snickered. "Mr. Thomas, naturally."

"Why the laugh?" I asked.

McDougal snorted. "Walt's starstruck. He thinks he should be runnin' things, has all sorts of ideas. He's got someone whispering in his ear, egging him on. But he's a sap. He ain't got the balls to run this gang."

Sam leaned forward. "Would that someone be Frances?"

McDougal said nothing, but I thought I detected a wary light in his eyes.

Sam must have as well, 'cause if anything he leaned in further. "You've got a choice, McDougal. You think you're going to walk on this numbers charge. What you don't know is the case against young Liam Tillotson has fallen apart. That means I've got you at a murder scene, with motive."

McDougal paled. "You ain't got nothing on me."

Sam sat back and spread his hands. "You've said all along that you're a loyal foot soldier. Tillotson was stealing from Blackie. He blackmailed the boss's girl, which could make them both look bad."

"We were just s'posed to rough him up." McDougal swallowed. "Get Tillotson to cough up the lettuce and that was it. Hopefully, the beating would teach him a lesson about stealing. I'm telling you Blackie didn't give a darn about Frances. Heck, he'd be glad of an excuse to get rid of her sooner."

I picked up the thread. "Sure, but what if things got out of hand? Maybe you were too good at your job. Or you got distracted when Frances showed up. You told her to get lost, landed one misplaced punch and Mr. Tillotson wound up in the canal. Bam, you've gone from assault to murder and gotten your boss in hotter water than he figured."

McDougal half rose. "That's not how it happened. Me and Danny, we had things in hand. Then that dumb broad shows up, madder than a wet hen over whatever cockamamie scheme Tillotson was runnin' on her and Walt, she—" He sank back in his chair. "I ain't saying no more. You cops ain't got squat on me. I'll be out by tomorrow and Mr. Thomas will smooth it all over. He'll put things in their place."

I stared at McDougal in his prison duds. He'd almost let it slip. Frances Corbett was in this up to her pretty little neck, but only one person could force out the details.

And it wasn't us.

Chapter Forty-Three

Sam and I left the jail and drove straight to the club on Abbott Road where Blackie Thomas did business. "Are you thinkin' the same as me?" I asked after we parked.

"Walt Reynolds takes orders from his boss," Sam said. "He arranged for Steve Daletzki to be at the cider house in the Fruit Belt. Blackie Thomas gave the orders for Howley and McDougal to collect from Tillotson."

"But Frances is involved, too. In both murders." I slammed the car door shut. "She was at the docks that night. She was mad at Tillotson on two counts, the blackmail and ruinin' the setup with Mr. Thomas. After all, the way she saw it, things were sweet. She had Mr. Thomas's money and a young pretty boy. She wouldn't want that gettin' messed up."

"Except McDougal said Blackie was getting rid of her."

"Either she didn't know that or she thought she could fix it."

Sam paused. "And she killed Daletzki because…why?"

"He was there, he was a witness. She goes down to the canals. Howley and McDougal are followin' orders, working over Mr. Tillotson. But she's not satisfied with a beating. Either directly or indirectly, she causes Mr. Tillotson to fall into the water. She thinks she's home free, but then she finds out Mr. Daletzki saw everything, maybe from hangin' around the others. At first, he's just scared so he goes into hiding. Frances sends Walt to squeeze Mrs. Wiese for information and while he's there, Mr. Daletzki calls her to check in. Walt gets in touch with Frances, who tells her pretty boy to set Mr. Daletzki up, meets him at the cider press, and shoots him. Problem solved."

Sam stuffed his hands in his pockets and tapped his foot, as though he was thinkin' over my idea. "It's just as likely Blackie ordered a hit on Tillotson, found out about Daletzki, and took care of the witness himself. Remember, Reynolds doesn't take orders from Frances."

I almost pitied Sam. "If Walt Reynolds is as smitten with Frances as everybody says he is, willing to pay twenty-five dollars to keep Mr. Tillotson quiet, do you really think he wouldn't do what Frances said? After all, she might not even have told him the whole story. Maybe she only said to get Mr. Daletzki up to the Fruit Belt so she could talk to him."

"Have you ever seen Frances with a gun?"

"No, but she's a bookie's moll. How hard can it be to lay her hands on one?"

"True." Sam looked at the doors to the club. "Let's go shake the tree and see what falls out."

As we approached the building, I noticed something I hadn't before. A shiny, black car was parked in front of the doors. I backhanded Sam lightly on the arm. "Do you see that?"

We stopped. I could hear the ticking of the cooling engine in the quiet of the street. I laid my hand on the hood. "Still warm."

He pointed at the windshield. "It has an A card. Who do you think it belongs to?"

"Mr. Thomas or someone who works for him. Gotta be."

"Don't you think he'd have a different card so he can get the gasoline?"

"Anything other than an A card might draw attention. It could be he knows a guy who can get him more than his gas ration. He's got his hands in a lot of pies." I crouched down and dragged my fingers across the ground. When I stood, they were black and sticky. "Fresh oil."

Sam's mouth turned down. "Didn't Blackie say something about a car that needed an oil pan fixed?"

"On our first visit, yeah." I pulled a bandanna out of my pocket and wiped my fingers. "This was the car in the Fruit Belt where Mr. Daletzki was shot. I'd bet good money on that."

"But who was driving it?" Sam drummed his fingers on the car's windshield. "It wasn't Walt Reynolds. He was sitting at Margaret Wiese's house."

"Mr. Thomas?"

Sam shook his head. "I don't know. On the one hand, he might want to meet Daletzki, but stay away from any shooting. On the other, he might be running out of people he can trust."

"Only one way to find out."

We went inside the club. I tamped down a bit of a surprise that the doors were still unlocked. Then again, if this was Blackie Thomas's main place of business, he'd prob'ly leave the place open, 'specially if he was expecting someone. There were fewer people about. No bartender was visible. But as soon as we took a step toward the corner booth, a hulking bodyguard rose up to stop us. "You aren't welcome here."

Before I could retort, Mr. Thomas's light voice came from the back. "That's okay, Ernest. Let them through."

We edged around the bodyguard. Okay, I edged. Sam laid a hand on his gun and strode past.

Mr. Thomas occupied the same booth he had before, an ashtray by his right hand, a plate with a half-finished roast beef on kimmelweck in front of him, and a tumbler of whiskey next to it. "Good evening. You'd better have a good reason for interrupting my dinner, Detective."

I summoned my moxie. "You coulda told us to scram."

Mr. Thomas chuckled. "As bold as ever, Miss Ahern. I was curious. I don't get many visitors on a Sunday and definitely not policemen."

A figure moved in the shadows and inched closer to the table. It was Walt Reynolds. He didn't look as confident as he had earlier, not even when we'd talked to him at his house. His deference to his boss was obvious and, truth be told, a little sickening. A man ought to carry himself better.

"Hiya, Walt," I said.

He flinched.

Mr. Thomas had been lifting the sandwich to take a bite, but stopped with it halfway to his mouth. "You know these people, Walt?"

"Oh, sure." I relished the discomfort on Walt's face. "We've talked a couple of times. In fact, we saw each other earlier today, isn't that right?"

Mr. Thomas laid down his food. "Where was this?"

The gangster had no idea what his junior lieutenant was up to. "Why it was at a friend's house. Mrs. Wiese, right? And then again at Walt's place."

"Oh really?" Mr. Thomas withdrew a pack of thin cigars and lit one. "You and I are going to have to talk about your friends, Walt. Let me get to know them. Now, Detective, I let you in because I was curious. But that's rapidly waning. Unless you want me to call your captain, I suggest you and the young lady get to the point or leave."

Sam stood with his feet spread slightly apart. "I think you'll find Captain Finley a little less open to your calls. In fact, I expect he'll be out of a job soon."

Mr. Thomas blew out a cloud of smoke and ashed his cigar. "Pity. And he was so promising. Ah, well, you can't win them all. Still, unless you tell me your story, and quickly, I'm going to ask Ernest to escort you out."

I glanced around the club. "Where's Frances Corbett?"

"At home packing her things, I expect." Mr. Thomas took a sip of whiskey. "I informed her earlier that her company was no longer desired."

"Ah." I glanced at Walt. A thin sheen of sweat lay on his forehead. "Because of young Walt here?" I hoisted my thumb in his direction.

He paled, making his shiner stand out a little more, even in the dim light.

"Oh, that." Mr. Thomas waved his hand. "Walt and I have had a talk and that's all settled. No, I'd tired of Frances before she took up with him."

"You did, huh?"

"Yes. I wouldn't be surprised if she saw it coming and that's why she turned to Walt." He finished his whiskey.

I glanced at Sam. He tipped his head slightly, giving me the go ahead. "I think maybe you're not as wise to the state of things as you think you are. John Tillotson knew about these two quite a while ago. Did you know he was asking both of 'em for money to keep his trap shut?"

The rest of the color from Walt's face drained.

Mr. Thomas turned, slowly. "Is this true?"

For the first time, I really looked at Walt Reynolds. He had a bit of a very young Gary Cooper in him, the smooth cheeks and full lips, although he was a little weak in the chin. Slap a cowboy hat on Walt and he coulda played Cooper's role in *The Winning of Barbara Worth*. When I compared Walt to Mr. Thomas, with his slicked hair, gap-tooth smile, and sallow face, it was easy to see why Frances had strayed. Blackie Thomas had money, but Walt was definitely prettier. "Are you gonna tell him or do you want me to?"

Walt slid away from his boss. "We, uh, we're real sorry, Mr. Thomas. I told Frances we needed to be honest and I was gonna tell you. But she said no, she'd take care of it. I guess she didn't." He gave a weak laugh.

Mr. Thomas didn't crack a smile. "We'll talk about this later, just you and me." His tone of voice would have frozen the lake.

"Ye...yes, sir."

Poor kid. I almost felt sorry for him.

The numbers man turned back to Sam and me. "Regardless, Frances is not here," he said. "Now, if you'll excuse me, it seems I have some matters that need attention."

"Sure thing," Sam said. "One question. Is that your car outside?"

A flash of confusion showed on Mr. Thomas's face. "Yes."

"Did you know it's leaking oil?"

He clenched his fist. "Walt, why is the car not repaired?"

Walt could hardly stand, he was quivering so hard.

I played a long shot. "I think it's 'cause someone's been using it. Right, Walt?"

The poor guy nearly fainted away.

Sam, bless him, played along, even though he couldn't have known what I was thinkin'. "Someone like Frances Corbett maybe?"

Mr. Thomas faced us again, his eyes like smoldering coals. "What did you say?"

"You said you wanted a story, Mr. Thomas. I've got one for you." That's all it would be, but instinct told me this was our last shot. I had to give it my best. "The night Mr. Tillotson disappeared, you had your boys Howley and McDougal meet him at the grain elevator canals to rough him up a little." I edged back from the table, not enough to be noticed, just enough to put me out of reach. "See, folks thought Mr. Tillotson was running around with Frances, but even if that had been true, you wouldn't have cared. Mr. Tillotson was one of your runners, but he was dipping into the till, wasn't he? You wanted your money."

Mr. Thomas inhaled on his cigar, sandwich forgotten, and watched me the way Cat watched a mouse hole.

"The problem was Mr. Tillotson needed cash more than you thought. He'd lost his job at GM. His family life was in shambles. Not only was he filching from you, he'd figured out Walt here and Frances were a couple, and he was putting the squeeze on 'em in exchange for keeping quiet. I think he really wanted out of this life, but that's only a guess. Before he went, he was gonna get as much as he could. But you turned your dogs on him. Frances found out where they were all gonna be and she showed up at the docks."

"Fascinating," Mr. Thomas said in a low voice that dripped venom and danger.

Sam took up the story. "What none of them knew at the time was that there were two other people on the docks. One was Liam Tillotson, John's son. He tailed his father from their house, curious to see what his dad was up to. The other was a man named Steve Daletzki. He'd covered for John at GM, something that had cost Daletzki his job. He knew his old friend was connected to money and wanted a piece of the action. Tillotson kept him away, but he saw his chance that night and followed his friend to the meeting."

"Him saying no to Mr. Daletzki is why I think Mr. Tillotson wanted to end his involvement here. That and a conversation he had with my pop." I took stock of the area. Mr. Thomas remained in his booth, but no one approached, not Ernest the doorman or anybody else. I didn't know how Walt was staying upright. I kept talking. "So there's Howley and McDougal, giving Mr. Tillotson you-know-what, when Frances sashays up. Now, Lee, that's Mr. Tillotson's son and a very good friend of mine, said he heard a thud, two splashes, and one of your boys say 'the boss ain't gonna be happy.' Want to know what I think happened?"

"I'm all ears," Mr. Thomas said in that same dangerous voice.

"You'd never have told Howley or McDougal to kill Mr. Tillotson. No, you wanted your dough back. But Frances, she's angry. Her plush life is at risk. Your money and her pretty boy here. She was desperate to hang onto both." I pointed at Walt, who wasn't looking at all pretty. "She hits Mr. Tilloton, maybe with a pipe from a stack nearby, or something else. It doesn't matter. Mr. Tillotson falls into the canal."

"Howley and McDougal wouldn't protect Miss Corbett."

"I agree, they don't give a fig for her. But they'd do anything for you. If a woman known to be your girl, even if you were gettin' rid of her, was pinched for murder, it might put unwanted attention on you and your operations. Howley and McDougal figure they gotta cover for you. They throw the murder weapon in the water and scatter the rest of the pipe to distract people. They scram."

Mr. Thomas exhaled. "I knew I should have sent her packing weeks ago."

Sam spoke again. "Except there are two problems. One, Steve Daletzki is a witness. He isn't sure what he overheard, but he knows it's not good. He also thinks it's just a matter of time before he's discovered so he runs. Also, Lee thinks the woman might have been his mother. He cleans up the scene, leaving his fingerprints everywhere, and prepares to take the rap for her. If he's in jail and then gets convicted, all's well for everyone."

I thought fast. It was a story from whole cloth, as my grandma would say, but the pieces clicked. "Your boys told us they thought they saw someone earlier and dismissed it. Mr. Daletzki, he told us he waited until everybody had gone, but I don't think that's true. He bolted as soon as he could after he heard Mr. Tillotson's body hit the water. My guess is Howley and McDougal stayed around long enough to see if anyone else appeared, they saw him, told you, and you found him."

Mr. Thomas narrowed his peepers, but remained silent. He was a snake, ready to strike.

I had to hurry this along. "Frances woulda known about Lee from the paper. She found out about Mr. Daletzki somehow. She coulda heard it from someone here, or I think I might have tipped her off when I went to see her at her home. Maybe he called her to hit her up for money. But once she knew about him, she tracked down his sister. She sent Walt here to sit on Mrs. Wiese. He happened to be there when her brother called and bam, Walt convinces Mrs. Wiese to set up a meeting. Only it's Frances waiting for him when he shows. She pops Mr. Daletzki, scrams, and thinks she's in the clear. You're left to pick up any pieces left behind. She was there in your car, so if anyone saw it, it'll trace back to you."

Mr. Thomas stared at me. After a second, he gave a slow clap. "I'm impressed. You are quite the storyteller, Miss Ahern. I'll give you that. However, Frances doesn't have a gun."

Drat. He would hone in on that. I gave it half a second. "Do you?"

"Of course. A thirty-eight. It's in my office."

"Are you sure about that? Using your gun for murder would be even better than driving your car. One more piece of evidence pointing your way."

A fleeting look of concern crossed his mug. He snapped his fingers twice. "Ernest."

The doorman lumbered over. "Yeah, boss?"

"Go check my office for my piece. You know where it is."

Ernest went off to the back.

Mr. Thomas buffed his nails on his lapel. "She wouldn't dare implicate me."

"Don't count on it," Sam said. He stepped over and turned his back to Mr. Thomas. Then he leaned in, close to my ear. "I don't suppose you can prove any of that, can you?"

I covered my mouth with my hand. "Almost none of it."

Sam groaned.

It didn't take long for Ernest to come back. "It ain't there, boss. I looked twice."

Mr. Thomas crooked his finger at Walt. "Come here."

Poor Walt looked like he was gonna upchuck. "Yes, sir?"

"You heard the girl. Is that what happened?"

Walt looked to me, then his boss, and ran his tongue over his lips. He had to be weighing his choices. "Pretty much. I think Frances went to the grain elevators that night to…I don't know, say her piece or whatever. I don't think she meant to kill Tillotson. Howley and McDougal, they covered for her 'cause they didn't want it coming back on you. We, Frances and I, thought it would end when Tillotson's son got pinched, but then we learned about Daletzki. Frances overheard Howley talking about him, before he got picked up at that game. After Miss Ahern visited her, Frances knew he had to go."

My stomach tightened. I hadn't mentioned Mr. Daletzki's name, but I'd contributed to his death, even if it was accidental.

Mr. Thomas got real quiet. If this had been the cartoon before a picture, there'd be steam comin' outta his ears. "Where's the gun?"

Walt swallowed. "I don't know."

I glanced at Sam. "It wasn't in the cider house. Is it in the car?"

"Who drove the car here?" Sam asked.

Walt hung his head. "I did. I picked it up from Frances's place."

Mr. Thomas didn't stop staring at Walt. "Ernest. Check the car." He paused. "Why leave it there?"

By now my thoughts were spinnin' as fast as a runaway freight engine. "To pin it on you. If the cops tie your gun to the murder and learn Mr. Daletzki knew about your operation, they might finger you. She might go as far as to tip them off. She gets her revenge for you dumpin' her. Woman scorned and all that."

"Definitely," Sam added. "At that point, we'd also review the Tillotson case."

Ernest returned. "It's in the glove box, boss. I didn't move it in case the cops want it."

I would not have expected such intelligence from the big guy. "Sam, you'd better nab it and get it into evidence. I'll bet anything any fingerprints have been wiped off, but you'll match it to Mr. Daletzki's shooting. Wait, do you have that handkerchief?"

"Here." He handed the evidence bag to me and left.

I held it out to Mr. Thomas. "This was in a spot of fresh oil up in the Fruit Belt where Mr. Daletzki was shot. Is it yours?"

He looked. "No, mine are initialed."

I turned to Walt. "What about you?"

He didn't say anything, but the sick look on his face was answer enough. The hankie was his.

Mr. Thomas leaned back. "Will you be wanting Walt any longer?"

There were many ways to take that statement and none of 'em good. "I'm sure Detective MacKinnon will need him at some point, preferably in one piece. But right now, we gotta get to Frances." I started to walk away.

"Do you want the address?"

I stopped and turned. "No thanks. I know exactly where I'm going."

Chapter Forty-Four

After Sam bagged the thirty-eight and put it in his trunk, and radioed for someone to come get the car, we sped over to the boarding house where Frances lived. This time, I didn't even mention Sam's driving.

When we arrived, though, we were too late. "Frances Corbett?" the house mother said. "She left an hour ago. And good riddance."

"Why do you say that?" I asked.

"The type of men she had here." The woman sniffed. "Oh, not in her room, mind you. I wouldn't allow that. But the cars she got into, you could tell. Besides, all the nice boys are overseas. All that's left are old men, invalids, and scoundrels."

"Could we see her room, please?" Sam asked.

The house mother eyed him suspiciously. Even a police detective wasn't entirely acceptable in her estimation, I could tell. But she relented. "This way."

Frances's room was small but clean. A bed filled one corner. A dresser stood against the opposite wall next to an aging wardrobe, and a small writing desk was under the window. The white muslin curtains framed a window that looked over an alley that held a row of metal trash cans. She didn't have much of a view. She hadn't bothered to make the bed before she vamoosed.

I knelt on the floor and inspected under it. The only things I saw were bits of fluff. Behind me, I could hear Sam going through the wardrobe, then each dresser drawer. I stood and brushed off my hands. "Have you found anything?"

"Some pins, a couple of loose coins, and not much else." He kept looking. "Why don't you take the desk?"

I didn't have much hope. Frances had never struck me as the letter-writing type. There was a fountain pen, ink, a packet of untouched stationery, and a calendar. Each day had an "x" on it. Today was circled. "She was counting down to something." I held out the calendar to Sam.

He flipped the pages. "What was special about today?"

"When she wanted to skip town? The day she and Walt were gonna come clean about their relationship?"

"The former, I think." He slapped the calendar against his palm. He turned to the house mother. "Did she say anything to you? Maybe if it was a birthday or special in some way?"

"I didn't talk to her much." The woman folded her hands, the prim librarian.

"Did you know she was leaving?"

She sniffed. "No. She did ask about train schedules yesterday. I couldn't help her and she didn't bring it up again."

While Sam questioned the house mother, I continued to search. I didn't find anything until I peeked in the trash. "Sam, look." I pulled three pamphlets out of the bin. "Schedules for the Wolverine, Ohio State Limited, and the Lakeshore Limited."

Sam turned them over. "She might be headed to Canada, Cleveland, or New York City. That really narrows it down."

I started to speak, but then noticed the house mother hovering. She might not have approved of Frances, but she wouldn't turn down a bit of juicy gossip. "You don't mind if we take these, right?"

Disappointment showed on her face. "Of course not."

"Swell. Thanks for your help." I led Sam out of the room and we returned to the car.

He waved the pamphlets. "Which did she take?"

"Let's be logical." I plucked the Lakeshore Limited schedule from him. "This runs to New York. Good choice if you want to lose yourself. Big city, no one's gonna bat an eye at a girl coming from Buffalo and getting off with a case."

"But Lakeshore is a luxury carriage. You think Frances has the money for that?"

"I think maybe she could, if she'd saved up any pocket money Mr. Thomas gave her. I don't see her doing that, although she'd like traveling in first class. More important, look at the schedule." I pointed. "It left at nine this morning. We know she was in the Fruit Belt shooting Mr. Daletzki around four o'clock this afternoon. She missed today's train. This one's out." I tossed it into the car.

Sam scanned the list of departure times for the Wolverine. "If she left here an hour ago, she *might* have made the six o'clock to Toronto."

"If she's in Canada, we're sunk."

"Not necessarily. The Royal Canadian Mounted Police are usually more than happy to return American fugitives. I'd have to make a call to their Toronto office."

I sagged against the car. "Are there any other Wolverine trains leaving tonight?"

He ran his finger down the page. "Yes, the last one is at midnight." He looked up. "What about Ohio?"

I pushed thoughts that without Frances, Lee would be stuck in jail forever from my mind. I didn't need pessimism. "One left at five. The next train out is at nine."

"Two options. She might think it'll be harder to extradite her from Ontario and head north. Or she might want to get out of Buffalo as soon as possible, which means she'd hop the train to Cleveland." He paused. "She didn't take Reynolds. Why?"

"Could be they agreed to meet up later when the heat was off. Or she no longer had any use for him."

Sam rounded the car. "Well, I don't want to go back and grill him to find out. We don't have time."

"Next stop, Central Terminal." I pushed off the car, opened the passenger door, and said a quick prayer. Sam was right. We had to find Frances before

269

she skipped town. All we could do was head to the train station and pray for a little luck.

* * *

Had I not been in a rush, or not been so distracted, I would have spent some time admiring Buffalo's Central Terminal. Everybody knew about Grand Central Station in New York City, but I bet Central Terminal coulda given it a run for its money in terms of beauty. Built in 1929, it boasted the bold, geometric shapes and sleek lines of popular art. A large shiny clock took pride of place on the tower and the last rays of the sun gleamed off the windows by the main entrance off Paderewski Drive.

Sam parked in a restricted zone. One of these days, he'd pay for that. We entered the lobby with its vaulted ceiling and the stuffed bison. There weren't a lot of people there, but every once in a while one of 'em would rub the bison before heading off to whatever platform they were departing from. I had a fleeting memory of seeing both Sean and Tom rub it, for luck, before they left. *Focus, Betty. It's Lee who needs you now.*

Sam shook the departure schedules. "The platform for the Wolverine is over there, Ohio State Limited is that way." He pointed to each location as he spoke. "I think we should split up. Are you okay with that?"

"Yeah. There aren't a lot of people around, but enough that if she pulls any funny business, there will be plenty of witnesses. I don't want to run the risk of picking wrong, and her jumping on a train and we lose her. Not when we've come so far."

"Got a preference?"

Maybe it was my female intuition, but I didn't see Frances going to Canada. "I'll take the Ohio. If one of us nabs her, we what? Send a redcap to the other platform?"

"Best we can do. Good luck." He headed off toward the Wolverine.

I didn't have a snap of Frances to show around, but I questioned just about every person I passed if they'd seen a green-eyed blonde. Other passengers, ticket-takers, porters with luggage trolleys, none of 'em had spied her. I had started to think I'd guessed wrong when I hit pay dirt with a shoe-shine boy at his station about ten yards away from the Ohio State platform.

"Yeah, I seen her. She asked if there was a place she could grab a bite before the train left. I sent her to the snack stand." He pointed.

I flipped him a quarter. "Thanks." I took a look at the overhead clock. It was nearly quarter to seven. Frances would be conspicuous hanging around the platform for two hours. No wonder she wanted a place to go.

The stand was deserted, 'cept for the vendor. "Hey, I'll take a box of Cracker Jack," I said. "I'm lookin' for a friend of mine, we were s'posed to meet up to catch the nine o'clock Ohio Limited. But I haven't found her. You see a green-eyed blonde, slim, nice clothes around here?"

The man handed over my box. "Yep. You just missed her. She bought a hot dog and went that way." He nodded down the terminal, away from where I'd walked on my way from the lobby.

"Thanks. Keep the change." I pried open the box, suddenly ravenous. I'd missed dinner and this box of caramel popcorn might be all I got to eat that evening. I strolled past the platforms, keeping my eyes peeled. Families, businessmen, even a few hobos. No mobster molls.

I was about to give it up as a bad job when I caught a flash of blonde hair. I took a second look. "Frances Corbett!" I called. "I need to talk to you."

She froze for a second, then took off.

Between the lead she had and my need to dodge a couple of travelers, she could have lost me. Unfortunately, for her, she was wearing heels. In no time, I'd caught up to her. I didn't bother tryin' to be ladylike. I launched myself like a football linebacker and tackled her. "Stop makin' a fuss," I said as her purse made contact with my head.

"Let go of me, you blasted busybody. How dare you?" She writhed in my grasp like a greased pig.

People gathered around us, but no one dared get involved. I stopped tryin' to dodge the blows and focused on keeping my grip. Surely someone would call for a railroad cop, wouldn't they?

I'd taken two more blows by purse and felt Frances's nails scrape my hands before help arrived. "All right ladies, break it up, break it up." A burly man in a railroad uniform pulled Frances away from me. Another officer grabbed me and yanked me to my feet. "What's the fuss? I'm gonna call the police if you don't knock it off," the first officer said.

Sam's voice floated over the crowd. "No need." He pushed his way through and showed his badge. "Detective Sam MacKinnon."

The railroad official pushed his hat back. "Evening, sir. You'll want to take these ladies into custody, I expect."

I freed myself from the grip of the man holding me and brushed dirt and cinders from my clothes. What I thought was not fit for words.

Sam reached for Frances. "Just this one." He fastened her arms behind her back with a pair of handcuffs. "Frances Corbett, you're under arrest for the murders of John Tillotson and Steven Daletzki."

I brushed my hair outta my face. "Frances. Why in heaven's name didn't you take off the shoes?"

She shot me a sullen look. "And ruin my stockings?" She pulled against Sam's hold. "Take these things off. I haven't done anything."

I swear Sam wanted to bust out laughing, but he held back.

"Give it up," I said. "We already talked to Walt. We know everything."

She let out a very unladylike oath. "He's a stupid little boy."

"Did you really think you could get away with it?"

She tossed her curls. "Why not? I knew Blackie was getting tired of me. I was determined to get every penny from him I could before my time was up. John Tillotson put that at risk. He was a useless drunk, but he could have ruined my plans."

"And Steve Daletzki? How'd you know about him?"

"I heard the men talking about him." She smirked. "When they think you have nothing but air between your ears, it's amazing what they'll say around you. You should try it sometime." She looked me up and down. "He's another who could have ruined everything. Plus, pinning that murder on Blackie was an opportunity to pay him back for cutting me off."

"Use his gun and car, and leave it for the cops to find." I shook my head. She was a shrewd operator. I turned to Sam. "Your timing was swell."

"I came up empty with the Wolverine, so I decided to check on your progress," he said. "I arrived to see you do the best flying tackle I've seen outside collegiate football. Teddy Roosevelt would have approved."

"And all you did was watch?"

"You had things well under control."

I dusted the last of the cinders from my knees. "Well, count your lucky stars, mister."

He nudged Frances forward and we headed to the lobby. "Why do you say that?"

"'Cause if I'd torn my slacks you'd owe me the dough for a new pair, that's why." Outside, I inhaled a lungful of the crisp night air. "You'll be dropping all charges against Lee, right?"

"Of course." He opened the rear door of the car and put Frances, who hadn't uttered another word, inside. "This late, I don't expect him to be released until early tomorrow morning, I'd say around eight. You and Miss Kilbride can meet him at the jail. Unless you need to be at work."

I'd make up an excuse for Bell. There was no way I'd miss one of my best friends getting sprung from the pokey. And I was sure Dot would be right at my side.

Chapter Forty-Five

Dot and I swapped our shifts at Bell so we could be at the city jail bright and early Monday morning. "When will Lee get out?" she asked, nibbling on her lip as we walked up to the front door.

I swatted her shoulder lightly. "Detective MacKinnon said to be here around eight. We got ten minutes to wait. Now stop makin' ground meat outta your lip. Lee won't wanna smooch that."

Her cheeks turned a bright red. "Aw, stop it, Betty. He's not gonna kiss me in front of all these people." She waved her hand at the crowd around us, mostly men in business suits hustling off to their offices. "I can't believe Frances was behind everything. Didn't everybody describe her as dumb?"

I thought Lee might do exactly that, but I didn't argue. "I guess there's a lesson there. A pretty face doesn't always mean an empty head." I'd told Dot all about the details of my weekend adventures with Sam while we rode the bus. I checked the time. "You want to grab a coffee?"

"Nah, I don't wanna miss him." She hurried inside the jail.

I followed her. "Detective MacKinnon? What are you doin' here?"

Sam walked over and smiled. He held an envelope. "I had to submit the paperwork and I didn't want to miss the grand reunion. Plus, I have something for you." He held out the envelope.

I took it. "What is this?"

"Just open it." He tapped a smoke out of his pack and lit it.

I did as he said. Inside was a magazine clipping. "An order form for a decoder ring? Are we startin' a spy organization?"

Sam scoffed, took the paper, flipped it, and handed it back. "Don't be ridiculous. I meant this."

It was an advertisement for a correspondence course to become a private investigator. "Why would I be interested in this?"

"I thought you were sharp." He exhaled a cloud of smoke and tapped the words. "It's so you can get your license."

"I can't afford to take a class." I looked up. "Besides, I don't need it. Lee's cleared and I don't have to present anything to that lawyer. At least I don't think I do."

"Well, if you want your money, you still have to go sign that contract." He winked. "I paid for the course. You should get the book in four to six weeks. I recommend telling Mr. Williams that your license is new and you'll bring him a copy as soon as you get it in the mail. Since the charges have been dropped, he should accept that. At least I hope he does."

"Sam, thanks, but...I have a job. Or did you forget?"

"Betty, listen to me." He flicked some ash off his cigarette. "I know you do good work at Bell, you're contributing to the war effort and that's admirable. But I watched you all weekend. You have the makings of a great detective."

"You think so?"

"Yes. You're smart, but more than that, you have a great deal of common sense. Not every investigator does. You're bold, too. When you tackled Frances Corbett, did it even occur to you that she might be armed, either with a knife or another gun?"

I thought. "Not really. All I was thinkin' about was not lettin' her get away. I s'pose I shoulda considered that possibility, but the most important thing was nabbing her, not whether I got hurt. Is that bravery or stupidity?"

He grinned. "No comment. There's a third thing, perhaps the most important one." He stared at me.

"What?"

"You have heart. You see something wrong and you want to fix it. Anne Linden, Emmie Brewka's grandmother, and now your oldest friend."

"Not all my cases have turned out the way I expected."

"It doesn't matter. I honestly believe that even if someone couldn't pay you a nickel, you'd help them out, just because you could." He looked around the lobby. "Look, if you don't want to do the course, that's your call. But think about it. You're good. I'd like to be able to say I knew you when."

I stared at the clipping. I'd dreamed of this, sure. But suddenly it was reality. Sam believed in me. I'd keep working at Bell until I got my license, but maybe it wasn't such a far-fetched idea. "A correspondence course, huh?"

"Work at your own pace." He dropped his cigarette on the floor and ground it out with his heel. "Let's go. Lee ought to be down any minute now."

I followed him over to where Dot paced by the main desk. "It's eight o'clock," she said. "Where is he?"

"Relax. Detective MacKinnon said Lee will be out soon." I slipped the clipping into my purse and gave her a one-armed squeeze. I didn't need her asking questions I didn't have the answers to right now.

Lee appeared five minutes later, wearin' the same clothes he'd had on when he was arrested. He made a beeline for me and crushed me in a hug. "You did it, Betty, you did it! I knew you would."

I returned his hug. "Good to see you, Lee." I pushed him away. "There's someone else who insisted on comin' with me." I turned him around.

The minute he saw Dot, he took two strides, swept her into his arms, and planted a smacker right on her lips. That sealed it. I'd have to remind Dot I'd been right. I let the kiss go on for ten seconds. "All right, break it up, you two."

Lee faced me, but he didn't take his arm from around Dot's shoulders. "Do you girls need to get back to work?"

"Not right now. Let's go. I think this calls for a celebratory breakfast and a cup of joe." I looked for Sam to thank him for his help, but he'd disappeared.

"What did you put in your purse just now?" Dot asked as we made our way out of the jail.

"I'll tell you later." The March sun still didn't give a lot of warmth, but the light had never looked so beautiful. I had my two best friends and the prospect of the job I'd always wanted. If the war was over and Tom was home, things would be perfect.

* * *

After breakfast, I went to Mr. Williams's office to sign the contract. Lee and Dot went with me, holding hands the whole time. Those two were gonna be inseparable, I could see it.

The secretary frowned a bit when I told her the story about the license. "I don't know, I should talk to Mr. Williams," she said.

"Look, the charges were dropped. What's the problem?"

She hesitated, then gave me a conspiratorial wink and pushed over the contract. "What he doesn't know won't hurt him. Sign here."

I did and collected my dough, smothering a grin.

Back in the First Ward, Dot announced that she and Lee were headed for a walk, maybe to the park. "Do you want to come with us, Betty?"

I studied the pair of 'em. Dot had one of those sappy, romance-movie smiles on her face and Lee's puss had never been happier. Whatever Mr. Kilbride thought of Lee as a potential son-in-law, I suspected it wasn't gonna matter much. "I'd only be a third wheel. You two enjoy the day. I'm gonna go write a letter to Tom."

They started walkin' away before I finished speaking and their goodbyes were a little mumbled. They only had eyes for each other. I remembered feeling that way around Tom when we first started goin' together. I'd better get used to being an outsider.

Cat sat on the front step to my house, washing his paws. He stopped to look up at me. *Meow.* He sounded a bit put out.

I bent and rubbed his ears. "Sorry, buddy. I had to help my friend. I'll make it up to you with an extra goodie at dinner, how's that?"

He gave me a typical feline stare, then went back to washing his paws. I took that as acceptance.

The kids were at school. Mom came out of the kitchen, dryin' her hands on her apron. "Is Lee home?"

I hung up my coat. "He and Dot went to the park. I'm sure they'll stop at the Tillotson house on their way so Mrs. T can fuss over him. You need any help?"

"Not especially, but I'd welcome the company if you want to join me."

"I got a letter to write to Tom first, but I'll be with you in a jiffy." I went to my room, where I sat and pulled out the V-mail envelope and some paper. I set the magazine clipping on the corner of my desk. Then I wrote.

Dear Tom,

I hope this letter finds you safe and well. I don't know where you are right now, and you probably can't tell me, but it has to be hotter than Buffalo. That stupid groundhog down in Pennsylvania said it was gonna be an early spring. He's never seen a Western New York winter, that's for sure. Bet you hardly even remember those, huh?

It's been busy here since I last wrote. Lee's father died. Murdered, actually. Lee had a bit of a dust-up with the law. I'm sure he'll write and tell you all about it. All I can say is I've learned a lot of lessons about people I thought I knew, and some I just met, in the past few days. I guess it goes to show that you never can tell about folks.

I learned a lot about myself, too. Turns out I'm a pretty good investigator. My new friend, Detective MacKinnon at the Buffalo Police Department thinks so, too. He bought me a correspondence course to get a private investigator's license. At first, I wasn't sure what to think. It'd mean leaving Bell and my work there, at least after I got my license. You can't do investigations if you don't start until four o'clock in the afternoon. I'd miss all the girls there. I'd miss feeling like I was helping out the war effort. On the other hand, I've told you before how much I like being a detective. It's a different kind of helping. Closer to home, and maybe that's just as, if not more, important than the war.

I paused and looked at the clipping. What would he think? What if he wrote to break off our engagement and said he didn't want to be married to a private dick? Then again, did I want to be with a guy who didn't support my dreams? I looked down at the paper.

I've decided to do it, become a private detective. I hope you're okay with that. I don't think it'll change me much. After all, more than anything else, I'm still your girl.

  Love,
  Betty

A Note from the Author

This story comes from my family history. In the 1970s, my father's Uncle Fran really did drown the way John Tillotson did. Uncle Fran wasn't murdered, though. The theory is he fell off a barge tied up in the grain elevator canals. But his body did float down the Buffalo River and was not recovered for almost two weeks.

Child Street is still there, but you won't find it on a map. It was renamed to Austin Street a number of years ago. But the geographic location is accurate.

The US Coast Guard still has a station in Buffalo. A lot of their work involves search and rescue along Lake Erie, as well as the Buffalo and Niagara Rivers. They also are involved in investigating and preventing smuggling operations between the United States and Canada.

Buffalo's Fruit District is also still in the city and was originally occupied by German immigrants, many of whom came from agricultural settings in the Old Country, as I described in the novel. They planted numerous gardens, including apple and pear orchards. Both of those fruits flourish in Western New York. The funny thing about the neighborhood is that none of the fruit-themed streets are called Apple or Pear. Within the district there are streets named Lemon, Orange, Grape, Mulberry, and Peach, as well as a few "tree" names (Maple, Oak, Elm, and Locust). While grapes are abundant along the shores of Lake Erie and there are numerous peach orchards up on Lake Ontario, as far as I know, nobody has ever been able to grow citrus trees outside of the Botanical Gardens and those wouldn't have been cultivated when the German immigrants settled the area—so I'm not sure what inspired those names.

Acknowledgements

Writing acknowledgements always seems a little repetitive, but that's because I have a solid crew of people who help me carry these books across the finish line.

Many thanks to my wonderful critique group—Annette Dashofy, Peter W.J. Hayes, and Jeff Boarts—for lending me their ears, their brains, and their shoulders. I always tell people I could not do this without them and that's the truth.

A million thanks to my father, Gary Lederman, for helping me with the historical research into Buffalo. It's a good thing he doesn't charge me by the question.

A shout-out to Ramona DeFelice-Long's Sprint Club for holding me accountable to my daily goals.

Thanks to Harriette Sackler and Shawn Reilly Simmons at Level Best Books for their support and assistance with everything from editing to cover design. Also thanks to Kathy Deyell for her sharp-eyed proofreading and her friendship.

And last, but certainly not least, thanks to my husband, Paul, encouraging me when I wonder if I'm any good at this writing thing. I love you.

About the Author

Liz Milliron is the author of **The Laurel Highlands Mysteries** series, set in the scenic Laurel Highlands of Southwestern Pennsylvania, and **The Homefront Mysteries**, set in Buffalo, NY during the early years of World War II. She is a member of Sisters in Crime, Pennwriters, and International Thriller Writers. A recent empty-nester, Liz lives outside Pittsburgh with her husband and a retired-racer greyhound.